Living Jim Crow

Living Jim Crow

Modern American Literature and the New Twentieth Century
Series Editors: Martin Halliwell and Mark Whalan

Published Titles
Writing Nature in Cold War American Literature
Sarah Daw

F. Scott Fitzgerald's Short Fiction and American Popular Culture: From Ragtime to Swing Time
Jade Broughton Adams

The Labour of Laziness in Twentieth-Century American Literature
Zuzanna Ladyga

The Literature of Suburban Change: Narrating Spatial Complexity in Metropolitan America
Martin Dines

The Literary Afterlife of Raymond Carver: Influence and Craftsmanship in the Neoliberal Era
Jonathan Pountney

Living Jim Crow: The Segregated Town in Mid-Century Southern Fiction
Gavan Lennon

Forthcoming Titles
The Big Red Little Magazine: New Masses, 1926–1948
Susan Currell

US Modernism at Continents End: Carmel, Provincetown, Taos
Geneva Gano

The Reproductive Politics of American Literature and Film, 1959–1973
Sophie Jones

Ordinary Pursuits in American Writing after Modernism
Rachel Malkin

Sensing Willa Cather: The Writer and the Body in Transition
Guy Reynolds

The Plastic Theatre of Tennessee Williams: Expressionist Drama and the Visual Arts
Henry I. Schvey

Class, Culture and the Making of US Modernism
Michael Collins

Black Childhood in Modern African American Fiction
Nicole King

Visit our website at www.edinburghuniversitypress.com/series/MALTNTC

Living Jim Crow

The Segregated Town in Mid-Century Southern Fiction

GAVAN LENNON

EDINBURGH
University Press

Edinburgh University Press is one of the leading university presses in the UK. We publish academic books and journals in our selected subject areas across the humanities and social sciences, combining cutting-edge scholarship with high editorial and production values to produce academic works of lasting importance. For more information visit our website: edinburghuniversitypress.com

Edinburgh University Press Ltd
The Tun – Holyrood Road
12(2f) Jackson's Entry
Edinburgh EH8 8PJ

First published in hardback by Edinburgh University Press 2020

Typeset in 10/13 ITC Giovanni Std Book by
Servis Filmsetting Ltd, Stockport, Cheshire

A CIP record for this book is available from the British Library

ISBN 978 1 4744 6157 3 (hardback)
ISBN 978 1 4744 6158 0 (paperback)
ISBN 978 1 4744 6159 7 (webready PDF)
ISBN 978 1 4744 6160 3 (epub)

CONTENTS

ACKNOWLEDGEMENTS

This book started in a small town in Ireland, where I grew up reading the ways in which space and people are organised. It reappeared much later when I started a PhD at the University of Nottingham, where I was lucky to have the support and expertise of three supervisors. I am very grateful to Graham Thompson, Celeste-Marie Bernier and especially Sharon Monteith for modelling a generosity of expert knowledge and understanding that I can only hope to show my own students. Owen Robinson and Zoe Trodd offered invaluable feedback and support at an early stage. I am grateful to the Arts and Humanities Research Council, and the Sir Francis Hill Postgraduate Scholarship for their generous funding of my PhD, and to the University of Nottingham and Canterbury Christ Church University for funding research trips to the USA. Edinburgh University Press has been a very welcoming home for this project, and I would like to thank Michelle Houston and Ersev Ersoy at the Press as well series editors Martin Halliwell and Mark Whalen. Feedback provided by two anonymous reviewers was invaluable, and this book is the better for it.

I've come to learn that southern literary studies is sustained by generous advocates, archivists and supporters. Nancy Smith Fichter kindly allowed me access to the Lillian Smith papers in Georgia, and I am grateful for her generosity. The archivists at the University of Georgia's Hargrett Rare Book and Manuscript Library, especially Mary Palmer Linneman and Steven Brown, and everybody at the Harry Ransom Center, the University of Texas at Austin were extraordinarily welcoming and helpful. Isadora Wagner and the Carson McCullers Society, Matthew Teutsch at the Lillian E. Smith Center, and Debra March, John Kay and Jim Clark from the Byron Herbert Reece Society went above and beyond the call of duty, and I appreciate all their work. Selections from Lillian Smith's *Strange Fruit* (1944) are reproduced with the permission of Houghton Mifflin Harcourt. Selections from Carson McCullers's *Clock Without Hands* (1961) are reproduced with the permission of Andrew Nurnberg Associates.

I am lucky to have smart friends and it is difficult to separate out the people who have supported me personally and intellectually, so I won't try. In no particular order, and with the usual (reluctant) caveat that I can't blame them for this book's shortcomings, I am grateful to the following people: Christina Duffy, Conor Carolan, Fionnghuala Sweeney, Nerys Williams, Hannah Hawkins, Gillian Roberts, Nicole King, Mitch Goodrum, Kath Abiker, Ali Eyden, Gillian Youngs, Dave Connolly, Neil Guerin, Martin Halliwell (again), George Lewis, Travis Smith (for driving me through the Mississippi Delta), Lydia Plath, Nick Witham, Jude Riley, Michael Bibler (who always offers the best advice), Martyn Bone, Harriet Pollack, Amy Clukey, Erich Nunn, Gina Caison and Brian Ward.

I would like to thank my family, especially my parents, Mary and Malachi, for encouraging me to read. Finally, to Zalfa Feghali, my partner in everything. Writing this book was very difficult. It is an understatement to say that I could not have done it without your constant love, support and immeasurable effort. I wish I could say more than 'thank you'.

Introduction:
Uncovering a Poetics of Protest

Immediately following the opening credits of Frank Capra's 1946 film *It's a Wonderful Life*, a close-up shot of a street sign informs the imagined viewer 'You are Now in Bedford Falls'.[1] The sign is a visual symbol of inclusion in an archetypal small American town. A montage of Bedford Falls' institutions follows this shot, including a pharmacy, a bank and a boarding house, while the voice of each proprietor is heard petitioning God for mercy for George Bailey, played by James Stewart. In these images, Capra presents a typology of the American town, suggesting that Bedford Falls (and, later, its perverse mirror image, Pottersville) is socially integral and economically effective because the community and its infrastructure of buildings and services operate seamlessly.

The litany of the town's offices that Capra presents suggests a model for reading cultural representations of the American town. *It's a Wonderful Life* depicts a supposedly typical American town in the immediate post-war period as the site of personal difficulties (the plot's catalyst is Bailey's decision to commit suicide) that can be overcome through the successful cooperation of each of the town's inhabitants and the spaces they occupy personally and professionally. Racial segregation remains just out of view in Capra's film. Bailey's peregrinations through Bedford Falls and Pottersville bring him to working-class and immigrant neighbourhoods but never to the section of town where, presumably, Bailey's African American housekeeper Annie lives. While this mid-century American town is not innocent of racism or racial segregation, its creators can turn away from racism as a structuring principle in small-town space and society. In cultural representations of the United States South from the 1940s to the early 1960s, racial segregation is not only a foundational component of the typical town but also the central prism through which artists enact social critique. In amplifying the role of the town as both setting and mode of critique, *Living Jim Crow: The Segregated Town in Mid-Century Southern Fiction* models a critical practice for recognising and articulating the role of aesthetics in racial protest.

In this book, I identify and outline a typology of the fictional southern town specific to mid-century writing emerging from and concerned with the US South. The typology I reveal is different from Capra's American archetype because it is governed by the legal and structural frameworks of *de jure* racial segregation. By exploring the work of seven mid-century southern novelists in detail, I codify the ways in which these authors use the setting of the town as a narrative strategy and political staging ground to critique racial segregation in the Jim Crow era, finding that authors imbue their fictional towns with such deeply embedded and insurmountable racial paradoxes as to dismantle the South's abiding myth of 'separate but equal'. The first extended study to explore the trope of the small southern town, this book argues that the imaginary, fictional space is consistently figured as a mechanism for exposing the ideological and practical failings of white supremacy and Jim Crow racial segregation. I define a distinct anti-segregationist literary tradition that only becomes clear through a sustained critical analysis of the overlooked trope of the small town as an anti-segregationist conceit at work in both major and overlooked mid-century southern fiction.

Examining the continued construction of the town in narrative strategies developed by William Faulkner, Zora Neale Hurston, William Melvin Kelley, Carson McCullers, Byron Herbert Reece, Lillian Smith and Richard Wright exposes new ways of reading the mid-century literature of the US South. In so doing, I cast this tradition as a literature preoccupied with depicting and critiquing segregation. Because, as southern novelist Eudora Welty wrote in 1965, a plot cannot be answered where an argument can, novelists were able to explore the injustices of segregation by putting them under scrutiny within the limits of the small, coercive and close-knit southern community. In closely examining the work of seven novelists, this book also reframes the literary history of the black freedom struggle among canonical and non-canonical authors. Well-known texts by Hurston, Smith and Wright are read along-side lesser-known texts by Faulkner, Kelley, McCullers and Reece to map the unexplored terrain of literary and narrative strategies used to resist segregation. In the most revealing fiction of the period, authors expose and critique the failure of the region's dominant racial politics and resist the racial status quo of their period by imagining a setting that showcases its own instability. I illustrate how authors deployed the setting of the town as part of an aes-thetics of anti-segregation that ran parallel to a spectrum of racial liberalism and radicalism.

In a 1967 essay, African American novelist Kelley asserted: 'There is no such thing as a good white liberal – not because of the evil of whiteness, but because of the evil of the concept of liberalism itself.'[2] For Kelley, the problem with white liberalism was rooted in class relations and exploitation as well as in racism: 'the white liberal [. . .] is not usually a white of the lower-class, but of the middle-class [. . .] within the white world, he must stay on the good side of the Big White Man, for he hopes to one day be one himself.'[3] In her 1949 memoir *Killers of the Dream*, white novelist and activist Smith articulated the intra-racial class dynamic in the form of a fable: 'Once upon a time, down South, Mr. Rich White made a bar-gain with Mr. Poor White.'[4] While Smith condemns wealthy whites who manipulate poor whites to exploit blacks, Kelley expands on the metaphor to articulate his distrust for well-intentioned middle-class whites as well. Smith suggests that the bargain could be altered: 'It never occurred to Mr. Rich White that with a bargain the Negro could help him make money. It never occurred to Mr. Poor White that with a bargain the Negro could help him raise wages.'[5] In contrast, Kelley would reject the terms of the bargain entirely in favour of a newly conceived economic unit that can bring an end to exploitation. [6] These very different authors, whose respective debut novels reveal the distinct uses of the trope of the town in the 1940s and early 1960s, offer evidence of literary critic Michael Szalay's contention that mid-century American novelists were among the most important political strategists of their time.[7] Reading Smith and Kelley together at opposite ends of chronological and ideological spectra shows how authors' avowedly politicised aesthetics can effectively undermine the privileging of the experience of whiteness in the twentieth-century USA. Indeed, the authors I explore represent a range of nodes on the broad ideological spectrum that opposed segregation from within the South. For the most part, these novelists are racial liberals, but they represent a diverse range of thinking – from the 'go-slow' gradualism of Faulkner and McCullers, through Reece's political contrarianism and Hurston's political ambivalence, to Smith's insistence on an immediate and total end to segregation, to Kelley's radical racial separatism. Despite these divergent political positions, these writers coalesce on the same aesthetic and political tool, the fictional town, as their preferred setting. Each author is representative of a broader political impetus, and, to that end, these novels illustrate the varieties of use to which the setting is put, though the list is far from exhaustive. The modes of reading that I outline here – the specific uses of a symbolic and material typology – can be perceived in a wide range of southern texts and sheds light on the myriad ways the setting of the small town is mobilised to social, political and aesthetic innovation.

Smith, Kelley and their contemporaries developed their imaginary, archetypal towns at precisely the moment at which, as sociologist Howard W. Odum argued in 1943, 'the South and the Negro [. . .] faced their greatest crisis since the days of reconstruction'.[8] Scholarship of this period consistently returns to this sense of immediacy, casting it as what historians John Egerton, Grace Elizabeth Hale and Neil McMillen respectively term the generation before the civil rights movement, a period that saw a project of racial making, and the age of Jim Crow.[9] In literary criticism, the period is no less significant, and Michael Bibler's study of the southern plantation during the same period holds that the cultural economic, social, racial and political landscapes of the South experienced profound change in the middle decades of the twentieth century.[10] *Living Jim Crow* begins from the premise that racism and segregation are not merely reflected or recorded in mid-century literary writing; mid-century authors developed formal settings in order to actively resist white supremacist 'ideals'. Such authors consistently figure their towns – and the racial orders that shape them –on the cusp of decisive change.

In creating fictional towns, therefore, southern authors did not simply select a setting that offered verisimilitude for their narratives, but took advantage of what literary critic Brian Norman has identified as a cartography of racial division, one of three characteristics that define what he terms the 'segregation narrative'.[11] As I show over the course of this book, these fictional towns, like their real-world referents, feature a divided geography that supposedly maintains distance between the town's two racial groups. But these divided geographies are mapped in order that they are bridged; each of the authors I examine provides a model for social and racial critique at the historical moment when segregation was most deeply entrenched in the South.[12] Norman maps the tradition of the segregation narrative in brief and in order to construct a framework through which to read twenty-first-century historical fiction set in the twentieth century. As a result, his conception of the segregation narrative neglects that tradition's political agency at mid-century. In particular, Norman – and other scholars who ably mobilise the mid-century period to explicate contemporary African American writing – neglects the stylistic strategies through which anti-segregationist authors develop their respective aesthetics of protest. In this respect, I am guided more by southern studies scholarship that focuses on the intersection of literary form and racial politics in the years between American involvement in the Second World War and the rise of the non-violent civil rights movement.

The place of the small town has been understood in southern literary studies as challenging the notion that the South moves at a different pace from the rest of the nation or, as Lucinda MacKethan summarises in *The Dream of Arcady: Place and Time in Southern Literature* (1980): 'time and progress belong to the world outside, or so the myth goes on the plantations or in the small, sleepy Southern towns that are popular images of the South, time is held back by the places themselves.'[13] In these novels, time is held back *temporarily*, but the South is not exempt from modernity nor from the conventional passage of time and the authors under study consistently invent representatives of a younger generation of southerners who are poised to effect racial change.[14] The myth that MacKethan identifies is inadequate for a study of how segregation is explored by writers of the fictional southern town at mid-century, and, as critic Robert H. Brinkmeyer Jr writes, to celebrate place suggests celebrating stasis and the status quo, perhaps one reason that segregation, with its barriers controlling not only movement in space but also within the social and economic spheres, seemed so natural in the South.[15]

But the novelists I study do not celebrate place or the social status quo in their depictions of the small town, and *Living Jim Crow* is by no means a celebration of the life of the small town. Rather, the novelists manoeuvre the trope of the small town to make of it a critique of the status quo. And while each of the fictional towns I explore reverts to the existing racial order to greater or lesser degrees, the novelists do succeed in undermining the stability and morality of that order, and expose the injustice and dysfunction of segregation. *Living Jim Crow* argues that the physical shape of an invented southern town should be read as a critique of segregation, and that authors invented semi-urban communities and spaces that depict the instability of segregation as an organising principle. By 'semi-urban' I mean that the fictional towns I explore feature the services and amenities expected of an urban centre but without the anonymity of the city: people in these towns have access to modern facilities and institutions but are also known by – or at least known to – all of their neighbours. By using the term 'town', then, my analysis incorporates a range of spaces and communities between large villages and small cities – nodes on a spectrum that includes 'a wide range of settlements between the traditional poles of the country and the city', in Raymond Williams's terms – in the South.[16] A characteristic that each of these fictional spaces has in common is a reliance on an architecture of segregation that seeks to maintain a solid southern identity, often through the implicit threat of racial violence.

In the popular imagination, the southern town is defined by the public courthouse square that often marks the spatial and organisational centre of community. Almost as ubiquitous a feature in the southern town as the square itself is the Confederate monument it houses. Novelist and avowed racial gradualist Hodding Carter writes fondly of these memorials, apparently considering them signifiers of the noble efforts of the Confederacy: 'These weather-stained guardians, doing sentry duty above the inscriptions to the beloved dead, have earned the right to an unending vigil.'[17] While Carter imagines these statues as deserving of respect, the monuments tend more often to be signifiers of a history of violence, white supremacy and alienation. For instance, white novelist Ben Haas juxtaposes respect for the Confederate dead with the disenfranchisement of poor southerners when he opens his novel *Look Away, Look Away* (1964) with a description of the Great Depression in the 'typical' southern town: 'You could see them in the courthouse square of every little Southern town, then, in the spring of 1932 – the dispossessed. With stunned eyes and unshaven faces, they lounged in ragged overalls and worn-out shoes on the courthouse steps or on the benches around the inevitable bronze Confederate soldier.'[18] The recurring trope of the monument to the Confederate dead that persists in fictional and non-fictional depictions of southern towns throughout this period signifies racialised southern memory. Courthouse squares and Confederate monuments anchor their towns civically and historically within a racialised and implicitly violent social structure. As historian Karen Cox writes: 'Confederate monuments were not simply about honoring the past; they had come to serve as symbols of the present, helping to ensure a continuity of values held by the generation that had instituted Jim Crow.'[19] The typical southern town in fiction radiates outwards from a centre that is designed to be legible in two different ways by the members of the community: hospitable to the majority of the town's white denizens, and overtly hostile and threatening to its black population.

While I draw on southernist Scott Romine's 'first rule of community', that 'insofar as it is cohesive, a community will tend to be coercive', I depart from his contention that a community 'resists mapping in a strict sense'.[20] On the contrary, a combination of textual mapping and close textual analysis reveals the ways in which these fictional towns coerce their populations, black and white, to maintain a space constituted according to white supremacist ideology and expectations. In so doing I reveal how the imagined shapes and structures upon which these fictional towns are designed represent a range of symbolic and material interrogations of the ideology of racial segregation. These towns are rendered as whole, integral units – many of these authors go to great lengths to ensure that their spatial design is consistent and comprehensive. The conventions through which such fictional towns are described are also the means through which their anti-segregationist potential can be outlined: mapping serves a simultaneously artistic and social function, as authors outline precisely how these towns are constructed, at the same time as presenting – just as precisely – why such racist constructions cannot persist.

As literary critic Stéphane Robolin argues in his comparative study of African American and black South African writing, 'the art of mapping is not the exclusive prerogative of the dominant culture', especially when marginalised authors 'engage in cultural counter-cartography' as a mode of aesthetic resistance to white supremacy.[21] In this way, the chapters that follow begin with careful textual mappings of the physical, metaphorical and ideological dimensions of the fictional town under study. The typology I identify includes the offices, institutions and public spaces that work in tandem to ensure the smooth running of the town, notably set around a town square or main street where the courthouse, police station, bank, restaurant, pharmacy, post office and lawyer's office are typically located. In my usage, the term 'office' denotes a local institution that is a component of the town and reflects both a building (such as the town jail) and the townsperson responsible for it (the county sheriff, for example). The office of the sheriff, in fact, is revealing of how these towns tend to operate. As critic Nahem Yousaf has written, the fictional southern sheriff is characteristically 'mired in moral dilemma', and torn between commitment to the law, and commitment to racist social orders that thrive on extra-legal and illegal racial violence.[22] The office of the sheriff reflects how the small town intersects with the political entity of the county (or the parish, in Louisiana-set novels) as an organising principle of southern space.[23] The county reflects the ways in which the structure of the town is at once an extension of the civic organisation of territory and at odds with it. When all offices are taken together and amalgamated, they form a typology that is recognisable across depictions of the southern town in mid-century fiction, even while it is adapted from text to text. More importantly, reading mid-century novels through this typology allows the critical identification of an aesthetics of desegregation.

As this book textually excavates how conventions of the fictional town develop in the work of individual authors, and how these conventions cohere into a literary tradition of protest, my analysis is led by the internal logic of each fictional space. Annette Trefzer argues that 'In the South, [the] Native American signifier is often buried under a symbolic creation of the region that minimizes its importance or even negates its presence altogether.'[24] Indeed, I would be remiss if I failed to acknowledge the indigenous foundations and the ongoing indigenous experience of these real and imaginary spaces, shaped as they are by a history of conflict and colonialism. Such spaces are always-already contested and ideologically designed. In critic Thadious Davis's work, for example, the notion of the 'southscape' or 'a geography of race and region' positions the South as 'a social, political, cultural, and economic construct but one with the geographic "fact of the land"'.[25] *Living Jim Crow* uncovers how the 'construct' of the fictional town can operate as an aesthetic protest against racial segregation because the ways in which fictional institutions and spaces of the towns are depicted unsettle their respective racial orders. I read spaces textually, as in what Homi Bhabha terms the 'third space of enunciation', which 'makes the structure of meaning and reference an ambivalent process', or Doreen Massey's idea of space as 'the sphere of continuous production and reconfiguration of heterogeneity in all its forms'.[26] These fictional spaces are certainly ambivalent and heterogeneous, but, more pointedly, they are also potentially productive and resistant. Anti-segregationist southern novelists do not simply expose the inconsistencies of the segregated, but integral, communal spaces; their formal interventions amount to political struggle against segregation. As geographers Ruth Wilson Gilmore and Katherine McKittrick argue, respectively: 'geographical imperatives [lie] at the heart of every struggle for social justice' and 'space and place give black lives meaning in a world that has, for the most part, incorrectly deemed black populations and their attendant geographies as "ungeographic" and/or philosophically undeveloped'.[27] If space is inherently contested and racialised, then authors who choose to foreground such struggled-over spaces, in such granular detail, do so in order to make a political and social stand. The literary forms of the southern town, then, are an extension of the racial activism of the twentieth century that otherwise mobilised conflicts over space to do civic work. Demonstrations, marches, picket lines and sit-ins all work to unsettle the typical and orderly conventions of southern place. The literary conventions of the town do similar activist work.

Such racial activism is only discernible at the level of literary form, even while some spatial theory presupposes limitations on aesthetic spatiality. Theorist Henri Lefebvre, for example, identifies what he deems a weakness in literary critical explorations of space: 'The problem is that any search for space in literary texts will find it everywhere and in every guise: enclosed, described, projected, dreamt of, speculated about.'[28] The trick, then, is to be selective about which guise a literary critic is interested in. While the fictional town is obviously in conversation with wider spaces – connections to other towns, cities and rural areas, to say nothing of crucial transnational connections – and is composed of a multitude of smaller ones – streets, buildings, rooms, bodies – it is the composition of the lived space, drawn along racially restrictive and socially coercive lines, that make the setting revealing to scholars interested in how segregation is imagined and challenged by American writers. In contrast to Lefebvre, Marxist geographer David Harvey recognises that certain novels 'typically recognize that societies and spatialities are shaped by continuous processes of struggle. The novel form lends itself, if need be, to a much stronger sense of spatiotemporal dynamics.'[29] Harvey does not expand on what this formal response might look like, but I do. The 'spatiotemporal dynamics' of these towns both reflect the continuous racial struggle of their fictional inhabitants and constitute a similar variety of racial struggle on the part of their authors. Narrative form becomes a means through which authors advance a set of progressive racial politics.

In her cultural history of segregation signs, *Signs of the Times: The Visual Politics of Jim Crow* (2010), Elizabeth Abel notes the peculiar physical intimacy that eating spaces represented for the segregationist:

> Both integrated and differentiated, bounded yet partially permeable, the physical body is a central image of the social body; bodily orifices stage and represent defining, vulnerable, hence carefully regulated, points of entrance to or exit from social wholes.[30]

In this formulation, shared social space equates to intimate cross-racial interaction. If the careful regulation of the physical body correlates to the regulation of the social body, this contravenes racial etiquette, a structuring principle of southern community that I turn to in Chapter 1. This sensual anxiety on the part of white diners corroborates Mark Smith's argument that segregationist ideology was emotional and sensual before it was intellectual: 'People supported segregation without really thinking why. They simply "felt" it was right. Feeling, not thinking, was segregation's best friend' and the intimate public eating space had an especially acute impact on segregationists' feelings about race.[31] In my definition of semi-urbanity, the 'powerful feelings' that Raymond Williams identifies as having attached to both the rural country and sophisticated city coexist in their worst attributes: 'On the country has gathered the idea of a natural way of life: of peace, innocence, and simple virtue. On the city has gathered the idea of an achieved centre: of learning, communication, light.'[32] To Williams, each of these ideas is subject to 'powerful hostile associations', namely 'as a place of backwardness, ignorance, limitation' and 'of noise, worldliness and ambition', respectively.[33] In spatial terms, this manifests in geographer Yi-Fu Tuan's concept of topophilia, or 'affective bond between people and place or setting'.[34] In fictional southern towns, these feelings manifest in implicit and explicit defences of the South's racial status quo, and authors deploy complex and agile narrative strategies to interrogate and weaken such racial thinking.

By turning to neglected texts and authors, critics of southern literature can uncover trends in politicised writing. Simultaneously, while engaging more closely with texts that suggest the diversity of anti-segregationist ideologies that characterised the post-war South through extensive literary mapping, I uncover techniques and stylistic flourishes in individual texts that constitute subtle and granular interventions against the racial status quo. While literary theorist Franco Moretti deploys literary maps in his practice of 'distant reading' as a means of subjecting 'the reality of a text' to 'a process of deliberate reduction and abstraction',[35] I prefer to model a practice of *racially calibrated* close textual analysis that elaborates the formal strategies that authors employ to undermine segregation. In doing so, these authors also interrogate the doctrine of southern exceptionalism that operates, according to Leigh Anne Duck, to bolster a national myth of progressivism:

> On the one hand, images of the region provided a venue through which national audiences could imagine restrictive but stable and sustaining bonds, and, on the other, they represented the conflict between U.S. democratic rhetoric and discriminatory practice as a difference between national and regional cultures.[36]

The South – and the southern town – features as a political and social construct, albeit one with meaningful and material resonance. These towns are constructed within an economy of violence and resistance, their capitalist organisations thriving on racialised codes and laws and on the violent means through which compliance is achieved and resistance is punished. While the white novelists considered in this book were under significantly less immediate physical threat than their colleagues of colour, they were not entirely safe from white supremacist violence. Smith's home in Clayton, Georgia, was the target of an arson attack in 1955 in response to her outspoken resistance to segregation.[37] Smith's construction of an imagined southern space made her a very real target for individuals who had a vested interest in maintaining a specific racial order in the 'real' southern space she occupied.

It is no longer possible to say, as Tara McPherson did in 2003, that 'The South today is as much a fiction, a story we tell and are told, as it is a fixed geographic space below the Mason–Dixon line.'[38] It is now clear, thanks to McPherson and others, that the South is indeed *much more* a fiction than it is a reality. The South is, as Jennifer Rae Greeson has it, a 'possessive fantasia, alternately exhilarating and terrifying'.[39] It is not, however, 'a meaningless term, naming nothing but fantasies', as Jon Smith asserts, because such fantasies are meaningful, productive and imbued with complementary and contradictory ideologies.[40] The fantasy of the South is a starting point rather than a line of limitation. It is precisely because of this trend in southern studies towards dismembering a region that is, in Scott Romine's argument, 'increasingly sustained as a virtual, commodified, built, themed, invented, or otherwise artificial territoriality' that dismantling a central image of the southern novel – the segregated town – is so timely.[41] For the same reason, a critical methodology that unpacks, interrogates and navigates textual and structural building blocks is demanded for such a study. In a public speech in 1965, Lillian Smith declared that 'men imitate art, art does not imitate men; everyday reality is bred from dreams, not dreams from everyday reality'.[42] As such, the aesthetic building blocks of the 'dreams', 'fantasies', and, most importantly, 'fictions' of the US South suggest precisely the means through which such harmful narratives can be troubled.

In the American context, close reading has been contaminated by its origins among the southern conservative New Critics of mid-century. These critics – including Cleanth Brooks, John Crowe Ransom and Robert Penn Warren – were so apolitical in divorcing literature from its social, political and historical influences as to constitute a radically conservative approach to text. Instead of consigning this approach to literary reading to the annals of literary history, this book recovers a racially calibrated mode of close textual analysis, attuned to strategies of protest that are present in texts but have been overlooked by earlier scholars. For example, while, as an editor, Ransom admonishes critics not to 'content themselves with what is manifest and for everyone to see', this sense of the interrogatory does not extend to uncovering covert negotiations of racial politics in southern texts.[43] The New Critics obscured or derided elements of political and racial protest in the novels and poems they studied. In the early 1960s, during a moment of escalation in the black freedom movement, Brooks establishes a view of the text as something necessarily divorced from its political context: 'it is for something else that one looks when he comes to estimate the achievement of the serious writers of our times – something more inward than a tract – something deeper and more resonant than a tirade against a particular abuse.'[44] Brooks's romanticised description of literature in the 1960s rings hollow. By describing in such vague terms what literature 'ought to do', Brooks highlights his conviction that literature should not engage with politics or protest (either as a tract or a, presumably shallow, tirade).

Where some scholars consider the innovations of the New Critics as a 'revolution in criticism' or 'brilliant and courageous', I do not.[45] Self-consciously formalist literary criticism long served to propel an implicitly reactionary approach to interpretation. It would not be feasible to understand the political and social implications of literary style that the writers I explore evidence here through the critical practice developed by the Fugitive/agrarian/New Critical intellectual tradition. Like critic Frank Letricchia and historian Angie Maxwell, I critique the New Criticism as 'an imposing and repressive father-figure' to contemporary literary scholarship that was 'almost-fundamentalist' in its efforts to divorce aesthetics from issues of race, gender and class.[46] As such, this book is interested both in the work of ideological opposition to agrarianism and neo-Agrarianism through close textual analysis. More recent southernists have adapted close reading methodologies in explicit service of Marxist and/or racially progressive critical programmes. Richard Godden describes how: 'close reading yields not some new account that the text may be made to bear, nor even an expression of interpretive freedom born in a spirit of ludic dialogue between author and recipient.'[47] This book takes up Godden's directive that critics should attend to 'inferences of a tale that is not being told' in order to craft an understanding of the narrative strategies of racial resistance.[48] My analysis of representative texts shows that reactionary scholarship of the period is decidedly at odds with the uses to which mid-century novelists put literary place. The small town, in this body of fiction, resists precisely the reactionary discourses that celebrate a nostalgic and welcoming (white) southern community. Meryl Altman makes a similar case, specifically in reference to Faulkner, when she argues that 'often, when we castigate "Faulkner" for adherence to a small-town Southern parochial view about black people or women staying in their rightful "place," it is really Brooks we should be attacking.'[49] In fact, this book shows that small-town southern parochialism needs to be refigured.

Drawing on theories of narrative and space, intellectual and cultural history, and deploying original archival research, *Living Jim Crow* enquires after what I call 'segregated integrity', the paradox at the centre of the fictional southern town. The integral character of the small town is rooted in its place in a capitalist system. As sociologist Georg Simmel remarked at the turn of the last century: 'The sphere of the life of the small town is, in the main, enclosed within itself.'[50] This capitalist integrity is incompatible with a social system defined by division. More recently, theorist Sharon Patricia Holland argues 'Racism dismembers the "real" – so robs and eviscerates it that nothing and no one can appear as "whole."'[51] The problem that mid-century authors reveal is the paradox of a town that is at once necessarily whole and (just as necessarily) split. Critic and historian Sharon Monteith articulates paradox as a defining feature of the setting, when she asserts that

> the small-town that is celebrated in much American fiction is revealed as a paradox in its southern incarnation: as beloved but benighted, close but repressive, coercive and resistant; a complex constellation of class and racial clashes and collaborations.[52]

These tensions are not merely present in the fictional towns discussed in the following chapters: they are guiding principles in each town's fictive design. The authors under study map the interstitial, messy, complex spaces between these ideological positions in order to develop aesthetics of anti-segregation. I do not claim to offer a uniform mode of reading for racist and ant-racist ideologies during this period; rather these towns stand as monuments to the paradoxes and compromises that simultaneously structure and fail to structure southern community in the middle of the twentieth century. The town is an adequate aesthetic model for exposing the inadequacies of segregationist ideology. Each of the chapters that follows, with the exception of Chapter 1, examines one particular fictional southern town to show how its author establishes a surface image of integrity, only to demonstrate that such wholeness is impossible if it relies on white supremacy.

Chapters 1 and 2 establish the intellectual history of the fictional southern town and outline the representative typology that I deploy throughout. Beginning with an overview of the intellectual and literary history of the 1930s, I argue that American novelists turn to the small town as a means of implicitly and explicitly articulating the ideological and material failings of racial segregation. In Chapter 1, I explore the origins of the small southern town as a trope deployed by anti-segregationist writers and outline a typology of the fictional southern town that these authors consistently deploy in their literary critiques. Through close textual analysis of Zora Neale Hurston's *Their Eyes Were Watching God* (1937) and Richard Wright's collection *Uncle Tom's Children* (1938/1940) I develop a model for African American literary resistance to segregation that takes place at the level of form. The 1930s saw an unprecedented intellectual engagement with the ideas of the American and US southern small towns, in landmark studies by Helen Merrell Lynd and Robert Staughton Lynd, John Dollard and Hortense Powdermaker, that advanced theories of the 'typical' small town in ways that inadvertently produced metonymic fictions. In order to discuss what is 'typical' in America and in the South, these anthropologists treat their subjects as *pars pro toto* synecdoches. In the same decade, reactionary intellectuals, including the Nashville agrarians, W. T. Couch, Bertrand Wilbur Doyle and Edd Winfield Parks, set about imagining a South predicated on 'natural' racial structures, guided by 'racial etiquette'. These distinct but simultaneous intellectual projects produce an inadvertent fiction of southern community that is remedied by innovative representations in contemporary African American fiction.

In 1944, author and activist Lillian Smith takes the trope of the small town further by imagining it as at once the site of entrenched racial violence and as loaded with the potential for progressive change. Following the intellectual and literary *pre-history* of the fictional southern town explored in Chapter 1, Chapter 2 argues that Smith's *Strange Fruit* (1944) offers a paradigmatic segregated town that operates according to the interaction of a wide range of offices. Smith develops a town, Maxwell, Georgia, that features virtually every aspect of my typology of the fictional southern town. Smith, more than her contemporaries, was forthright and uncompromising in her anti-segregationist activism, and the relationship between her stylistic invention and her political convictions are clear and pronounced. Later in her career, Smith would be an active and significant member of civil rights organisations including the Congress of Racial Equality and Student Non-Violent Coordinating

Committee, and her public writing is notable for critiquing racial gradualists with as much force as segregationists. Because of this deep and well-documented political engagement and because of the detail with which Maxwell is depicted, Smith's work is paradigmatic. Smith's steadfast refusal, as an activist, public intellectual and citizen, to capitulate to segregation is made explicit in the novel, where she invents a town through which to confront an imagined reader with the injustice of racial segregation.

Chapters 3 and 4 explore authors' aesthetic engagements with racial violence during the period in which the non-violent civil rights movement became increasingly central to the South's place in the national imaginary. In the work of Appalachian novelist Byron Herbert Reece, the subject of Chapter 3, anti-lynching aesthetics undermine a prevailing notion of the mountain South as uniformly white and pre-modern. Reece has been ignored in scholarly narratives of post-war American and southern fiction. The manner of the author's dismissal echoes the strategies through which his native southern Appalachia has been marginalised and wilfully misunderstood. Today, Reece is remembered – if at all – as the model of a rustic, apolitical 'mountain bard'. This model reinforces received notions of Appalachia as primitive and unsophisticated, but intellectually 'pure' and bucolic. In fact, Reece's fiction and the archival sources that survive him evidence a politically and socially engaged intellectual contrarian. Nowhere is this more evident than in Reece's second novel, *The Hawk and the Sun* (1952): a highly sophisticated anti-racist text that builds on wide and cosmopolitan influences in order to expose racial terrorism as a southern illness. I argue that Reece establishes a distinctive anti-lynching poetics based on the twinned emphases on symbolic representation and material consequence and his construction of the town of Tilden, Georgia, through a range of metaphors of disease and illness. Reece constructs a town-as-organism that is imperilled by the invasive and toxic presence of white supremacist violence. Reece portrays a community built on segregation that is physically and morally rotting in order to explore how individuals may nevertheless resist racial conformity.

Chapter 4 argues that Carson McCullers's novels are best understood as individual parts of a narrative cycle that is made coherent by a shared setting, and that *Clock without Hands* (1961) operates as the culmination of what I term the 'Milan Cycle'. Through close textual analysis of McCullers's final novel I show that the author's earlier fiction should be retrospectively understood as contingent parts of a larger narrative, one that is consistently driven by the representation of a developing black freedom struggle. Drawing on archival research, I uncover motifs and patterns through the whole of McCullers's oeuvre, and especially her first novel, *The Heart is a Lonely Hunter* (1940), that have gone unexplored by critics. It is only with the publication of *Clock without Hands* that the town is attributed with a name: Milan, Peach County, Georgia. The town is only discernible in the moment that the town's legal order is forced to change because of the announcement of the Supreme Court decision in *Brown v. Board of Education of Topeka* in 1954. By representing the town of Milan at various points on a trajectory of racial progress, McCullers implicitly reflects a gradualist ideology in which desegregation can be realised by attrition over a period of time. McCullers dramatises the gradual shift of an entire town and exposes that town's social and physical architecture to the gradually changing racial politics of the region. McCullers depicts a community and a town in increasing flux over the course of four novels. Although Milan is a stable feature across McCullers's fiction, it is nonetheless a town in process, as it moves gradually away from white supremacy. By tracing similarities of setting and characterisation across novels, I assert that McCullers not only returns to the same locale for all of her major fictions but that the town develops with the South's shifting racial politics.

Chapters 5 and 6 explore the ways in which the trope of the town had begun to shift, in political and aesthetic terms, during the early 1960s. In two very different novels from 1962, William Faulkner and William Melvin Kelley are able to position the fictional town in vastly different ways as ideological expressions of, respectively, reactionary nostalgia and radical futurity. In Chapter 5, I argue that Faulkner's final novel, *The Reivers* (1962), offers a veiled but nonetheless potent critique of racial segregation that has managed to go relatively unnoticed in the years since its publication. Faulkner's final novel has long been understood, thanks in part to the intervention of the author, as a more easily digestible and humorous work by an otherwise 'difficult' modernist. This chapter interrogates this impression of the novel by offering a reading of *The Reivers* as a complex and ironic exploration of backward-looking white supremacist narratives of southern history. By comparing depictions of characters across numerous novels and by mapping the changing terrain of the town, I argue that Faulkner relies on an existing understanding of Jefferson as a defence against white supremacist revisionist history. In particular, Faulkner depicts Jefferson's courthouse square, the centre of the town's social and physical landscape, as a contested space that defines the collective identity of the town. A comparative reading of narrator Lucius Priest's description of the town against representations elsewhere in Faulkner's oeuvre reveals that Priest is intentionally misleading his grandson by offering an idealised narrative of the segregated South in the early twentieth century. By leaving textual 'clues' for an imaginative reader to follow, Faulkner reasserts the racially brutal history of the town that Priest attempts to suppress. As such, the chapter proposes a corrective to the implicitly reactionary critical readings of the novel that still, largely, abide.

In Chapter 6, I explore a literary intervention that is simultaneous to Faulkner's but goes much further in its radical racial politics. New York–born William Melvin Kelley positions his imagined town of Sutton, in an unnamed southern state, at a moment of historic change when the state's white citizens are forced to consider the events that led their African American neighbours to abandon the South entirely. To do this, Kelley imagines the porch of a general store as a town's social hub that brings together white men in a wide array of social positions. Kelley's representation of the southern town is a radical reimagining of the typical segregated town in fiction. While each of the white authors explored in earlier chapters imagines, to one degree or another, how the southern town can progress beyond segregation, Kelley's *A Different Drummer* depicts a resolute rejection of liberal principles in favour of a massive black exodus from a fictional southern state. While Kelley, like the white authors I explore, imagines the town of Sutton as 'typical' of southern towns, the larger context in which he places the town is atypical. Kelley imagines an entire American state that is decidedly different from any recognisable, existing state in the Union.

He deliberately eschews representation of an identifiable southern state in order to better imagine the hypothetical ramifications of his invented exodus on the South and the rest of the nation. Through this expansion of narrative focus, I read Kelley as extending the practices of imagining fictional small towns in order to explore the ramifications of desegregation, not simply on a single, representative community, but on the entire Union. Kelley's aesthetic and political development of the fictional southern town is more wide-ranging than the literary projects of the white novelists I discuss in earlier chapters, and his departure from an ameliorative, integrationist mode of thought on desegregation coincides with his decision to construct a broader imaginative landscape through which to explore those ideas.

My conclusion returns to each of the representative texts from the earlier chapters in order to articulate a narrative of aesthetic and political development between the 1930s and the early 1960s. Specifically, the ways in which each author represents the image of the field – a discrete unit of productive agricultural land – reveals a given fictional town's capacity for racial progress that moves beyond and, often, against agrarian and neo-Agrarian conceptions of space and the South. Developing connections between extant theories of space and place – especially those by Bhabha and McKittrick – this conclusion posits a new means of understanding the racialised space of agriculture in the twentieth-century United States. Across the novels studied, the metaphor of gradual progress becomes increasingly inadequate and this is mirrored in the authors' need for a total reappraisal of the typology of the segregated town. This shift in thought is also, I argue, a productive metaphor for the study of the US South, as it continues to struggle with the legacies of reactionary and exceptionalist ideologies. Across these chapters, I develop a narrative in which progressive ideology, ethical social engagement and literary critique coalesce at the level of literary form. I identify a distinct literary tradition at mid-century that consistently, in terms by turn explicit and implicit, rejects the notion that segregation is a permanent or practicable principle for defining southern – or American – identity.

CHAPTER 1

Creators of the Small Town: Anthropology, Racial Etiquette and African American Fiction in the 1930s

Robert Penn Warren regretted writing 'The Briar Patch', his contribution to the southern agrarians' manifesto *I'll Take my Stand* (1930). As the poet, novelist and critic's politics developed through the middle decades of the twentieth century, he shifted from the implicitly white supremacist, reactionary ideology of the agrarians towards racial liberalism. By the 1950s, and the publication of *Segregation: The Inner Conflict of the South* (1956), Warren offered an intellectual contribution to civil rights activism. His collection of interviews with civil rights activists, *Who Speaks for the Negro?* (1965), included a frank rejection of the earlier essay: '... even then, thirty-five years ago, I uncomfortably suspected [. . .] that no segregation was, in the end, humane. But it never crossed my mind that anybody could do anything about it.'[1] Nevertheless, when the younger Warren, the reactionary agrarian, declared that 'The Southern Negro has always been a creature of the small town and farm. That is where he still chiefly belongs, by temperament and capacity',[2] he was describing two complementary, if inadvertent, fictions. The first fiction positions the small southern town as an archetype: a discrete, representative unit of community and space. The figure of the town that Warren constructs stands as an integer that is at once recognisable and resistant to specificity. The second fiction relates to the system of racial etiquette through which such towns operated. Warren implies that this system of 'appropriate behaviour' is both a natural offshoot of African Americans' essentialist 'temperament and capacity', and that it is beneficial, contributing to a sense of 'belonging'. But southern towns were not stable integers awaiting objective study; nor was racial etiquette either natural or beneficial.

Warren was not unique among his contemporary intellectuals. The 1930s saw a crystallisation of these two narratives, as put forward in discourses from both the social sciences and the humanities. The former thrived through an unprecedented turning inward of American anthropology and ethnography: pivotal works by John Dollard, Helen Merrell Lynd and Robert Staughton Lynd, and Hortense Powdermaker invented fictions of the typical American and southern towns. Alongside and including the agrarians, historians and social commentators – from ideologies spanning white supremacy and reactionary conservatism to gradualist racial liberalism – identified racial etiquette as a healthy and necessary structuring principle of southern community during the same period. Together, these narratives developed understandings of the southern town as a coherent and functional whole that operates more or less beneficially for all its inhabitants.

The same decade, however, saw concerted efforts on the part of novelists to undermine, discredit and satirise these intellectual trends. Such literary responses served to represent 'typical' southern towns as inherently and detrimentally built on racial violence and coercive community systems and novelists including Zora Neale Hurston and Richard Wright authored correctives to the abiding discursive constructs of the Southern town. In so doing, they paved the way for later southern writers to further mobilise the setting of the town as a means of protesting segregation, as I show in the chapters to come. While the personal and artistic differences between Hurston and Wright have been well documented, the fictional towns described in *Their Eyes Were Watching God* (1937) and *Uncle Tom's Children* (1938) each combat the toxic narratives in circulation that idealised the segregated town.

This chapter examines the intellectual *pre-history* of the fictional southern town at mid-century by exploring the intellectual and literary constructions upon which subsequent novelists build. Beginning with a discussion of intellectual history of the small town in mid-century ethnography, I argue that social scientists developed metonymic fictions of 'typical' towns. These archetypes limit diversity of experience and, in some cases, marginalise the lived experience of African Americans. Hurston, a trained anthropologist, offers an ironic retelling of these metonymic fictions in her depiction of a fictionalised Eatonville, Florida. The chapter then proceeds to uncover how reactionary intellectuals, including Warren and the Nashville agrarians as well as W. T. Couch, and Edd Winfield Parks, set about imagining a South predicated on 'natural' racial structures of etiquette. In Wright's fiction, the racial and gendered violence through which racial etiquette is constituted and policed is indistinguishable from the structure of the southern town itself. By reading these works of fiction alongside the *inadvertent* fictions rendered in anthropology and intellectual commentary, I expose an implicit intellectual and artistic conflict over the right to describe the 'typical' town. Novelists like Hurston and Wright are better able than their scholarly contemporaries to reshape their representative southern towns to achieve their desired anti-racist social aims.

The Town as Ethnographic Object:
Zora Neale Hurston's Eatonville

Beginning in the 1920s, social scientific studies advanced theories of the 'typical' small town in ways that inadvertently produced metonymic fictions. In order to discuss what is 'typical' in the United States and in the South, these anthropologists treat their subjects as *pars pro toto* synecdoches: they suggest that the experience of these specific towns is representative of the experiences of similar towns throughout the nation or the region. This new tendency, while not without precedent, represented a sea change in a discipline that had been characterised by its focus on supposedly less-developed communities outside the United States. Earlier in the twentieth century, academic considerations of the American small town tended to be less sustained, but they were characterised by an insistence on reading a specific exemplar as representative of a particular type. Even while scholars centre social inequality in their discussions of towns, they tend to evade the structuring principle of race through careful selection of 'average' towns.

Philosopher Randolph S. Bourne asserted in 1913 that 'The

suburban town is a sort of last stronghold of Americanism.'[3] Bourne's description of the American town anticipates my coinage of the term semi-urban when he classifies his subject as sufficient in size to 'contain a fairly complete representation of the different classes and types of people and social organizations, and yet not so large that individualities are submerged in the general mass, or the lines between the classes blurred and made indistinct'. A community this size is, to Bourne, a 'real epitome of American life'.[4] Central to his conception is a rigid sense of social stratification; Bourne consciously avoids spaces in which 'the lines between classes' are rigid and legible, and his archetypal town is carefully – if implicitly – northern.[5] Bourne offers an entreaty to scholars who follow to continue to mine the significance of the small town: 'Only by understanding [the town] and all its workings, shall we understand our country. One can begin by understanding that little cross-section of American life, the suburban town.'[6] But here, Bourne takes an intellectual short cut: the synecdoche of the small town becomes a key through which scholars and readers can understand the whole of the United States. Despite the inherent flaws in this line of thinking, scholars would continue to make archetypal American towns the object of study.

Following Bourne's example, sociologist Thorstein Veblen privileges the 'country town' as an emblem for US identity and as 'one of the great American institutions, perhaps the greatest, in the sense that it has had and continues to have a greater part than any other in shaping public sentiment and giving character to American culture'.[7] Veblen's conception of the town is pointedly rural, but regionally non-specific: 'The country town of the great American farming region is the perfect flower of self-help and cupidity standardised on the American plan. Its name may be Spoon River or Gopher Prairie, or it may be Emporia or Centralia or Columbia.'[8] Among the towns listed, Columbia, Emporia and Spoon River could reasonably found in any state, while Gopher Prairie and Centralia suggest the Midwest. Crucially, in order for Veblen's discussion of the town to work, each town must closely resemble the last: 'The pattern is substantially the same and is repeated several thousand times with a faithful perfection which argues that there is no help for it.'[9] Veblen allows his methodology to prove its own value: through the study of a single town, all towns become legible – reaffirming the choice to focus attention on a single town.

Following Bourne's and Veblen's respective brief essays, sustained and methodologically rigorous social scientific studies of the American town began to indicate a disciplinary shift in anthropological thought. Helen Merrell Lynd and Robert Staughton Lynd's *Middletown: A Study in Modern American Culture* (1929) and *Middletown in Transition: A Study in Cultural Conflict* (1937) revised the focus of American anthropology away from what they termed 'uncivilised peoples'.[10] Taken together, these studies represent 'the most exhaustive studies of small-town life ever undertaken' and helped to make their subject, Muncie, Indiana, 'the most studied of American towns'.[11] The Lynds's rationale for studying the town, however, embodied a paradox:

> Two main considerations guided the selection of a location for the study: (1) that the city be as representative as possible of contemporary American life, and (2) that it be at the same time compact and homogeneous enough to be manageable in such a total-situation study.[12]

Of course, homogeneity – especially in racial terms – is rarely characteristic of American life or community at mid-century. It is not even as characteristic of life in Muncie as the authors assert, and the Lynds consistently marginalise Muncie's non-white population in their description of the town.

One criterion for the selection of Muncie as Middletown is that it has a 'small Negro and foreign-born population'.[13] Even while this homogeneity is thought desirable for the study of a 'representative' American town, the Lynds acknowledge that it is not typical: 'In a difficult study of this sort it is a distinct advantage to deal with a homogeneous, native-born population, even though such a population is unusual in an American industrial city'.[14] Their statement almost amounts to an admission of fictionalising the subject at hand. The Lynds recognise the gap their study leaves based on the selection of an unusually homogenous town. Anthropologists would return to the site of the Middletown studies to correct the misleading account of race in Muncie, but the Lynds' studies remain deeply engrained in conceptions of the small town.[15]

The school of anthropological studies of the southern – rather than typically American – town at roughly the same time as *Middletown* does not and cannot evade discussion of race so completely. Such studies nevertheless inadvertently render their real objects of study as representative fictions. The two landmarks in the field of anthropological ethnography of the southern town, John Dollard's *Caste and Class in a Southern Town* (1937) and Hortense Powdermaker's *After Freedom: A Cultural Study in the Deep South* (1939), have a shared subject: the town of Indianola, Mississippi. Indianola is rendered in Dollard's book as 'Southerntown' and in Powdermaker's as 'Cottonville'. Each author describes the names they apply to Indianola as 'fictitious', thereby implicitly recognising the element of artifice employed in these acts of renaming.[16] These names immediately indicate the authors' differences in methodology and focus: 'Southerntown' seems chosen to align more clearly with the *Middletown* paradigm, while 'Cottonville' highlights the structuring principle of the plantation economy. Each of these studies, which diverge in key respects, presents a different town, and neither 'faithfully' represents the real Indianola.

Dollard's interest is not only in commercial and financial infrastructures within (and surrounding) the town but also with the 'emotional structure' of the community. Dollard recognises the futility of arbitrarily dividing the inhabitants of the town along racial lines and instead calls for a greater focus on the network of interracial communications: 'The lives of white and Negro people are so dynamically joined and fixed in one system that neither can be understood without the other.'[17] He articulates this relationship in terms of fixed categories of race, albeit with an asymmetrical balance of economic and social power: 'whites and whiteness form an inseparable part of the mental life of the Negro. He has a white employer, often white ancestors, sometimes white playmates, and he lives by a set of rules which are imposed by white society.'[18] Dollard identifies two characteristics of interracial exchange here, firstly that whiteness and blackness are 'inseparable' from each other and, secondly, that the black inhabitants of Southerntown are subject to the 'imposition' of white rules and customs. Dollard describes an integral system, one based on the inseparable cooperation of its constituent parts. He also makes clear that this 'integrity' is constructed in favour of the white inhabitants, particularly the white employers, of the town.

The focus of Powdermaker's study is methodologically centred more fixedly on the African American inhabitants of Cottonville. The author outlines the 'interests' of her research as being 'the process of acculturation and in problems concerning the Negro'.[19] While in Powdermaker's research 'the emphasis is on the Negro', she recognises the inseparability of the town's inhabitants along a racial binary: 'Today, as in the past, the Negro lives in no isolated black community. To understand his life there must be an understanding of the Whites who form so large a part of it.'[20] Just as African American life in the town is inextricably enmeshed with white life, the structure of the town is dependent on broader agricultural space: 'Cottonville [. . .] is fused with that portion of the countryside which focuses upon it as a center into an organic unit with a population which drifts in and out of town, pausing for an hour, a day, a season.'[21] Powdermaker's description of the town in quasi-biological terms suggests a generally integrative functional social and spatial system. Both studies position their respective towns as whole and complete, but Powdermaker's translation of Indianola's racial infrastructure is markedly more critical than Dollard's. That the same subject of study could influence two vastly different scientific descriptions is understandable, but it also points to a potential lacuna in the writing of anthropology that recalls the conventions of prose fiction.

The decades following these studies saw a thorough re-examination of the role of narrative – and of figurative language – in the ethnographic method. Contemporary scholars have a stronger sense of the inadvertent fiction-making that is necessarily part of the social scientific methodology. James Clifford warns that 'To call ethnographies fictions may raise empiricist hackles' but locates his use of the term within a discourse in which the term 'fiction' 'has lost its connotation of falsehood, of something merely opposed to truth'.[22] Clifford's realisation that 'even the best ethnographic texts – serious, true fictions – are systems, or economies, of truth' and that '[p]ower and history work through them, in ways their authors cannot fully control' is intuitive to literary scholars and bolsters my argument that self-conscious fictions of the town are correctives to the domineering ethnographic narratives.[23] Clifford's conception of the 'partial truth' still suggests a stable spectrum of truth and falsehood: 'Ethnographic truths are thus inherently *partial* – committed and incomplete [. . .] But once [this assertion is] accepted and built into ethnographic art, a rigorous sense of partiality can be a source of representational tact.'[24]

Novelists like Hurston and Wright, then, are able to disengage totally from these processes of representation. While each of the fictional towns examined in *Living Jim Crow* has one or more real-world touchstones – a town in which an author may have lived, or that has otherwise influenced a fictional geography – the settings are obviously and self-consciously invented spaces. This is especially true of Lillian Smith's Maxwell, Georgia – the subject of the next chapter – a town with clear connections to the real South, and equally clear processes of authorial invention. Through the rest of *Living Jim Crow*, I argue that novelists craft towns that do things real towns simply could not. The act of invention allows authors to more fully explore the ideological and material fallout of segregated community. Unlike the ethnographers to whom Clifford directs his analysis, the novelists I discuss have no burden of directly accurate or 'faithful' representation, but are instead empowered to invent an exemplar that is more representative than any brick-and-mortar town could be. Novelists, unlike anthropologists, may develop their towns as representative synecdoches without fear of academic or intellectual dishonesty.

The cross-pollination of Hurston's work in fiction and ethnography is well documented, and, as anthropologist Kamala Visweswaran summarises, 'there is not a clear-cut demarcation of [the author's] work into novelistic, autobiographical, or ethnographic genres.'[25] Hurston would anticipates Clifford Geertz's call for 'thick description' in ethnography by several decades.[26] Hurston studied under the so-called 'father of American anthropology', Franz Boas, who is most famous for undermining the supposedly scientific rationale for racism. Boas became a target for segregationists seeking to attack the intellectual underpinnings of desegregation throughout mid-century. Arch-segregationist Theodore Bilbo warned against the 'damnable and blighting teachings of these disciples of Boas' and white supremacist pseudo-intellectual Carleton

Putnam termed Boasian thought 'the rotten core of [the] rosy apple [. . .] upon which integration feeds'.[27] Boas was certainly influential in Hurston's development as an anti-racist anthropologist, but she consistently went further in her innovation in the form of ethnographic writing. Hurston's anthropological work was addressed not only to the professional audience who responded to Boas's work but, according to literary critic Cynthia Ward, to 'another audience, a vernacular one, which values not fixed truth but transforming and transformative "lies" and indeterminacy'.[28] In his very brief preface to Hurston's anthropological study *Mules and Men* (1935), Boas twice makes reference to Hurston's ability to access the 'true inner life' of the African Americans under study.[29] Boas is keen to affirm the relationship between the anthropological method and clear, unambiguous truth. In contrast, Hurston's success as an anthropologist is defined precisely by her writing's capacity for ambiguity and her figurative, vernacular style of discourse.

Hurston invents Eatonville as a space that both is and is not typical of other southern towns. Eatonville is mired in the segregated social order that surrounds it, even as the town itself is more or less isolated from cross-racial violence and racial etiquette. By exploring in detail the origins of the town – chiefly in *Their Eyes Were Watching God*, but also in the early piece 'The Eatonville Anthology' (1926) and the play *De Turkey and De Law* (1930) – I show that Hurston extends and improves existing narrative means of developing the town as the site of scientific study. Hurston's stated views on segregation vary greatly in the period between the 1920s and 1950s, but her construction of Eatonville represents a town that is at once distinct from and built upon the governing principle of segregation.

In the 1929 essay 'How It Feels to be Colored Me', Hurston reflects on becoming raced only upon leaving her real hometown: 'I left Eatonville, the town of the oleanders, as Zora. When I disembarked from the river-boat at Jacksonville, she was no more . . . I was not Zora of Orange County any more, I was now a little colored girl.'[30] As Cheryl Wall writes, the essay is driven by a 'rejection of race as an immutable condition' that, in turn, 'represents a crucial turn in the development of the twentieth-century African American essay'.[31] Here and elsewhere in her public writing, Hurston identifies northern racism as more insidious and harmful, in her experience at least, than the *de jure* racial segregation in Florida. In 'My Worst Jim Crow Experience', for example, the author explains how her 'most humiliating Jim Crow experience came in New York instead of the South as one would have expected'.[32] Hurston consistently, if implicitly, critiques the ideology of southern exceptionalism by locating the worst of racial abuses in the urban North.

The author's treatment of segregation in the South can verge on the dismissive. Hurston's experience of black autonomy in Eatonville provides some rationale for her surprisingly reactionary response to *Brown v. Board of Education of Topeka*. Perhaps infamously, in a letter to the *Orlando Sentinel* dated 11 August 1955, she asks: 'How much satisfaction can I get from a court order for somebody to associate with me who does not wish me near them?' and reads the second *Brown* decision, handed down on 31 May 1955, as 'insulting rather than honoring [her] race'.[33] In an essay published a decade earlier, Hurston was more staunchly opposed to segregation and vocally in favour of legislative action: '. . . I am all for the repeal of every Jim Crow law in the nation here and now. Not in another generation or so.'[34] In this earlier essay, Hurston shares Lillian Smith's frustration with gradualism and repeatedly insists on the immediate overturn of segregationist laws: 'I crave to sample this gorgeous thing [democracy]. So I cannot say anything different from repeal of all Jim Crow laws! Not in some future generation, but repeal *now* and forever!!'[35] Hurston's collected writings on segregation are more complex than the *Brown* letter alone might suggest, but she consistently affirms black self-definition in favour of what she might consider self-pity. She offers a consistent critique of African American authors – including and even especially Wright – who contribute to what she calls, 'the sobbing school of Negrohood who hold that nature somehow has given them a low-down dirty deal and whose feelings are all hurt about it'.[36] Hurston's tone is dismissive, but her conception of cross-racial contact is clearly influenced by her experiences growing up in the decidedly atypical southern town of Eatonville.

To the young Hurston, whiteness is defined through the lens of Eatonville: 'During this period, white people differed from colored to me only in that they rode through town and never lived there.'[37]

If the real town of Eatonville protected Hurston from the worst experiences of segregation – at least in her public reflections on her childhood – Janie, the protagonist of *Their Eyes Were Watching God*, is afforded no such protection. Unlike Hurston, Janie enters the all-black Eatonville having already matured in a segregated community, and Hurston is careful throughout the novel to reflect Janie's origins in segregated West Florida. While Eatonville itself is not developed – physically, at least – along a geography of the colour line, its population is influenced by the lived experience of segregation. Janie's account of her development, for example, places an equal emphasis on the efforts of her grandmother and the white family for whom Nanny worked: 'Mah grandma raised me. Mah grandma and de white folks she worked wid. She had a house out in de back-yard and dat's where Ah wuz born. They was quality white folks up dere in West Florida.'[38] Janie softens the impact of segregation by insisting that her grandmother works with, and not for, the white Washburn family. Equally, she insists that the Washburns are exempt from the moral compromise of segregation, because they are 'quality'. Despite Janie's moves to modulate the significance of segregation on her childhood – a move that Hurston undermines by maintaining inferences of the damage of segregation – the psychological impact is clear. Elsewhere, the same segregated labour-based dynamic in which Janie is raised is figured more obviously as coercive. Janie is, for example, the subject of bullying because of her proximity to whiteness: 'de chillun at school got to teasin' me 'bout livin' in de white folks back-yard' (22). Hurston represents the social harm of segregation through intra-racial – rather than cross-racial – conflict that develops as a result of the exploitative labour relations between black and white southerners.

As an indirect result of the mediation of black agency in the unnamed Florida town, Nanny is figured as unable to fathom a black-run community, or black empowerment, even on a global scale: 'Maybe it's some place way off in de ocean where de black man is in power, but we don't know nothin' but what we see' (29). Nanny articulates a social-scientific maxim by warning against developing theses based on unobserved data. Hurston is ambiguous as to whether Eatonville disproves Nanny's statement – by being a place where 'the black man is in power' – or affirms by remaining indebted to white patronage.[39] At the very least, Eatonville operates within a broader segregated Florida as, at best, an anomaly or, at worst, a measure of containment. Joe Starks, the character who most clearly fits Nanny's hypothetical paradigm, is clearly compromised by his exploitation in segregated Georgia. Starks's domineering presence imbues the town he designs with similar, though mono-racial, spatial power dynamics.

Starks's introduction is rhetorically figured as a process of urbanisation: 'She [Janie] had been there a long time when she heard whistling coming down the road. It was a cityfied, stylish dressed man with his hat set at an angle that didn't belong in these parts' (47). As well as being urbanised ('citified'), Starks is presented in the first instance as a *pars pro toto* synecdoche. The 'whistling' – a sound for which Starks is responsible – 'was' the man who made the sound. The absence of punctuation following the phrase 'at an angle' suggests ambiguity regarding whether it is Joe, a migrant from Georgia, or his sartorial style that is alien to the region. If the phrase 'with his hat set at an angle' were a subclause within the sentence, separated by commas, the statement would be clear. By presenting this ambiguity, Hurston suggests a connection between appearance and belonging, both of which are fundamentally sited and prefigured by a process of 'citifying'.

Starks's authoritarian presence in the novel is consistently constructed, at the formal level, through recourse to languages of space and power. Following his introduction, the narrative continues in the same mode of free-indirect discourse to explicate Starks's ambitions: 'Joe Starks was the name, yeah Joe Starks from in and through Georgy. Been workin; for white folks all his life. Saved up some money – round three hundred dollars, yes indeed, right here in his pocket' (47). Hurston deploys the technique of deixis to embed the free indirect discourse – the phrase 'right here in his pocket' underscores the spatiality of Starks's introduction at the same time as it underscores his role as both a synecdoche and a quasi-anthropological architect of an archetypal southern town. Henry Louis Gates reads Hurston's experimentation with free indirect discourse as one of her defining stylistic contributions, that 'not only to represent[s] an individual character's speech and thought but also [. . .] the collective black community's speech and thoughts'.[40]

Gates calls Starks 'the master of metonym', and Hurston consistently positions him as representative of the inhabitants and spaces of the town.[41] Before setting foot in Eatonville, Starks conceptualises the town as literally constructed on the bodies and labour of African Americans: 'But when he heard all about 'em makin' a town all outa colored folks, he knowed dat was de place he wanted to be' (48). In this formulation, 'colored folks' are the objectified building blocks of the town, while Starks is positioned as a participant in the town rather than its raw material.

Joe's forceful personality has the immediate effect of galvanising and subduing the residents of the town: 'There was something about Joe Starks that cowed the town' (75). The inhabitants of Eatonville are brought together as a population because of a shared subservience to Starks. Just as he overwhelms the town's social landscape, Starks takes ownership of the physical, commercial and official apparatuses of Eatonville, becoming 'all set as the Mayor-post master-landlord-storekeeper' in short order (75). The residents of Eatonville are collectively ambivalent about the position of power Starks creates for himself, but lack the individual power to resist him: 'The town had a basketful of feelings good and bad about Joe's positions and possessions, but none had the temerity to challenge him' (79–80). By exerting his dominance over residential property, the social space of the store, and the civic offices of mayor and postmaster, Starks shapes Eatonville in his own image. Starks's authority in the town speaks to a paradox of power in the community: 'They bowed down to him rather, because he was all of these things, and then again he was all of these things because the town bowed down' (80). Hurston dramatises the paradox of Starks as architect and beneficiary of the town, and he is figured as alternately founder and interloper at crucial moments in Eatonville's development.

Hurston is explicit in her representation of Joe's internalised, performed whiteness. To cement his standing in the town he buys 'a spittoon just like his used-to-be bossman used to have in his bank up there in Atlanta' (76). The repeated word 'used' shifts meaning in this short passage from a temporal indicator to a verb that suggests exploitation. Hurston deploys the shift in meaning to highlight similarities in behaviour between Starks's racist former employer and Starks himself. Such overt displays of dominance inevitably lead to discontent in the town and the people of Eatonville consider their antipathy towards Starks in terms of the logic of segregation: 'It was bad enough for white people, but when one of your own color could be so different it put you on a wonder' (76). Starks, like the anthropologists I discuss above, comes to Eatonville with an idea of how power structures in typical towns work, and then sets about replicating those old structures where they need not exist. Starks's privilege is unsettling to the people of the town, and Hurston enhances this paradigm through a distinctly *unheimlich* metaphor: 'It was like seeing your sister turn into a 'gator. A familiar strangeness. You keep seeing your sister in the 'gator and the 'gator in your sister, and you'd rather not' (76). The unsettling metaphor of the alligator begins to suggest the unstable place Starks holds in the town's imagination: 'There was no doubt that the town respected him and even admired him in a way. But any man who walks in the way of power and property is bound to meet hate' (77). Hurston suggests that power and property are inevitably contingent concepts and Starks's ambitions to (racialised) power are necessarily connected to his domination of the landscape of the town. Stark's first encounter with the town is defined by precisely this motif of walking in power.

Starks and Janie's first act upon arriving at Eatonville is to survey the landscape: 'Joe said they must walk over the place and look around. They locked arms and strolled from end to end of the town' (56). With the few buildings overwhelmed by natural overgrowth and 'scattered in the sand and palmetto roots' Joe dismissively asserts the absence of the facilities of semi-urbanity: 'God, they call this a town? Why, 'taint nothing but a raw place in the woods' (56). Joe's corrective to the bioregional character of the space, defined by its undisturbed Floridian landscape, is to prioritise residential buildings: 'You cannot have no town without some land to build it on' and he immediately 'ups and buys two hundred acres uh land at one whack and pays cash for it' (60, 62). Starks seems to echo Veblen's attention to property as a galvanising factor in a town's social life: 'Real estate is the one community interest that binds the townsmen with a common bond.'[42] Like the social scientists I discuss earlier in this chapter, Starks paradoxically sets out to invent a new town based on his existing understanding of what a town ought to be. Eatonville is Starks's simulacrum of an all-black segregated town, and Hurston's critique of innovation that reaffirms inequality. Starks's insistence on a recognisable model undermines his own conception of Eatonville as genuinely innovative and unique. As a result, the space of the town is created in the image of pre-existing southern spaces that feature the architecture of inequality: 'The rest of the town looked like servant's quarters surrounding the "big house"' (75). Joe is forthright in his plans 'tuh make dis our town de metropolis uh de state' while he acknowledges that establishing integrity, based again on an existing model, is of utmost importance: 'if we expect tuh move on, us got tuh incorporate lak every other town. Us got tuh incorporate and us got tuh have uh mayor, if things is tuh be done right' (68–9). Starks's imposition of a racialised geography contributes to what Patricia Yaeger has termed the 'incredible instability of place' in the novel.[43]

Starks's ambitions to the office of mayor is signalled by the word's etymology. The modern English 'mayor' derives from the Latin *māior* and Old French *maire* meaning both 'elder' and 'greater'. To Starks, the official process of incorporation is also articulated as a structure of feeling: 'Ah kin see dat dis town is full uh union and love' (68). The practical structure of the town – the incorporation suggested by 'union' – is not differentiated from the coercive emotional baggage Starks deploys. Hurston reflects the tension that derives from Starks's position through Janie's discomfort: 'Janie soon began to feel the impact of awe and envy against her sensibilities [. . .] She slept with authority and so she was part of it in the town mind' (74). Eatonville is compromised by its architect's internalised power dynamics, and Janie is equally compromised by her unwilling role in the embedding of those power dynamics into the town's physical shape.

Starks recognises that his position of authority in the town must also function at broader state- and nation-wide scales. Through his founding of a post office, Starks ensures that his local domination has a wider impact. His wider ambitions are a source of both scepticism and awe among the people of Eatonville, who describe his plan in terms of resource extraction: 'He's gointuh put up uh store and git uh post office from de Goven'ment' (62). The post office is understood to be a particularly bold assertion of the town's status, as one townsperson articulates scepticism against another's perceived naivety: 'Yo' common sense oughta tell yuh de white folks ain't goin' tuh 'low him tuh run no post office' (63). The other responds with a show of faith in Starks's ability to put the town on the map: 'Ah reckon if colored folks got they own town they kin have post offices and whatsoever they please, regardless. And then agin, ah don't speck the white folks way off yonder give uh damn' (63). Segregation still influences the way the people of the town think about power and inclusion in the body politic and continues to dictate what constitutes 'common sense' for black southerners. What the disagreement above suggests is that proximity to whiteness is a crucial indicator. The perceived distance from a figurative colour line allows the optimistic speaker to believe in Starks's ability to run the town. Hurston makes sure that the faith is not completely returned and that Eatonville's inclusion under the auspices of the federal government remains mediated by neighbouring white community: 'When the mail came in from Maitland and [Joe] went inside to sort it' (77). The community's inclusion within both the nation and the circulation of information is twice mediated: first by the authority of the neighbouring white community that acts as a conduit and filter for the town's mail and second by Starks himself, who acts as an additional authority. Eatonville is independent and autonomous, but on in the terms dictated by white Florida and enacted by Starks.

Repeatedly, and earlier in her career, Hurston articulates the post office as the public centre of Eatonville. In the early text 'The Eatonville Anthology', which has been classed alternately as a short story and an ethnographic essay, she rehearses the use of 'the town' as synecdoche that would characterise *Their Eyes Were Watching God*: 'The *town* was collected at the store-postoffice as is customary on Saturday nights. The *town* has had its bath and with its week's pay in pocket fares forth to be merry.'[44] Using the same technique of hyphenated compound words she would later deploy to describe Starks's multiple role, Hurston identifies the post office's dual responsibility as a hub for communication beyond the confines of the town and as a commercial centre within the space of the town. In a brief description of the town as a *totem pro parte* synecdoche (the whole of the town represents its individual inhabitants), Hurston establishes the complex balance between the community as at once a component in a larger, state and federal, context and an insular unit that is commercially self-sufficient.[45] Hurston appropriates the techniques of ethnographic studies that isolate their subjects, but she positions them as components in an antiracist critique.

If Starks builds the town – in terms of its landscapes, its social life, it offices of authority, and its relationship to the federal government – then Hurston presents us with Eatonville as imbued with a range of toxic social mechanisms from the start. Janie, perhaps, offers a means of taking the town away from the inherent vice of Joe's influence. In Hurston's novel, as in novels by Byron Herbert Reece and William Melvin Kelley discussed later in this book, the absence of a literal colour line is not the absence of segregation. Power dynamics – especially those that proscribe cross-racial interaction – remain fundamental to the ontological life of Eatonville. Such dynamics were clearly defined in the segregated South and were ideologically supported by a group of white intellectuals. Hurston challenges dominant academic discourses about race and the southern town in part by reimagining anthropological methodologies, but also by exposing racial etiquette as a toxic and prevalent narrative.

Synecdoche, Survival and Racial Etiquette in *Uncle Tom's Children*

The metonymic fictions developed by the social sciences are insidious in so far as they produce misleading objects of study. They threaten to undermine the specificity of lived experience in southern and American towns and, as such, can serve to undermine activism and political organising in those towns. The fictions of racial etiquette that circulated during the same period, with roots much earlier, are clearly more dangerous. Systems of racial etiquette, buttressed by acts of racial violence and terrorism, organised southern towns socially and geographically. Racial etiquette maintained the psychology and architecture of apartheid through which white southerners organised the region. During the 1930s a range of non-fiction writers from a variety of ideological positions attempted to articulate racial etiquette as both organic and beneficial. To them, the systems that governed cross-racial encounters explicitly bene-fited white and black southerners. African American intellectuals and writers – including Hurston and Richard Wright – articulated resistance to this ideological position and rationale for racial segre-gation. Wright's first book, *Uncle Tom's Children*, explores the lived experience of racial etiquette in fiction and memoir. For Wright, and across the stories and essay collected in the volume, racial etiquette is an extension of the physical landscape of the archetypal southern town.

The construction of fictional towns allows authors to engage with harmful paradigms of racial etiquette at both narrowly and broadly defined geographical scales. Historian J. William Harris summarises the significance of individual communities in forging codes of racial conduct that are replicated more broadly: 'laws of etiquette were largely informal and a part of "local knowledge," varying from place to place and time to time' but remained 'rel-atively consistent' across localities.[46] Confrontation with racial etiquette was a valuable tool of protest for both African American and white southerners during the civil rights movement. Historian Benjamin Houston, in a study of Nashville at mid-century, argues that civil rights activists and proponents of massive resistance 'simultaneously provided whites with self-justification for their racial beliefs while channeling black resistance'.[47] To Houston, racial etiquette is designed along spatial and economic axes as it 'preserve[d] social hierarchies in the spaces where the races inter-acted' and 'reinforce[d] black economic dependence on whites'.[48] It goes without saying that racial etiquette was designed to the advantage of white southerners, and to the disadvantage of black southerners. Commentators and academics in the 1930s devel-oped tenuous intellectual foundations for the racial social struc-ture of small communities.

In 1937 African American historian Bertram Wilbur Doyle iden-tified the process by which 'forms of deference and recognition, repeated and imitated, soon crystallize into those conventional and obligatory forms of expression we call "etiquette" or "social ritual" in the antebellum period'.[49] Doyle reflects somewhat coldly on how the rules of etiquette defined contemporary southern life: 'A society or community [. . .] may be said to have obtained stable equilibrium when all the social distances are known and every individual is in his place.'[50] Doyle's research does not explore the intellectual and psychological impact of etiquette on black southerners who are unwilling participants in racial etiquette. The politics of humiliation and resistance is powerfully articulated in the essay from which the current book takes its title, Wright's 'The Ethics of Living Jim Crow' (1938). Wright recalls a story in which he avoids either the distasteful option of deference to white men or the dangerous one of resistance. When expected to show gratitude for a small act of 'kindness' shown by a white southerner, Wright fumbles with a package he carries, thereby avoiding either humiliation or violent retribution.[51] The complex system of racial etiquette suggests why cultural historian of the American town Miles Orvell overlooks the subtext of demographic data: 'If blacks were tolerated in the southern town, they were restricted by Jim Crow practices to their own distinct places' while in other regions in the United States 'there was more typically no place at all for blacks'.[52] Rather than 'tolerating' an African American presence, white southerners in small towns required it. Instead, racial etiquette served to affirm the strict rules of interaction through which white Americans could maintain power over their black neighbours.

White southerners maintained this etiquette through acts of racial violence and terrorism, but forms of intellectual discourse that gained traction the 1930s supported their efforts. Each of the fictional towns I explore at length through the remainder of this book are spatially divided along racial lines. In Smith's *Strange Fruit* the division between 'White Town' and 'Colored Town' follows a common trend in naming. The 'niggertown' slum presented in Reece's *The Hawk and the Sun* (1955) is more overtly offensive, but accurately represents naming conventions in some southern towns and cities.[53] As conservative literary critic Edd Winfield Parks noted in 1934, racially proscribed cartographies characterise real southern towns: 'the most notable physical characteristic that differentiates these southern towns [. . .] is the presence of the Negro. Each town has its Negro section, usually given such expressive names as "Black Bottom," or "Nigger Hill."'[54] Aside from covertly supporting a myth of a racially homogenised North, Parks suggests that racial division is an organic and inevitable trait of southern towns. Parks's paternalistic analysis revolves around the fiction of functional southern community:

> These titles might imply that the Negro is badly treated, but this most certainly is far from true. He is segregated, socially, but in all other respects he is a normal, and generally, a happy part of the community, with his own school and churches. For the small-town Negro, also, is not philosophical, and he remains unworried over subtle distinctions of racial equality or of right and wrong.[55]

Parks, probably unintentionally, deploys the flawed analytical tool I identify in the work of anthropologists of the era: he invents a subject of study (a happy, unphilosophical and unworried black southerner), elevates that subject as an archetype, and draws a far-reaching scholarly conclusion based on an apparently representative case. In *Their Eyes Were Watching God*, Hurston implicitly critiques such intellectual rationales for cross-racial encounters in segregated Florida.

Janie's grandmother Nanny is formerly enslaved, but she also represents the development of segregation as a defining feature of black interactions with whiteness in the years following *Plessy v. Ferguson*. Nanny is able to own her own land only because of the system of white patronage that typically accompanied black landownership in the South: 'She got de land and everything and then Mis Washburn helped out uh whole heap wid things' (22–3). While Janie is characteristically reticent about what 'helping out' means, Hurston here suggests the paradigm of a white person vouching for an African American's economic and social stability. Power relationships in real southern towns routinely proscribed African Americans' capacity to own property. Publisher and Federal Writers Project administrator W. T. Couch observes, a black would-be farm-owner 'must first have the approval of the community. Often the purchase will have been made at the suggestion of a white man who wishes to do a favour to a Negro who he likes.'[56] Couch's description is uncritical, but Hurston's fictional portrayal of Nanny's homeownership constitutes an implicit critique. The passage constitutes a subtle allusion to the role of racial etiquette in the segregated South. An imagined reader is reasonably expected to infer that the 'help' included some guarantee of personal character and of financial reliability. Nanny is presented as well considered by white southerners for adopting an 'appropriate' role within the community, signifying complicity in or accommodation to the rules of racial etiquette.

While Parks and Couch, like Warren four years earlier, articulated a belief that African Americans were happiest in their proverbial place in the small-town South, they each described the black subject as the object of white organisation, rendered in the passive voice so that whites are implicitly staged as innocent of racially oppressing blacks. Parks's passive voice suggests that African Americans are 'badly treated' and 'segregated' by an unnamed force, and for Couch, 'bad conditions' exist independently of white southerners' design. That each of these essays appears in a collection titled *Culture in the South* (1934) indicates the degree to which white southern identity at mid-century was governed by a person's racial 'place' in the southern town. The analytical voice adopted by each of these writers indicates the degree to which racial etiquette is linguistically constructed. Without citing evidence, intellectuals rhetorically construct a stable social paradigm based on etiquette. As critic Richard Gray argues of the essayists of *I'll Take My Stand*, 'The case presented for the rural life by the Agrarians is inseparable, finally, from the words in which it is put [. . .] occupying a sort of unique hinterland between fact and fiction.'[57] Authors like Wright deploy similar rhetorical methods to dismantle the ideology of etiquette covertly outlined in conservative writing of the time. For Wright, the spatial organisation of the southern town is inexorably bound to the coercive social order of segregation and, especially, racial etiquette. When Wright's fictional towns emerge most clearly – often in a literal re-emergence after submersion or disguise – they are met with a firm assertion of racial violence as an organising principle. Alongside the pivotal essay, 'The Ethics of Living Jim Crow', the story 'Down by the Riverside' is most revealing of Wright's early treatment of racial etiquette as a guiding social principle of southern community.

The protagonist of 'Down by the Riverside', named simply Mann or 'Brother Mann', struggles to make an unnamed southern town legible as he works to survive the Great Mississippi Flood of 1927 and (under duress) rescue other townspeople. Navigating the town is almost impossible because recognisable geographical and structural features are obscured, unmoored or submerged by the extreme weather. Understanding of geography is always followed immediately by a reassertion – through violent or otherwise coercive means – of racial etiquette, as when Mann recognises the submerged 'Rose Street' and is immediately identified by a white authority figure as 'violating curfew' (83). Wright depicts a town that can *only be a town* if it is guided by violent racial order and constructs of two parallel geographies of the town – one at the surface of the flood and the other hidden by it. The geography of the town is also characterised by an aquatic motif, as in the names of Rose Street and Pikes' Road, and the character of Mr Bridges (83, 77, 99). Wright deploys 'Rose' as a pun signifying the past tense of 'to rise' as well as an ironic invocation of romance and natural beauty while Pikes' Road suggests aquatic life. The story opens, pointedly, with a consideration of foundations:

> Each step he took made the old house creak as though the earth beneath the foundations were soggy. He wondered how long the logs which supported the house could stand against the water. But what really worried him were the steps; they might wash away at any moment, and then they would be trapped. (62)

The 'foundation' of the house is a clear metaphor for the town that is being visited by a flood. It is fragile and likely to succumb to pressure. Mann is more concerned about the facility for upward (or downward) travel and the ability to escape. The stairs signify both a narrative of racial ascension and a simple right to movement. The foundations of the southern town are rotten, leaving escape or extraction as the only viable options for survival. The first story in the collection, 'Big Boy Leaves Home', immediately precedes 'Down by the Riverside' and ends with the eponymous African American youth leaving another unnamed southern town to avoid being lynched: 'The truck sped over the asphalt miles, sped northward, jolting him, shaking out of his bosom the crumbs of corn bread, making them dance with the splinters and sawdust in the golden blades of sunshine' (61). For Big Boy, physically and intellectually leaving the disintegrating southern town – symbolised by the falling crumbs of corn bread – is the only means of survival.

In the midst of disaster, racial dynamics of labour revert to a more obviously coercive and exploitative model: '[Mann] had heard that white folks were threatening to conscript all Negroes they could lay their hands on to pile sand- and cement-bags on the levee' (64). At the same time, the social order of the town becomes less easily legible to its black inhabitants, and the consistent threat of violence becomes still more acute:

> Yes, it was hard to tell just what was happening in town. Shucks, in times like these theyll shoota nigger down jus lika dog n think nothin of it. Tha shootin might mean anything. But likely as not its jus some po black man gone . . . (64, ellipses in original)

Wright offers an early example in the narrative of an important theme of Mann seeking to understand his town in order to survive it. Mann recognises that the black townspeople's already fragile personal safety from racial violence is immediately forfeit in the face of a natural emergency. His physical safety, and that of his family, is explicitly threatened by the subsumed architecture of the town as he navigates above it in a stolen boat:

> To all sides of Mann the flood rustled, gurgled, droned, glistening blackly like an ocean of bubbling oil. Above his head the sky was streaked with faint grey light [. . .] all around he was ringed in by walls of solid darkness. He knew that houses and trees were hidden by those walls and he knew he had to be careful. (74)

Mann experiences two contradictory, but simultaneous, landscapes. His navigation of the flooded town is facilitated by a DuBoisian double-consciousness and Mann must navigate both the undifferentiated landscape in which the grey sky and black walls of water merge and simultaneously rely on his knowledge of the hidden landscape of the town to avoid collision. Either landscape could kill him, and both ontological positions are necessary for survival. The racial ontology imposed by racial etiquette is similarly necessary for African Americans to survive segregation.

Mann tries desperately to locate himself in the geography of the town by seeking signifiers of the racially coercive capitalist economy of the town: 'he began to look for the cotton-seed mill that stood to the left of the railroad. He peered, longing to see the black stack-pipes' (75). While the cotton economy was a factor of the town that Mann, presumably, had to struggle to survive prior to the flood, he now turns to his understanding of that spatial and social structure to survive the natural disaster: '[He] wondered what could be on the ground, what landmarks the water hid [. . .] Westward *would be* houses. And straight down *would be* Pikes' Road. That *would be* the shortest way' (75, emphasis added). Wright dramatises the conditional existence of African Americans in a segregated community, just as he recalls a similar pattern in 'The Ethics of Living Jim Crow'. In the essay, Wright recalls being frightened into silence by 'the mere idea of what would happen to' him if he were to 'snitc[h]' on two white co-workers or if he were to inadvertently call one of those co-workers a liar (5, 6). The very real threat that the submerged buildings pose to Mann as he navigates the flooded town echoes a similar fear of residential properties that Wright recalls in his essay: 'Even today when I think of white folks, the hard, sharp, outlines of white houses surrounded by trees, lawns, and hedges are present somewhere in the background of my mind [growing] into an overreaching symbol of fear' (3). Wright's phobia is defined by the conflation of race and space, and the 'sharpness' of the buildings marks them as weapons. Literary critic Stéphane Robolin describes how 'an acute spatial consciousness was more frequently the province of black subjects who could ill afford to be indifferent to the layout of their surrounding environments' whose 'finely tuned geographic knowledge and spatial literacy in a segregated land served as essential tools for black subjects'.[58] In memoir and fiction Wright depicts, rather than describes, this process. He positions rhetoric and narrative form as correctives to the abiding intellectual narratives of racial etiquette.

Mann, upon feeling a wooden object in the water, attempts to site his experience of the flood within his racialised understanding of the altered landscape. His desperation to locate himself highlights what geographer Katherine McKittrick identifies as 'the classificatory *where* of race'.[59] Wright appeals to metaphors of the built environment with a pointed vocabulary of construction when he describes Mann's attempts to ground himself: 'He breathed hard, trying to build in his mind something familiar around the cold, wet, smooth pieces of wood. A series of pictures flashed through his mind, but none fitted. He groped higher, thinking with his fingers' (76). Wright depicts Mann's experience of the town through a synaesthesia of the tactile and visual. The passage represents an ontological exercise and Mann seeks the specific knowledge he needs to survive the unusual conditions he has encountered. This synaesthesia becomes more acute as Mann comes to locate himself more certainly in the physical town: 'Then suddenly he saw the whole street: sunshine, wagons and buggies tied to a water trough. This is old man Toms sto. And these were the railings that went around the front porch he was holding in his hands' (76–7). Mann's familiarity with the territory of the town must be complete in order to survive this catastrophe, but also to effectively navigate threats of violence that pre-exist the flood. He deploys his geographical awareness of the submerged town in an attempt to navigate the boat away from danger:

> He righted [the boat], striving to keep away from the houses, seeking for the street. He strained his eyes till they ached; but all he could see were dark bulks threatening on either side. Yet, that was enough to steer him clear of them. And he rowed, giving his strength to the right oar and then to the left, trying to keep in the middle. (77)

It is unclear whether Mann is navigating the middle of the current or the middle of the unseen – but imagined – Pikes' Road. Repeatedly, the space of the town, and black characters' knowledge of its geography, is figured as necessary to survival. When, slightly later, Mann approaches the Heartfield house, he strives for a racialised understanding of geography: 'His mind groped frantically in the past, sought for other times on Pikes' Road and for other nights to tell him who lived where those yellow lights gleamed. But the lights remained alone and the past would tell him nothing' (78). Wright consistently depicts the town as an ontological construct as much as it is a geographical and social structure.

Throughout this extended scene of navigation, Wright dramatises simultaneous feelings of anxiety and optimism in the same way that Mann is forced to navigate two simultaneous and contradictory landscapes. This is especially evident when Mann notices the first sign of habitation in the flood: 'They helped him, those lights. For awhile he rowed without effort. Where there were lights there were people and where there were people there was help' (77). Rhetorically, this passage exemplifies chiasmus, a technique in which phrases are repeated and reversed.[60] No sooner does Mann draw the conclusion that the lights suggest safety than he considers them to be equally suggestive of the threat of violence: 'Wondah whose house is tha? Is they white folks? Fear dimmed the lights for a moment; but he rowed on and they glowed again, their soft sheen helping him to sweep the oars' (77–8). Wright deploys internal rhyme and sibilance in the third-person narration to mirror the rhythmic flow, and deep uncertainty, of the flood and the moving boat. Mann's anxiety is likewise represented as subject to the ebb and flow of the flooded street, foreshadowing how his attempt to survive the flood forces him to break racial etiquette.

After Mann kills Heartfield in self-defence, the geography of the town takes on a still more menacing dimension in Mann's experience. After being conscripted to rescue stranded whites, Mann is terrified when Brinkley – a similarly conscripted black local – identifies the position of their government-issued boat: '"Its Pikes Road!" Its the Pos Office! Its Miz Heartfiel . . .' (105). As in *Their Eyes Were Watching God*, the post office ties the town to a broader federal identity. Ironically, this figurative anchoring to the US government persists even as the physical office is literally unmoored. Mann is forced to join the rescue effort by the federal-mandated military presence, and Wright carefully implicates the whole nation – not simply the South – in Mann's violent exploitation. The Heartfield house becomes literally untethered from the submerged geography of the town, becoming more identifiably a feature of the grey, inhospitable landscape of the flood: 'The house was moving down the street. Mann held his breath, feeling himself suspended over a black void. The house reached the center of the street and turned violently' (108). Wright deploys pathetic fallacy to describe the house as violent, and suggests that Mann is being attacked by the town itself. Faced with the likelihood of being discovered during the rescue mission, Mann's terror is again rendered in terms of landscape: 'They got me now, he thought. He stumbled on dry land. He took a step and a twig snapped [. . .] The landscape lay before his eyes with a surprising and fateful solidity. It was like a picture which might break' (114). The fragility expressed in this passage echoes the description of the unstable foundations early in the story. Mann's desperate attempts to make sense of the shifting landscape are ultimately unsuccessful. He is unable to survive the threat posed by town's system of etiquette, while his wife dies because the flood restricts her access to medical care. Wright locates the construct of the segregated town as a necessary corollary to white supremacist violence.

These texts set a template that would be followed by later white and black novelists who choose the South as their setting. Key features of this template include the importance of the synecdoche as both a rhetorical device and a representation of ideology. Fiction is the only form of narrative in which a 'typical' town can be said to exist. The town undermines white supremacist ideology and action. Hurston and Wright develop a paradigm for race and protest that later writers are judged against. For example, the protagonist in Chester Himes's novel *If He Hollers Let Him Go* (1945) disagrees with a white character about the relative merits of Wright and Lillian Smith:

> 'Of course, I think Richard Wright makes the point better in *Native Son*.'
> 'Oh, but what Lillian Smith does is condemn the white southerner,' Arlene said. 'All Wright did was write a vicious crime story.'
> 'Personally, I think the white southerner doesn't mind being just how Lillian Smith describes him,' I said.[61]

Himes's novel explores the threat posed by racial etiquette in Los Angeles, rather than the South, but Himes is careful to align his protest with Wright's model. Smith's novel, the subject of the next chapter, does condemn some white southerners but it also offers a model for the fictional southern town that is more clearly figured as a tool of protest than either Hurston's or Wright's. In the 1940s the same reactionary intellectual trends persist, but novelists like Smith take the principles outlined in the previous decade further in service of desegregation.

The inadvertent narratives I outline in this chapter – of racial etiquette as a healthy feature of the southern town and the archetypal town as a stable metonym in sociological study – are articulated and critiqued in the 1930s. They form an intellectual background against which the authors I explore in the remainder of this book focus their energies. While only Faulkner published significant fiction during the decade – indeed, Kelley was not born until 1937 – they each resist and satirise these notions of the town in their fiction. In outlining some of the aesthetic techniques that Wright and Hurston developed to undermine and critique these narratives, I also expose a blueprint for reading the fictional southern town as inherently sceptical of the social and intellectual underpinnings of the imagined American town. Smith, already an established figure in the South's literary culture as editor of a series of literary magazines from 1936, would establish herself as the region's most popular and unrelenting critic of segregation in fiction. The aesthetic and political tactics that Wright, Hurston and other African American writers of the period mobilised in the setting of the town received a more thorough, even painstaking, application in Smith's *Strange Fruit*.

The White Town/ Coloured Town Paradigm: Lillian Smith's Maxwell

On 27 May 1961 Lillian Smith received a telegram from James Farmer, national director of the Congress of Racial Equality (CORE), urging her to attend an 'emergency meeting of [the] CORE advisory committee' in New York. Farmer requested Smith's 'immediate advice and help' because the Freedom Rides[1] were at 'a decisive stage'.[2] Three years later, shortly before the signing of the Civil Rights Act of 1964, Smith received another telegram, this one from President Lyndon B. Johnson, informing her that he would be establishing a 'community relations service [to] assist communities in preventing and resolving racial disputes'.[3] Johnson asks Smith to join, writing: 'I urge you as a private citizen to use your leadership in the meantime to prom[o]te a spirit of acceptance and observance in your own community and business area.'[4] In pencil, on the reverse of Johnson's telegram, Smith drafted a response indicating that she would be 'honored' to serve in such a capacity and that she would do all she could 'as a citizen and a writer to help'.[5] What emerges from this correspondence is an image of Smith as repeatedly called upon to offer a practical contribution to the movement in the early 1960s. That Smith considered her efforts to relate to the roles of 'citizen and writer' begins to suggest how the novelist, memoirist and journalist understood her written output to be an extension of her moral and practical commitment to desegregation.

This commitment to activism and writing is anticipated in the novel through which Smith rose to national prominence, the controversial and popular *Strange Fruit* (1944). Within a month of its publication, 140,000 copies were in print and within ten months the novel had sold almost half a million copies, figures that Lawrence P. Jackson identifies as 'blockbuster statistics'.[6] Indeed, it was the number-one fiction bestseller of the year.[7] Along with high sales figures came more than a little notoriety; Smith's indictment of the South's segregated system meant the novel was banned in Boston on 20 March 1944, from the mail by the Post Office Department in May, and unofficially in Detroit by 'gentleman's agreement'.[8] In her later non-fiction writing, Smith was vocal in seeking an immediate and uncompromising end to segregation, rather than a gradual decline. While *Strange Fruit*'s role as an extension of Smith's politics has been examined by critics including Richard King, Will Brantley and Robert Brinkmeyer Jr, the novel's paradigmatic setting of the small southern town has yet to be fully explored.[9]

Smith's focus in *Strange Fruit* is on the entirety of Maxwell's landscape, from the uninhabited swamp that delimits the town inwards to points at Maxwell's centre where the nominally divided 'White Town' and 'Colored Town' meet. Every element of the landscape is imagined as facilitating segregation, even as Smith continually exposes the town's failure to effectively separate the races. By exploring Smith's conception of Maxwell as similar to, but distinct from, real southern towns and by charting how *Strange Fruit* depicts the failure of segregation as a structuring principle, I argue that Maxwell constitutes a typology of the fictional southern town that would be replicated in novels I examine later in this book. Smith draws on her lived experience in small southern towns while remaining a work of the imagination. Smith consistently exposes the racial barrier as porous: the division between 'White Town' and 'Colored Town' is artificial and permeable, as exemplified in scenes that take place on the borders of the two supposedly distinct spaces.

The novel traces the consequences of an interracial relationship between black domestic servant Nonnie Anderson and white doctor's son Tracy Deen. Nonnie is pregnant with Tracy's child and wants to have the baby. Tracy, whose relationship with Nonnie has largely been a diversion from the expectation of his mother and Maxwell's white community that he will marry Dorothy Pusey, decides to pay Henry, his family's black employee and Tracy's childhood friend, to marry Nonnie and raise the child as his own.

Nonnie's brother Ed, recently returned from his job in Washington, DC, in order to take Nonnie north, discovers the pregnancy and the plan and murders Tracy. While Ed flees north alone, Maxwell's white community must find a scapegoat for the murder. Henry is lynched by a mob of poor white workers, and this reinstates the social order of the town that had been threatened by Tracy's relationship with Nonnie.

Every element of Maxwell's social order contributes to its apparent integrity, both in the sense of the town as a functioning whole, and its shared morality. Tracy, a veteran of the First World War, is struggling to find a place within Maxwell appropriate to his family's prestige and Alma's expectations. The Deens live in a 'yellow' house on College Street, at the centre of 'White Town', suggesting tarnished whiteness or political and social cowardice.[10] Conversely, Nonnie and her family live at the very edge of Maxwell, in 'Colored Town'.

Everyday Reality is Bred from Dreams: Making Maxwell

Smith's Maxwell is an invented space. Any resemblance it may bear to real towns that the author lived in is secondary to the construction of a unique fictional identity. Maxwell is constructed at every level to approximate the working social order of a typical southern town. Smith locates Maxwell within a real American geography but establishes its shape, population and collective identity by charting the personality of the town and its population in great detail. She is painstaking in texturing the layers of economic, social and cultural facilities appropriate to its size in order to maintain racial division and uphold a white supremacist ideology. The town's white supremacist identity (and progressive threats to that identity) are mapped in the space of the fictional town.

The novel's opening line introduces a symbolically divided town: 'She stood at the gate, waiting; behind her the swamp, in front of her Colored Town, beyond it, all Maxwell' (1). The line enacts a spatial symbolism of the town, establishing a divided Maxwell. The syntax engages directly with the town's ironic name. The phrasing of the sentence – '. . . Colored Town, beyond it, all Maxwell . . .' – removes African American domestic space and social experience from the sanctioned definition of the town proper. Smith's syntax suggests that, other than the geography of racial segregation ('beyond Colored Town'), everything in the social order of the South is faultless ('all [is] Maxwell'). Smith's town is integral: it is a complete and coherent unit. At the same time, this cohesion depends on racial division. This paradox, of segregated integrity, forms the crux of Smith's aesthetic critique of segregation, and it is a paradox that defines each of the towns explored later in *Living Jim Crow*. The threshold at which Nonnie stands as the novel opens can allow progress in either direction and thresholds proliferate in the novel, and Maxwell is consistently depicted as a town on the brink of either racial progress or a reassertion of racial coercion.

Nonnie, as yet identified only by the pronoun 'she', occupies a liminal space, both in the geography of the town and in the town's shifting racial and sexual ideologies. The paragraphs that follow this opening sentence establish a coercive composite voice for the town that defines Nonnie in its own terms and denies her the privilege of self-identification. She is described and defined by different groups of the town's population in turn over the course of the novel's opening pages. Smith thereby introduces Nonnie as her protagonist while also offering a cumulative portrait of the population of the town. Each of the voices imposes a rigid definition upon Nonnie and, taken together, the ad hoc chorus forms a panoramic introduction to the social order of the town. The first group given a voice is obviously white:

> 'That's Nonnie Anderson,' they would tell you, 'that's one of the Anderson niggers. Been to college. Yeah! Whole family been to college! All right niggers though, even if they have. Had a good mother who raised her children to work hard and know their place. Anderson niggers is alright. Good as we have in the county I reckon.' (1)

In being the first to name her in the text, this section of the white population of Maxwell establishes its right to judge Nonnie and her family personally and socially within the parameters set by race. Nonnie is considered a constituent of the town ('good as we have in the county') but not on equal terms. She is not part of 'they' who define her, nor is she the 'you' who would be told. The passage supposes an individual white speaker (as suggested by the first-person singular pronoun in 'I reckon'). However, this individual is representative of a much larger group of which he or she is a member, addressing another person or persons ('they would tell you').

Nonnie is evaluated, by residents on either side of the colour line and across the social spectrum, according to her compliance with Maxwell's system of racial etiquette. Black residents identify Nonnie as aloof, alternately in pejorative or affirmative tones: she is either 'stuck up like Almighty' or it is a 'pity ain mo like her' (1). Nonnie is compared negatively to her sister Bess, who is identified as more 'friendly with folks' and a better domestic servant by black and white Maxwellians, respectively (1–2). Bess, whom I discuss at length below, is praised for better complying with the gendered structure of racial etiquette that defines the town. To white Maxwell, Nonnie is likewise judged based on her labour and her disposition. She is both 'biggety' and 'the best servant in Maxwell' other than Bess. Her employers describe her as 'a good nigger', further establishing her worth as mediated by her ability to function within rigidly defined racial and gendered parameters (2).

Because racial etiquette always, and necessarily, intersects with coercive gender norms, Nonnie is especially prone to scrutiny by sexually predatory white men:

> And white boys whistled softly when she walked down the street, and said low words and rubbed the back of their hands across their mouths, for Nonnie Anderson was something to look at twice, with her soft black hair blowing off her face, and black eyes set in a face that God knows should have belonged to a white girl. (2)

The phrase 'low words' can be interpreted either as whispered words or base swearing. In Smith's construction of the passage, the men seem to be at once individuated and part of a mob. They are described rubbing 'the back of their hands across their mouths', rather than the backs of their hands: the number of persons is confused. The men have multiple mouths but act as if with a shared hand, and Smith deploys a linguistic synecdoche during the same passage that establishes Maxwell as a representative synecdoche for the segregated town as a type. Each of these descriptions of

Nonnie occur extra-diagetically while, in narrative time, she has not moved from her symbolically loaded space at the threshold of her home. The social mores of segregation are carefully and deliberately inscribed on Nonnie's racialised body. An imagined reader first comes to know the character through a composite portrait offered by the town as a whole. Rather than a unified and cohesive voice – like the first-person plural narrative voice of William Faulkner's 'A Rose for Emily' – Smith's depiction of Nonnie is almost Cubist. The combined image takes shape based on a variety of divergent and conflicting perspectives.

Nonnie's position on the threshold at the beginning of the novel is also mirrored in Tracy's conception of their relationship as a path he chooses to take, which is thrown into relief when he learns of her pregnancy: 'Now sign says: *Road closed*. Better detour' (62). That Tracy thinks about his future as a linear path indicates his investment in white Maxwell's conventional racial narrative. Here, the reality of segregation prevents Tracy from considering a future with Nonnie. Later, after Tracy has committed to his plan to disown Nonnie, the imagery of the path is more aggressive and hostile: 'Nonnie was only a name today. A name and an obstacle. A colored girl blocking a white path' (97). While Nonnie is defined from the beginning of the text as poised at a moment of decision, Tracy is figured as subject to determinism because he is forced to follow the 'path' the town expects of him.

The verisimilitude with which Smith imposes her fictional town of Maxwell on an actual map of the United States is striking, with real Georgia towns and northern cities alluded to throughout the novel. While Maxwell is a construction of Smith's imagination, elements of its geography resemble towns in which the author lived and she sites her town within a recognisable US context. Real places are described in relation to Maxwell to locate the town geographically. For instance, Alma Deen's parents are from the town of Hawkinsville in the centre of Georgia, where Tracy spends time as a child (77). Tracy is defined by the racial structure of the invented, unreal, Maxwell, but he is partly raised within a real US geography. The tension implicit in this bi-location asserts itself in his relationship with Alma: 'Tracy never seemed quite hers after that' (78). Other real-world locations function as avenues of escape from

Maxwell. As a child, Henry lives in the Deens' back garden with his parents, who leave Maxwell for a cotton farm in Baxley when their son is a teenager (114). Smith presents the move as the result of a conflict arising from the racialisation of space in the town, and Henry's father tells his wife that he: 'hate[s] livin in Deen's back yard. Told you a hundard time it'd be better in the quarters where we'd be free to do as we like' (113). Proximity to whiteness, and the absence of self-determination, induce the McIntoshes to leave the town. Spaces outside the geography of Maxwell, and within the real-world geography of the state of Georgia, are sources of material wealth predicated on racial division. Alma Deen's wealth derives from 'nigger shanties' she owns in Macon, to the north of Maxwell (187, 332). Macon figures in the novel as a contact zone with real-world racial and social dynamics.

In her preface to *The Winner Names the Age: A Collection of Writings by Lillian Smith* (1978), Smith's partner, Paula Snelling, suggested an experiential, regionally derived grounding in much of Smith's writing:

> The sights, sounds, smells, the cadences of speech, body language, rituals and rotes of her region entered her bloodstream in childhood and give sensory verisimilitude to her writings. She did not sever this taproot, although her early, hometown search for the *whys* became a worldwide and lifelong quest.[11]

The verisimilitude Snelling discerns is drawn organically from Smith's 'hometown' experiences, not only her experiences in either Jasper, Florida, where Smith grew up, or the couple's chosen hometown of Clayton, Georgia, but from the 'taproot' of living in towns that are as 'typical' as these. Smith draws on her experiences for verisimilitude in her writing, but she does not engage in direct textual representations of her 'hometown' South.

Snelling suggests that '[t]he Maxwell Georgia, of her novel *Strange Fruit,* so far as it had specific geographical location and cultural milieu, was the town she left at age seventeen and to which she never returned'.[12] Smith herself described Jasper as an important touchstone in the novel's imaginative construction, even while the northern Florida town does not share a 'specific geographical location' with either Maxwell in central or Clayton in northern Georgia. The 'cultural milieu' Snelling describes is somewhat closer to the mark. Such real-world referents as Clayton and Jasper become 'touchstones' in the creation of fictional towns in that authors may draw on existing social and physical geographies, while maintaining a malleability of setting. In the theatrical programme for Smith's infamously unsuccessful 1945 Broadway adaptation of the novel, the author contributes a short introduction to the town of Maxwell.[13] In this piece, Smith erodes the division between the fictional Maxwell and her own experience of growing up in Florida: 'When I was a child in Maxwell, I lived on College Street where oak trees make cool paths for children to run on, and moss shuts the glare of sun from their eyes. [. . .] This was my town.'[14] In a letter from 1961, Smith also describes how she felt like a 'complete stranger' when she returned to Jasper as an adult.[15] In spite of the distance that the adult Smith felt from Jasper, the act of writing *Strange Fruit* strengthened her bond with that town, as when Smith describes the novel as 'removing a long amnesia about [her] hometown'.[16] By inventing a new town, Smith is able to access a relationship with a real town more fully, but the fictional town remains primary. As a result, Smith's construction of Maxwell allows her to rediscover Jasper in an ancillary sense. As she muses elsewhere, 'men imitate art, art does not imitate men; everyday reality is bred from dreams, not dreams from everyday reality.'[17] Jasper is, in Smith's description of it, modelled on Maxwell rather than the reverse. Only by inventing Maxwell as a synecdoche is Smith able to translate her personal development in the real segregated town of Jasper.

Smith's memory of Jasper does influence Maxwell's mapping in the novel as a series of concentric circles. As Smith remembers: 'Rimming the town like a shadow were the quarters where colored folk lived and at the edge of the Quarters a little unpainted church where they worshipped and sang.'[18] Elsewhere, Smith describes the same pattern: 'I can see even now the Negro shanties, rimming our town like a deep shadow and the big homes under oak trees on College Street.'[19] Smith uses strikingly similar language in the novel to describe how domestic servants return home to 'the cabins rimming the town, a shadow behind Maxwell' (117). Smith's locates the unincorporated space of the undeveloped swamp beyond even this outer rim of 'civilized' Maxwell.

The swamp is an ambivalent metaphor in the novel, at once representing the limitation and possibility of movement away from the town. It acts as a border, encircling the inhabitable space of the town with uninhabitable wilderness and contains Maxwell in spatial but also ideological terms. As Anthony Wilson argues in his cultural study, the swamp can be the site of 'alternative memory, independent of the white patriarchal master narrative'.[20] The swamp represents a space apart from the coercive and restrictive conventions of the town that empowers characters at least as much as it inhibits them. The swamp is the absence of the town offering less security, but greater freedom from the strictures of racial etiquette.

It is for this reason that Nonnie is attracted to the swamp; her attraction derives from a connection she appears to have to its wildness. It calls to Nonnie: 'it says, "come here, come here, come here"' (4). The affinity Nonnie feels is inaccessible to Tracy, though, who sees only the ecological fact of the landscape: '"You hear it?" she whispered. "Nope. Nothing but the frogs croaking, and the dogs"' (5). Tracy is unable either intellectually or emotionally to inhabit a space outside of the regulations of Maxwell, whereas, for Nonnie, a space distinct from those regulations is compelling. Tracy is afraid that Nonnie 'might get lost' in the swamp (5), but Nonnie is 'just visiting' the swamp as she would a neighbour (4). Smith implicates Tracy in the town's structure of racial etiquette through her invention of the space of the swamp. Tracy does not suffer the same burden of etiquette that Nonnie does, and he becomes anxious as a result of Nonnie's resistant engagement with space.

In the antebellum period, the southern swamp represented a dangerous space, but one which could be used by the enslaved to evade capture. Harriet Beecher Stowe's *Dred: A Tale of the Great Dismal Swamp* (1856) features a community of escaped slaves living in the Great Dismal Swamp area of Virginia and North Carolina.[21] In this reading of the swamp, Tracy remains contained by Maxwell, where Nonnie's place in the town is less fixed. Here, Smith's depiction of the swamp is what Wilson calls a 'signifier of subversive ambiguity' that 'presents subversion as a losing battle', and Smith makes it clear that the power in the town, as opposed to the swamp, sits with Tracy and not with Nonnie.[22]

As Smith's depiction of the swamp illustrates, Nonnie knows that 'Tracy lives in a white world', epitomised in the novel by the elite white enclave of College Street (123). Despite the name, characters who receive university educations have to travel elsewhere in the state or the country. Bess and Nonnie are educated at Spelman (20), and Smith's representation of college graduates working as domestic servants contributed to the controversy surrounding the novel. Then director of the National Association for the Advancement of Colored People, Walter White, expressed disbelief that an educated black woman like Nonnie would submit herself to Tracy as she does in the novel. Smith, formerly a welcome guest at Spelman, was discouraged from visiting after her portrayal of Bess and Nonnie.[23] Laura, among the most educated characters in the novel, studies at Columbia University (51), while Sam has studied medicine in Philadelphia (38). The absence of a centre for higher learning in the town contributes to scepticism among the people of the town, who see education as a dangerous asset to black southerners, and even to progressive whites. Both Sam and the Anderson sisters are judged according to the effect their education has on their personalities: Sam is described as 'one nigger a college education didn't ruin', because he 'knows his place' in the social environment shaped by racial etiquette (37). Despite the absence of a centre for learning, the 'College Street crowd' is at the top of Maxwell's social order, along both intra-racial and inter-racial lines (44). Poor white mill worker, and leader of the lynch mob, Willie Echols despises 'College Street folks with their airs and their money!' (117).

Smith's depiction of the white upper class intersects with her indictment of racial gradualism. Prentiss Reid, described as 'Maxwell's radical', is the editor of the local newspaper but does not print his own political views in the *Maxwell Press* (45). The newspaper is described, rather, as furnishing the needs of the local community and propagating the political and social integrity of segregation:

Prentiss Reid's *Maxwell Press* observed the publishing amenities of southern tradition, with proper space given to church news, to Society, to the

> Democratic party, to White Supremacy, to the protection of the freedom
> of big business, to farm interests, home hints, and obituaries. Only upon
> younger and less powerful ears than those of his advertisers and readers
> did his tongue drip its acid. (46)

Reid flatters southern traditionalists while proclaiming a more radical set of beliefs in private. Smith portrays Reid as a hypocrite rather than a proponent of change: the 'acid' that his tongue drips lacks the impact that his newspaper would otherwise allow. Other novels of the southern and American small town figure the office of the local newspaper in three distinct ways. Small-town journalists can be figured as narrative centres through which entire communities may be understood and focalised, as in Sherwood Anderson's *Winesburg, Ohio* (1919); idealised as the source of racial change, as in journalist and southern white gradualist Hodding Carter's *The Winds of Fear* (1945);[24] or figures of hypocrisy through which authors can satirise racial and social mores, as in Colorado-born southern novelist Mary Fassett Hunt's *Joanna Lord*. Smith's influence on Hunt's work is clear, and Smith's representation of Reid satirises moderate southern journalists, a theme Smith would continue to explore in her public writing and speeches. In the 1956 speech published under the title 'The Right Way is Not the Moderate Way', for example, she asserts that 'moderation never mastered ordeal or met a crisis successfully'.[25] In this exploration of local media in the novel, Smith establishes the newspaper as a part of the typology of the fictional southern town that fails to challenge its racial status quo.

As well as presenting the illicit and hidden lives of the College Street crowd, Smith represents the segregation of the business area of the street as undermining its more generally appealing image. Ed considers Maxwell in the context of other American urban centres and notices a single defining difference:

> Ed stood on the sidewalk. In front of him was the garbage-heaped alley
> of stores facing College Street. He could have been looking into a back
> alley of Washington, New York, anywhere. To the right of him four stores
> separated Salamander's Lunch Counter (colored) from the white people's
> Deen's Corner Drug Store. Now he looked straight into Georgia. (8)

The town's segregated business centre is visualised as an example of how College Street's image of itself is fragmented. The 'garbage-heaped alley' suggests refuse and unsanitary conditions, and the separate eating facilities on the street signal fracture. Ed's cynical presence at the centre of College Street indicates a failure of the integrity of Maxwell's wealthy whites. The repetition of the verb 'look' also highlights Ed's role as an observer. Having returned to the town after an absence, Ed recognises the details of the coercive structure upon which Maxwell is built. The explicit signposting of segregation is the key difference between Maxwell and Ed's adopted home of Washington, DC.

Ed's presence on College Street is an example of uncontrolled black presence within Maxwell. This undermines the apparently racially discrete integral design of 'White Town'. Ed's visible racial-isation as black highlights the contrast in Maxwell's social system. He is described as 'a black digit marked out in white chalk', recalling Zora Neale Hurston's assertion that she 'feel[s] most colored when [she is] thrown against a sharp white background' (8).[26] Ed's visibil-ity is at odds with white Maxwell's reluctance to see him: 'he wasn't there on the sidewalk. He never had been there . . . he just wasn't anywhere – where those eyes looked – where those damned eyes –' (8). Even in his childhood, Ed represents a threat to the town. Tillie sends him to Washington, DC, at the advice of Pug Pusey, Dorothy's father and Ed's employer at the grocery store: '"Better get your boy out of town, Tillie," he'd said, "the boy's itching for trouble. He's not a bad boy – just restless"' (21). This description suggests Ed is an irritant and his 'itching' a threat to himself and to the stability of white Maxwell. His return foreshadows a destabilis-ing of the town's social order, and his perspective on College Street signals a failure in the racial division on which the town is built.

College Street represents the heart of Maxwell's white collective identity, and Ed's presence exposes the inherent instability of racial division as an organising principle in the fictional town's geog-raphy. Further from the town's social centre, the spaces in which 'White Town' and 'Colored Town' meet consistently undermine the supposed separation of white and black. Through the interstitial spaces of racial intersection, Smith develops a counternarrative to the town's collective identity that interrogates Maxwell's fiction of racial separation by exposing the town's colour line as characteristically and necessarily porous.

The Bifocal South and the Porous Colour Line

While the division of Maxwell into 'White Town' and 'Colored Town' is a vital component of white residents' conception of their town, it is a convenient fiction. The social, economic and spatial shapes of Maxwell are too contingent on black and white interactions to be effectively, practically, racially divided. Smith's representation of College Street undermines the myth of 'separate but equal' because it is both necessarily integrated, and shaped by racial inequality. The division of the town along racial lines is as implausible as it is necessary. Throughout the novel Smith offers examples of the inherent permeability of the colour line. The specific geographical point at which 'White Town' and 'Colored Town' meet is the home of white spinster and 'dope fiend' Miss Ada (128). This section explores points of intersection between and within 'White Town' and 'Colored Town', and I argue that Smith mobilises the fictive space of Maxwell to articulate the impossibility of rigid separation in small-town space and community.

While a relatively minor character, Miss Ada and her house occupy singularly significant roles in the racial geography of the town. Because her home marks the point at which 'White Town' and 'Colored Town' meet, it lies on the periphery of – and is disowned by – each. Socially and geographically, Miss Ada and her house represent a line of demarcation between Maxwell's two halves. As the most socially marginalised white resident of Maxwell, she is not included in the community of 'White Town' and yet, as a white woman, she cannot be included in the community of 'Colored Town'. As an unmarried older woman, Miss Ada fits the trope of the spinster that is common in southern fiction in this era. An unmarried woman may represent an investment in the South's confederate past, as in the case of William Faulkner's Emily Grierson, who lives in a 'big, squarish frame house that had once been white [. . .] set on what had once been our most select street', or the development of a progressive southern racial politics, as in the case of Faulkner's Miss Eunice Habersham, 'a kinless spinster of seventy living in the columned colonial house on the edge of town.'[27] Miss Ada's rejection by the town is less reminiscent of either of these 'types' of 'spinster'. However, Smith's representation of Ada anticipates the widow Mrs Dubose in Harper Lee's *To Kill a Mockingbird* (1961), who is described as 'nasty'.[28] Miss Ada's position between the two populations makes of her an object of fear and curiosity. Ed, walking home from College Street, remembers 'his boyhood habit' of ceasing to whistle as he walked past the ironically named Evergreen Cemetery and the equally haunting home of Miss Ada (13). Ada and Ed differ in the degree to which they are rehabilitated: before her death, Mrs Dubose overcomes her morphine addiction and her role in the town of Maycomb, Alabama, changes. After her death, she is described as 'a lady'.[29] While Lee's character is eventually reincorporated into the white community, Smith's Miss Ada remains abject and frightening throughout.

At this location between 'White Town' and 'Colored Town', Henry coerces naïve domestic servant Dessie into having sex with him. In order to have illicit sex, the couple must remove themselves from their own black milieu without penetrating the white area of the town:

> They went out by the A.M.E. Church, past the white graveyard, arms around each other, walking more slowly now, Dessie hesitating, dragged back by a conscience never long at ease. Under the cedars in front of Miss Ada's she paused. (239)

Dessie's sense of gendered propriety, which 'drag[s]' her backwards towards 'Colored Town', is appeased by the liminal space of Miss Ada's property. The pair have sex in the ill-defined space between 'White Town' and 'Colored Town', while the gender norms that would prevent such an act are spatially located in 'Colored Town'. The vantage point of Ada's house allows Dessie a view of Tracy's corpse (239). The path by Miss Ada's facilitates both intra-racial sex and the hiding of Tracy's body.

While the wealthy homes on College Street epitomise the surface identity that defines Maxwell, this façade conceals sexual, racial and gender tensions. As the Deen family sits down to breakfast, the scene is almost idyllic: 'It was the kind of dining room one associates, perhaps too glibly, with a southern accent' (63). The room epitomises the genteel myth of the South while also satirising the 'glib' way in which northerners may have imagined the South. The scene is undermined by the family's secret lives: Tracy's romance with Nonnie and Laura's secret lesbianism are incongruous with the superficial image of the wealthy southern home. Another staple of the southern myth is satirised in this scene as a means of challenging the commonly held image of southern gentility. Tut has to change his clothes before work because 'his seersucker coat looked mussed' (63). The seersucker suit, which suggests a certain kind of southern masculinity, is 'mussed' and, as a result, the image falters. Just as Tut's coat fails to live up to its purpose, so does the image of the happy southern family home. Laura, who has been educated in New York and lives uneasily now in the southern town, wears 'bifocal glasses' at breakfast (64), which present two parallel but different images to the wearer and the duality of the white southern home. Laura, unlike the rest of her family, has tried to rectify her poor sight and insight. As a result, she sees two distinct images simultaneously. The white home, as it is represented in *Strange Fruit*, operates as a similarly bifocal paradigm. Beneath the surface image of racial homogeneity, wealth and a happy family life, the white home is compromised and haunted by a repressed black presence.

What I term the 'bifocal paradigm' borrows from and extends literary critic Tara McPherson's concept of the 'lenticular logic' that abides in the South as a means of describing the 'racial economy of visibility'.[30] Describing a shifting three-dimensional image on a postcard, McPherson describes how the image represent either an idyllic scene of plantation whiteness or a stereotypical image of an African American woman, depending on the angle from which the image is viewed. McPherson reads this image as a metaphor for the 'covert' expression of 'the South's obsession with separating black from white and its long legacy of interwoven traditions, an interweaving characterized by both disgust and desire'.[31] Laura's bifocal perception of the southern town leaves more room for racial activism. If the overtly hostile stereotype is obscured by the idyll in McPherson's metaphor, they coexist in Smith's. Simultaneity allows an imagined observer to reflect on the paradox of race in the South more directly.

The compromising simultaneity of segregation in the space of the white home can be the scene of two concurrent but opposed narratives. The coincidence of each of the bifocal images silently testifies to the inherently non-segregated status of the white home, dependent as it is on black labour. Black cooks and maids are a feature of Maxwell's white homes, and their lives follow broadly similar patterns: 'Out of the back doors went the cooks home to Colored Town. Some with bundles under their arms for the family they'd left there' (116). The home lives and work lives of these women are divided, as suggested by the phrase 'the family they'd left there', indicating two separate personae. The presence of concurrent and oppositional narratives echoes W. E. B. Du Bois's concept of 'double-consciousness' that holds that African Americans, unlike whites, have access to how the United States is perceived by members of either race. [32] Blacks must simultaneously see themselves through their own eyes and as they are perceived by whites. Smith directly alludes to the concept in the text, when Bess expresses her frustration at being black in the segregated South to Sam: 'It *would* be so simple, Sam, to be white. I'm so tired of being two people! Sometimes I get mixed up myself' (293, emphasis in original). Bess's experience as a domestic worker, a job that requires her to perform roles defined by her race and gender at odds with the roles she plays in black Maxwell, is an overt engagement with Du Bois's theory. The houses on College Street are defined as much by the presence of these employees as by the whiteness of their inhabitants, making such homes another explicit point of racial crossing even as they are located deep within 'White Town'.

Sharon Monteith has described how white writers have typically depicted black domestic servants as extensions of, or foils for, the concerns of white characters: 'A shift toward recognizing and representing forms of resistance in the behaviour of black women working in white homes is not so discernible in white-authored literature' as it is in African American fiction of the same period.[33] In *Strange Fruit*, Bess's complexity marks her as an unconventional domestic servant in novels by white southern women because of the degree to which her thoughts are articulated both internally and in her dialogue with others. In other mid-century fiction of the segregated town, relationships between black domestic workers and their employees are represented through a failure of communication, as in Hunt's *Joanna Lord* (1954), in which a black domestic servant is described as 'so close to the family and yet apart. Always on the outside looking in, as puzzled by them as they by her.'[34] Critic Diane Roberts, in *The Myth of Aunt Jemima* (1994), argues that Smith 'reinscribed the quintessential racist image of the Mammy' even while she 'laboured to challenge the stereotypes of race and gender in the South'.[35] Bess is an exception, and Roberts allows that the character is 'an astute reader of how little her culture has changed'.[36] This imbues Bess with a level of insight and self-knowledge that is also atypical in white representations of black domestic workers, and, with the exception of Laura, a rare quality in a citizen of Maxwell. Evidence of the complexity of Smith's development of Bess comes in a depiction of Bess recovering from a day's work: 'Bess laid the wet cloth across her eyes. Coolness drove the pain into her neck' (15). Smith depicts Bess through the same motifs of sight and insight as she does Laura. Bess's act of temporarily blinding herself by placing the cloth on her eyes highlights her capacity for insight. By covering her eyes, Bess privileges her internal life and her insight into the lives of her family members.

After Tracy's death, Nonnie's grief and that of her employer Mrs Brown are presented as simultaneous but asymmetrical. Smith deploys this juxtaposition to underscore both the 'bifocal' nature of race in Maxwell, and the role of the white home as a necessarily un-segregated space of labour. Mrs Brown, who has very little claim to grieve for Tracy compared to Nonnie, is very vocal about the personal difficulty his death has caused her. Conversely, Nonnie grieves in silence. Mrs Brown's grief is represented in counterpoint to Nonnie's internal recollection of recent conversation with Tracy and Ed:

'I'm sorry, Nonnie, to c-cry–before y-you–like thi–this – It's–I'm up-upset – A death always up–I try–so hard–not to–give in–know Boysie's my-my cross–t-to bear–he's such a sweet b-baby–I–shouldn't–'

'He is, Mrs. Brown.' . . . *you can't think things out down here that's the Bible name for it there're others you'll hear them all I'm going clean from now on Dorothy a ring back to Washington to live decently I've fixed that* . . . (316, ellipses in original)

While Mrs Brown loudly protests her grief, Nonnie's is presented as being literally unspeakable: even in her interior monologue Nonnie does not articulate her mourning but is only able to repeat, and dwell upon, fragments of other people's words.

Nonnie and Tracy's affair is a taboo in each of their respective communities. Their sexual relationship must be hidden from Maxwell's white and black communities even after Tracy has died. Tracy's behaviour is prohibited, but tolerated, by white Maxwell. He must take pains to hide his affair, despite the fact that sexual encounters between white men and black women form part of the expected development of Maxwell's white youth, and are accommodated within the town's system of racial etiquette in a way that the inverse is not. The location most often used by Tracy and Nonnie for their affair is unincorporated, even into peripheral 'Colored Town'. An abandoned cabin to the rear of the Anderson house is a viable space for an interracial affair because it, like Ada's house, is fully incorporated by neither 'White Town' nor 'Colored Town'. Closer to the swamp than any other property described in the novel, Aunt Tyse's cabin – named for a character who does not otherwise appear in the novel – is as far removed from the social conventions of Maxwell as one can go without leaving the incorporated space of the town. When Tracy returns from service in the First World War, he and Nonnie resume their relationship in their private space: 'Down the old path, beyond the grape arbor, through the field, to old Aunt Tyse's deserted cabin. The grass had grown high around it, as if no one had been there in the years he had been away' (55). The repetition of the word 'old' in the passage above may indicate that the cabin is a relic of the antebellum period. The undisturbed physical landscape suggests that the only function of the space is to facilitate illicit sexual encounters between Nonnie and Tracy. The cabin is incorporated in the town, then, as a space of greater sexual freedom for white men like Tracy, who take advantage of the imbalanced power dynamic proscribed by racial etiquette. Tracy is always 'glad to be back in a world where nothing was ordered as in white Maxwell' when he visits the cabin with Nonnie (135).

In a conversation with Tracy, Brother Dunwoodie acknowledges the illicit behaviour afforded by the etiquette of the colour line: 'Now there's another sin. Lot of men, when they're young, sneak off to Colored Town. [. . .] Get to lusting – burning up! And they get to thinking . . . they'd rather have that kind of thing than marriage' (87). The less than egregious 'sin' of exploiting black women is expected among young white men like Tracy, and implicitly condoned by the white townspeople at large. The greater transgression in Dunwoodie's warning is that coercive cross-racial sexual encounters would inhibit intra-racial marriage. Dunwoodie offers a solution to the issue of Nonnie's pregnancy that can be easily accommodated within the strictures of racial etiquette: 'Find some good nigger you can count on to marry her. Give [. . .] her some money. They all like money – all women like money, no matter what color!' (100).

Just as Aunt Tyse's cabin is available to meet Tracy's personal needs, the moral order of white Maxwell secretly accommodates his affair with Nonnie, and when Tracy's body is found, there is a tacit understanding among Maxwell's white men as to the circumstances of Tracy's death: 'Many a man in Maxwell knew why Tracy was killed on the Old Town road, though of course the women didn't. Yes, she must have done it. That Anderson girl' (300–301). Although secrecy is a necessary part of Tracy's relationship with Nonnie, it is essentially another one of Maxwell's social conventions. That Maxwell's white men know not only that Tracy is having an affair but also with whom indicates the specific role cross-racial sex plays for the town's white men and the degree to which it is mediated by racial etiquette. Elsewhere in the novel, however, Smith develops spaces in which segregation's reach is interrogated. While Smith presents a permeable colour line as a means of exposing the fiction of the separation of the races, it is at the level of the individual that she begins to propose the means for resisting the system. The purpose of the Methodist revival is to unite Maxwell's white community exclusively and to support the town's structures of white supremacy, but the inherent permeability of the town's racial divide means that the sermons and music are audible to Maxwell's black inhabitants, too.

African American religion in Maxwell operates on a principle of inclusion, even when it is, by necessity, segregated. The naming of the town's leading black church, the African Methodist Episcopal Church, suggests an erosion of theological difference (12). The white population of the town is religiously divided between Methodists and Episcopalians, whereas, for Maxwell's African Americans, Christianity is unified by race and but not subject to a denominational divide. The name of the church also suggests Pan-Africanism in its privileging of the term 'African' at the same time as it merges the theological positions of the Methodist and Episcopalian faiths.[37] If, then, Christianity in 'Colored Town' operates on a principle of inclusion within the black community, the white religious revival is pointedly established in isolation from the rest of the town.

The revival is held in a large, white tent, a construction that serves to contain a select group within an emblem of whiteness. The tent, filled with white worshippers and 'white singing to Jesus' (3), is erected at a spatial, ideological and theological remove from Maxwell's black population. It is intended to bring people together despite differences in class but within carefully defined racial and religious terms. Intra-racial class disparity remains central to the work of the revival, and Dunwoodie exploits this disparity for his own gain while wealthy whites take the opportunity to feel superior. With more than a hint of condescension, Alma tells Laura: 'It's a community project [. . .] All of Maxwell has not had your opportunities. [. . .] It is especially those poor mill people who need God' (66). Dunwoodie's financial motives are barely concealed, and he sees the class dynamic within the tent as an indicator of his own success, and his sermons are 'slanted to appeal to the more solid portion of Maxwell's citizenry. For, however many mill people were converted, a revival could not be called a success in Maxwell until the prominent citizens [. . .] were returned to the fold' (248–9). Dunwoodie is more salesman or political demagogue than a religious leader, driven by making 'the Lord's business' a lucrative one (248). The revival tent stands as an emblem of white integrity and isolation, embodied by carefully staged religious music that Dunwoodie intends to affect Maxwell's white elite. Sound cannot be segregated.

The sounds of the whole of the town of Maxwell travel indiscriminately to its most extreme point, the Anderson home at the edge of the swamp. For instance, that the clock of the town courthouse can be heard striking the hour incorporates the Andersons into Maxwell

(41). The implication is that black characters are included within the symbolism of American justice and integrity but are resolutely situated on the periphery. Similarly, the sounds of 'White Town' permeate the barrier between the races in a manner that undermines their separateness. Nonnie, standing at the gate, becomes incidentally involved in what is intended as an entirely white social interaction: 'Across the town came the singing. A white singing to Jesus. An August singing of lost souls. A God-moaning. August is the time folks give up their sins. August is a time of trouble' (3). 'August' here has multiple meanings. As an adjective, it evokes the seriousness of southern Protestantism while also echoing the narrative's temporal setting in the month of August, when the southern climate is most overbearing and oppressive. It is also, of course, suggestive of another southern novel about lynching, though Smith was no admirer of Faulkner or *Light in August* (1932).[38] The religious singing permeates the town and is present throughout the events of the plot. The singing, which represents the failure of separating the town's white and black populations, contributes to the structure of the text. Although this 'white singing' is presented as exclusionary, it is uninhibited by the symbolic barriers of segregation. It is accessible even to those it attempts to exclude.

Sound, a sensory experience beyond the remit of segregation, is incompatible with the revival's exclusionary methods. Just as music refuses to abide by the town's division, so does silence:

> The town was quiet now. White Town. Colored Town. And Nonnie standing there at the gate had not heard the preacher's words. But her mind was full of revival sounds as after a fire bits of ash float for a long time through the air. (132)

The singing is given a racial identity, a property alien to something as ephemeral and bodiless. The potential for singing to permeate the barriers of race travels in both directions, and Laura can hear black music from her home: 'Sometimes across town you'd hear the colored folks singing, and the slow rise and fall of it would be [. . .] sweet to your ear' (246). Religious music is an experience shared by southerners on either side of the colour line: 'you could fill in the words you couldn't hear. Anybody born in Georgia could fill in the words' (125). To Smith, local identity is a more significant factor than racial identity in cultural understanding.

The black population of the town, exemplified by Nonnie, is unintentionally incorporated into the revival. In some cases this incorporation can take the form of voyeurism. Ed, the black character who feels most divorced from the conventions of life in Maxwell because he has experienced city life elsewhere, has a fascination with the revival that develops from his antagonism towards the town's white population:

> Eddie watched the meeting. Night after night he came and watched the meeting. As you'd see the boys around town watch the screened box at Rainey's market, where sometimes there'd be a captured coon, or a rattler coiled in a corner, or some rabbits. You'd stand there and watch the animal, maybe feed it something. Maybe just watch. Not thinking much. Not feeling much. (215)

In this metaphor, Ed's perception of Maxwell's whites is alternately as a threat (a rattlesnake), benign (a rabbit) or restrictive (captured). The phrase 'captured coon' resonates with coon's double meaning as an abbreviation of racoon and as a derogatory term for a black person. The 'captured coon' in this extended metaphor anticipates the eventual capture and murder of Henry later in the novel and, when coupled with the image of the snake coiled in readiness to attack, suggests the nascent lynch mob present at the revival meeting. The combination of the second-person pronoun 'you' and the conditional tense, as in 'you'd', in this passage extends the act of voyeurism beyond Ed's experience of the revival meeting. By using the second-person pronoun, Smith also implicates her imagined reader within the disinterested spectatorship of the captured animal.

The compulsive way in which Ed watches the revival meeting, 'night after night' suggests a curiosity, bordering on fascination, with white Maxwell. Ed finds himself at turns affected by the community atmosphere of the meeting and indifferent to it: 'And sometimes Ed didn't feel, didn't think, then sometimes he felt what he believed the white folks were feeling. [. . .] Sometimes you felt against your mind. Against all you knew. Against all you believed. Yet, there it was' (215–16). Ed is emotionally involved in the revival against his will and against the apparent segregation of the revival's congregation. Ed's emotional response runs contrary to his rational distaste for the revival – 'against [his] mind' – however, it is inevitable. Ed's experience of the revival shows the colour line to be unavoidably permeable both to those, like Brother Dunwoodie, who want to maintain a racially integral religious congregation and to Ed, who seeks to remove himself from the confines of Maxwell and its racial order.

At least one member of the congregation is vocally unwilling to remain complicit in Dunwoodie's fear-inspiring lectures.[39] The congregation, with one exception, raucously appreciates a speech that capitalises on Tracy's: 'Mrs. Henderson laid down her hymn-book and gathered up her gloves. It was only her civic sense of duty that had made her attend the revival services. This, tonight, was too much' (309). Henderson refuses to be complicit in dema-goguery, and her protest signifies a refusal to imply consent by her continued presence. She is compelled to participate in the revival due to a 'civic sense of duty' towards the town's collective social rituals, despite the fact that her Episcopalian faith marks her as already ideologically opposed to the Methodist revival.[40] As she leaves, she is mocked by the preacher and the congregants: '"For some," Brother Dunwoodie spoke at last, slowly, "the Gospel of Jesus is too strong meat for their po' sick souls to stummick". Mill folks tittered[.]' (310). Dunwoodie maintains authority over his congregation by expanding his rhetoric to include scorn for those who find him unconvincing. Moreover, he increases the level to which his audience is attracted to his rhetoric by indulging their desire to humiliate one of their number. Through the figure of Mrs Henderson, Smith presents a model of Christian protest against segregation. By presenting a character willing to suffer scorn for maintaining moral principles, Smith shows how the rhetoric of demagogues can be manipulative and compelling but also how it may be resisted.

In Smith's depiction of the revival tent, an apparently exclu-sionary space is shown to contain the seeds potential for individ-ual resistance. Smith suggests that the segregated institutions of the South inevitably incorporate all southerners. Nonnie's and

Ed's experience of the revival indicates its failure as a model for segregation. In the figure of Mrs Henderson, Smith reduces the space of resistance to an individual subject and develops an aesthetic of empathy at the levels of narration and characterisation. Through this aesthetic of empathy, Smith incorporates an imagined reader into her desegregationist project. The result is a novel that also works as an incitement to political engagement and even activism.

The (Inter-)Personal Pronoun

Although *Strange Fruit* is ostensibly a third-person narrative, the second-person singular personal pronoun, 'you', is deployed liberally throughout. It typically acts as a conversational replacement for the more formal third-person, gender-neutral personal pronoun 'one'. However, the function of this pronoun in *Strange Fruit* is purposefully ambiguous. As well as signifying the thoughts of an individual character, it addresses the novel's imagined readership directly. Consistently, Smith deploys the pronoun to trouble ideas of regional and racial separation and to invoke a public space for the novel's political concerns. Literary critic Scott Romine describes Smith's *Killers of the Dream* as a 'rubric of the Southern Sociological autobiography, a genre that places the autobiographical "I" in a certain varying relation to "the South" as a dual act of self-expression and social commentary.'[41] Where *Killers of the Dream* deploys the first-person singular pronoun to simultaneously express and comment, *Strange Fruit* deploys 'you' to describe a wide range of characters while contributing to Smith's wider desegregationist social commentary.

In her foreword to the 1961 reissue of *Killers of the Dream*, Smith describes that text in terms that solidify this conflation of personal and public experience: 'this is personal memoir, in one sense; in another sense, it is Every Southerner's memoir.'[42] *Strange Fruit* challenges the southern exceptionalism that marks the South as the nation's problem region in contrast to the cosmopolitan North. Writing in the programme for the novel's Broadway adaptation, Smith explicitly expands the harmfully divisive racial system of the segregated southern town to the larger United States:

> It may be that these characters have a lot of kinfolks up North . . . Or it may be that Maxwell is not just the town in Georgia they came from but every place on earth where there are walls, rough and jagged or smooth and invisible, which shut human beings away from each other and from a world in which they should feel at home.[43]

Smith figures Maxwell as a synecdoche for any number of places built on the premise of segregation. While Smith extends the metaphor to 'every place on earth', her primary example is with segregation's 'kinfolks up North'. Given that the play was performed, and therefore the programme read, in New York, her imagined readership in this case is easy to identify. The novel could be read in any part of the country; the play is specifically sited in the North, and the people of Maxwell are consistently referred to as 'they'.

In the novel, lynching is described, through Laura, as a disturbing but undeniable fact of southern community: 'her mind knew that this is what happens down here in our South sometimes. This is what happens. And she had wondered which of the boys and men she knew belonged to the Ku Klux Klan . . .' (325). The statement that 'this is what happens' and the first-person plural pronoun 'our' function together to include an imagined reader in the narrative of southern racial violence.[44] It incorporates, or implicates, a community external to the South within the social structures that facilitate racial violence within the region. Smith troubles the conception of the South, discussed later by Leigh Anne Duck, as 'an effective container for the nation's disavowed antiliberalism'.[45] Smith removes the geographical distance between the reader and the southern town in order to prevent the deferring of responsibility.

In discussing the intersection of space and temporality in the novel, Duck argues that: 'Disputing the idea of absolute cultural barriers between the U.S. South and other spaces, *Strange Fruit* nonetheless insists on the experience of temporal distance in shaping one's responses to others and even one's sense of self.'[46] For Duck, Smith represents an alternative means of addressing the region in her writing. Smith's novel evokes a 'provincial cosmopolitanism' that constitutes 'more limited, varying, and contingent forms of local affiliation, including the ways in which people in nonmetropolitan areas may be nonetheless interested in or attached to diverse broader social networks.'[47] Smith's adaptation of the second-person voice serves to play with distance. While the temporal remove that Duck describes contributes to self-reflection, the linguistic move of the second-person voice evidences an empathetic impulse. By simultaneously expressing a third-person and a second-person narrative voice, Smith develops a framework of inclusion that implicitly critiques the myth of personal and social integrity upon which segregation is founded.

For example, Nonnie's feelings about her pregnancy (3), Ed's conflicted feelings about returning home (8), and his feelings of grief at the passing of his mother (10) are all rendered through the second-person voice. Pregnancy, grief and ambivalent feelings about one's home are not racialised experiences. By using these prisms to present her African American characters, Smith erodes racial difference as an obstacle to empathy. The experiences of the town's wealthy white population, such as Alma's menopause (71), Tracy's memory of military service (48), and Laura's growing awareness of her own queer sexuality (241) also implicate an imagined reader within Maxwell's white community. This act of inclusion creates an imaginative space for cross-racial identification. In response to Tracy's murder, the use of this technique implicates an imagined reader both within a process of community grieving and, again, erases the supposed emotional, intellectual and physical distance from southern segregation in which a non-southern reader might take refuge. Laura's grief and her regret that she and Tracy were not closer is rendered in the second person in order to encourage empathy (190–1). Tracy's murder causes Tom Harris to consider his own children and whether or not his parenting has been effective in keeping them safe: 'Tom sighed. It made you wonder about your own boys. Wonder if you had done as well by them as you might' (301). The above passage begins by identifying Tom in the third person. Immediately, however, the voice shifts to the second. The subject of these sentences begins as the fictional Tom Harris before shifting to address an archetypal anxious parent. By representing feelings of parental responsibility, Smith extends moral culpability for Tracy's death.

Although examples proliferate, a scene in which Tracy recalls combat in France during the First World War is characteristic of the manner in which Smith's 'you' transcends the divide between the personal and the public. Tracy's fellow soldier, an idealist from New Jersey, anticipates an egalitarian America after the war:

> That sounds good, you [Tracy] said, but you [the New Jersey native] don't know the South, you don't understand us. We'd never let the Negro into that world and I'm not so sure you up in Newark would either. We'd never let the Jews in, a Swede from Chicago said, not in my town. We'd never let the Japs and Chinks in, somebody from California yelled. (49)

This passage suggests a standard of white bigotry across the United States, even though the groups excluded differ regionally. The absence of quotation marks and the manner by which the dialogue runs together formally suggest a blurring of regionalism as a container for racism. The passage constructs an American psychology of exclusion throughout the nation and not only in the South. The first sentence's ambiguous inclusion of the word 'you' both implicates the reader in Tracy's thoughts and accuses the same reader of ignorance over the southern racial dilemma. The supposed 'you' is simultaneously included as a southerner and as a northerner in the same sentence. The implication is that a reader of *Strange Fruit* is asked to exercise empathy with a diverse range of characters, regardless of the contexts of region or race. Linguistically, this suggests a didacticism that makes use of the novelistic narrative form to promote empathy for southerners living under segregation. The conflation of persons (and of reader and fictive subject) is evident in the novel's depictions of racial and sexual violence. The disturbing consequences of the system of southern apartheid are also represented such that the reader is implicated by their inaction in efforts to dismantle such systems. This situates the novel's formal strategies within a paradigm of empathy that encourages the imagined reader to consider the agenda expressed in Smith's narrative style.

While critical attention to the novel's formal strategies has tended to be lacking, literary critic Judith Giblin James highlights the 'subtle and adroitly managed narrative techniques' that Smith employs, 'particularly the use of close third-person narration to produce an effectively controlled stream of consciousness for the principal characters'.[48] What James describes as 'tightly controlled',

I would describe as mediated: the narrative voices of these primary characters are inflected and manipulated by a third-person narrator using the techniques I have described. This mediation both mirrors the coercive social patterns of the southern town and encourages resistance to segregation.

As well as appealing to commonly shared experiences, Smith's use of 'you' also implicates her reader in some characters' horrific behaviour. When Tracy visits Nonnie to unburden his own conscience and to deliver money in exchange for her silence, he arrives in a drunken state. He drinks heavily in advance to psychologically distance himself from the implications of his behaviour (196). Tracy tries to ignore his romantic history with Nonnie and to dissociate himself from his affection for her by referring to her as 'nigger' (197). Tracy defers his sense of responsibility, both as an individual and as a beneficiary of infrastructures of inequality. Tellingly, while he is preparing to confront Nonnie and evade responsibility for his unborn child, 'Maxwell was on his side' (184). Rather than a transgression of personal and social responsibility, Tracy's decision to hide his indiscretion solidifies his role in the town's structure of racial etiquette. Bolstered by the consensus of the town's white elite, he succeeds in altering his perception of Nonnie, dehumanising her and allowing himself to think of their intimacy in terms of property and ownership: 'You're mine – even if you're just a little nigger, you're mine and I love every inch of you' (198).

Ultimately, Tracy's objectification of Nonnie – and his drunkenness – emboldens him to commit sexual assault. The description of the attempted rape is presented as though Tracy is having an out-of-body experience: 'He saw somebody pulling at her dress, fumbling with buttons, tearing it from her shoulders' (198). Tracy is able to avoid responsibility by deferring agency and action onto another person, the 'somebody' he apparently witnesses assaulting Nonnie. Tracy convinces himself that not only is he innocent of assaulting Nonnie but that he is also morally vindicated by imagining that he is resists the aggressor:

> Saw somebody tearing her blouse off, tearing her skirt off, pulling at cloth until there was nothing between his hands and her body. He saw a man – couldn't see much, couldn't see much – a man above her, saw him

press her down against the floor – don't do that! – saw him press her body hard – saw him try and fail, try and fail, try and fail . . . (198)

Tracy reassures himself of his innocence by claiming that his vision is impaired ('couldn't see much, couldn't see much') and by silently ordering the 'man' to desist ('don't do that!'). Tracy is a parody of Americans who nominally advocate racial equality while remaining complicit in national structures of white supremacy. Tracy, the person completely responsible for this assault, allows himself to believe in his own innocence. By presenting this scene in the second person, Smith makes analogous personal responsibility more difficult to evade for her reader and removes the balm of regional distance from the problem of segregation.

The scene culminates with Tracy's realisation of his own culpability. Tracy performs remorse over his brutal acts while remaining at a psychological distance from his actions. He hears: 'a deep harsh cry – she's crying – no, it's you crying – it's you – you couldn't – you – couldn't – couldn't . . . you couldn't – you couldn't – you couldn't –' (198–9). The abundance of dashes and ellipses in this passage denotes psychological turmoil and the failure of Tracy's attempt to distance himself from his actions.

'You' also creates empathy in Smith's depiction of Laura's lesbian desire for her friend Jane. Alma's description of lesbianism is vehement in its disgust and rigid in its enactment of sexual normativity: 'Now Mother lowered her voice: "There're women who are – unnatural. They're like vultures – women like that." Mother's face had grown stony. "They do – terrible things to young girls"' (243). The word 'Mother' operates, in this passage, in a manner comparable to the expansion of the second person elsewhere. By designating Alma as 'Mother' the text directly invokes Laura's subject position by using a term that denotes their personal relationship. As her name – which recalls the phrase *Alma Mater* – suggests, Alma's position of matriarch in the Deen family is total. She is not only the family's primary breadwinner but she is also the family's most powerful person. Alma's maternity is expanded by the capitalisation of 'Mother' to become an archetype of domineering motherhood. By articulating an archetypal lesbian relationship that is inherently predatory, Alma suggests homosexuality is intrinsically exploitative, especially towards vulnerable 'young' women. By focalising this scene through Laura, Smith constructs a pattern of empathy between the imagined reader and a queer character as she is exposed to homophobia.

Laura's developing understanding of her own sexuality is described using the second-person personal pronoun in order to create understanding of the paradoxical normalness of her queerness. This suggests the turmoil that her sexual identity causes: 'Laura moved restlessly. Lying awake, like this, did your feelings no good' (241). Jane represents romantic and platonic intimacy to Laura, as well as an escape from Maxwell's codes of racial and gendered etiquette: 'There was so much you could say to Jane that you had never been able to say to anyone' (243). The pair is marked as different for their artistic and intellectual tendencies, as well as Laura's representation as different due to her sexual attraction to Jane.[49] Laura's refusal of intellectual and sexual normativity also intersects with her racial politics, as when she visits Tom Harris in an effort to protect Henry from lynching (295). By shifting focalisation, Smith undertakes a clear exposition of the problem of lynching from the perspectives of two white southern liberals. Where Smith creates empathy with racially liberal positions, she also explores the exploitative use of the direct address.

Smith is not uncritical of the power of her narrative strategy, and she offers and implicit warning that demagogues can manipulate the same empathetic technique she deploys. The tension arising from Tracy's murder suspends the town's social rituals and temporarily disrupts the permeability of racial barriers that the singing services had heretofore represented. Brother Dunwoodie's sermon makes use of recent events to further compel his congregation into contributing financially. At this point the narrative shifts into a free-indirect association with the preacher and confuses the barrier between direct and indirect speech (307). As the sermon becomes more aggressive, Dunwoodie exploits the anxieties of Maxwell's white parents:

> 'Oh, my friends . . . my heart is bleeding for the unsaved of this town
> . . .
>
> 'You wives . . . where are your husbands . . . ?

'You mothers . . . where are your boys . . . ?

'Where were they last night, and the night before . . . and the night before? Do you know?'

His despairing eyes plunged into the white faces straining up toward him. (308, ellipses in original)

Dunwoodie feigns personal attachment ('my heart is bleeding') before accusing the women of the town of ignorance regarding their own families. By continuing to move the parameters of what constitutes sufficient knowledge ('last night, and the night before . . . and the night before'), Dunwoodie makes it more difficult for mothers to be completely certain that their sons are safe and morally secure. The mass of 'white faces' into which Dunwoodie speaks suggests a unified community, drawn together by race, their faith in his rhetoric, and a shared obligation to their children: 'You Christian mothers would go down into hell to save your boys' souls. Wouldn't you?' (308). It is at this point in the sermon that Mrs Henderson takes her leave, as I discuss above.

While Smith is cognisant of the conservative ends to which he aesthetics innovations may be put, she simultaneously proposes a means of resisting that coercion. Dunwoodie's rhetorical techniques are superficially similar to Smith's, but Smith is careful to contrast the ways rhetoric can be co-opted for different agendas. Although Smith describes sites in Maxwell with the potential to facilitate resistance, at the novel's close the town's segregation remains intact and unthreatened. While this return to relative harmony appears to suggest the impossibility of change, Smith's narrative temporality provides the space for change in the future.

Smith ends the novel with a series of vignettes that show the population of the town accommodating the emotional trauma of the murders of Tracy and Henry. Notably, only characters who remain within the confines of the town at the novel's end are represented; Ed, who has escaped to the North, is unobserved by the omniscient narrator. Henry's death acts as a pressure valve for the white community's racial tensions and allows the town's industries to maintain their captive and subservient black labour force. The town has experienced, to borrow Richard Slotkin's term for the 'settling' of the West, 'regeneration through violence'.[50] In the southern context, generative violence strengthens the power of white men, for, as Bertram Wyatt-Brown observes, 'Southern males sometimes believed that a little home violence went a long way to ensure loyalty and inspire healthy respect. If it worked with blacks, it surely would help with meddlesome women.'[51] W. Fitzhugh Brundage has interpreted this white male violence as upholding what he terms 'community honor'.[52] As these historical perspectives suggest, violence in Maxwell shores up the town's segregated social order and buttresses wealthy white men's position at the top of that order.

Where the novel's opening narration establishes Nonnie's role in the community through an almost Cubist portrait of how she is perceived by the town's residents, Smith's closing narration mirrors this technique by creating a series of static images of the town as it would like to be seen. However, the symmetry of the novel's opening and closing is disturbed. While the opening description of Nonnie presents a composite image of the perception of the character by the town at large, the closing images combine to present a composite image of the town itself. The latter is undermined by readerly knowledge of its secrets. An imagined reader passively receives Maxwell's description of itself in the opening passage, but is empowered to interrogate a similar description at the novel's end.

This series of vignettes begins with the architects of Henry's murder, and the lynching party is described returning home: 'As night fell, Bill Talley and Dee and the others went to their homes back in the county or to the sawmill and Ellatown' (346). The lynching party is marked, through the town's geography, as belonging to a poor and working-class population. These white men are agricultural and industrial workers, and their return home signals the re-inscription of the town's economic system. Talley's return is a performance of superiority and inferiority as well as the most acute example in these closing portraits of the division between the town's surface identity and the submerged truth of events. Talley, who has clearly been central to the lynching, feigns ignorance to his black domestic worker Lias: '"Well, Lias," Bill said, "I heard they burned a nigger over to town today," voice mighty casual' (346). Talley intimidates Lias while simultaneously performing his innocence. Lias, in turn, performs the role of a dedicated and submissive servant, even while his actions indicate an underlying unease or anger: 'Lias's hand fumbled for the bridle' (346). While Talley is threatening his employee in a 'mighty casual' way, Dee listens to the exchange and laughs twice (347). Talley's innocence is, to Lias, as clearly a performance as Lias's nonchalance is to Bill and Dee. Bill's pretence at ignorance is facilitated by Dee's laughter: through Dee's subtle indication of his own part in the lynching, Talley is able to simultaneously protest his innocence and exhibit his guilt. The underlying threat in Talley's behaviour is understood by Lias as a means of ensuring a stable black workforce for Talley's cotton crop:

> 'Well,' said Bill, 'Reckon we better get to pickin, a Monday.'
> 'Yessuh, Boss.'
> 'Reckon you can round up plenty hands, don't you? Won't be no trouble about gittin plenty?'
> 'Nossuh, Boss. Can get all we can use, yassah.'
> Dee laughed, walked away. (347)

This ostensibly simple exchange between a white landowner and the black manservant seeing to his horses is, typically in *Strange Fruit*, laden with meaningful subtext. While the lynching itself is not described in the text, its aftermath is shown in the relationship between an employer and his labour. Beyond the heinous act, the lynching works as a boon to Maxwell's structure of segregation. For Bill Talley, the lynching of Henry has served its proper function. His previously waning pool of labour has been intimidated. The return to this relationship between employer and employees marks a re-inscription of the South's coercive agricultural system.

The other branches of Maxwell's social infrastructure are shown to return to a state of normality. In the Echols family, poor white employees at the lumber mill, the proliferation of cheap, terrorised black labour threatens their ability to earn a living wage: 'Willie's all time talkin bout organizin. I tell him he's wastin his breath. All Tom Harris ud do would be to turn him off and hire a nigger in his place' (351). Simultaneously, the lynching is celebrated for maintaining the order of white supremacy: 'It was a sight that nigger! Swingin there. Got what he deserved. What every one of em deserve' (352). While the Echols family recognises the importance of organised labour in gaining greater financial security for themselves, they subscribe to the racial structures that enable their own exploitation.

Despite his 'radical' politics, Prentiss Reid is shown preparing another diluted issue of his local newspaper even in the aftermath of a lynching. Although Reid is perturbed by the lynching, he refuses to change his practice of accommodating white supremacy: '*The Maxwell Press* aims to please' (367). Dunwoodie is concerned only with the potential impact of 'this trouble' on the success of his revival (358). While Sam is clearly disturbed by the events of the preceding days, he is shown working in his medical practice as usual, suggesting that the work of racial progress and black survival is ongoing (358–9).

After the individuals and families of the town are visited in their homes, the narrative adopts a broader perspective and examines the town as a whole, exploring the integral typology of the town after having examined a range of its component offices. In a passage that recalls my reading of Frank Capra's *It's a Wonderful Life* in this book's introduction, Smith blends the people and places of Maxwell to offer an image of their collective will. The town is presented using pathetic fallacy:

> [A]nd after a time Maxwell Georgia slept. As still as only the weary can be, it lay – splotched dark against flat stretches of cotton; tied to them by roads which wound their white threads through cotton fields, past black pinelands, around ponds, under great oaks, on, on, on, in the night. (368)

The town's deep sleep suggests peace. The town and surrounding rural areas are presented as either black or white. The whiteness of the cotton and blackness of the pine are fundamentally connected. Although this image seems to support the premise that the town's corrupted order will remain unchanged, there is some doubt: 'Covered by darkness, Maxwell slept ... in tired peace' (368). Although the sleep described is deep, the town's peace is 'tired'. The town in repose suggests that the 'weary' system of segregation might in the future come to an end. Smith's choice to set the novel some twenty years before its date of publication can be read in this light to indicate the possibility for change in the author's present. While change might be progressive or regressive, the novel's temporality can be interpreted as optimistic, and, writing more than a decade later, Smith would be in a position to assert that 'Men have dreamed, for thousands of years, of a time when all people would be accepted as persons; [. . .] That age has now come. We have all we need to make it a reality for the earth's people.'[53] Smith's optimism in the wake of the decision in *Brown v. Board* (1954) is anticipated by *Strange Fruit*.

Following this series of vignettes, the narrative shifts to consider the Anderson sisters to underscore the novel's sense of cautious optimism. As another day's work begins for them, the rhythms of the town return to normal: 'Everything would be the same – as it always was' (371). This sentiment of a lack of change is at odds with other images in this closing scene. Dessie arrives at the Anderson house with her clothes covered in dirt. At Bess's instruction, she washes her skirt before going to work: '"I'd wash *good* if I were you. It'll make you feel better." Dessie washed good' (370). This is an image of cleansing and of renewal. While Maxwell has, for the moment, returned to its old system, the implication is that southerners like Dessie, Bess and Nonnie are working to improve their lives. The novel's closing image is of Dessie, the youngest of the three women, crossing the threshold of the Anderson house:

> Dessie stumbled on the rickety steps, righted herself, came running down the path. She had gone back for her hat. It was perched on the side of her head, three roses bobbing up and down as she walked, breasts bobbing up and down in soft unison. (371)

The path to the Anderson home, which represented Nonnie's indecision in the novel's opening scene, is now being navigated by a younger generation of black southern women. The three roses on Dessie's hat echo the three women depicted in this final scene. That the novel closes with an image of Dessie's body, active and in motion, reads as an indicator of hope in positive future change.

Providing a broad panorama of the offices that underpin the typology of fictional southern town, *Strange Fruit* establishes a paradigm for understanding a body of fiction that uses the setting of the southern town as a tool for exploring racial segregation. Narrative techniques that incorporate the diverse voices of the people of

Maxwell coincide throughout with scenes that represent the crucial spaces of the typical southern town. As a result, Maxwell is navigable: its landmarks are positioned in relation to one another, and an imagined reader is invited to participate in the social life of a southern town. To the same degree that Smith provides a thorough overview of the workings of the fictional town, Byron Herbert Reece, whose novel *The Hawk and the Sun* (1955) is the subject of the next chapter, offers a town that is built upon a framework of symbolism. The offices of Reece's town of Tilden, particularly those relating to organised religion, banking and education, can all be read as symbolic rather than as the type of figuratively 'typical' institutions that Smith imagines in *Strange Fruit*.

CHAPTER 3

An Anatomy of Critique:
Byron Herbert Reece's Tilden

Driving along US Route 19 between the Neels Gap mountain pass and the small north Georgia town of Blairsville, a traveller would pass through a stretch of road that was named the Byron Herbert Reece Memorial Highway in 2005.[1] Reaching Blairsville, the same traveller could visit Reece's home on a nearby farm, a state heritage site, to walk a trail through the beautiful surroundings and purchase Appalachian crafts in the gift shop.[2] Despite this evidence suggesting that the novelist and poet is remembered as an icon of northern Georgia's cultural heritage, Reece's work has had little place in southern literary studies. Literary critics rarely turn to him as a significant southern poet, let alone as a novelist. The abiding image that has so far formed of Reece is that of a rustic mountain bard, whose writing is somehow 'authentically' simple. Many of the mistakes made in reading and remembering Reece are parallel to the mistakes made in considering southern Appalachia, and this chapter offers a corrective to each of these misconceptions. The focus of this chapter, Reece's second novel, *The Hawk and the Sun* (1955), is a complex indictment of racial violence in the life of the fictional town of Tilden, Georgia, on the day in which the white community bands together to lynch the town's last African American resident.

Despite its critical neglect, the novel is a sophisticated anti-racist text that builds on wide and cosmopolitan influences, and is deeply engaged with Reece's contemporary moment. My reading complements and extends a body of scholarship in Appalachian

Studies that reads the region as racially and politically diverse as a corrective to marginalising narratives of the mountain South. As literary critic Rodger Cunningham argues, the Appalachian mountain range holds a precarious geographical and ideological position in the United States as it is 'not only an internal Other to the South as the South is the internal Other of America, but it is also the occupier of a simultaneous gap and overlap *between* North and South'.[3] By reading Reece's exploration of racial segregation through a typology of the southern town, I argue that he is an author who is both experimental and engaged with contemporary racial politics. Locating Reece in this way contributes to a growing scholarly understanding of southern Appalachia. *The Hawk and the Sun* tends to be read, if at all, as an example of trends in southern literature at mid-century more often than it is explored at length on its own.

Writing in 1968, literary critic Nancy Tishler reads the novel as emblematic in writing about lynching, and in her interpretation the novel's central black character, Dandelion, is figured as a 'sacrificial hero'.[4] Two years later conservative critic Floyd Watkins describes the novel as one that 'idealizes the Negro and condemns the white' and goes so far as to term such representations 'racism' in southern fiction.[5] Watkins criticises what he describes as an imbalance in novels like *The Hawk and the Sun* that 'depict a number of bad white people but no bad Negroes and no wrongs committed by Negroes at all'.[6] The problems with this line of argument are too obvious to explore in depth. More recently, Sharon Monteith interprets the novel as an example of a racial conscience in white southern fiction, with Reece 'making visible the ideology according to which lynching crimes could be ritualised as the white community's defense against a mythologised racial enemy within and allowed to go unpunished – though not forgotten'.[7] In part, the novel's appearance in little more than overviews of southern fiction stems from a misconception at mid-century that Appalachia did not share the same racial dynamics as the rest of the South. For example, James McBride Dabbs, in a brief overview of Wilma Dykeman's *The Tall Woman* (1962), contends that 'one would hardly expect a story of Southern Appalachia to be concerned with the civil rights movement; there are too few Negroes there.'[8] Scholarship on Reece's work in fiction is slim, but a small but significant body of writing has emerged that positions his life as a two-dimensional metaphor for Appalachia.

Regional memory of Reece is conflated with tired stereotypes of the 'traditional' mountain South, as in Tom DeTitta's biographical play *The Reach of Song: An Appalachian Drama* (1990). Billed as 'Georgia's state historical drama', the play suggests a state-level sanctioning of its image of Reece.[9] The play represents southern Appalachia in the middle of the twentieth century as a rural space reluctantly undergoing a transition into modernity. Reece serves as the play's 'ghost narrator', and observes the rural community.[10] The characters, all of whom are contemporaries of Reece, remember him nostalgically:

> Byron Herbert Reece could best tell the story of our mountains. His words hold the truth of yesteryear; his life was our lives, too [. . .] But what made him different started with him standing and watching, noticing – seeing the spirit into every little thing he came upon.[11]

This speech unironically catalogues a number of clichés of southern Appalachia, all of which are refracted through Reece and his work as a poet. The play is an unapologetic, if undeclared, adherent to Appalachian exceptionalism, despite an ever-growing scholarly consensus that the region is 'no longer the other America. It is America.'[12] DeTitta fetishises oral storytelling as an almost sacred, and firmly rooted, art form by asserting that Reece's words 'hold the truth' of the region's history, but Appalachia may only be understood in retrospect or, at best, as a extant contemporary view of 'yesteryear'.

Southernist Elizabeth Engelhardt has argued that the region's treatment as a 'cultural scapegoat' frequently takes precisely this temporal turn, as 'again and again Appalachia is relegated to the past tense: 'out of time' and out of step with any contemporary present, much less a progressive future'.[13] To DeTitta, Reece is an extension of the landscape, which itself is made sacred by the character Reece who 'see[s] the spirit into' it. The play consistently portrays Reece as a romanticised figure almost indistinguishable from the equally romanticised region. As DeTitta's Reece says: 'A man's got to be married to something in this life, and I suppose I am married – to farming and writing.'[14] 'Marrying' Reece to a distorted, pre-modern image of southern Appalachia holds his career in suspended animation; his work cannot be read as progressive or probing so long as it is merely a signifier of a lost past. Similarly, the idea of Appalachia as a region that, in popular historian Elizabeth Catte's terms, 'can be condemned or redeemed to suit one's purpose' has been consistently challenged by scholars of Appalachia and, implicitly, by the work of anti-racist Appalachian authors such as Reece.[15]

As the novel opens, the town of Tilden has been shaped by a racial scandal. When a white woman, Hester McCracken, gives birth to a biracial child the town's white population terrorises Tilden's black population in an ultimately fruitless search for the father. In protest and in order to survive, the town's black population flees Tilden. On the day on which the novel is set, Tilden's population is entirely white with the exceptions of McCracken's son, Gin, and a physically disabled man named Dandelion who is unable to migrate with the others. The social order includes respected leaders like Reverend Carhorn and a banker named Darlington, and marginalised figures including a bookish, single woman named Ella. A neighbour accuses Dandelion of rape after she mistakes noises coming from Ella's home as evidence of a sexual encounter. The majority of the men of the town band together to find and lynch Dandelion, while a local teacher tries to prevent the murder and a respected farmer makes a moral stand.

Through racially calibrated close textual analysis I show that Reece invents and deploys the town of Tilden, Georgia, to offer a critique of segregation and racial violence in three distinct but connected ways. First, Reece constructs his town through biological language, making Tilden symbolically analogous to a living body. Reece signals Tilden as a space diseased by racial violence, in what I read as an implicit critique of segregation. Secondly, the biological underpinnings of the town are supplemented by a symbolic framework in which Reece stages forces of insight and brightness (typified by the farmer Abraham), against those of imperception and darkness (embodied by the lynch mob). Finally Gaines, the town's history teacher, represents the limitations of exploring racism through an entirely symbolic lens. Because, as I note above, scholarship on Reece is scarce, I draw on archival sources that evidence Reece's anti-racist thinking.

'A Network of Exposed Bowels':
Tilden's Biology of Resistance

Reece represents the town of Tilden as a complex organism with a number of social and economic regulatory systems, and imagines the shapes and circulatory systems of the town as functions of an organic body. In doing this, he represents segregation as akin to physical threat. Reece's white townspeople act as a body with a single will to uphold Tilden's white supremacist sensibilities. Reece uses biological imagery to depict a town that acts as one to repel Dandelion, who is figured in the extended metaphor of the body as a dangerous, infectious irritant. Reece's use of organic language makes Tilden a community that perceives itself as 'diseased' by the presence of Dandelion when it is really suffering from the effects of vicious rumour and mob violence.

The town is represented as an autonomous urban unit within a decidedly rural setting, and its components work to facilitate its operation like the interconnected organs of a complex organism. While each of the towns examined in this book is, to varying degrees, self-contained, Tilden is notable for being isolated and is not described in physical, social or governmental relation to other places in the South or the United States. The town's restrictive design and the containment of its population are more acute than, for example, in Smith's Maxwell, which is contained by the swamp. In Tilden, 'There was little in the town to lure outsiders into it, but for all of that the inhabitants could think of no very good reason for leaving it' (19). The population is in 'balance' and 'remain[s] constant' (19). The geographical fact of the North Georgia mountains limits the town spatially: 'Behind Tilden mountains low and rounded rose on three sides. Not close, but like a distant irregular semicircular wall thrown up against invasion from the outside world' (19). The language of 'invasion' suggests a town under siege, figuring it as isolated, embattled and demanding protection. 'Invasion' also suggests infection from outside sources, and the mountainous landscape functions as the town's immune system. That the mountains are 'thrown up' against invasion imbues the abstract town with agency and suggests that the town has engineered its own defences. The phrase also suggests a common, if unpleasant, physical response to disease or infection. Ironically, the depiction of a 'siege' within the novel occurs inside the limits of the town with the 'invading' presence the town's white population, not outsiders.

In this structuring metaphor, Reece's Tilden is an integral, functioning organism, as is the 'disease' that threatens it. There is a constant tension in the novel between Dandelion as a disease that threatens the white body of the town and the lynch mob as a malevolent organism threatening the moral structure of the town. Reece's own body was under attack from a malevolent organism while he composed the novel, and archival evidence suggests that ideas of illness shaped the practice of the author's writing. In a July 1954 letter to Elliott Beach Macrae, president of his publisher, E. P. Dutton and Company, Reece asked for an advance to pay for tuberculosis treatment:

> I can see why you might be reluctant to invest more in the manuscript under the circumstance of my illness. The fact is, though, that the novel stands a better chance of coming to completion now than it ever did before. I can't do anything but write now. I can do that, though of course I must go slowly. I can't afford to break down any of the hard-earned healing that has taken place in my lung.[16]

Without wanting to overstate the effect of Reece's illness on the vocabulary of the body used in the novel, the letter clearly indicates that sickness and the ability of a single component of an organism – in his own case, the lung – to endanger the entire body was painfully resonant for Reece. The novel was written in part while Reece was resident in a sanatorium receiving treatment for tuberculosis, and, in this letter, he is acutely aware of his own body's vulnerability. Reece would leave the sanatorium, against the wishes of his doctor, shortly after writing this letter. Four years later, following an aggressive return of symptoms, he committed suicide.

Reece struggled with disease during the composition of *The Hawk and the Sun*, and disease is a structuring principle of the town. Tilden itself is decaying, and individual components are described using metaphors of organic systems in disrepair. The confrontation of any particular character with their own mortality is not central, and terminal disease is not a plot device – as it is in Carson McCullers's *Clock Without Hands* (1961), the subject of the next chapter. In the case of Dandelion's mother, Hattie, her syphilis is understood by the town's white population to be a manifestation of her sin: 'It was said that [Dandelion's] lameness resulted from the pleasure his mother took in men' (16). The disease from which Hattie suffers, and its imagined eugenic properties, highlights the cross-racial sexual practices common in the town, because her disease has also 'withered the pride of many white men' (16).[17] The taboo of racial mixing that leads in turn to the 'Exodus' of the black population several years prior to the novel's fictive present only prohibits sexual relationships between black men and white women. Reece's depiction of sexuality and racial etiquette echoes the same dynamics discussed in Lillian Smith's *Strange Fruit* in Chapter 2.

Hattie's disease is mirrored in the squalid living conditions she and her son endure. The nameless street on which Dandelion lives is described as a 'poor street, pocked with potholes', accenting the town's unequal infrastructure as visible scarring (24). The first house Dandelion passes on his 'circuit' (17) of white Tilden has plumbing like 'a network of exposed bowels' (22). The house belongs to a working-class white woman, who fantasises that Dandelion commits a taboo act so that she can have him lynched. In an instance of pathetic fallacy, her house is given a physical intimacy like that of a human body: 'The Negro kept his eyes averted from the house as he passed out a sense of innate decency, turning his gaze from it as he would from a wind-lifted skirt' (22). Reece depicts the physical structure of the house using a metaphor of racial sexual politics to underscore Dandelion's vulnerability early in the narrative. Dandelion's house is 'ill-kept', suggesting both his poverty and the town's decision to 'quarantine' him; this phrase could refer to a poorly maintained property, or to an illness maintained by the white community who keep Dandelion 'ill'.

In contrast to the 'niggertown' area of Tilden, Maple Street is 'the heart of the town', suggesting both its centrality in the organism of the town and its role in circulating malevolent bodies through the rest of Tilden (17). The fictional history of the town charts its development from a single-cell organism: 'The nucleus of the town had been an inn, a gristmill, and a forge' (46). The description of Tilden as a growing organism underscores the 'blight' of segregation on southern community, and Reece highlights this inequality by depicting the varying degrees of decay from Tilden's most affluent 'heart' to its rotting edge.

Just as Smith's *Strange Fruit* begins with a lone figure on a threshold surveying a segregated town, *The Hawk and the Sun* opens with Tilden being surveyed by a lone, unidentified man. Unlike in *Strange Fruit*, this man will not be identified in the course of the narrative. Rather, he is a *pars pro toto* synecdoche representing any and every white man resident in the town. The opening line of the novel establishes an atmosphere of vulnerability, while also shaping the town: 'It was three o'clock, and as the tide of darkness rose again over Tilden and flowed westward after the ebbing moon a man stood in his open doorway and looked out upon the dark street' (13). The man is not identified but the town is, privileging the collective unit rather than the individual component. The unnamed man and the named town operate together, and neither would be legible if not for the presence of the other, as is the case in theorist Michel de Certeau's idea that space 'occurs as the effect produced by the operations that orient it' and is 'actuated by the ensemble of movements deployed within it'.[18] The 'open doorway', the 'tide of darkness and the 'ebbing' of the moon foreshadow change. Throughout the representative novels explored in *Living Jim Crow*, fictional segregated towns are always on the brink, about to collapse or explode.

The scene precedes the dawn of the day on which the novel is set, and Reece establishes his fictional town as at peace, before compelling it into conflict. The unnamed figure who observes the town is associated with the unregulated natural world and with the highly regulated town: 'He had planted the maples when they were seedlings along the frontage of his own lot and remembered the whole file of them along the street, from leapfrog height' (13). While the neat line of trees may contribute to the order and even the homeliness of the town, disordered woodland is symbolic of the space beyond the reach of the town. Past the point on the town's periphery to which Dandelion has been consigned, a path 'los[es] its character as a street a hundred yards beyond, becoming suddenly a winding dirt road that idled into the countryside' (24). That Maple Street runs through the centre of the town further accentuates the peripheral identity of the nameless street on which Dandelion lives: 'A quarter of a mile beyond the white woman's box-square house the street of no name on which the Negro Dandelion walked entered Maple Street, street of the best houses in Tilden, which ran all the way through the town, serving as its central axis' (29). The term 'axis' indicates both dynamism and machinery; Maple Street is the stretch upon which the rest of the town turns. The 'white woman's box-square house' that Dandelion must pass as he enters the 'enemy territory' of white Tilden marks the outer limit of the white centre, and signals the threat that centre poses to Dandelion (21). Reece designs the streets, roads and paths of the town along a rhizomatic – rather than gridded – pattern. The lines that define the town, and facilitate movement, meander like the veins in a body. The roads that service the town and its economy have developed organically, and the body of the town is presented as in the process of absorbing physical change.

The mass migration of the town's black inhabitants has caused an enormous demographic shrinkage in the 'niggertown' slum, leaving Dandelion alone and the slum neglected without a population to maintain it. As a result, the white centre of the town is afforded increased purchase on the town's social and cultural identity. Dandelion alone lives on 'Tilden's decaying edge', a precarious location where 'edge' is redolent of tension and of blades, including the one that is used to emasculate Dandelion at the novel's end (48). By cutting off its diseased edges, the white supremacist 'heart' of the town rejuvenates itself and strengthens the geographic and ideological core of its identity. It becomes stronger as a body, having eliminated the threat to its racist ideals. Its quasi-biological systems of circulation and regulation thrive after the destruction of the 'threat'. The economic life of the town moves along a 'one-way flow' into the centre, suggesting the flow of blood in the cardiovascular system and recalling Dandelion's 'circuit' of the town (54).

This circulatory system disseminates information throughout the town, as Reece describes the propagation of the rumour of Ella's rape: 'This news, for it was no longer rumor, with a will and strength of its own and almost as if it had a tangible presence, traveled from the side streets of Tilden inward toward the centre of the town' (95). The 'news' is caught in the flow of the biological system towards the town's central nervous system: 'at last it reached the square itself' (96). If racial anxieties are passed through the body of the town like a virus, then the disease is aided by Tilden's southern climate. Without the heat of the August day, the maintenance of Tilden's 'life' would be less volatile: '[Abraham] thought of the time when winter would hold sterile dominion over the earth' (27).[19] In contrast to 'sterile' winter, Reece reminds the reader with a pun that 'This was August', hinting at the stifling conditions in which a disease can thrive (27). Heat encourages the growth of organisms such as bacteria, and Reece positions white racial terrorism as the disease most threatening to the southern town.

The town's social 'systems' regulate its conscience by deferring responsibility. The white widow Aunt Angelicia's place in the social economy of Tilden is fixed and clear. Her charity to dozens of unwanted cats is a sanctioned safety valve for a culture of neglect:

> neither she nor anyone in Tilden thought it was strange that she should keep so many. She was able to keep them and it seemed to Tilden that she was only doing right by the homeless when she adopted the stray cats of the town. (34)

By choosing the phrase 'it seemed to Tilden', Reece combines the opinion of each individual resident into a single collective person in a *totem pro parte* linguistic synecdoche that highlights white Tilden's collective perception. Angelicia is the caretaker of the town's biological nuisance and takes care of its abdication of responsibility for the animals. While she is aware that her neighbours 'quietly' abandon unwanted cats on her property, she does not confront them.

Angelicia's home is a sanctioned, but unacknowledged, repository for unwanted bodies when cats are 'dropped ... over the wall of the garden' (35). Reece's choice of the passive voice further removes individual responsibility from owners. Angelicia's home is a regulatory system that maintains the balance of Tilden's cat population. She absorbs the biological refuse of the town, but she is nonetheless entrenched within the community's collective will. Indeed, she is as invested in her community's norms as any other resident of Tilden: 'Aunt Angelicia was not a thoughtless woman, yet she accepted for her own the mores of her group without undue examination to determine whether they were right or wrong, just or unjust, merciful or unkind' (35). Reece grants other members of the community – including Abraham and Gaines – the capacity to dissent, but withholds it from Angelicia. Angelicia embodies the collective by carrying out her function and refusing to resist her place in the town. By specifying that she is 'not thoughtless' Reece represents her conformity as a wilful act, and Angelicia as, at best, complicit in the Tilden's toxic social economy.

Reece implicitly criticises Angelicia's unexamined adherence to Tilden's white supremacist norms by describing it as a superficial trait: 'She wore the status quo as a cloak, and the cloak changed little in style, only gathering a frill here and there or dropping a pleat or pucker, alterations that could be effected without change in the basic cut of the garment' (35). Angelicia's 'cloak' of normalcy is contrasted to the individualism Reece celebrates in the teacher and the farmer. The verb form of the word 'cloak' suggests masking and the avoidance of the moral insight that Reece advocates. The town is figured as obscuring or cloaking questions of what is 'right or wrong, just or unjust'. The implication for the working organism of the town is that intolerance is a garment that changes little over time but may ultimately be removed. Patricia Yaeger articulates the difference between 'rubbish' and 'waste' as a matter of community standards: 'Rubbish is something people look at all the time without onus or shame or desire, whereas waste is something that must be secreted away, hidden, a matter of attraction and shame.'[20] Angelicia's role as a sanctioned but marginalised collector of the town's waste (rather than its rubbish) both extends the metaphor of the town as body and positions her as a regulatory presence in the town's systems, but one that does not threaten its ideological identity.

Angelicia's missing cat, Tawm, is described as 'fixed' in another foreshadowing of Dandelion's emasculation. The language of function suggests that Tawm's ability to reproduce made him 'broken' and that his role in the town is governed by eugenics (42). Tawm and Dandelion are each prevented from procreating because they threaten to change the town's demographic character and threatens its tightly controlled character. Similarly, Gin is forced to live in a 'shed-room of the pastor's house' because having a home in either the white or black section of town would commit him to a racial identity (189). The town instead contains the problem of his identification, ensuring that each of the town's groups is consigned to a discrete and definite space in a defined racial geography. The black escapees remove themselves, en masse, from the town. This process of 'amputation' results in the town adapting itself physically to compensate. The town also shrinks to conceal its loss, and it is only from the outside that the organism's workings are seen clearly.

As a result, the countryside that circles the town and marks its limits is ideologically distinct from the town proper. As the African American residents of Tilden leave the confines of the town, they curse it: 'Once beyond the abruptly ended street, in reach of the woods to hide, they turned and shouted a volley of curses back into the town' (32).[21] The African American population is neither in the woods nor in the town. They level their curses from a space neither incorporated into nor external to the limits of the town. The proximity of the woods to Tilden offers security from violent retaliation, but the black population's literal position not-yet-in-the-woods allows their curses to be heard by Tilden's white inhabitants. Neither fully included in the town, nor yet fully clear of it, they are able to curse from a perfectly balanced place granted by their situation beyond the town's literal and figurative periphery.

The black population leaving Tilden sees it most clearly as they curse it. The local hunter Nimrod Anse, who refuses to take part in Dandelion's murder, is also granted perspective due to his vocational situation on these mountains to the west of the town. On the day in question, unlike the other residents, who are increasingly aware that Dandelion will be murdered, Anse is 'awake and aware' from the beginning of the day (18). Nimrod's name is a biblical allusion to Noah's great-grandson who is described as 'a mighty hunter before the Lord', suggesting a similar degree of sight to his namesake in Tilden.[22] Both the hunter and the fleeing black citizens stand on the mountains, which are simultaneously of and not of the town, and see the workings of its organs, and another biblical allusion makes sense of this similarity. The biblical Nimrod is grandson to Ham, who is 'cursed' by his father and sentenced to being 'a servant of servants' in what was interpreted by slave-owners and segregationists as a biblical endorsement for white supremacy.[23] Theologian Everett Tilson, writing in 1958, rejects a similar interpretation of Ham's story as a defence of segregation: 'Specialists in the interpretation of biblical literature insist that the author of [the Genesis] narrative never intended or attempted to give us an account of the separation of men on the basis of their physical characteristics.' Tilson elaborates that on the rare occasions in which the Genesis author 'takes note of any racial difference at all' it is 'not from the viewpoint of racial purist, [but] of the geographer'.[24] Tilson, like Reece, critiques the ideological abuse of the Book of Genesis in support of white supremacy.

The 'exodus' of Tilden's black population is preceded by a siege of 'niggertown'. The white population sections off the black population, isolating it within the already carefully contained space of Tilden. To borrow the novel's discourse of the body: 'niggertown' is a limb starved of blood. Because no individual 'culprit' is found to be the father of McCracken's child, blackness itself is criminalised. McCracken's sexual encounter with a black man has so thoroughly undermined the town's system of racial etiquette that it must be wholly revised, and the racial make-up of the town radically altered. In the absence of a single 'guilty' party, all black residents are made entirely guilty and the slum is made a prison: 'The second night after Hester McCracken's death a file of cars drove slowly through niggertown and wherever there was a black face at a window or behind a door watching, the fear [. . .] sprang full blown into obsession' (31). Residents are forced to hide in fear, cut off from the amenities at the centre of the town. Just as racial etiquette has collapsed, Tilden's semi-urbanity is no longer available to its black residents, who are denied access to the facilities that make the town a town.

The infrastructure of segregation outlasts the town's black population, but continues to undergo a process of erasure. The town inherits the curses of its former black residents along with Gin McCracken. After the African American population has left the town, their former homes remain empty and uncared for. On the morning of the lynching, Abraham stands outside Dandelion's shack and looks upon 'the empty shanties that had comprised niggertown before all the colored people had left suddenly in the night' (51). Linguistically, 'niggertown' has ceased to exist: the shanties 'had' comprised the area, but do so no longer even though they remain standing. The past tense in this passage of free-indirect discourse, focalised through Abraham, supposes that it is the population, 'all the colored people' of Tilden, that defines the character of an area, and, in turn, that area's relationship to the town as a whole. In this synecdoche, the presence of a black population *had* constituted a racialisation of space within the town. However, the shanties that comprised the racialised infrastructure have persisted, and, with them, a physical structure of racial division. This has left the town of Tilden ambiguously segregated: the infrastructure of segregation, particularly the second-class housing, endures as does the designation of that area despite the absence of the black population that defined the town as segregated. In their absence, the homes fall into increasing disrepair. This abjection is described in terms that suggest the decomposition of a body: Dandelion lives in a 'rotted house on the outskirts of Tilden' (15). After the forced migration, the slum is left to rot and, presumably, fall away from the 'healthy' body of the white town. This very visceral symbol is supplemented by symbolic motifs that Reece borrows from his reading in ancient and medieval literatures. For Reece, allusion is a means of exploring the positions of his characters and to recast the ethical question of segregation.

The Man at the Centre and the Man at the Edge: Symbolic Tilden

Reece's depiction of the town as a physical body is simultaneously symbolic and material. The physical shape of the town is presented as organic, while its organic structures are also metaphors for segregation. Reece develops his critique of racial violence along the twin axes of materialism and symbolism. As a contingent part of the body of the town, the lynch mob is itself a single organism composed of component individuals. In Reece's depiction of the mob's formation, he repeats the symbolism of a working organism on a smaller scale. As each person joins the mob, the mass becomes increasingly distinct from any of its component parts:

> Those first to arrive had formed a nucleus and the cluster grew by additions to its periphery. Soon the group began to move, the man at the centre turning in an effort to see each new arrival at the circle's edge and each man in his place, until the whole mass was a great spring winding itself. (122)

The mob resembles a single-cell organism, with a nucleus around which the mass of white men collects. As the cell grows outward, the organism becomes more complex. The mass is self-sustaining, capable of 'winding itself' and driven by a single representative, 'the man at the centre', who maintains his individuality as a means to focus and galvanise the shared will of the mob.

Shortly before Dandelion's lynching, Abraham takes his moral stand and the organism adapts to losing one of its parts: '"Wait!" a voice said, and looking up the Negro Dandelion saw that the mob-face had spawned out of itself a new face, a face like its own but different, kinder' (165). Abraham's individual body is differentiated from the body of the mob only after he voices resistance. The description of the lynch mob as a synecdoche is anticipated by the circumstances surrounding the black 'exodus' of Tilden:

> The [African American] reverend Elder Pate went among his flock and exhorted but no one, man nor boy, came forth to claim fatherhood of the half-black child and the scapegoat that was secret among them bloated on the fear of the guilty until it grew out of size and became them all. (31)

The father's unwillingness to come forward spreads the guilt to all of the town's black men. A (real or imagined) contravention of the sexual taboos that define racial etiquette forces a consolidation of the town's white population. Abraham's act of resistance to the mob mentality, and his suddenly acute separation from the group, puts him in temporary danger: 'He moved without fear but with slow, deliberate care from the menace that had shifted momentarily from the Negro to himself', and his movements are tracked by a man aiming a shotgun (166). Abraham's defiance neither defines nor influences the shared will of the mob; its focus continues to be directed by its charismatic leader.

That leader, a man named Harker, rallies the town's white male population into a unified whole with the express purpose of lynching Dandelion. Harker is literally and figuratively at the centre of the expanding mass of the mob when he instigates the hunt for Dandelion through charismatic speech: 'It was as if by centripetal force he had been thrown to the center of the circle and by this given authority. His name was Harker, and he was a big, dark man whose voice rang resonant and deep as if it came out of a well' (122). In a novel in which audible speech is consistently obscured or made ambiguous by narrative strategy, the emphasis on Harker's voice is telling. His 'authority' comes as much from his deep and resonant voice as from his locating himself at the centre of the mob. His voice, more than any actual words he speaks, allows him to direct the actions: 'The first word he spoke was not a word. It was a heavy raw command that sounded something like *Haak!*' (122–3).

Although it is rooted in the vocal, Harker's charisma is also silently physical. After a member of the mob makes a sick joke about hanging Dandelion, Harker silences the crowd: 'Harker lifted his hands and held them palms down at the height of his breast for a long moment. The eyes of the crowd fastened upon the stalled hands that remained poised until they had drawn the last shred of sound from the men' (123). This physical gesture demands silence from the crowd and marks Harker's authority as predicated on the physicality of the 'big, dark man'. Even while his physicality demands compliance, his power over his own speech, and that of the other men assembled in the mob, forms the core of his authority and charisma: 'When all was silent, Harker pushed his hands downward with a sudden violent motion and spoke: "All right, let's go get him!" he said' (123). Harker has absorbed the power of speech from those around him and consolidated it. Through a violent physical gesture, he channels the collective voice of the mob into a violent linguistic gesture. He is a conduit for the will of the mob, absorbing and emitting the raw material provided by its members.

Harker is made symbolic of English-language traditions of oral storytelling. 'Haak!'– the word that was not a word – is a modern variation of the Anglo-Saxon word *hwæt*, an exclamation used to begin Old English narrative poetry. Like Harker's 'Haak!', *hwæt* is a word that is not a word: it is no longer used in modern English, and its traditional usage communicated urgency and demanded attention rather than carrying out a descriptive function. The most celebrated instance of *hwæt* in English literature is the opening line of *Beowulf*, the story of a hero slaying a monster. Reece ironically figures Harker – whose name can thus be read as a noun meaning a person who harks – as the instigator of a heroic narrative poised to vanquish the 'monstrous' Dandelion.[25] The very name of the town also has a medieval provenance: in Middle English, *tilden* is a verb meaning 'pitch', as one would a tent. The name of the town works in concert with the novel's original title, *Tents toward Sodom*, to suggest that Tilden, like Sodom, is a doomed and wicked city. Another precedent for the town's name arises from more recent, and more local, historical sources. Samuel J. Tilden's closely contested presidential campaign against Rutherford B. Hayes precipitated the Compromise of 1877 that officially ended Reconstruction. Tilden, a New York Democrat, conceded the election to Republican Hayes in exchange for the removal of federal troops from the former Confederacy.

Among mid-century historians of the South, Tilden and the Compromise were understood to signal a moment of transition in the relationship between North and South. C. Vann Woodward viewed the election as a turning point in the developing identity of the postbellum South: 'A great deal more was at stake in the winter of 1876–1877 than the question of which of two citizens, Samuel J. Tilden or Rutherford B. Hayes, would occupy the White House.'[26] John Hope Franklin figures Tilden as an electable dem-ocratic candidate with progressive potential, calling him a 'widely respected reform governor of New York' who had 'no taint of dis-loyalty or wartime Copperheadism'.[27] The town, like the New York governor, is representative of a moment of potential progressive change and a potential shifting of ideologies in the South. With similar resonance, Shelby Foote names a small-town bank manager Lawrence Tilden in *Love in a Dry Season* (1951).[28] These twinned allusions in Reece's choice of the town's name represent an interrogation of southern traditionalism, either as medieval inheritance or nineteenth-century Lost Cause. Reece refracts this interrogation through a character who epitomises continued belief in these principles.

Harker's rhetorical power constitutes a nuanced allusion to medieval narrative conventions. While Reece's reading in medieval literature is evident from this passage, so too is his immersion in a mid-century southern intellectual life. Reece's depiction of Harker's place 'in the center' of the mob is also reminiscent of W. J. Cash's *The Mind of the South* (1941), which includes a chapter entitled 'Of the Man at the Center'.[29] Cash's chapter addresses the almost mythical figure of the southern agrarian ideal: 'a backcountry pioneer farmer or the descendant of such a farmer'.[30] Cash's description of this ideal, one he implicitly rejects, is markedly inflected by the South's supposed medieval inheritance. Cash criticises the Nashville agrarians' attempts to 'reassimilate' the medieval English 'squire' into the image of the man at the centre.[31] In Michael O'Brien's terms, *The Mind of the South* 'is a book about the southern Zeitgeist and its ability to transform both the perception of the individual and socioeconomic realities', while James C. Cobb writes that 'Cash's book would become the most widely read and influential attempt to unravel the mystery of southern white identity'.[32] Reece's allusion to Cash's 'man at the centre' bears out each of these interpretations of *The Mind of the South*, because it focuses on the perception of the individual and collective white identities of Harker and the men who surround him. Reece reimagines Cash's famous phrase to critique the agrarian romanticisation of the medieval.

While an instructor at Young Harris College in northern Georgia, Reece taught classes on the history and development of the modern English language from a number of sources, including Latin. In his lecture notes, Reece outlines the influence of Anglo-Saxon language and history on Modern English:

There are about two thousand Anglo-Saxon words in the language. The Romans left Britain in 449 A.D. By 600 three tribes, the Angles, the

Saxons, and the Jutes had established themselves on the island. Their fused dialects became the English Language.[33]

Reece clearly knew, and taught, early-medieval English and his readings of medieval literature influenced his invention of Tilden, and the speech patterns of its inhabitants.

Tracing trends in literature of southern Appalachia from the 1920s, Richard Gray identifies the 'originating interest in speech' as a defining feature in the construction of Appalachian characters. Speech, specifically idiom, comes to denote regional specificity as it 'anchored the hymn to the mountain man in something very basic and quite specific: the words of the southern highlander *were* his world'. 'His way of life', Gray goes on to say, 'was caught and explained in the still living tissue of his language' in what the critic describes as 'a story of survival against the odds'.[34] Reece upends these conventions by making his characters' speech ambiguous and dangerous. If the 'mountain man' as constituted through speech is typically a metaphor for 'survival', Dandelion's predestined death implies a failure of this metaphor. As a southern intellectual, Reece manipulates motifs of southern personhood to better reflect the region's ambiguity. Reece's reading in medieval literature and language lends his representation of the lynching an allusive dimension. By intervening in sophisticated contemporary discourses, Reece evidences the complex and cosmopolitan undercurrents of Appalachian thought that are all too easily ignored in conceptions of the region. As cultural theorist Kwame Anthony Appiah warns, 'celebrations of the "cosmopolitan" can suggest an unpleasant posture of superiority toward the putative provincial'.[35] To Appiah, and in my reading of Reece, cosmopolitanism that exceeds the term's exclusionary baggage is a necessarily ethical state of being, predicated on the assumptions that 'we have obligations to others' and that 'we take seriously the value not just of human life but of particular human lives'.[36] In the literary context, and as critic Gillian Roberts explores, cosmopolitanism is manifested in 'the overlaying of host and guest status' in specific fictional characters 'that emphasizes global citizenship's rights and duties'.[37] Reece's association with Appalachia might conventionally exclude him from understandings of cosmopolitanism, but *The Hawk and the Sun* engages with each of these definitions of the term. The novel is deeply concerned with the ethical responsibility of neighbours and with how characters, especially Abraham and Gaines, attempt to meet those obligations.

Through an understanding of Harker as symbolic of an oral narrative tradition, Reece inflects his interrogation of the lynch mob with a symbolic criticism. Reece conceived of the novel as highly symbolic. It is through this symbolism that Reece positions his novel as a critique of segregation in the 1950s. While Reece made few public comments on segregation, his private correspondence is valuable in extrapolating the intersection of symbolism and race in his conception of *The Hawk and the Sun*.

In a letter to a former student at Emory University in 1956, Reece explicated the novel's symbolism and subtext and deliberately cautioned his student against relying too much on an author's interpretation of a work: 'I would preface these few remarks by saying that whatever light a statement from me may throw on THE HAWK AND THE SUN it will not be the whole meaning which is illuminated.'[38] While Reece made no attempt to fully explain the 'meaning' of the novel, he does shed a 'light' on the structure of the text, 'illuminat[ing]' his use of certain motifs in the novel. Southern novelist William Goyen, in a review of the novel, highlights this symbolic binary, writing that the novel 'is a frozen landscape of blocks of color and textures where light breaks over and darkens over' and likens Reece to a 'checker player' who moves his characters along the dark and light squares of a board.[39] Significantly, the language of 'illumination' foreshadows the 'deliberately symbolic' allusive project Reece outlined:

As for its symbolic structure, I have read about, or perhaps seen a picture, of a representation of Ammon-Re that once stood in Thebes. This representation shows Ammon-Re with a sun symbol and a falcon. No doubt the attribute assigned to Re shifted over a period of time, but Re is the Father-god and the sun god and is or may be interpreted to be time. The sun illuminates. As for the falcon, or hawk, it is noted for its power of sight, hence its use in hunting. The falcon, then sees what the sun illuminates. Illumination and perception are both joined in Ammon-Re.[40]

Reece's assertion that the novel is 'deliberately' steeped in symbolic imagery suggests this schema as a prism through which to understand the text. Alongside his engagement with medieval texts, Reece draws symbolic language from ancient Egyptian mythology. His attention to the two particular symbols that are clearly reflected in the novel's title, a sun and a falcon, suggests how individual objects within the novel are specifically resonant.

Reece named his novel *The Hawk and the Sun* shortly before it went to press, but he continued to use the working title, *Tents toward Sodom*, until a very late stage in the composition. In January 1955 Reece received a letter from Louise Townsend Nicholl, his editor at E. P. Dutton, requesting that he give the novel a title that will 'make it easier to sell!'[41] Reece considered a number of alternative titles for the work and made the decision in collaboration with Nicholl. Among his ideas were titles that mirrored the syntax of *The Hawk and the Sun*, including 'The Seed and the Harvest', 'The Shadow and the Substance' and, more explicitly, 'The Nigger in the Hills', each of which suggest balance or division as does the syntax of the phrase 'the hawk and the sun'.[42] Other options that Reece feared had the 'Wrong Emphasis [*sic*]' included 'The Lynching' and 'The Lynchers', titles that would highlight racial violence as a structuring principle in the novel.[43] Reece was less sure of another option, 'Dream of Darkness', writing that it 'seems vaguely familiar, but perhaps I have in mind [William] Styron's "Lie Down in Darkness"'.[44] In his letter to Nicholl, he indicates a preference for 'The Hawk and the Sun', despite the author's facetious concern that the title's description of the novel's dénouement amounted to 'accessory after the fact'.[45] A final draft of the novel, marked 'Copy for the Press' and dated '1/25/55', has the title *Tents toward Sodom* typed and struck through, with the final title *The Hawk and the Sun* handwritten underneath.[46] The letter in which Reece suggested the final title, *The Hawk and the Sun*, is dated 26 January 1955, so it is likely that change was carried out after the date on which the draft was received. In making his eventual choice, Reece foregrounded the novel's symbolic schema and, specifically, the imagery of light and vision that persists throughout the day on which the novel is set. If the statue of Ammon-Re that Reece describes compares to any figure in the text, it is Abraham. Like Ammon-Re, Abraham is distinguished as a father, and his recognition of the hawk at the novel's end signifies insight.

Reece structures the novel to reflect the principles of illumination and perception, as he describes how the novel

> begins in darkness but progresses as the sun rises and reaches a climax shortly after noon, while there is plenty of illumination to aid perception. It closes in darkness. But this darkness is of night, and of course it will be dispelled with the return of the sun.[47]

Reece's description of the sun not only echoes his statements about Ammon-Re, but also throws the author's portrayal of Abraham into relief. Abraham's decision to leave the lynch mob will improve the moral standards of future generations of his family: 'something was added to the heritage of Abraham's sons, and his sons' sons and daughters still unborn, that would bestead them in dark hours in the future that was theirs' (191). Abraham's ability to recognise, or 'perceive', what has been 'illuminated' is a trait that will assist future 'chosen' generations in recognising good and evil. Abraham believes that the hawk he sees at Dandelion's lynching is a manifestation of God – 'Well, I can say what I believe. I saw the hawk and it was not a hawk' – his phrasing recalling Harker's 'word that was not a word' and positioning Abraham as Harker's moral opposite (191). This symbolic divinity is very different from the religion exemplified by Tilden's organised institutions. Reece reconfigures a spiritual and moral response to segregation through this imagery.

Reece's reading of darkness as temporary and 'dispelled' by the sun may suggest that the novel ends on a note of optimism; Abraham's ethical stand and his commitment to his sons mark a positive shift for the future of the town. However, just as the sun will rise the following day, it is bound to set. The ending, then, is ambivalent and denies either optimism or pessimism in isolation. Abraham's sons and their families are, however, granted the necessary tools to compete with shadow and darkness. Reece also describes Abraham as biologically attuned to this ethical shift, and he and Gaines are alike in their capacity for moral insight and growth, a capacity reflected in the latter's name. In contemplating this aspect of the novel, Reece expands on his conception of the two characters:

> I think I needn't pursue this symbolism any further except perhaps to say that at the scene of the lynching the farmer Abraham (the father of the strong sons) has the power to believe the truth only after the arrival of the hawk, the power to see. It doesn't seem inconsistent to me to say that he got this power from the impulse of life in his cells while the professor of history got it from the study of history.[48]

Abraham, simultaneously witnessing the sun and the bird of prey, is analogous to the mythical figure of Ammon-Re in Reece's conception of the Egyptian deity. Amun was initially a local deity associated with Thebes but was fused with the sun god Ra in the fifteenth century BCE, taking on pan-Egyptian significance. Ammon-Re represents the twin traits of historical insight, indicated throughout the novel with Gaines's interest in Thebes, and the illumination of the sun. When petitioning Carhorn for assistance, Gaines thinks of Ra within a pantheon of ancient gods who 'wore averted faces' in the presence of 'the shrine of the Unknown God' represented by Carhorn's inaction (140). The sun god, in Gaines's imagination, refuses to see the injustice of Carhorn's religion. Here, the symbolic illumination of the sun is hindered by the refusal to perceive.

On the other hand, the symbolic interaction of illumination and sight combine in Abraham who is depicted as deeply invested in the cultivation of the landscape and of the next generation of white southerners. Professor Gaines, albeit in a different way, is also invested in the education of a new generation, because he sees his job as 'the cultivation of the mind' (181). He and Abraham mirror each other in their roles as symbolic cultivators. As a farmer and a teacher, each cultivates a culture of moral insight in the segregated South, and Reece, who worked as both a farmer and a teacher, was well placed to identify this connection.[49] These 'cultivator' characters are committed to using their insight to improve the material social order of the town. Nimrod Anse is aware from the novel's beginning that the lynching of Dandelion is a threat to the moral centre of the white community. Anse is singularly resistant to joining the amalgamated body of the mob precisely because he is a

hunter: 'Finally, with the exception of Anse the hunter who preferred the blood of the fox, the men were all going in the direction
of Clifton Mill' (98). As a hunter, Anse is made analogous to a bird
of prey, because he is already invested with insight, as is the hawk of
the novel's title. As well as lending Anse similarities to his biblical
counterpart, Reece positions the hunter in symbolic opposition to
Harker. Nimrod from the Book of Genesis appears as a character
in the *Inferno* section of Dante Alighieri's allegorical epic poem *The
Divine Comedy* (c. 1320) and is blamed for the fall of the Tower of
Babel, being described as 'Nimrod, to whose evil thought is due /
that more than one tongue in the world is spoken'.[50] When read
in light of Harker's similarity to the *Beowulf* poet, Dante's Nimrod
signifies both a failure of speech (contrasted to Harker's capacity to
speak for the community), and the invention of dissenting perspectives. Each of these resonances with Dante is manifested in Reece's
Nimrod, who silently refuses to join the single-minded mob.

In contrast to Anse, Gaines and Abraham voice their resistance,
rather than expressing it through silence. Reece, in a personal letter,
claimed that 'the book is not primarily a statement on the race
question' but nevertheless located Gaines and Abraham at the
novel's moral centre:

> There is professor Gaines, steeped in history which is at once the lesson
> itself and the instrument for viewing the lesson of men's living together.
> There is the farmer Abraham, the father of life (you remember the prom-
> ise made to Abraham on the plains of Ur) who has the strength to believe
> the truth.[51]

While Reece concedes that the novel might be interpreted as 'pretty
pessimistic', he also asserts that 'there is no room in it for hopeless-
ness' because of the actions taken by these two characters.[52] With
this letter, Reece intervened in a wider conversation about art's role
in the face of segregation at mid-century. Rather than race being
merely symbolic, he also explored the symbolic and material issues
that arise from segregation.

The fictional siege of 'niggertown', which may have a biblical
analogue in a number of sieges of Jerusalem, is a narrative set-piece
that illustrates Reece's treatment of the material through symbol-

ism. The first potential biblical intertext, the siege of the city of Jebus by King David, resulted in the city being renamed Jerusalem.[53] The Babylonian king Nebuchadnezzar II twice lay siege to and sacked the city: the first such siege led to exile in Babylon and is described in 2 Kings 24:10–16. The second results in the destruction of the city and of the Temple of Solomon.[54] After it was ended, the people of Jerusalem began to starve: 'The famine was sore in the city so that there was no bread for the people of the land.'[55] The theme of starvation is echoed in *The Hawk and the Sun* when white racial terrorism erupts: 'from that time no colored person dared go into Tilden for supplies and finally all began to starve' (31). However, given Reece's acknowledged debt to the story of Ammon-Re in the composition of the novel, the Egyptian forces' siege of Jerusalem is a more likely analogy. Gaines's mind turns to stories of 'Ammonite kings' at various points in the text, and they become an analogy to the white inhabitants of Tilden who starve out the town's black population.

Reece recounts the stories of Genesis in his novel and adds to them a genesis of his own: he depicts the inception and growth of the town of Tilden through an oral narrative passed down through generations. As well as a physical mapping of the town, Reece adopts a historical mapping from its founding and situates Abraham as the arbiter of the town's history from its inception to the fictive present. Observing the landscape of the town compels Abraham to consider its development. He 'could see the town, now bathed in light, lying below him and he began to cast back in his mind to bring together all the fragments of its history which he knew' (46). The narrative shifts from Abraham's thinking about the town's development into the direct representation of a conversation between its founders, which 'Abraham knew from the telling of an ancestor' (48). In spite of Abraham's temporal remove from Tilden's founding, the story includes direct speech between the town's namesake, Melvin Tilden, and a 'damn good' blacksmith named Anders, whose name means 'man' or 'humankind', who work together to build the foundations of the town (49).

Abraham's understanding of the history of Tilden emerges from an immersion in oral storytelling: 'Abraham remembered his ancestor telling and telling of it with repetition of the minutest detail in the manner of the very old' (50). The 'very old' recalls medieval and biblical conventions of storytelling. The history of Tilden is constructed through the repetition of oral narrative, just as Melvin Tilden makes the settlement a town by building an inn named The Traveller's Rest (50). The naming of this inn, which suggests both migration and the interruption of mobility, ironically transforms an area through which people passed into an organised community. This oral narrative is an act of invention as it relates how the 'the crossroads became a town', and indicates the role of moral choice in the town's identity (50). The way that the white community treats Gin McCracken is an indicator of its collective moral decision-making.

Gin McCracken is left behind by the African American residents just as their curses are. Abraham's conception of the 'exodus' and of McCracken are synchronised when he considers the remnants of 'niggertown' and considers how the African American inhabitants of the town:

> [. . .] left suddenly in the night
> And left their curses upon the town, thought Abraham.
> And left as Tilden's ward Hester McCracken's bastard, a whinny-voiced idiot who had a purplish-black skin, in color like the face of a strangulated man. (51)

The passage is spread across three paragraphs, the latter two beginning with the word 'and'. It is grammatically irregular to begin a sentence, let alone a paragraph, with a conjunction. However, it is common in the Bible for verses to begin with 'and', another stylistic flourish that connects Reece's text with Genesis, and it is deeply tied to his depiction of the patriarch Abraham. As well as this allusive effect, his choice of 'and' highlights the contingency of each of the passage's three statements, allowing it to read as an inventory of the town's inheritance from the departed black population: the abandoned shanties, their curses, and the care of the 'ward' Gin McCracken. The repetition of 'and' also makes each of these three factors contingent on the last: the emptying of residential space leads to the cursing of the town, and Gin McCracken is implicitly figured as a curse. The word 'ward' denotes responsibility, at least as much as it does an educational relationship. Gin's similarity in appearance to a 'strangulated man' marks the affiliation between the town and its 'ward' as constraint at the very least, as when a hand constricts a throat, and as death at the very worst, as well as foreshadowing Dandelion's later death by hanging. Gin's continuing presence in the town makes impossible an evasion of the racial terrorism of the past.

Tellingly, Abraham conceives of Gin in physical opposition to his own sons: 'To balance and outweigh the vision of the misshapen half-black child, Abraham thought of his own strong sons, each of them sturdy and straight and the flesh of them barley-gold in colour' (51). This comparative description operates on the principles of balance and imbalance. Abraham's effort to 'balance' the images of Gin and his sons draws on similar rhetorical formulations: while Gin is 'purplish-black', Abraham's sons are 'barley-gold'. These descriptive compound words, held in balance by a hyphen, lie on opposite sides of a colour spectrum. However, as well as trying to balance his thoughts, Abraham attempts equally to 'outweigh' these thoughts, a term that suggests imbalance. Gin's description is consequently marked by asymmetry: imbalance exists in conjunction with balance. Gin's physical asymmetry, his 'misshapen' body, is outweighed by the physical stability of Abraham's 'sturdy and straight' sons.

As much as Gin is physically differentiated from Abraham's sons, he is marked as different from Dandelion. When they meet, Dandelion taunts Gin about his indeterminate racial identity and neither recognises kinship in the other. Their respective physical disabilities (rather than their shared racial heritage) place them on shared ground: 'the two, both maimed, stood a moment in immortal light and stared meanly at each other' (76). Their 'maimed' bodies mark out these characters as different from the rest of the community, at least as much as their racial identification. Their physical impairments also symbolise their threat to the structural security of white Tilden's conception of the town. Gin's persistence in the town symbolises a continuing politics of oppression in the South. Abraham's 'strong sons', however, symbolise a parallel continuation of resistance to oppression. While Dandelion's story is a tragic one, Reece provides a framework for progressive change even while he presents the graphic brutality of segregation.

'Let Him be Dandelion': Reece's Material Recourse

Even while Reece embeds his social critique in a web of symbolism, he refuses to allow this symbolism to displace material implications. His construction of the town as a metaphorical body that regulates itself through lynching reflects a combined approach to anti-racism that relies on esoteric and realistic tactics. Reece's characters, particularly Ella and Gaines, resist the diffusion of their circumstances into abstraction by eschewing the romantic allure of medieval precedents. Reece presents the immediate and physical concerns of the town, in terms of its economic and religious systems, as antithetical to solid moral positions. Reece does not allow the symbolic schema that structures his narrative to become an alibi for the racial concerns that it reflects and explores. By focusing on the South's economic and religious institutions, embodied in the physical buildings of a bank and a church, Reece pointedly aligns his symbolic narrative with the region's material infrastructure.

When Ella remembers a past romance she thinks herself to have been 'A silly girl to be setting a man a love-trial and he no knight nor of the age of knighthood' (106). Ella, who is unusually well educated by the standards of the community, has insight into the medieval code's incompatibility with contemporary society. Harker, by contrast, symbolises an investment in the persistence of outmoded mores.[56] Ella's home marks her out from the rest of the community. The physical conditions and spatial location of her house signal her discomfort within the social and geographical constraints of Tilden: 'Where she lived alone near the widening of the world into the limitless country beyond the borders of Tilden, her neat small house bulged with books' (59). The syntax itself 'bulges' with alliteration, echoing Ella's pushing of Tilden's ideological boundaries and complementing Reece's rhetoric of the body. The word 'limitless' not only re-inscribes the space beyond Tilden as free of ideological constraint but also underscores the town's spatial and intellectual limits as the widening of the world suggests the narrowness of Tilden.

Just as Lillian Smith's Miss Ada lives on the line of demarcation between Maxwell's 'White Town' and 'Colored Town', Reece's Ella and the otherwise unnamed 'iron-jawed woman' live at the outer limit of Tilden's white community. Each woman is somewhat removed from the rest of white Tilden: Miss Ella by her creative and intellectual personality, and the iron-jawed woman by her social class. As Reece writes: 'Miss Ella lived on a cross street that connected Center Street with the fringe of the town where the Negro himself lived' (76–7). Her home lies at the literal and figurative intersection of Tilden's 'best houses' and its slum at the fringe. She is literally placed off-centre, suggesting that her personality is incompatible with white Tilden's preferred self-image, and Reece, like the other novelists I discuss, imagines a pointedly anti-racist geography for his fictional town. The ambivalence of this interstitial space in Tilden is made manifest in the depiction of the incident in which Dandelion observes Ella suffering an episode of psychosis. The encounter, which precipitates the lynching, is described in two succeeding chapters from two different perspectives, each of which deploys a markedly different formal strategy. Chapters 15 (85–8) and 16 (89–92) portray the scene differently, and these differences in perspective lead to Dandelion's punishment for a crime that has not been committed.

The earlier chapter is marked by uncertainty and focalised through an unreliable character when Ella 'lay in the rigors of madness' (85). Although the omniscient narration is precise about the scene's temporal setting at 'eight o'clock on that morning of August 19th', this specificity does not penetrate the consciousness of the scene's primary subject: 'Time meant nothing to Miss Ella because she could not extricate the present from the past' (85). Ella's physical location, as suggestive of her place on the social periphery, is something of which she is only dimly aware during the episode: 'Sometimes it occurred to her briefly that she was in her house on the extreme edge of Tilden' (86). Ella is largely unaware of her own place in Tilden's structure and even less aware of a visit from Dandelion when an erotic memory causes her to shout ecstatically: 'She saw the burning face before her and because of the urge to affirm, she said loudly: Yes, yes, yes' (88).[57] Although her speech is audible, even 'loud', it is not rendered in quotation marks, leaving the act of speech as ambiguous and confused as her state of mind. In counterpoint, the later account of the same scene is characterised by a false certainty: the poor white woman who 'witnesses' Dandelion's attack is adamant about the crime. When Dandelion innocently carries out his regular chores for Ella, she suddenly screams, making Dandelion flee in panic (90).

The purposefully ambiguous events of the novel's previous chapter are interpreted here, in no uncertain terms, as an imperative to lynch Dandelion. Seeing Dandelion leaving the house provides her with all the evidence she needs to make the accusation: 'As he ran he glanced at the house nearest Miss Ella's and saw that the iron-jawed woman who did the cleaning there was standing on the back stoop with a broom in her hand. She was looking directly at him, her broom poised. Suddenly she shouted to him' (91). Before the woman speaks to Dandelion, her broom is 'poised' to carry out a violent act of rebuke. The woman, who lives in the first house Dandelion encounters on his daily circuit, is compelled by a perverse desire for Dandelion to have raped Ella and to be murdered for it:

> Meanwhile the iron-jawed woman from the house next door hurried into Miss Ella's house, and when she saw her lying senseless among the dishevelled covers she was sure that her dreadful hope had been realized. But because she needed corroboration she began to question Miss Ella. (91)

The woman is so motivated by the desire to have been witness to sexual violence that her 'dreadful hope' affirms her belief; Miss Ella is sought out only to corroborate 'the facts' as she has already interpreted them.

When she asks if Ella has been raped, she interprets Ella's ecstatic utterance as affirmation: '"Yes, yes, yes," Miss Ella said. But she spoke to the figure with the face of fire that moved in her fantasy' (92). While the rendering of this same act of speech in the previous chapter does not include quotation marks and is understood as certainty, 'Yes, yes, yes' is expressed in this scene with the punctuation of direct speech. The woman who interrupts Dandelion's chores in Ella's house is invested in his 'crime' to the degree that the ambiguity of the exclamation in the earlier chapter is eroded. In her eagerness to criminalise Dandelion, the woman imposes certainty both on her interpretation of the events and by the manner through which her interpretation is conveyed in the mirroring of the incidents in the text. Reece deploys this experimental technique as a means of reflecting the confusion inherent in the working of racial etiquette.

This fractured representation of Dandelion's visit to Miss Ella's home facilitates the act of violence that ends the fracture of the town along racial lines. With Dandelion's murder, 'niggertown' is no longer a container for the town's disenfranchised black community and, ironically, the iron-jawed woman will now occupy the town's least prestigious peripheral space. Reece makes it clear that her act of witnessing stems from her insecurity about her place in the racial order of the town. Earlier in the novel she watches Dandelion as he begins his circuit of jobs and is enraged that their positions are similarly on the fringes of the town: 'And I a white woman, she thought in a final flare of rage against the Negro Dandelion. She had equated their tasks in her mind and found them the same except that his were a little the more menial' (23). The woman resents Dandelion because she is forced to work as a domestic servant despite her race, and her low prestige in the town's social order is mirrored in her physical situation and underlined by the absence of an exploitable black workforce in the town. She is both geographically and socially peripheral; Farley, a representative of elite Tilden, thinks of her only as 'a large raw-boned woman he had never seen', suggesting a distinct lack of importance to the rest of white Tilden (102). Reece positions the woman's own material poverty as a corollary to the racist structure she is so keen to support.

Reece depicts the lynching of Dandelion as intrinsic to the economic and cultural life of the town. The web in which Dandelion has been caught is bound up in the economic and material systems of the town that demand his death in payment for his supposed crime. For example, Gaines is initially reluctant to involve himself with the practical workings of the town because he is more comfortable in his internal, intellectual life but sees himself as duty-bound to attempt to save Dandelion's life: 'He was not by nature a Samaritan. He felt that it was his duty to try to save the Negro Dandelion, to try to extricate him from the web which not justice but circumstance had woven about him' (125). Gaines commits to intervening in the physical, rather than symbolic, realm in order to save Dandelion. In his efforts to prevent the lynching, Gaines, known most frequently in the text as 'The professor of History at Tilden High' or 'the father of the boy Farley', appeals first to the Reverend Mr Carhorn, pastor of the local Baptist church, who is unwilling to involve himself in preventing the lynching.

Carhorn, second only to the banker Mr Darlington in the town's esteem, is a highly respected member of the white community. The 'imposing stone church' that constitutes the office of the pastor attests to his prestige, and the building 'stood as befitted its place of importance in the lives of the people of Tilden, only a block away from Mr. Darlington's bank which occupied the central position of the south side of the square' (138). Carhorn's spiritual authority is understood as secondary to Darlington's material and economic authority; his church's prestige is defined by its proximity to the bank. Carhorn and his church are, combined, a telling example of my contention that fictional towns are shaped around 'offices' – a label that incorporates both a building and an individual. As Carhorn welcomes Gaines and Farley into the church, he and the building form a single body: 'He began to swing his big body about as if it were hinged to the door jamb and he was opening himself inward' (139). Carhorn's self is made indistinguishable from the material edifice of his office, the church. The phrase 'the church' is a common *pars pro toto* synecdoche because a single building comes to represent the whole of the religious institution. In this portrayal, religion is figured as a concrete, worldly institution rather than the metaphysical spirituality Abraham experiences at the novel's close. The church is morally compromised by its physical location in the confines of Tilden.

Carhorn is unwilling to reconcile physical violence with the eso-teric spiritualism of his congregants: 'He could not bring himself to believe that the people of Tilden who sat in his congregation with such quiet hands could turn them to the lynching of Dandelion' (142–3).[58] Carhorn refuses to help Gaines in any material way and simply prays for Dandelion's safety (143). Carhorn is comforted by the symbolic implications of the lynching, and allows them to override the material implications of the act: 'I am going to let him be Stephen and be stoned, and be Paul and be persecuted, and be as Christ and be crucified' (144). Throughout the novel, Gaines's knowledge of history has allowed him to defer engagement with the material world. Gaines constantly 'repatriate[s] all people he met to the kingdom of Thebes' (57). In his meeting with Carhorn, and faced with Dandelion's murder, he now refuses symbolism and allegory. Rather than allowing Dandelion's death to remain a symbolic act for Carhorn, Gaines insists on keeping it within the material realm: 'Let him be Dandelion and be saved' (144). Like Ella, Gaines's education allows him to pragmatically engage with tradition. Gaines's appeal is unsuccessful, but he has rejected the esoteric defence of lynching offered by Carhorn. Through Carhorn and his personification of the church, Reece critiques the religious institution for its collective inaction in the face of racial terrorism while simultaneously suggesting that anti-racism is a Christian imperative.

Following his meeting with Carhorn, Gaines meets with the local banker Mr Darlington and appeals for his help in an obtuse manner. Gaines uses the metaphor of economic commodities to attempt to convince Darlington to intervene to prevent the lynching. In another instance of nominative determinism in the novel, the banker's name marks him as a 'darling of the town', and suggests that he is empowered to challenge the mob mentality of its constituents. Darlington is initially confused at the absence of customers in his bank because the impending lynching has emptied the town centre of its population, with most of the men who would ordinarily be contributing to the economic life of the town hunting Dandelion. Darlington walks through the square in an attempt to understand the change that has come over the town's population:

> A little before the professor of History at Tilden High left the Reverend Mr. Carhorn kneeling in the sanctuary of the great stone church, Mr. Darlington summoned his second vice-president to watch the tellers while he made a discreet excursion into the streets to see what he could learn about the odd circumstances that had emptied the square of the town and left the bank inactive, like a piece of machinery made idle because the raw material that poured into its maw to be transformed in its noisy interior into shapes strict and foreign had ceased flowing from its source. (154)

This long sentence, which opens a chapter, describes the simultaneous actions of three of the novel's characters: Gaines, Carhorn and

Darlington. The length of the sentence reflects the ways in which the individual actions of the people of the town interact with and inform each other. Reece's choice of verbs to describe the movements of these characters highlight their respective roles within the community. Gaines 'leaves', suggesting both his continuing action on Dandelion's behalf and his habit of removing himself from the life of the town to the safety of 'history'. Carhorn 'kneels', marking him as the person responsible for the spiritual health of the community but also as unwilling to take any decisive action against the men of the town in order to save Dandelion. Finally, Darlington 'summons' his employee, marking him as a leader within the community, his position at the economic apex of the town affording him authority over the behaviour of others. The beginning of the sentence portrays the town as a unit that is intrinsically dependent upon the cooperation of its members. A significant effect of the sentence's length is that it marks out Darlington, who is the subject following the first clause, as a dynamic personality; he is a central component of the mechanism of the town and is continually moving to maintain and exploit Tilden's economic resources. Stylistically, the sentence is kinetic, moving quickly through the events of a short period of time. Two of the three men addressed, Gaines and Darlington, are similarly kinetic and are represented in motion.

The people of the town are described in a simile as akin to commodities within an industrial framework; they are like 'raw material' fed through a machine to produce an end product. The machine is further described through a metaphor. Reece uses the word 'maw' to denote the point of entrance into the industrial mechanism, suggesting a carnivorous animal feeding on the 'raw material' of the people of the town. The bank, at the figurative and literal centre of the town, is here a metonym for the economic order of American capitalism in the mid-1950s. Through free-indirect discourse, Reece shows Darlington as limited by his small community: 'He always felt somewhat cramped in his activities by the smallness of the town of Tilden' (154). Despite the limitations of the small town, Darlington sees himself as a component in the economic function of the entire nation: 'Ah, well, he was really part of the financial machinery that geared contemporary life and time.

He was a vital cog in a vast machine' (155). Darlington sees his role in the town's financial life as a defining feature of 'contemporary life and time'. While 'life' refers to the commonplace interactions of people in capitalism, contemporary 'time' has perhaps a more sinister resonance. Darlington's vision of working people as raw materials to feed a machine is indicative of a contemporary ethos and the ideological basis of the contemporary moment. Just as the time of a single day defines the narrative's parameters, the economic systems of both the United States and the South define the contemporary moment of Dandelion's lynching.

Because Darlington sees each of the members of the community as interchangeable commodities contributing to the functioning of his 'machine', Gaines couches his request for assistance as an exchange of commodities when he appeals to Darlington's sense of himself by calling him 'master of both those who buy and sell' (156). Gaines stages his appeal to save Dandelion's life as a commercial transaction, asking Darlington to sell him a bucket of blood or buy from him a bone (156). In order to impress upon the banker the importance of his intervention, Gaines facetiously figures Dandelion's life as a commodity to be bought and sold: 'The body of a man is capital also. It is invested in the labor that produces wealth' (158). By engaging the banker in his own logic, that of the machine requiring raw materials, Gaines reimagines the lynching as an entirely material transaction in order to (unsuccessfully) co-opt the town's capitalist centre to his own ends.

Darlington is ultimately frightened and bemused by Gaines's offer to buy or sell the life of Dandelion. The banker's refusal to enter into such a contract, reminiscent as it is of Shylock's 'pound of flesh' in William Shakespeare's *The Merchant of Venice*, but answers in the same incongruous tone that Gaines established: 'His voice was cold, remote, and withdrawn; he spoke in the tone he used to deny a loan to a man he considered a bad financial risk' (158). Darlington accepts Gaines's premise because it is offered in the appropriate register, but refuses to help. Darlington's tone of voice suggests finance capitalism; it is 'withdrawn' like money from his own bank. Even while Gaines's reduction of Dandelion's life to a financial opportunity is made in bad taste and in bad faith, it is not for this reason that the transaction is declined: Darlington does not deny the fact that Dandelion's body and labour are commodities, only that they are valuable enough to save.

Reece figures Dandelion ironically as a financial commodity throughout the novel. His lynching, rather than constituting a digression from the town's capitalist order, is an extension of it. At the beginning of the novel, the sleeping inhabitants dream about their personal desires fitting in a figurative and literal economy of the town. They are figurative in that the commodities they desire can be understood as pertaining to emotional fulfilment, and literal because the items desired are also commodities available to consumers within the town:

> Somewhere in the town, one dreamed of Thebes. One dreamed of a tin of snuff, another of the cat Tawm's arch and spit of pride; and one, sleeping or waking, dreamed of the flesh and bones of the blonde boy Jonathan as he, integer, moved separate but indivisible from the life of the town which the sun created anew each day into the definition of light. (14)

This passage is a catalogue of the desires of some of the novel's primary characters. It is Dandelion who dreams of snuff, the one luxury item on which he spends the small profit from his labour. An undated draft of the novel, fairly close to completion, shows Reece's handwritten changes to a small number of such scenes. At this point in the composition of the novel, it was still titled *Tents toward Sodom*. The description of Dandelion's labour, as it relates to his ability to purchase snuff, is expanded in the draft. The typed description reads: 'Without snuff it was a long time until eight o'clock.' Underneath it in pencil, Reece added: 'It was a shed to clean, it was a chicken to dress, it was wood to cart; without snuff, etc.'[59] The passage, appearing in the final text, reads: 'It was a shed to clean, it was a chicken to dress, it was wood to cart; without snuff it was a long time till eight o'clock' (17).

Reece changed the statement from a short, declarative sentence, to an inventory of jobs. The addition of a semicolon, which brings the sentence's two separate clauses together, makes the sentence a narrative of time and effort being spent. In this formulation, both time and effort are commodities. The time 'until eight o'clock' is more difficult for Dandelion to pass because he lacks the funds to buy his luxury item and the expansion of the sentence reiterates the duration of that time. By lengthening the sentence, Reece highlights the length of the time between sunrise and 8am. The expanded sentence also clarifies the translation of Dandelion's labour (cleaning sheds, dressing chickens, carrying wood) into its equivalent purchasing power, the snuff, marking Dandelion and his labour as commodities within the economic structure of the town equal to the value of the tobacco. Fittingly, Dandelion must complete his circuit of jobs before 8am because this is when the town's shops open: his working day precedes the beginning of the working day for the town's shop owners and his physical comfort is dependent on the 'circuit' of their workday as much as that of his own.

Dandelion's fixation on snuff is echoed disturbingly towards the novel's end. After Harker has brutally emasculated the beaten and dying Dandelion and 'cast[s] away' his dismembered penis, Dandelion's heart stops. After his masculinity has been symbolically and materially effaced, Dandelion is bodily and spiritually removed from the town: 'With his heart's stoppage whatever meager dreams had animated his spirit were snuffed utterly' (176). Dandelion's death is described as the 'snuffing' of a candle, while the novel's opening makes clear that his one 'meager dream' was snuff. Although the word 'snuff' appears alternately as a noun and a verb, Reece echoes 'snuff' as a signifier of a tobacco product with 'snuffing out a life'. Reece imbues Dandelion's death with the traces of his life as a commodity in the economic structure of the town and his dependence on the smallest of commodities provided by that same structure. As a result, Reece's appeal against racial violence enacted through a schema of symbolism is never divorced from the economic reality of the South during segregation. While Dandelion's death is a symbol of a morally bankrupt southern town, it is also a representation of the inherent violence of an economic system in which lynching is a means of regulating labour and consumption.

Reece represents characters in the roles of farmer and educator in an aesthetic that combines a concern with both the physical and the metaphysical. By having each of these characters act against type, Reece calls for a reimagining of the southern town's cultural systems and by merging the characters' material and intellectual vocations. The two characters are treated as synecdoches for individuals who wish to make material change in the segregated South, and they represent two components of a typology of the fictional town that refuse to capitulate to the collective identity that is enforced by other elements of the same typology, especially the banker and reverend. As Reece wrote in a letter in 1956, 'all books worth a damn are symbolic at least to the extent that their characters and incidents stand for something beyond themselves, stand for the experience common to us all.'[60] Reece's characters 'make a stand' for racial justice and in turn they 'stand' for other white southerners' capacity to slowly change the segregated racial structure of the region.

In this novel, the fictional southern town is built from the ground up on a structure of symbolism and allusion. Reece imbues the typology of the southern town with an allusive subtext drawn from ancient and medieval literary texts, and every element of Tilden and its population can be mapped onto the symbolic schema that the author outlines in his correspondence. However, this detailed symbolism does not exist in a contextual vacuum. Reece's Abraham represents a symbolic cultivation of racial change in the segregated South just as Gaines stands for non-symbolic, direct individual action against racism. In Carson McCullers's *Clock Without Hands* (1961), the individual's responsibility in the face of racial terrorism is still more explicitly explored. McCullers's final novel puts all of her previous fiction into perspective as an extended portrayal of a single community. Only with the announcement of the Supreme Court ruling in the case of *Brown v. Board* is the author's fictional town of Milan, Georgia, fully defined. Where Reece's farmer and teacher represent symbolic types, McCullers invents a pharmacist and three lawyers through whose stories she maps gradual racial change.

CHAPTER 4

The Milan Cycle:
Carson McCullers's Milan

One of Carson McCullers's earliest short stories, published posthumously as 'Untitled Piece' in *The Mortgaged Heart* (1972), rehearses some of the characters and scenarios that would form the basis of the author's first novel, *The Heart is a Lonely Hunter* (1940).[1] In the story, a white man named Andrew Leander arrives, drunk and aimless, in a small southern town. Leander emerges at the railway station restaurant 'in a drunken turmoil', and bears more than a passing resemblance to Jake Blount in McCullers's later novel.[2] In the story's closing dialogue, Leander approaches a young boy working in the restaurant, uncertain where he has found himself: 'I got off the bus half drunk. Will you tell me the name of this place?'[3] If Leander gets an answer, it is not reported in the story. In *The Heart is a Lonely Hunter*, too, the small town setting is not named, nor is the small-town setting in any of McCullers's subsequent long works, *Reflections in a Golden Eye* (1941), *The Member of the Wedding* (1946) or 'The Ballad of the Sad Café' (1952). Ostensibly, these texts share similarities of setting and of theme, but are set in distinct, separate archetypal southern towns. To the contrary, I argue that McCullers's novels are best understood as components in a narrative cycle that is made coherent by a shared setting in or around the fictional town of Milan, Georgia. Her final novel, *Clock Without Hands* (1961), makes these connections legible and acts as a capstone to what I term the 'Milan Cycle'.

The novel centres on the lives of four southern men and culminates with the announcement of the Supreme Court decision in

Brown v. Board of Education of Topeka on 17 May 1954. The four men – J. T. Malone, Sherman Pew, Jester Clane and Fox Clane – represent various points on the town's spectrum of racial politics. These characters represent the final stages in a political trajectory in Milan that McCullers begins charting in her earliest published fiction. Milan is only named in the novel that most overtly engages with the region's real history of civil rights activism. I argue that the symbiotic relationship between McCullers's cycle and the black freedom struggle is necessary to make sense of the cycle *as a* cycle. Milan, in short, can only be named when it is seen alongside an extended narrative of anti-racist activism.

Clock Without Hands is relatively seldom discussed in McCullers's criticism, although her engagement with political activism has been well documented. Robert H. Brinkmeyer Jr celebrates the author's 'savaging of southern authoritarianism'.[4] A common theme of scholarship is McCullers's often combined engagements with queer sexualities and the grotesque. Rachel Adams explores 'the intersection between the freak, queer sexuality, and racial hybridity', and Sarah Gleeson-White argues that McCullers 'points to the difficulty of accessing a new language and a new body of images with which to represent grotesque desires'.[5] The narrative techniques of McCullers's earlier fiction led to the author becoming a literary celebrity of the era. Oliver Evans, in one of the earliest sustained studies of her work, described McCullers as 'a "writer's writer" [. . .] whose work requires, or at least lends itself to, a considerable amount of explication'.[6] In contrast, *Clock Without Hands* was judged a disappointment by its 'hordes of eager readers' upon publication in 1961.[7]

Reviewers were sympathetic to McCullers herself and tended to celebrate her past achievements even while they considered the novel a failure. One book critic lamented that 'to praise her book would be a pleasure. Unfortunately that is not possible. *Clock Without Hands* is not a successful novel.'[8] Another reviewer articulated the novel as an explicit waning of talent: 'in her past work she could carry off almost anything through the virtuosity of her language [but *Clock Without Hands* is] an unadorned and scrappy scenario for a not-yet-written novel.'[9] Contemporary literary critics specifically cited McCullers's renewed interest in racial politics as a weakness. Neo-Agrarian scholar Louis D. Rubin termed it 'the annotation of an idea instead of something involving created characters and a story',[10] and Donald Emerson claimed that McCullers's engagement with politics was detrimental to her established style when he wrote that 'Mrs. McCullers is most herself as the novelist of inward experience, but in *Clock Without Hands* she attempts to add another dimension by making her characters stand for the whole South. It is a mistake.'[11] Even among McCullers' friends and peers in southern literature, the novel was roundly criticised. Tennessee Williams only relented from 'begging' her to delay publication over fears that her poor health could not take the rejection.[12] Less delicately, Flannery O'Connor believed it to be 'the worst novel [she had] ever read'.[13] Even Lillian Smith, a close friend who had received similar dismissals of her work, judged it to be 'the least real of any' of McCullers's novels and queried whether McCullers was 'so much a part of the intellectual and psychological climate of New York City' that she had lost her ability to write convincingly about the South.[14]

This consistent disappointment in the novel compared to her earlier work is ironic because, as I argue, the novel develops and extends literary motifs and settings that McCullers had long explored. Specific places, including the First Baptist Church, the New York Café and the outlying hamlet of Forks Falls, all of which appear in her last novel, are also mentioned or described in earlier narratives. By tracing the continuity of these individual locations, a larger continuity of setting becomes apparent. As well as mapping McCullers's setting and offering comparative character studies of John Singer from *The Heart is a Lonely Hunter* and J. T. Malone in *Clock Without Hands*, I demonstrate that the town of Milan as inextricably connected to the protagonists of novels also set there. Across the novels, but especially in *Clock Without Hands*, the town's racial politics undergoes a process of continuous gradual change. McCullers's final novel is a culmination of an extended experiment on the relationship between literary aesthetics and racial activism, and her career ends with a southern community on the brink of momentous racial change.

Resetting McCullers's Novels

In this chapter I propose a model for reading McCullers's fiction as an extended narrative cycle that ends with a novel depicting a major shift in the town's segregated order. Charting the process of the town's construction across novels leads to an exploration of connections across texts that suggest spatial continuity and provides textual evidence that the town with which McCullers has been concerned in her fiction has always been Milan. Such continuity is meaningful only in the context of *Clock Without Hands*, the novel that connects these threads and most overtly portrays Milan as a town undergoing a process of desegregation. Through close textual analysis of the novel and the narratives that precede it in the cycle, I identify a pattern of continuity in both setting and character development that is contingent because each insight into the town is influenced by earlier portrayals and McCullers shows a typology of the fictional southern town in the process of evolving.

In the opening line of her first novel, *The Heart is a Lonely Hunter*, she foregrounds the importance of the town in that novel's structure: 'In the town there were two mutes, and they were always together.'[15] Although not named, the town is introduced to an imagined reader before even 'the mutes', Singer and Antonopoulos. The novel begins with an allusion to the fairy-tale form; two declarative statements are joined, with each providing the essential details of setting and *dramatis personae* without designating either with names. The definite article suggests the conventions of fairy tale by underscoring 'the' town as representative of all towns.[16] McCullers draws on fairy-tale narrative conventions in order to underscore the archetypal characters of the town and the representative nature of the characters. McCullers returns to the same unnamed town repeatedly to explicate its dimensions in greater detail in subsequent novels, examining different dimensions of the social life of the town from text to text. Even when Milan is not the primary setting for a novel, as is the case in *Reflections in a Golden Eye*, the town is never entirely absent. This novel is set in the years before the outbreak of the Second World War in a military camp in the South, located near an unnamed small town described as 'a dull place'.[17] The setting compares with the real Fort Benning, a military outpost outside Columbus and can be read as McCullers's thinking through the broader social landscape of her fictional town-in-process. The town that serves as the setting for McCullers's other novels is looked at askance in this novel, which is set in federally operated space just outside of the incorporated limits.[18] Only by having established Milan as a setting in her previous novel is McCullers able to obscure it in her second to explore a space contingent upon but separate from the town.

Elsewhere in her fiction, McCullers depicts the town in a state of flux as a pathetic fallacy that mirrors her characters' development. For example, Frankie Addams, the protagonist of *The Member of the Wedding*, makes her personal confusion manifest in the town's constituent parts: 'She went around town, and the things she saw and heard seemed to be left somehow unfinished, and there was the tightness in her that would not break.'[19] The 'unfinished' feeling is a projection of the adolescent Frankie's insecurities. Frankie's feeling of incompleteness may also be read as a self-conscious allusion to McCullers's ongoing project of elaborating her 'unfinished' fictional town as it evolves from text to text. Later in the novel, as Frankie leaves for her brother's wedding, her emotional relationship to the town is again suggestive of McCullers's invention of the setting: 'At that still hour the sky was the dim silver of a mirror, and beneath it the grey town looked, not a real town, but like an exact reflection of itself, and to this unreal town she also said farewell.'[20] By figuring the town as a simulacrum, McCullers allows Milan to move with the developing needs of her characters. A sense of narrative stability allows texts that appear to move away from Milan as a setting to remain grounded geographically and thematically by the structures put in place in earlier novels.

A smaller population and sparse distribution of amenities mark the setting of 'The Ballad of the Sad Café' as different from Milan but McCullers situates the novella's hamlet in the same fictionalised geography. 'The Ballad of the Sad Café' opens with a description of all of the systems and amenities present in the larger town but in condensed form. The hamlet in which the novella is set does not conform to the schema of semi-urbanity I outline elsewhere in this study. Like William Faulkner's Frenchman's Bend, McCullers's community has significantly reduced access to the facilities of modernity and is centred on a single commercial and social hub. The hamlet is described in relation to other places in the state and, crucially, is connected to its neighbouring towns by transport infrastructure: 'The nearest train stop is Society City, and the Greyhound and White Bus Lines use the Forks Falls Road which is three miles away.'[21] The town is indirectly connected to 'society' by these avenues of movement that are accessible to residents even while they are some distance away. The community, which lacks any explicit geographical detail, is almost certainly in Georgia: when the characters imagine Amelia being executed, she is 'electro-cuted in Atlanta'.[22] Society City and Forks Falls are not locations in a real Georgia geography as is Atlanta. Instead, their names suggest community and divergence respectively and locate this hamlet on the same map of McCullers's Georgia as Milan.

As well as establishing the parameters of this smaller town, the opening scene of 'The Ballad of the Sad Café' returns to a feature of the fictionalised landscape first established in an earlier novel. Forks Falls appears in a number of stories told to Frankie Adams by her housekeeper Berenice in *The Member of the Wedding*. In one such story, Berenice visits family in Forks Falls and feels like an out-sider 'praying in a church where the congregation was strangers to [her]'.[23] This positions the town of Forks Falls as distant both from the town of Milan in which Frankie lives, and the setting of 'The Ballad of the Sad Café'. In both cases Forks Falls represents a neigh-bouring town through which to define the primary setting in both texts and against which the population of either town defines itself. Forks Falls is a shared coordinate in a fictional cartography, which suggests that the two novels share the same imagined map. These two fictional locales are positioned in geographical relation to each other more clearly than to any recognisable location in the real state of Georgia. Highlighting this connection rather than placing the towns in relation to real-world locations suggests McCullers's primary engagement with inventing rather than representing the southern town. The unseen Forks Falls does not appear in *Clock Without Hands* but is the earliest appearance of recurring locations in her work through which an attentive reader is able to chart a continuity of setting across her fiction.

One building in Milan to recur across novels is the First Baptist church. It appears in both *The Member of the Wedding* and *Clock Without Hands*. As in Reece's Tilden, Milan's religious centre plays a significant role as monument to wealth and social standing rather than as an avenue for spiritual deliverance. The First Baptist church is represented as an important social and geographic anchor for the people of Milan in both texts. Literary critic Jan Whitt draws attention to the confluence between the churches in both novels, noting that 'churches were a central part of McCullers' fiction, just as they were the centre of the southern communities she knew'.[24] In *The Member of the Wedding*, the First Baptist church is described briefly but its role in controlling the town's profitability is highlighted: 'The clock in the tower of the First Baptist Church clanged twelve, the mill whistle wailed.'[25] The church works in tandem with the town's centre of industry to mediate time for the workers; lunch is announced with spiritual as well as commercial authority.

In *Clock Without Hands*, the architectural detail of the church is described in far greater depth. Facing his mortality early in the novel, Malone takes comfort in the physical building of the church rather than in faith in the religion it symbolises. The material façade of faith is more reassuring to Malone than promises of salvation:

> Malone sought comfort in the church. When tormented by the unreality of both death and life, it helped him to know that the First Baptist church was real enough. [. . .] A church like that was bound to be real. The pillars of the church were men of substance and leading citizens. Butch Henderson, the realtor and one of the shrewdest traders in the town, was a deacon and never missed a service from one year to the next – and was Butch Henderson a likely man to waste his time and trouble on anything that was not as real as dirt?[26]

The phrase 'real as dirt' serves as a reminder of Malone's mortality in spite of his attempts to seek solace in the material world. Malone's faith has no spiritual basis; it is built on pragmatism and a desire to be successful in the community.

The 'white columns' holding up Milan's church do not denote the architectural element popular in Greek Revival churches throughout the South but, rather, race and social prestige. McCullers puns on the racial group to whom respect in the church is afforded, as well as conflating the social and architectural properties of the building.[27] The church is also a source of reassurance to Malone when he learns of his disease: the stability of the building and its respectable congregants re-inscribe Malone's belief in the 'real'. The repetition is also a pun on 'real' property, the real estate on which the church is built and the industry in which one such 'pillar' of the community, the realtor, makes his living. Malone's reaction to the social infrastructure of the small town is consistent with a paradigm McCullers develops in earlier work: the church is a means of critique in *Clock Without Hands* in a way that it was not in *The Member of the Wedding*.

The New York Café, another node of continuity in the cycle, provides a social hub for maladjusted characters in *The Heart is a Lonely Hunter*, but when the café reappears in *Clock Without Hands*, it does not serve the same narrative function. In the later novel, the judge meets his friends for drinks and to play poker in the 'back room' of the café (53, 164, 177). The New York Café is one of a number of places in which the judge expresses his politics to his neighbours, as when he speaks to 'audiences in Malone's pharmacy, in the courthouse, in the back room of the New York Café and in the barbershop' (164). Because of the judge's influence on the space, it has a more conservative atmosphere than when Biff Brannon operates it in *The Heart is a Lonely Hunter*. By 1953, when *Clock Without Hands* begins, the café is not connected to Brannon as proprietor, the implication being that the café's role as a meeting place for the town's misunderstood and oppressed residents has been overcome by white supremacy. In *The Heart is a Lonely Hunter*, Biff defends his benevolence in opening his doors to misfits and the oppressed, and offering service on credit, telling his pragmatic wife, 'I like freaks.'[28] In *Clock Without Hands* the atmosphere Biff created of diversity and tolerance is replaced by the judge's white supremacy. The changing role of the café in Milan is a measure of the community's political temperament.

In contrast to the café as a haven for Clane's bigotry, its namesake city is persistently figured as the judge's idea of a decadent 'Babel' (40). The judge recalls with horror how he saw an interracial couple in New York, casting the city as the spatial representative of his deepest racial anxieties (40). The judge is astounded by a conversation with his son: 'it was as if he were talking to a panel of

New York Jew lawyers' (169). The judge's racism and anti-Semitism require the idea of New York as a foil, and the judge's imagination fixates on the city as the antithesis of his beliefs, a horrifying but distant space of racial and sexual permissiveness. The judge finds it unthinkable when his grandson expresses eagerness to visit New York City as soon as he can (40). For Jester, the northern city is a valuable proving ground for his ideals even if its namesake café is presided over by his grandfather. A comparison between characters' developments in McCullers' first and final novels indicates that *Clock Without Hands* represents a point of transition in which progressive change is more tangible than at any previous point in the town's fictional history. McCullers consistently deploys Milan as a staging ground for exploring contemporary social issues. In Robert Brinkmeyer's view, in *The Heart is a Lonely Hunter*, McCullers 'recasts the rise of Fascism in Europe in a small southern town fractured by change and beset with numbing alienation', making that novel and *The Member of the Wedding* 'the clearest example of the portrayal of the South as something close to a Fascist state'.[29] McCullers effects this warning against fascism in part by representing the failure of *The Heart is a Lonely Hunter*'s most politically motivated, progressive characters – alcoholic white drifter Jake Blount and African American physician Benedict Mady Copeland – to consolidate their efforts to organise against racial segregation.

Blount and Copeland are isolated by social beliefs, but when they have the opportunity to meet and discuss Marxist ideas,[30] all that results is a 'long, exhausting dialogue' during which they are unable to agree.[31] If Jake Blount bemoans 'The strangled South. The wasted South. The slavish South', but is unable to effect radical change, his failure is overwritten by Jester Clane.[32] In *Clock Without Hands*, Jester has the potential to effect legislative change in the racial order of the South. Jester is a corrective to the well-intentioned but impotent Blount and Copeland and has a greater degree of insight than either of his predecessors. At the end of the Milan cycle, he is in a unique position to foster (albeit still gradual) racial change. Towards the end of the novel, while flying his family's plane, Jester sees the town from above. From the plane, Jester sees Milan as a productive whole and is better able to understand its flawed workings. The altered vantage point allows Jester to rethink his conception of

Milan: 'From this height you do not see a man and the details of his humiliation. The earth from a great distance is perfect and whole' (202). Jester's aerial view is 'grounded' when he considers the rift between his idea of Milan and that of his grandfather:

> Looking downward from an altitude of two thousand feet, the earth assumes order. A town, even Milan, is symmetrical, exact in a small grey honeycomb, complete. The surrounding terrain seems designed by a law more just and mathematical than the laws of property and bigotry: a dark parallelogram of pine wood, square fields, rectangles of sward. (202)

In this scene, McCullers confronts what I term the 'paradox of segregated integrity'. While the symmetry might be interpreted as an allusion to the racial myth of 'separate but equal', the design of the town from this perspective overcomes its design along segregationist 'laws of property and bigotry'. This perspective throws into relief the view of the town from closer to the ground, defined by the decidedly and fundamentally asymmetrical principles of segregationist law, overseen by Jester's grandfather. Jester's unique insight and his intention to translate his political convictions into a legal career modelled on his father's position him as capable of effecting change with more success than the quarrelling radicals of *The Heart is a Lonely Hunter*. The activism that is germinal in McCullers's first novel has the potential to be actualised in her last.

The typology of the fictional southern town that I identify in earlier chapters is shown, in analysis of McCullers's work, to develop over time when the author returns to individual offices during different historical moments. Milan's racial identity changes in parallel to the recurring offices, and *Clock Without Hands* is the novel in which these narratives of racial and formal development are simultaneously visible. Only by understanding each novel as a point on a trajectory can this narrative be charted and the trajectory understood as it is woven through the texts.

Sartre's Knife and Sherman's Eyes in Malone's Milan

Despite Jester's unique perspective at the end of the novel, the character who most closely reflects the town's unexamined white supremacy is J. T. Malone, whose name differs from 'Milan' only in the placement of vowels. Malone is the character at the social centre of the novel, and his struggle with racial politics provides an insight into the waning power of white supremacy in McCullers's town. His is not the 'conversion ... from racism to something approaching racial enlightenment' that Fred Hobson identifies in white southern autobiographies, but he represents the town's shifting politics.[33] By his death, Malone is unwilling and unable to take action against white supremacy, but he has also lost the will to support it. The implication of Malone's political ambivalence is that the passing of his generation will allow a new generation of southern whites, typified by Jester, to mature along the same ideological trajectory.

Malone's development is paralleled by the town of Milan, which is poised for gradual but progressive change. But, because Malone experiences the changes in his personality, he also witnesses the shifts the town is undergoing and undergoes a process of defamiliarisation as the town and his own body become increasingly alien to him. McCullers develops Malone in contrast to an earlier anchor of Milan's social sphere, *The Heart is a Lonely Hunter*'s John Singer. Singer and Malone are points at different ends of the town's literary life. Malone is more internally focalised than Singer, and this allows McCullers to structure her final novel around his personal development. *The Heart is a Lonely Hunter*, on the other hand, is driven by other characters' misguided perceptions of Singer. In his review of the novel, book critic Orville Prescott describes the novel as 'about death, the fear of death and the approach of death, and also about the necessity of self-realization in the midst of life'.[34] This observation hints at McCullers's preoccupation with existentialist philosophy in her construction of Malone. The dynamic by which the health of the town is mirrored in Malone extends to his place of work. Malone's pharmacy is a building around which the rest of the town orients itself and through which the people of the town navigate Milan spatially. It is a public social venue in which people meet to drink Coca-Cola and gossip but also as a medium through which to understand Malone's confused mentality in the months following his diagnosis.[35]

While Singer negotiates Milan's political crises at an earlier point in the town's fictive chronology, his character is developed along decidedly different lines from Malone's. An unexpected change in the town's weather anticipates a significant change in each character's personality in the months leading up to his death. The change in Singer is anticipated by an unusually ferocious season: 'The town had not known a winter as cold as this one for years [. . .] A change came over Singer.'[36] Midway through the narrative, this change denotes the beginning of a severe depression that leads eventually to Singer's suicide. Malone's pivotal change also signals his mortality and is anticipated not only by an extreme winter but by an equally extreme shift in seasons:

> The winter of his fortieth year was an unusually cold one for the Southern town – with icy, pastel days and radiant nights. The spring came violently in middle March in that year of 1953 [. . .] diagnosing spring fever, he prescribed himself a liver and iron tonic. (7)

In both cases, the men's experiences of extreme winter are mediated by the personified town: the first is described as being 'known' by the town while the second winter is judged by the standards of Milan rather than any objective measure. While in each novel exceptional weather patterns symbolise a turning point for a major character, in Malone's case this technique is elaborated through the 'violent' arrival of spring. By erroneously prescribing medicine for spring fever, Malone actively works against these changes in his character and his home to hinder the passage of time and he is figured as arresting change both in himself and Milan.

McCullers's stated conception of Singer is decidedly at odds with her later treatment of Malone as the subject, rather than object, of narrative attention. The shift in narrative focalisation from Singer to Malone is the same as a simultaneous shift from a character upon whom meaning is imposed by the population of Milan to one who is self-constituted. In an outline for the novel that would become *The Heart is a Lonely Hunter*, McCullers describes her idea of Singer:

> The parts concerning Singer are never treated in a subjective manner. The style is oblique. [. . .] Except when he is understood through the eyes of other people the style is for the main part simple and declarative. No

attempt will be made to enter intimately into his subconscious. He is a flat character in that from the second chapter on through the rest of the book his essential self does not change.[37]

Singer has a gravitational pull that attracts the other characters in the town, anchoring them emotionally and spatially. Competing interpretations of Singer's personality orient the rest of the novel's characters and structure the social geography of Milan: 'all the characters are singly drawn toward one man [. . .] who stands bewilderedly at the novel's centre.'[38] When Singer writes a letter to his institutionalised companion Antonapoulos, he addresses it to 'My Only Friend', suggesting that the bond the other characters feel to Singer is one-sided.[39] His own feelings towards the group that relies on him become clearer as he thinks about its members coldly as 'the black man, the young girl, the one with the moustache, and the man who owns the New York Café'.[40] Singer's candour is only reported when *The Heart is a Lonely Hunter*'s omniscient narrator observes a written account of his feelings. Where Singer's subjective experience of the town is not directly rendered in the narrative, the omniscient narrator of *Clock Without Hands* consistently depicts the narrative through Malone's subjective understanding.

This divergence is highlighted through McCullers's engagement with European existentialism, especially as a means of understanding the impulse towards white supremacy. McCullers anticipates Malone's quasi-existentialism in an essay in which she discusses the psychological roots of white supremacy:

> For fear is a primary source of evil. And when the question 'Who am I?' recurs and is unanswered, then fear and frustration project a negative attitude. The bewildered soul can answer only: 'Since I do not understand "who I am," I only know what I am *not*.' The corollary of this emotional incertitude is snobbism, intolerance and racial hate. The xenophobic individual can only reject and destroy, as the xenophobic nation inevitably makes war.[41]

In what is perhaps the author's most searing published indictment of racism, she locates the imperative to racial violence within a perverted subjective experience of the world without absolving 'the xenophobic individual' of responsibility for their actions. The violent affirmation of identity based on opposition – what one is not – leads, in McCullers's argument, to a community of shared xenophobic principles:

> After the first establishment of identity there comes the imperative need to lose this new-found sense of separateness and to belong to something larger and more powerful than the weak, lonely self. The sense of moral isolation is intolerable to us.[42]

In this description, the existentialist impulse to self-determination can lead to bigotry in an unthinking adherence to harmful and hateful social conventions. When Malone is initially diagnosed with leukaemia he conforms to this mentality. As his illness demands a reconsideration of the social principles he has taken for granted, he remains afraid of moral isolation and maintains his friendship with the judge and his unspoken adherence to white supremacy. [43] Malone's forename, J. T., is not an abbreviation of two other names. The initials – like the character in the early part of the novel – do not 'stand for' anything. Malone's surname, given that his mortality is a central theme of the novel, is an obvious reference to Irish novelist and playwright Samuel Beckett's *Malone Dies* (1951).[44] I read the character as an engagement with the existentialist movement of which Beckett was a part, and McCullers signals this philosophical grounding with the character's name.

McCullers draws on the philosophies of Jean-Paul Sartre and Søren Kierkegaard in her construction of Malone in order to figure him as a character undergoing an ideological change. Sartre's philosophy serves not only as a lens through which to understand Malone's awareness of his mortality, but also as an ethical paradigm. In *Existentialism and Humanism* (1948), Sartre explains his epistemology with the assertion that existence precedes essence and uses the example of a paper knife. The paper knife, for Sartre, is an object for which essence precedes existence because the function of cutting paper is incorporated into the knife's design before the object itself is made:

> If one considers an article of manufacture – as, for example, a book or
> a paper-knife – one sees that it has been made by an artisan who had a
> conception of it; and he has paid attention, equally, to the conception of
> a paper-knife and to the pre-existent technique of production which is a
> part of that conception and is, at bottom, a formula.[45]

In counterpoint, people are not created by design and each individual's essence is developed after birth. Ethically, this means that each individual is responsible for how their actions impact others and forces personal moral responsibility.

McCullers explores this set of ideas by depicting Malone, by the end of his life, as at last able to confront his past beliefs rather than unthinkingly taking them for granted. When Malone learns of his leukaemia, he fixates on a paper knife in his doctor's office becoming 'fascinated and obscurely distressed' by it (10). McCullers's choice of this particular is more than coincidental. The knife is alluded to a total of eight times in the opening chapter alone, making the paper knife an emblem of Malone's leukaemia and his discovery of his illness. Initially, Dr Hayden avoids making eye contact with Malone by distracting himself as he 'handled a paper knife, gazing intently at it as he passed it from hand to hand' (8). The seemingly innocuous object fascinates both doctor and patient at precisely the moment when neither feels able to comprehend the gravity of Malone's diagnosis.

Malone attempts to mediate his reaction to the news through recourse to a stable narrative of white supremacy. It is a desperate attempt to reaffirm essentialist beliefs after being confronted by the fact of his mortality. Remembering the 'Jew grinds' who supposedly robbed him of a 'fair chance' of succeeding in medical school, Malone suddenly recognises Hayden's Jewishness (12). Striking out against the difficult-to-process diagnosis, Malone directs his prejudice to Hayden in order to invalidate the abilities of his diagnostician. Malone's defamiliarisation of his relationship with Hayden is an initial coping mechanism:

> Hayden was a good customer and a friend – they had worked in the same
> building for years and saw each other daily. Why had he failed to notice?
> Maybe the doctor's given name had tricked him – Kenneth Hale. Malone

said to himself he had no prejudice, but when Jews used the good old Anglo-Saxon, Southern names like that, he felt it was somehow wrong. (12)

Malone's familiarity with Hayden is expressed through their shared geography; they each work in the building that houses Malone's pharmacy. Despite this familiarity, the free indirect narration makes it clear that Malone now feels 'tricked' by Hayden's religious background, which runs contrary to Malone's misguided notion of an imagined Anglo-Saxon heritage.

As well as being 'mesmerised by the paper knife', Malone's discomfort manifests itself physically: 'Malone sat taut and waiting, one leg wrapped around the other and his Adam's apple struggling in his frail throat' (8, 9). The conspicuous allusion to Malone's Adam's apple draws attention to the biblical creation story in juxtaposition to his fixation on the Sartrean paper knife. These two forces operate against each other in the scene as Malone is torn between essentialist and existentialist epistemologies. The description of his Adam's apple 'struggling' suggests an insecure grasp on the faith and belief systems on which Malone has previously relied. Indeed, discomfort with his Adam's apple is among the initial symptoms that cause Malone to seek medical advice, suggesting insecurity in essentialist preconceptions: 'His temples were shrunken so that the veins pulsed visibly when he chewed or swallowed and his Adam's apple struggled in his thin neck' (7). Malone's leukaemia is presented repeatedly as a threat to the traditionalist, white supremacist modes of perception upon which he has always relied. The moment of Malone's diagnosis is rendered via two totems or fetishes – the paper knife and the Adam's apple – each of which represents an epistemological decision that the character must make in the face of his illness. His diagnosis can be read as the failure of an engrained belief system to process the shock of mortality, demanding that he reassess that which he has taken for granted.

During a meeting with Clane shortly after, Malone's anxiety about his illness is reflected in how he dwells again on the image of the knife: 'Malone paled at the unconscious image of a doctor's office with the smell of ether, the children's cries, Dr. Hayden's knife and a treatment table' (57). The paper knife looms in Malone's anxiety, implicitly embodying the existential decisions his disease will force him to make. These unsettling thoughts make Malone 'pale', drawing attention to the connection between his mortality and his whiteness, as the verb and adjective forms of the word coincide. Malone reacts physically to his disease as his complexion changes and reacts psychologically by becoming more racially whitened. Leukaemia itself denotes a symbolic failure of whiteness, as the disease leads to the production of defective and harmful white blood cells. The word itself derives from the ancient Greek terms *leukós* and *haîma*, meaning 'white' and 'blood', respectively.

Through the depiction of Malone's leukaemia, McCullers inverts blood's typical racial-metaphorical cargo. Where the anxiety of visibly white southern bodies being contaminated by non-white heritage, or 'blood', is commonplace in the twentieth-century South, Malone's body is diseased by whiteness itself: his white blood cells attack his body. Because Malone is a symbol of Milan, the leukaemia can also be read as the failure of whiteness to regulate the racial order of the town. Judge Clane is unwilling to see the common metaphor subverted, and is unable to comprehend Malone's illness as arising from his blood: 'A *blood* disease! Why that's ridiculous – you have some of the best blood in this State' (18). By wilfully confusing the figurative and literal connotations of the word 'blood', the judge demonstrates the degree to which whiteness and wellness are conflated in white supremacist thought. McCullers parodies this common southern myth in order to highlight the anachronism of traditionalism in her rapidly changing town.

Whiteness and blood are equally potent symbolic markers for race in the twentieth-century South. This is especially true in the early part of the century when 'blood', as Jay Watson summarises, 'was the most dangerous thing going, the culture's most loaded and coercive metaphor'.[46] Watson's statement is grounded in a wide-ranging body of scholarship that addresses the figurative meaning of blood in southern historical and literary contexts as a metaphor, in John Duval's terms, for 'a belief that identity is a hereditary essence [that] moves through the pages of southern literature'.[47] This trope of an essential identity is undercut in *Clock Without Hands* when Malone's literal blood fails him while his figurative blood remains relatively stable. Commonly, the presence of 'black blood' threatens the supposed superiority of white heredity and figuratively burdens the identity of a visibly white character. As Werner Sollors describes in his writing on mixed-race characters in literature by white writers, 'black blood' when it is 'understood as genealogical essence is such a liability' to mixed-race characters as to inform their behaviour at every level.[48] The idea of blood is a corollary to the question of agency as it determines a character's identity without his or her volition. For Sollors, 'involuntary descent relations are associated with blood and material substance' while voluntary, or 'consent', relationships have no such association. This locates Malone's blood disease, metaphorical as it is, as a matter outside of his control.[49] Read this way, the reactionary idea of blood as inevitable essence is a literal threat to Malone's life, in tandem with the town of Milan's racial crisis, which is typified by Malone's growing self-awareness. His experiences, as both a health-care provider and health-care receiver, contribute to his depiction as an increasingly confused character struggling with a changing existential self-definition.

Sartre's covert presence in the novel's opening chapter establishes a pattern through which Malone's struggle with cancer can be interpreted as an unwilling engagement with existentialist angst. Later, during a stay in hospital, Malone begins to read Kierkegaard's *The Sickness unto Death* (1849).[50] In November 1953 Malone's third doctor, Dr Milton (whose name resonates with the English poetic tradition and, implicitly, an imagined Anglo-Saxon identity) insists on a second stay at the vaguely named City Hospital. Uninterested in a pulp detective novel that, by virtue of its genre, follows a linear and progressive plot, Malone is instead drawn to Kierkegaard's title: 'The next time the aide came around with the books, Malone returned the mystery and glanced at the other titles; his eyes were drawn to a book called *Sickness unto Death*' (129). Malone's terminal illness resonates with the book and its language. While skimming the dense work, Malone is struck by a particular passage:

> From the wilderness of print some lines struck his mind so that he was instantly awake. He read the lines again and then again: *The greatest danger, that of losing one's own self, may pass off quietly as if it were nothing; every other loss, that of an arm, a leg, five dollars, a wife, etc., is sure to be

noticed. If Malone had not had an incurable disease those words would have been only words and he wouldn't have reached for the book in the first place. (130, italics in original)

The statement has a transformative effect on Malone, causing him to become 'instantly awake', and the very language is defamiliarised in the process of the words becoming more than 'only words'. Just as the diagnosis compels him to consider Hayden's paper knife, his stay in the hospital compels him to learn about despair.[51] Repeatedly, then, a narrative of growing existential awareness characterises Malone's relationship with other characters and his town, as his progression towards death instigates significant changes in ideology and personality.

The novel's complex negotiation of the metaphor of blood is complemented by Malone's job as a pharmacist and his position in the typology of the town; his role in Milan and that of his pharmacy are both indicators of the changing attitude of the people and the town. McCullers designs Malone's drugstore as a social centre for the town and as a spatial representation of its proprietor's subjectivity, and the office of the pharmacy symbolises the town's collective moral health. The building that houses Malone's business takes on the characteristics of its proprietor in its internal division. As well as housing the doctor's office in which Malone is forced to reassess himself, the pharmacy is divided between the public, outward-facing storefront, and the shady, private 'compounding room' in which Malone meets with the judge and prepares prescription medicines (16). Sharing the space with the doctor who diagnoses his cancer is the earliest indication in the novel of the building's symbiotic relationship to Malone, underscoring the degree to which building and inhabitant are merged in a single 'office'.

When Jester walks through the town, the pharmacy is featured as a locus for the town's activity:

He left the bus at the corner of J.T. Malone's drugstore which was in the centre of town. He looked at the town. On the next block was the Wedwell Spinning Mill [. . .] Just to stretch his legs he strolled around the business section of town [. . .] Jester circled back to Malone's drugstore thinking of a cherry coke with cool crushed ice. (90)

As he takes in the town, Jester uses the pharmacy to anchor his walk through its 'centre'. Shortly afterwards, Jester contemplates the inherently segregated structure of Milan's physical layout: 'So it would go on, Jester knew [. . .] Tipped panama hats, the separate fountains for white and coloured people in the courthouse square [. . .] muslin and white linen and raggedy overalls. Milan. Milan. Milan' (91). The detail of segregated water fountains in the courthouse square underscores racial segregation's place at the civic and legislative heart of the town. The local seat of governmental oversight and of justice upholds the physical framework of segregation that defines Milan, and the clothes the townsfolk wear are material indicators of class and racial inequality, whether muslin, linen or overalls. Before the announcement of the *Brown* decision, the town seems to Jester to be irredeemably engineered by racial segregation.

Segregation is at the centre of Milan's architectural design, just as Malone's business is the locus for its social and business dealings. Following his diagnosis, a 'restless' Malone seeks reassurance in the physicality of the town:

> Often he would walk aimlessly around the streets of the town – down through the shambling, crowded slums and the cotton mill, or through the Negro sections, or the middle class streets of houses set in careful lawns. On these walks he had the bewildered look of an absent-minded person who seeks something but has already forgotten the thing that is lost. Often, without cause, he would reach out and touch some random object; he would veer from his route to touch a lamp post or place his hands against a brick wall. (13)

This route marks out the social inequality in the organisation of the town, as he passes residential areas set out for poor whites, poor blacks and wealthy whites, respectively. The pathetic fallacy of the narrator's description of 'careful lawns' suggests a precarious social position for the town's middle-class community, whose status is dependent on the continued existence of crowded slums. The town is animated by the principles of racial and social inequality, and the description of the slums as 'shambling' suggests a neighbourhood in motion, presumably against the 'careful' middle-class homeowners. Seeking a tactile relationship with the town's lamp posts and brick walls, Malone reaffirms his connection, even as his route negotiates the town's economic and social imbalances. Defamiliarisation allows Malone to question the caste system according to which Milan operates. This is seen most clearly in his abrasive and disconcerting first meeting with Sherman.

In an 'unpaved alley' Malone believes he can hear strange footsteps and see unsettling shadows. Frightened, 'He turned so suddenly that he collided with his follower' (15). This meeting unnerves Malone in the same way that the presence of the paper knife in Dr Hayden's office has. Sherman's appearance is accusatory, signalling the inescapable fact of 'miscegenation' that threatens the discourses of white 'integrity':

> Except for his eyes, he looked like any other coloured boy. But his eyes were bluish-grey, and set in the dark face they had a bleak, violent look. Once those eyes were seen, the rest of the body seemed also unusual and out of proportion. (15)

Sherman's blue eyes arouse Malone's prejudice, and Malone criminalises his mixed-race heritage: 'the impression on Malone was such that he did not think of him in harmless terms as a *coloured boy* – his mind automatically used the harsh term *bad nigger*' (15). Malone and Sherman are represented as sinister doubles, sharing a particular and significant trait: 'the eyes of both were the same grey-blue and at first it seemed a contest to outstare each other' (16). Their shared trait implicates Malone, who usually thinks himself 'lenient' in matters of race (16). By featuring this meeting so close to the paper knife scene, McCullers implies a common theme in each encounter.

In a novel that McCullers dedicated to a psychotherapist, her friend Mary Mercer, it is easy to read the 'unpaved alley' in which Malone and Sherman meet as symbolising repressed psychology. The 'doubling' of the characters, who share *unheimlich* similarities in their eyes (their modes of perception), lends itself comfortably to a psychoanalytic reading. However, as compelling as such an approach might be, it runs the risk of deploying the idea of the 'gothic' as an umbrella term for racial and psychological tensions in southern fiction. As well as the psychoanalytic dimensions of

McCullers's description of this meeting, the architectural and material facets of the town contribute to a more nuanced perspective on race in the encounter and in the novel. Malone is unwilling to accept his similarity to Sherman and only the omniscient narrator observes that the characters share the same coloured eyes. Malone may be interacting with the racial structure of Milan in a new way, but his racist foundations remain. The place in which Malone and Sherman meet is figured as adjoining, but separated from, the familiar space of Malone's drugstore, to which he subsequently retreats: 'He was relieved to get out of the alley and enter his safe, ordinary, familiar pharmacy' (16). The abrupt and uncomfortable encounter in the alley underlines the process of defamiliarisation Malone begins in Dr Hayden's office, and marks the space around the pharmacy as a porous barrier between the racially bifurcated town and the strictly white interior of the pharmacy. As the novel proceeds, private space in the building is more sinister to Malone, especially when it becomes the meeting place for the lynch mob.

As in *Strange Fruit* and *The Hawk and the Sun*, the irreconcilable racial tension that builds in a town predicated on racial inequality eventually explodes in sanctioned racial violence. The meeting takes place in the compounding room in the rear of the pharmacy, rather than the public-facing part of the store in which customers are attended to and drinks served. The back room is described in terms that highlight its covert atmosphere: 'It was a very small room, separated from the rest of the store by a wall of medicine bottles. There was just enough room for a rocking chair and the prescription table' (16). The cramped, dark room signifies its proprietor's private impulses and is also the place where Malone and Clane discuss race. The wall of glass bottles suggests a fragile barrier, reiterating the porous division between the races throughout the rest of the town. The divided sections of the pharmacy have different atmospheres in a literal sense, and their separate aromas compete: 'The electric fans on the ceiling churned the mixed odours in the place – syrupy smells from the fountain with the bitter medicinal smells from the compounding section in the rear' (16). The smell of each distinct space signifies its specific role in the identity of the building. The saccharine smell of the public-facing storefront suggests an artificially pleasant atmosphere that is juxtaposed with the bitter and unpleasant odour of the back room. The pleasant smells hide the bitter processes that take place behind the proverbial curtain.

In the compounding room, Malone gains a new perspective on the men who meet in his store to decide Sherman's fate which 'compounds' earlier stages of self-realisation into a pronounced scepticism as he 'recalled something unpleasant about each of the men he met that night' (192). Having been assured by Judge Clane that the men are upstanding citizens, Malone is now able to see the men who make up the mob in a new light. Having seen them as 'ordinary people, so ordinary that he usually didn't think of them one way or the other', he now see also sees 'the weaknesses of these ordinary people, their little uglinesses', concluding 'No, they were not leading citizens' (192). Malone's life in the white community is once again defamiliarised as his condition worsens in what the omniscient narrator calls Malone's changed 'frame of mind' as he moves closer to death (192). Confronted by the 'fraternity of hate' the men symbolise, he is unable to carry out the murder that he has been chosen to commit (194). McCullers closes the existentialist arc of the narrative by bringing Malone to a revelation.

Malone's decision to refuse to commit murder is as much an act of self-preservation as it is evidence of developing tolerance: '"Gentlemen, I am too near death to sin, to murder" [. . .] He went on in a stronger voice, "I don't want to endanger my soul"' (195). The strengthening of Malone's voice signals a new-found willingness to confront the town's white supremacist ideology even though Malone has nothing left to lose, including his life. While this language of 'sin' appears to assert a Christian ideology, this is less than certain. Unable to understand Malone's change of mind, one of the conspirators asks: 'What the fuck is an immortal soul?' (194). Malone's response indicates his shift in thinking: 'I don't know . . . But if I have one, I don't want to lose it' (195). Malone remains uncertain about religious ethics but he is unwilling to 'sin' against either religious or secular morality, suggesting a moral turn from total intolerance to ambivalence.

Even as Malone refuses to personally carry out the bombing, it is clear to him that somebody else will do so in his place. Malone's decision not to murder Sherman falls short of a commitment to prevent the murder from happening at all. To compare Malone to the characters in *The Hawk and the Sun*, his 'stand' is closer to Abraham's than Gaines's. Malone's deepening understanding of his racist beliefs encourages a shift in his personal ethics, and the landscape of Milan that has been so closely connected to the character is, in my reading, poised to follow suit. This shift is indicated by Clane, who is unseated over the course of the novel from his position as the town's political and legal figurehead.

Political Currency in the Peach County Courthouse: The Three Houses of Fox Clane

At the beginning of the novel, the judge is dominant in every sphere of politics: the personal, the local and the national. Each political sphere is embodied by a building, namely, the judge's home, the Peach County Courthouse and the US Capitol Building. In each space, the judge's agenda is the presiding ideology and he is able to make his bigoted beliefs into political realities. As the novel progresses the judge's dominance in each space is irrevocably undermined. Clane imagines his beliefs as analogous to the physical structure of the South: 'The wind of revolution is rising to destroy the very foundations on which the South was built' (17). The metaphor of the foundations of the South makes the space of the town inextricable from the mentality that the judge propagates among the people of the town. As the judge's role as figurehead begins to shift, Milan undergoes similar changes. Clane's 'ornate Victorian house', an edifice to white supremacist politics, is known mockingly as 'The Judge's White Elephant' (155). The phrase 'white elephant' denotes an object for which cost exceeds value; it refers to an expensive burden whose cost is not proportionate to its worth. The house, then, is symbolic of the judge's outmoded, and increasingly costly, ideology of white supremacy being devalued nationally.

The sanctity of white supremacy in the judge's home is threatened when he employs Sherman as his secretary. Initially, the relationship between Sherman and the judge is cordial, as the elder statesman behaves paternalistically, and Sherman is content to work as his personal secretary and amanuensis. Despite an initially warm relationship, the judge does not hesitate to order Sherman's death for renting a home where white segregation mandates that he should not. According to southernist Sharon Monteith, author and activist Alice Walker was conflicted when reading the novel, wondering 'how [to] explain the seeming paradox of a man like the Judge' who treats Sherman 'as if he were his own son' before ordering his execution.[52] Walker did not answer her own question, but in Monteith's analysis the complex relationship between Judge Clane and Sherman is an example of how some white writers 'grapple most revealingly' with the 'apparent paradoxes' of cross-racial behavioural codes.[53] This is no paradox, but a coherent expression of racial etiquette. It is entirely consistent that Clane would treat Sherman paternalistically until the point that Sherman forges a distinctive activist persona.

Sherman's place within a progressive black cultural tradition is even more pronounced in earlier drafts of the novel. Archival sources indicate that one of McCullers's final decisions as she composed the novel was to remove him from a centre of African American higher learning. McCullers's handwritten amendments to a near-final typescript of the novel remove references to the Tuskegee Institute. In early drafts, Sherman is alternately described as 'a graduate of the singing school in Tuskeegee [sic] Institute' and 'a scholarship boy at Tuskeegee [sic] and one of the best singers in this town'.[54] In both cases, these allusions to an institution with a long tradition of black southern liberalism were crossed out in pencil shortly before the manuscript went to print. McCullers left no allusion to Sherman's education in the published novel. While this omission might seem trivial, it marginalises Sherman's self-identification as an activist and removes the influence of higher education from his character development. Reading Sherman as a university graduate would further underscore the irony of his position as a domestic labourer in Clane's home. Sherman increasingly exploits his position of domestic power to undermine the judge's authority and even his health: 'Finally he did something. When he gave the Judge his injections in the morning, he substituted water instead of insulin. For three days that went on and he waited. And again in that creepy way nothing seemed to happen' (186). Although ineffective, Sherman's attempt to harm the judge is a radical infiltration of the judge's most intimate space. Sherman uses his access to Clane against him and is able to threaten the integrity of the judge's very body by withholding insulin.

Leaving his job and renting a home in a white neighbourhood, Sherman ceases to be tolerable within the judge's conception of the town's racial order, and when Sherman purposefully inserts himself into the town's white spaces, in contravention of the norms of racial etiquette, he comes under threat of violence. Jester visits Sherman to urge him to leave his new home to avoid the bombing that will kill him, but he is met with disbelief: '"Leave my furniture?" With one of the wild swings of mood that Jester knew so well, Sherman began to talk about the furniture [. . .] in an ecstasy of ownership, Sherman seemed to have forgotten all about the fear' (196). Having invested in his own domestic space, Sherman is unwilling to forsake his home even for his own safety. Sherman is safe while at work in 'The Judge's White Elephant' but by creating his own monument to domesticity he is endangered by the town and the judge's racial double standards. While McCullers positions Sherman's decision not to flee as an implicit critique of racist values, she allows Jester to safely interrogate them within the protected space of the Clane family home.

Intra-racial and cross-generational conflict erupts during a debate between grandfather and grandson concerning the correct way to practise law. An epistemological rift emerges as the judge sees nothing contradictory in enforcing a two-tiered system of justice while Jester insists on change:

> Jester said: 'I still think that as a judge you judge one crime in two different ways – according to whether it is done by a Negro or a white man.'
>
> 'Naturally. They are two different things. White is white and black is black – and never the two shall meet if I can prevent it.' (39–40)

The judge's baldly racist ideas hold sway because he is in a position to practise his legislative agenda. In fact, the judge plans a return to Congress precisely in order to effect a change to national laws:

> I am going to have a bill introduced in the House of Representatives if
> I win the next election that will redeem all Confederate monies, with
> the proper adjustment for the increase of cost-of-living nowadays. It will
> be for the South what F.D.R. intended to do in his New Deal. It will
> revolutionise the economy of the South. And you, Jester, will be a wealthy
> young man. There are ten million dollars in that safety box. What do you
> say to that? (37)

The historical narrative of the Confederacy's defeat means that Jester will inherit always-already worthless objects. Even while the Confederate dollar was accepted in transactions, it was a currency by fiat. Its value was not tied to a stable economic resource such as gold but was imposed solely by governmental decree.[55] Ironically, then, the value that the judge is attempting to reassert in his plan for the currency was never fixed or stable, even in the Confederacy.

It is only in the judge's neo-Confederate mentality that Confederate dollars are of any value, and Jester, who has inherited more of his father's ideals than his grandfather's politics, knows that the bills lack any intrinsic worth. Judge Clane's plan – in a perversion of African American calls for reparations for slavery – is based on the principle of white southerners' inheritance of the profits of slavery.[56] The judge's proposed legislation revolves around his perceived right to be compensated as a white southerner: 'He began to talk about reparation for burnt houses, burnt cotton, and to Sherman's shame and horror, of reparation for slaves' (140). This strange plan is itself a Clane family heirloom: beginning with the judge's grandmother during Reconstruction, the Clane family has been amassing millions in Confederate dollars. The judge takes great pride in this history: 'There are ancestors of vision in our family – remember that, Jester' (37). His admonition to 'remember' his ancestors may serve just as well to promote a social conscience in Jester as to indoctrinate him. By rejecting his grandfather's intentions for him at the heart of the family home, Jester begins to subvert the abiding political identity of the house itself, challenging his grandfather for mastery of the ideological space. Jester's act of subverting the racial politics of the judge's house is preceded by a similar act of subversion carried out by his grandfather years earlier, albeit in a different type of house.

During the novel's fictive present, Judge Clane is a former congressman for Georgia in the US House of Representatives. As well as being a Representative, he is representative of a southern type within the town and society at large. But the judge is a former representative, maintaining the respect of the office while carrying little or no influence beyond the territory of Milan. His ability to speak for the South is waning. Like his white elephant home, the judge's value is decreasing. In the fictive past, however, when the judge leaves the physical space of the town of Milan to represent that same space in federal government, he infiltrates the federal space of Washington, DC, with his provincial ideology.

The judge describes himself as a 'Southern patriot', despite having been elected to the federal government. He sees his role in Washington as defending 'the noble standards of the South' under siege by the same federal government (29).[57] The judge is respected in Milan because he was a congressman, even though he was obstructionist during his time government. Jester explains his developing racial liberalism to the judge by remembering a story of the judge's time in Congress:

> That time I heard about when that Negro from Cuba was making a talk in the House I was so proud of you. When the other congressmen stood up you sat back farther in your chair, propped your feet up and lighted a cigar. I thought it was wonderful. I was so proud of you. But now I see it differently. It was rude and bad manners. (32)

In this story, the judge subverts the federal space of the Capitol Building in Washington by refusing to conduct himself appropriately. While in the Capitol, the judge represents the geographical territory in which Milan is located in order, also, to propagate white supremacy in the government. The judge minimises the spatial distance between Milan and Washington by replicating his small town's politics in the nation's capital.

The act of putting his feet on the bench is a performance of 'making himself at home'. The intimate, private acts of putting one's feet up and smoking delegitimise the space of the Capitol Building as a site for international diplomacy. By positioning a congressman as a governmental force in opposition to desegregation, McCullers reflects the degree to which each branch of federal government had moved, or failed to move, against segregation by her time of writing. As Mark Tushnet notes: 'President Harry S. Truman's order desegregating the armed forces placed one branch of government on the side of civil rights. *Brown* placed a second branch there, leaving Congress as the sole holdout.'[58] In Sherman's words, the judge's planned legal action, were he to return to Washington, would 'turn back the clock for a hundred years' (141). In an allusion to the novel's title, this statement also focuses the conflict between the judge and Sherman as a debate regarding the ownership of history.

In his plan to reinstate Confederate currency, the judge is represented as a neo-Confederate, using his political power in service of a twentieth-century version of Confederate nationalism. Paul Quigley has argued for an understanding of Confederate nationalism predicated on a psychological rationalisation: 'Surely here [in the Confederacy] more than anywhere nationalism was an artefact, the deliberate, self-conscious intellectual creation of cultural and political leaders, designed to rationalize political independence.'[59] In the judge's imagination, the South is a conquered 'nation', and he is attempting to employ the same techniques as Confederate leaders to galvanise a regional identity based on white supremacy over blacks and southern supremacy over the North. The judge is a fictional representative of the neo-Confederate imagination that Quigley describes as having a unique and myopic interpretation of the Civil War: 'White southerners used highly selective memories of slavery and images of the Confederate war effort as a romantic "lost cause" to fashion a new kind of regional identity', drawing on 'the belief that shared victimhood and suffering united white southerners in a sacred community of sacrifice'.[60] Published in the same year as *Clock Without Hands*, Robert Penn Warren's *The Legacy of the Civil War* (1961) treats the conflict as a singularly evocative historical event in the American imagination, writing that 'the Civil War is our only "felt" history – history lived in the national imagination'.[61] While the veracity of this claim is difficult to substantiate, Warren, whose politics had shifted further to the centre-left by this point in his career, acknowledges the racial successes of the war as partial: 'the Civil War abolished Slavery, even if it did little or nothing to abolish racism.'[62] An emotional engagement with the meaning of the Civil War is, according to Warren, a common response on either side of the colour line, depending on the degree to which race is considered a part of the Union directive during the war. This contestation of meaning further erodes the judge's intellectual ownership of the town's political mentality and its perception of the Civil War.

In the novel, African American memory of the same period focuses on heroic 'anti-slavery' figures. The Civil War plays a vastly different role in Sherman's imagination from the one it plays in the judge's. Union victory in the Civil War is intrinsic to Sherman's conception of American national identity and his own personal identity. For instance, when Sherman mails a letter to a celebrity he imagines to be his mother, he addresses it directly to 'Madam Marian Anderson, The steps of the Lincoln memorial' (96). McCullers is referring to a famous performance delivered by the African American singer and activist on the National Mall after she was denied the right to perform at Constitution Hall in April 1939. Sherman's fantasy family is tied up with his fantasy of American history, with Lincoln the Great Emancipator. His disgust with the judge's plan for 'reparations' is articulated through recourse to two historical figures who recur in the text: 'Well, Abe Lincoln freed the slaves and another Sherman burnt the cotton' (141).

Implicit in Sherman's naming is a celebration of the role played by General William Tecumseh Sherman in the destruction of the Old South. Sherman's name is acknowledged by the judge as being a common tribute to the Union general: 'After Sherman marched through Georgia many a colored boy was named for him. Personally I have known half a dozen in my lifetime' (173). McCullers positions the judge's and Sherman's narratives of the Civil War in direct and overt conflict. Clane's distaste for the 'half a dozen' Sherman namesakes echoes white supremacist writing of the period, as when journalist Daniel D. Workman conflates Sherman's role in southern history with cross-racial sex and mixed-race southerners: 'It is obvious that a number of half-breed Yankees were left among the Southern Negroes in the wake of marauding Federal troops who ranged the South under the command of William Tecumseh Sherman and other despoilers of the land.'[63] The judge and Sherman represent opposing perspectives on southern history that converge on the controversial figure of the Civil War general.

The themes of generational conflict and the law are decidedly related, as in the judge's memories of his son. In her portrayal of Johnny Clane, McCullers represents a new generation of southerners adopting more tolerant, liberal racial politics. The judge recalls how concern over his son's apparent 'Bolshevism' was allayed by his participation in traditional southern institutions: 'He had always consoled himself by the fact that Johnny was young, was a quarterback on the University of Georgia Football team, and that the fads and fancies of the young pass quickly when reality must be faced' (162). The judge understands the University of Georgia as an acceptable locus for the formation of a southern identity shared by himself and his son. The judge is unable to reconcile Johnny's identity with his own, and the generational rift remains a concept the elder Clane cannot accept. That such a generational rift is visible to the judge during Johnny's education suggests that the generational difference will manifest itself in the way each Clane conceives of the law. These differences come to a head in the Peach County courthouse, a symbolic site in Milan.

The stage for one of the novel's most significant cross-generational debates on race takes place in the Peach County courtroom during the judge's tenure. Johnny's interpretation of the law comes into conflict with the judge's when Johnny defends African American Sherman Jones, Sherman Pew's father, who killed a white man in self-defence. While the judge rationalises racist judgments by thinking of himself as 'only an instrument of the law', he makes legal decisions based on 'the law and the customs of the state' (158). On the contrary, when Johnny defends Jones, he appeals solely to the basic tenets of American law, urging his father and the jury to assess his client's guilt through recourse to federal law, rights and justice.

In the judge's estimation, Johnny makes the mistake of treating the people of Milan as if they are capable of understanding the law: 'He argued as if those Georgia crackers, millhands, and tenant farmers were trained jurors of the Supreme Court itself. Such talent. But not a grain of common sense' (166). The judge condemns Johnny's unwillingness to pander to the largely poor and entirely white jury. Johnny erodes the supposed difference between North and South and implores the people of Milan to reject southern exceptionalism to perform their civic duty (170). These arguments rely on the cornerstone of federal law and when Johnny appeals to the Constitution it reflects his desire to implement national conventions within the local sphere. McCullers depicts a rift in federal and local law that, at this point in the narrative chronology, Johnny is unable to overcome. The practical implementation of the Constitution is overwritten in the community by the mechanism through which the provisions of the Constitution are withheld from black citizens and 'no Negro in Peach County had ever voted' (143). The judge, in his role as adjudicator of the law, allows these racist facts of the legal system in Peach County to supersede the Fifteenth Amendment. Johnny commits suicide after losing the Jones case, effectively refusing to practise a law governed by racist southern traditions. McCullers implies that Jester's growing legal awareness will provide a continuation of Johnny's agenda, and she achieves this in part through the repetition of a particular document across each of the three generations: the Gettysburg Address.

McCullers deploys Lincoln's address as a mobile intertext at various points in *Clock Without Hands*. The changing narrative context alters the specific meaning of the otherwise unchanged text of Lincoln's speech, which is usually delivered within the confines of the courthouse. For Clane, the speech is worthy of respect primarily as an example of rhetoric. As a pseudo-intellectual, the judge is fond of reciting or paraphrasing 'great' works of literature and has Sherman read aloud to him. The judge's desire to be at the centre of a performance, and his affinity for pomp, lead him to recite even texts he finds politically distasteful: 'The Judge never needed a second invitation to sing or recite or otherwise exercise his voice for an audience' (171). He enjoys performing the speech because he believes it to be rhetorically accomplished, despite his political convictions to the contrary of Lincoln's. Johnny has a vastly different relationship to the speech and attempts to invoke it, alongside his appeal to the Constitution in his unsuccessful defence of Sherman Jones. In opposition to his father's superficial reading of the text, Johnny intends to employ the speech as a legal precedent in defence of Jones but is prevented when the judge raps his gavel in response to the opening phrase 'Four score and seven years ago –' (171). The judge's interruption prevents the remainder of the speech from being included in the court record. However, in retelling the story he piques Jester's curiosity and must continue the recital himself. At first, Jester is unfamiliar with the speech because he 'did not know clearly what the quote would be' after his grandfather begins (171). The speech is absent from Jester's education, which has been administered by his grandfather with a vested political and financial interest in the history of the Civil War. For Jester, hearing the speech for the first time is clearly affective: 'Jester listened with tears of glory in his eyes' (171). Despite the comically melodramatic description, the speech makes him feel closer to his father and signals his allegiance to progressively understanding the law. The most significant context in which the speech is reiterated is as a direct response to the *Brown* decision when the judge is ironically rendered speechless in the face of the announcement.

Clane anticipates the decision early in the novel, but as a fantasy event beyond the realms of the reasonable: 'Equal rights in education will be the next thing. Imagine a future where delicate little white girls must share their desks with coal black niggers in order to learn to read and write' (17). Later, the judge repeats his fears to his grandson, who queers the paradigm in response: 'How about a hulking white girl sharing a desk with a delicate little Negro boy?' (30). The judge's position is destabilised by Jester's inversion and by the very rhetorical forms that he manipulates to sway people. The proleptic detail of this allusion to the likelihood of the *Brown* decision mirrors the historical process that C. Vann Woodward articulates: 'never had the [Supreme] Court moved more deliberately' than with the *Brown* case, in order to ensure that the decision would be effective and far-reaching.[64] The *Brown* decision is anticipated even earlier in the novel, in the way in which Johnny conducts his defence of Sherman Jones by asserting to the jurors that 'the Constitution itself is on trial' and reciting the Thirteenth and Fourteenth Amendments to them (171). In the case of *the People v. Jones*, Johnny unwittingly predicts the same arguments that the Warren Court would later detail in the *Brown* case. The court's opinion in the latter case also cites the Fourteenth Amendment as the grounds on which African Americans are guaranteed equal provision under the law and specifically in education.[65] In an insult to the judge, Johnny begins to recite Lincoln's

Address, compounding his strict reading of the Constitution with a 'non-southern' reading of the history of the Civil War. McCullers deploys Johnny's defence of Jones as an unsuccessful rehearsal of the ideas of the desegregationist legislation that would follow in the wake of *Brown*. In this moment of intergenerational conflict, the judge retains the position of power in striking down the defence, although it is a power he will not hold later in the text when the Warren Court's decision is imposed.

The judge is much less willing than Malone to relinquish power over the character of the region and the town. By the middle of May 1954, following his refusal to murder Sherman, Malone's health is failing rapidly. Segregationists knew the day on which the novel's dénouement is set as 'Black Monday', and the phrase was the title of a segregationist pamphlet published in 1955.[66] Malone's anxieties of race and status appear to have faded as the *Brown* decision is announced and he nears death. McCullers underscores Malone's altered ideas because his imminent death has thrown into relief the pettiness of the judge's ideology: 'But his livingness was leaving him, and in dying, living assumed order and a simplicity that Malone had never known before' (208). In a state of frenzy, the judge visits Malone: 'Sputtering, incoherent with anger, the Judge told about the Supreme Court decision for school integration', but Malone is unmoved (206).

After receiving a cold reception from Malone, Clane rushes to the Peach County courthouse to take part in a radio broadcast condemning the *Brown* decision. In his state of agitation and in spite of himself, his powers of rhetoric and leadership fail him:

> So, angry, defiant – expecting at any moment a little seizure, or worse – the Judge stood with the microphone in his hand and no speech ready. Words – vile words, cuss words unsuitable for the radio – raged in his mind. But no historic speech. The only thing that came to him was the first speech he had memorized in law school. Knowing dimly that what he was going to say was wrong, he plunged in.
>
> 'Four score and seven years ago [. . .]' (207)

The judge is unable to reflect on the announcement of the Warren Court using any of the language with which he is most familiar. The

Brown decision forces the judge to abandon the rhetoric of race he has imposed on Peach County during his tenure as judge and he unwillingly falls back on the foundational texts of his education in law. The judge's confused mental state is rendered by McCullers's omniscient narrator in the phrase 'But no historic speech'. This line is not a sentence because it lacks both a verb and a subject. Two parenthetical clauses, removed from the main body of the text by dashes, signals the judge's failed attempt to think coherently about the announcement. With the *Brown* decision, the judge's interpretation of the law in Milan is overwritten by a federal edict, and he is left an intellectual blank slate, parroting the doctrine against which he has always struggled. The recurrence of the courthouse as a setting calls attention to Johnny's invocation of the Address in the earlier case and suggests the changing political context of the town in the intervening years. Having once stopped the Address from being spoken in his courtroom, the judge is now unable to stop himself from reciting it. He is an automatous mouthpiece in favour of the law that he despises because his political currency at home, in the town and in the nation has been eroded over the course of the narrative.

The judge recites as much of the Gettysburg Address as he can, even while being prodded off stage by his own supporters. As he recites, Clane divorces himself from his words as he stands 'at the microphone with the echo of his own words ringing in his ears' (208). He is subject to increasingly violent attacks from a crowd that mistakes his speech for a show of liberalism and he is eventually forced to realise the shift in roles: 'The shock of recognition made him crumble, yet immediately he shouted: "It's just the other way around! I mean it just the other way around! Don't cut me off!"' (208). The novel ends with the judge physically unable to articulate anything but a doctrine of federal government and racial change. If Clane continues to be a representative of Milan, his role has changed with the federal decision that will fundamentally undermine the system on which the town rests. McCullers charts the development of Milan's political identity by showing how three sites, the judge's home, the US House of Representatives and the Peach County courthouse adapt, in spite of the judge, to the changing racial politics of the South at mid-century. Tellingly, the potential black radical Sherman is killed while the white would-be lawyer Jester survives to fight for his convictions within a legislative rubric. As Rachel Adams argues, Jester survives the novel because his 'differences can eventually be assimilated in a way that the visible stigma of dark skin cannot'.[67] By representing the town of Milan at various points on a trajectory of racial progress, McCullers implicitly reflects a gradualist ideology in which desegregation can be realised by attrition over a period of time.

At the end of *Strange Fruit* the characters of Bessie, Nonnie and Dessie figuratively cleanse themselves of the town's racial violence in a scene I have interpreted as signalling an optimistic future for Maxwell. In *The Hawk and the Sun*, a moment of personal change is made more explicit when Abraham commits to extricating himself from the town's racial violence and to encouraging future generations of his family to promote racial tolerance. Where in Smith's and Reece's novels the ideological positions that underpin the typology of the typical southern town in fiction are challenged by the actions of a small minority of white characters, McCullers dramatises the gradual shift of an entire town. McCullers exposes her town's social and physical architecture to the gradually changing racial politics of the region in order to depict a community and a town in increasing flux over the course of four novels. Although Milan is a consistent feature across McCullers's fiction, it is nonetheless a town in process. McCullers depicts its gradual move away from the judge's attempts to conserve white supremacy, which are shown to fail in the character's final act of speech. The protagonist of William Faulkner's *The Reivers* (1962) also commits to speaking for his small-town home as a means of ensuring that Jefferson, Mississippi, maintains a white supremacist collective identity. While Faulkner's narrator, Lucius Priest, is more successful than Judge Clane, his backward-looking narrative is undermined by Faulkner's extensive mapping of the fictional town of Jefferson.

CHAPTER 5

Breaking the Pencil:
William Faulkner's Jefferson

On 14 June 1962 William Faulkner's publisher at Random House, Bennett Cerf, received a letter from entertainment lawyer Benjamin Aslan. Aslan was keen to discuss the 'musicalization of Mr. Faulkner's work' *The Reivers* (1962), published earlier that month.[1] The letter apparently followed a telephone conversation between Cerf and Aslan and negotiations for an adaptation were far enough along for Aslan to enclose copies of a proposed agreement. Faulkner was, to judge from Cerf's response, amenable to the suggestion. It seems likely that the adaptation would have gone ahead had the author not died following a horse-riding accident less than three weeks later on 6 July 1962.[2] The Nobel laureate's fiction does not, at first glance, seem appropriate subject matter for musical theatre, and it is difficult to imagine another of his novels being 'musicalised'.

Faulkner's final novel has long been understood, thanks in part to the intervention of the author, as a more easily digestible and humorous work by an otherwise 'difficult' modernist. In contrast, I argue that *The Reivers* is a complex and ironic indictment of backward-looking white supremacist narratives of southern history. By the early 1960s the typology of the fictional southern town that Faulkner had been exploring in the Yoknapatawpha cycle for decades had become a metafictional device through which an attentive reader could interrogate the reliability of a narrator. In particular, Faulkner depicts Jefferson's courthouse square, the centre of the town's social and physical landscape, as a contested space that defines the collective identity of the town.

The novel tells two stories. One, favoured by earlier and traditional Faulkner critics, is an adventure yarn about a young white boy who steals a car, loses it and tries to win it back in a horse race. The boy, Lucius Priest, is joined by Boon Hogganbeck, who featured in the earlier novel *Go Down, Moses* (1942), and Ned McCaslin, a member of the African American branch of the McCaslin family explored in the same novel. This story, I argue, serves to obscure a more insidious and politically reactionary narrative. Through a framing device, the phrase 'Grandfather said' with which the novel opens, Faulkner makes it clear that the adventure is being related by an elderly Priest to his grandson.[3] Priest's narrative goal is indoctrination, and the narrative present is not the prelapsarian, pre-modern Jefferson of 1905, but the fraught and violent South of the early 1960s. As southernist Brannon Costello argues, Priest's narrative 'moves in two directions at once: on the one hand, it is an attempt to recast his story and the history of his family [. . .] Yet at the same time, his narrative constantly speaks the truth that he wants to silence.'[4] Faulkner, in presenting these simultaneous narratives, deploys the trope of the segregated town as a narrative and political tool to undermine Priest's implicitly white supremacist revisionist history. The history that the elderly Priest seeks to revise is the same that Faulkner has painstakingly outlined in earlier narratives of Jefferson. I argue that, with *The Reivers*, reading for the town allows scholars to read otherwise unseen strategies of literary protest.

In an account of Faulkner's only public reading of *The Reivers*, at West Point on 19 April 1962, literary critic David L. G. Arnold describes the text as comparatively remarkable within Faulkner's oeuvre for its simplicity, especially in contrast to *Go Down, Moses* (1942): 'In *The Reivers*, Faulkner seems to be revisiting old scenes of tragedy and reshaping them, creating forms which will allow him to realize his greater sense of optimism for human fulfilment.'[5] Arnold's interpretation of the novel may be influenced by Faulkner's performance of the extract he chose to read, a relatively exciting passage depicting a high-stakes horserace. In his introduction to the reading, Faulkner prepared his military audience for an aesthetically uncomplicated scene: 'I will have to skip about a little to read about a horse race which to me is one of the funniest horse races I ever heard of.'[6] Aside from highlighting the scene's humour, Faulkner performs distance from the narrative when he suggests it is a story he 'heard of', rather than imagined. The impulse to read *The Reivers* as 'far removed' from the experimental, 'difficult' and complex novels of Faulkner's earlier career characterises much of the criticism written in immediate response to publication, as well as in the decades following. John E. Bassett, for instance, is misdirected by *The Reivers*' ostensible simplicity, despite acknowledging the novel's framing technique of 'Grandfather said' as a means of creating a critical distance within the text: 'Since no other signals in the book indicate irony between grandchildren and grandfather, or the reader and grandchildren, the narrative voice is fully reliable.'[7] That any narrative voice can be 'fully reliable' is a difficult claim to substantiate. At the very least, the tension between Priest's maturity and his staged adolescence is one source of narrative irony, because it creates a disconnect between the moment in which the narrative is staged and the moment that the narrative depicts. Bassett reinforces his contention by claiming that *The Reivers* is 'the least ironic of Faulkner's novels'.[8] In my reading, the divide between Priest and Lucius, the younger self he depicts, evidences of the dramatic irony at the centre of the novel's aesthetic strategy.

Faulkner stages a similar distance from his fiction elsewhere in his public writing, when he propagates an image of himself that is divorced from the 'intellectual' practice of writing novels. In an often-referenced letter to editor and critic Malcolm Cowley, Faulkner claims: 'It is my aim, and every effort bent, that the sum and history of my life, which in the same sentence is my obit and epitaph too, shall be them both: He made the books and he died.'[9] Faulkner performs a romantic view of his career as a novelist and short-story writer and, in his choice of the verb 'made', obfuscates the intellectual labour of writing fiction. Far from erasing his signature on the works, this letter is an effort to cement his name in the canon of American literary modernism. Faulkner's letter of protest is easy to dismiss, addressed as it is to the editor of *The Viking Portable Faulkner* (1949). Faulkner seeks to protect and promote his name in the same exercise.

Faulkner anticipated a response to his final novel that would interpret it at face value. Despite displacing himself from the act of writing, Faulkner facetiously insisted that the cycle's future would be comprehensive and encyclopaedic in an interview with Jean Stein for *The Paris Review*: 'My last book will be the Doomsday Book, the Golden Book, of Yoknapatawpha County. Then I shall break the pencil and I'll have to stop.'[10] Faulkner's humorous suggestion that a hypothetical novel that encyclopaedically depicts the history of Jefferson would force him to cease writing wilfully neglects the persistence of ambiguity and partial histories depicted across his work. The metaphorical breaking of Faulkner's figurative pencil underscores his singular claim to authority over Jefferson, the town of which he is 'sole owner and proprieter'.[11] In this formulation, only Faulkner, with his metonymic pencil, is entitled to develop the ongoing history of his fictional town, rendering Priest's attempts to do the same ultimately fruitless.

Readers were inclined to minimise or neglect the novel's racial subtext. A surface reading of *The Reivers* does not offer a significant engagement with the South's civil rights crisis, even though it is published at a moment of escalation. Among contemporary reviewers, a consensus emerged that *The Reivers* was a more easily digestible, less intellectually strenuous, version of 'Faulkner'. Novelist and literary critic Granville Hicks termed *The Reivers* a 'minor' text in Faulkner's corpus. To Hicks, the novel permitted, or even demanded, that a different set of criteria be employed to read it: 'Once one accepts the fact that *The Reivers* isn't a major Faulkner novel, nor, I should say, was meant to be, one can settle down to enjoy it, for minor Faulkner may be very good, and this is.'[12] In this reading, accepting that *The Reivers* is a superficial text is a prerequisite to reading it at all.

Hicks's imperative that a method of reading was needed for this novel was consistently expressed by reviewers on the novel's publication. They alternately highlighted the novel's pretensions to the adventure genre, calling it a 'gentle comedy of rustic rustlers', 'a boy's adventure story' and 'an excursion into the pleasures of fantasy',[13] or commended it as a departure from Faulkner's experimental modernism, describing it as 'a happy holiday' from Faulkner's characteristic style, lacking 'Faulknerian brooding' and representing 'low-voltage Faulkner'.[14] This impulse to read *The Reivers* as a superficial adventure tale has been replicated in the work of critics down the decades. In scholarship, too, critics are keen to highlight the novel's comedic tone. Lothar Hönnighausen identifies how 'most critics duly acknowledge the humour in Faulkner's last novel [. . .] while they tend to ignore its violence',[15] and Joseph Urgo celebrates comedy as an end in itself, describing it as 'a humorous book about automobile and horse theft' and asserting that 'the humor in *The Reivers* does not run too deep'.[16] The critical reception suggests that Priest's narrative misdirection achieves a degree of success in recasting the history of Jefferson in a sanitised, even harmonious light. Priest dilutes the existing history of Jefferson by selectively depicting elements from that history that he finds appealing and by revising those elements that he does not. As a result, Kevin Railey interprets the text as 'a deeply romantic, nostalgic vision of people's places and possibilities in society'.[17] In each of these assessments, the novel's generic involvement with the adventure tale supersedes readings of any possible political or racial subtext, and each reading overlooks the potential for irony discernible in the text that is made visible when the novel is read through the lens of the segregated town. I posit an expansion of the more sceptical readings of the novel, one in which Priest is understood as the implied villain of the novel.

I argue that Lucius Priest's 'reminiscence' of the southern town lacks veracity even while any depiction of Jefferson is necessarily – and obviously – fictional. Priest enters into a pedagogic contract with his grandson by supposedly imparting the wisdom of an older generation of white southerners. In turn, the grandson presents an imagined reader with a misrepresentation of the history of Jefferson. Debating which of these fictional characters is responsible for the presented text cannot yield a satisfactory conclusion without a representation of their meeting in a nursing home in 1961. The narrative of *The Reivers* studiously neglects such a representation. Regardless of which Lucius Priest, grandfather or grandson, is responsible for the narrative, its claim to fictive truth is more tenuous than almost any earlier story, precisely because Priest's tale is contradicted by pre-existing narratives of Jefferson in earlier novels and short stories. By reading the tension between *The Reivers* and the other instalments in the Yoknapatawpha cycle, the collective identity and composite history of the town itself are legible in opposition to the white supremacist surface narrative. In particular, the space of the town square, which recurs prominently across narratives of Jefferson, is positioned in this instance as the contested centre of the town's identity.

Squaring the Cycle: (Re-)Centring Jefferson

In his interview with Stein, Faulkner confided a realisation he had some way into writing the Yoknapatawpha cycle that 'by sublimating the actual into the apocryphal [he] would have complete liberty to use whatever talent [he] might have to its absolute top', particularly because of the freedom this would grant him with character development: 'I can move these people around like God, not only in space but in time too.'[18] Faulkner articulates the particular advantage of the small town as a literary setting. By constructing a series of spaces and offices that are fit for his aesthetic purpose, Jefferson can serve its author's political and narrative needs. What Priest achieves with his narrative is a similarly egotistical power over his relatives and neighbours, but Priest's ministrations are transparent in comparison. Priest recasts the history of Jefferson, shifting events and characters around to his own profit. Priest's intent is to compel his grandson to subscribe to the same set of beliefs to maintain his stake in the town's segregated social economy, in what Owen Robinson has termed 'a challenge to the younger man to attempt to empathise with the age gone by that he has little contemporary means of understanding, an age that is nevertheless crucial to his own life as a Southerner'.[19] I would add to Robinson's reading that Priest's monologue to his grandson is also a challenge to the grandson's 'means of understanding' contemporary Jefferson. Priest makes this challenge by reformulating the town's geography, specifically the courthouse square that represents the civic and social heart of Jefferson.

In his choice of Priest's name, Faulkner develops two complementary puns. The first is decidedly pre-modern, the second just as decidedly contemporary. In theology, a priest differs from another member of the clergy because their role includes ritual sacrifice. The difference between a Roman Catholic priest and a Protestant minister, for example, is the belief in transubstantiation, that Christ's literal body and blood are sacrificed in the Mass. Faulkner thereby imbues Priest with the didactic qualities of clergy while also underscoring the implicit violence his narrative perpetuates. The second pun derives from Priest's initials. Long-playing vinyl records, or LPs, began circulating in 1948 and surpassed 78 RPM shellac records in popularity by the late 1950s. Faulkner draws attention to Priest's narrative as an extended 'record' of the South in the early twentieth century. The pun simultaneously pokes fun at Priest as a boring and tedious mouthpiece for white supremacy and positions him in the contemporary context he is so careful to avoid.

Priest's name, an element of the narrative for which Faulkner is solely responsible, is an example of the intrusion of the contemporary moment. Elsewhere, too, Priest's conservative agenda intrudes on his nostalgic narrative. Priest describes Mr Binford in an aside that directly addresses the grandson narratee: '(You see? how much ahead of his time Mr Binford was? Already a Republican. I don't mean a 1905 Republican [. . .] I mean a 1961 Republican. He was more: he was a Conservative[)]' (103). Priest interrupts his narrative to celebrate contemporary conservatism just as, later in the tale, he interrupts to condemn social progressivism:

> In those days females didn't run in and out of gentlemen's rooms in hotels as, I am told, they do now, even wearing, I am told, what the advertisements call the shorts or scanties capable of giving women the freedom they need in their fight for freedom. (183)

Priest is very careful to distance himself from contemporary social politics, twice mediating his reactionary finger-wagging with the phrase 'I am told'. His tone is unmistakably dismissive of the feminist movement, even as several of the women he describes in his narratives are forced into sex work by economic need. In each of these cases, the sanitised pre-modern South that Priest has invented is held up as an idealised corrective to the overt politicisation that dominates the United States and Mississippi in the early 1960s. While these narrative intrusions comment on national and international politics during the period, Priest's focus is typically much more local, and he is especially interested in deploying a reactionary image of the town of Jefferson.

The economic, social and physical centre of Jefferson, the town square, is the site at which Priest makes his most direct claim to speak for the history of the town. Priest co-opts the history of the fictional town by foregrounding the elements of its development that suit his blinkered perspective, and evading or obscuring the moments in the town's history that trouble his nostalgia. A similar character in Shelby Foote's fictional Mississippi Delta town of Bristol also stands for a community's sense of progress: 'Major Malcolm Barcroft [. . .] was an institution in Bristol, one of the final representatives of what the town had progressed beyond.'[20] Unlike Barcroft, who has died by the beginning of the narrative, Priest actively seeks to reconstitute the narrative of his town in his final days by claiming ownership of its history by offering a compound narrative of the square. By compound narrative, I mean the aggregate representation of the square that is evident through reading its recurrence in the cycle. Aside from in Faulkner's work, the town square is among the most iconic signifiers of the small 'typical' southern town, and its deployment by Priest signals an attempt to co-opt the figurative foundation of the small southern town. Priest chooses to depict Jefferson's town square because it represents a nexus of commercial, social and administrative resources for the community.

Priest's is not a narrative of the community, but an idiosyncratic, personal narrative staged as community-sanctioned. The idiosyncrasy of Priest's story is apparent because earlier texts about Jefferson deploy this type of community-based narrative. The story 'A Rose for Emily' (1930) is narrated in the first-person plural narrative voice, depicting what 'we [the town] believed' about Emily Grierson's love life. 'Dry September' (1931) is narrated by a single member of a lynch mob, who records what 'the town' sees and says.[21] 'Death Drag' (1932) depicts the 'composite' narrative of the town as it witnesses an air show; the unnamed – representative, rather than individual – narrator describes the amassed spectators as 'groundlings, dwellers in and backbone of a small town interchangeable with and duplicate of ten thousand little dead clottings of human life about the land'.[22] In this depiction, the population of Jefferson is 'interchangeable' and ill-defined, making the town of Jefferson 'typical' and representative of southern towns at large. In contrast, Priest's rigidly individuated, imagined town is not the sum of a mass of parts but of his singular interpretation of its history.

The same community voice that provides the narrative foundations for the short stories is present in Priest's retelling of the town, but, crucially, his voice stands apart and his actions are not endorsed by its population. That Priest does not have the confidence of the town he represents is evidenced when Lucius surreptitiously prepares to steal his grandfather's car: 'I went back home, not running: Jefferson must not see me running: but as fast as I could without it' (55). Lucius must maintain appearances for the sake of the collective identity of the town, especially because his actions, in this case, are illicit. Paradoxically, then, Priest asserts his right to represent Jefferson while simultaneously depicting his younger self in negotiation with the rigid social expectations of the town, as symbolised by its central spatial hub. In *Requiem for a Nun* (1951), the construction of the courthouse and its square is represented as the foundational moment of the town of Jefferson:

> 'We're going to have a town,' Peabody said. 'We already got a church – that's Whitfield's cabin. And we're going to build a school too soon as we get around to it. But we're going to build the courthouse today . . . Then we'll have a town.'[23]

Peabody, a medical doctor, acknowledges the typology of the southern town as a benchmark for the settlement. The religious office of the church is given prestige over the civic and legislative office of the courthouse, but each is privileged over the educational office of the school. But it is with the construction of the courthouse square that Jefferson is defined as a town: 'We've already even named her.'[24] Faulkner positions the courthouse and the square in which it is built as the apex of the constellation of amenities that makes Jefferson a semi-urban space, as I define it in my Introduction.

At various points in the extended Yoknapatawpha narrative, the square is the site of major events in the life of the fictional town. Faulkner's annotations of the map of the fictional Jefferson published with *Absalom, Absalom!* describe the square in these terms: 'Courthouse square where Temple Drake testified, & Confederate Monument which Benjy had to pass on his <u>left</u> side.'[25] This commentary on the topography of Jefferson signals that the square, with its monument to the Confederate dead, is the focal point in the construction of the town's identity. Elsewhere, the square is the site of cross-racial tensions that threaten to spill into violence. In *Intruder in the Dust*, the town square is the venue for the intimidation of Lucius Beauchamp – another member of the extended Priest family – by a would-be member of a lynch mob: 'A car rushed from nowhere and circled the Square; a voice, a young man's voice squalled from it – no words, not even a shout: a squall significant and meaningless – and the car rushed on around the Square.'[26] This overt racial terrorism is absent from *The Reivers*, but the same square that plays host to it in *Intruder in the Dust* reappears. Faulkner marks the persistence of the town's capacity for racial violence, despite its role in the later novel as a stage for the performance of wealth and social standing. Despite Boss Priest's distaste for the car he is compelled by the town's expectations to purchase, the family drives daily through the town, 'always through the Square first', to ensure being seen by as many townspeople as possible (39).

Among contemporary anthropological accounts of the southern town, the ubiquitous town square is understood as integral to the commercial, local political and social functions of the town. Courthouse squares ground southern towns as political, social and economic entities, as when John Dollard describes the centre of 'Southerntown':

> Adjacent to the business block a domed courthouse is set in a little park-like space, a spigot for administrative services to the county, for Southerntown is the county seat. On the cool side of the building, on a summer's afternoon, a few white men lounge and talk.[27]

In this interpretation, the square is a landmark of the town's social and political identity as it is figured as a hub for commerce, local administration and intra-racial socialising. Writing about the same Mississippi town, but giving it a different name, Hortense Powdermaker describes 'the general layout of Cottonville' as 'very simple': 'The business district consists of four blocks grouped in a square. Running in three directions from it are the residential streets where the white people live.'[28] As I argue in Chapter 1,

Dollard, Powdermaker and other anthropologists of the small town craft inadvertent fictions when they make their subjects of study representative of a diverse range of southern towns. In *The Reivers*, Priest's narrative project is strikingly similar: he also develops Jefferson as a pre-existing proof of his political agenda. Like other ethnographers, Priest sites his description of the town in the square as a means of exploring the shifting and modernising trends of the southern town at mid-century.

Even when the iconic town square represents modernisation, it retains the dual significance of symbolising the town's economic and political lives. In his work of reportage *Segregation: The Inner Conflict of the South* (1956), Robert Penn Warren describes a return to Nashville, Tennessee, after a long absence to find the layout of the city changed in only one particular: 'going into the square where the big white stone boxlike, ugly and expensive Davidson County Court House now stands on the spot where the old brawling market once was'.[29] While Warren is clearly less than thrilled with the architectural change, the description of Nashville's centre signals the square's dual responsibility to the commercial life of the town – the market – and to local and federal laws. The ability to narrate the square, then, is equivalent to authority over the town. The book describes an encounter between Warren and a member of Mississippi's White Citizens' Council. Warren summarises the political aims of massive resistance as 'recreating an habitation for the values they would preserve, to achieve in unity some clarity of spirit, to envisage some healed image of their own identity'.[30] For his part in *The Reivers*, Priest attempts to foster the unity that Warren describes by co-opting the town's social history and encouraging its citizenry into accepting his agenda. Priest attempts to use his dialogue with his grandson to envision a fictional town that is as conducive as possible to the ideology of massive resistance to desegregation.

The archetype of the southern town square is often imagined with a Confederate monument standing in its centre. Novelist, journalist and racial gradualist Hodding Carter writes fondly of these memorials, apparently considering them signifiers of the noble efforts of the Confederacy: 'These weather-stained guardians, doing sentry duty above the inscriptions to the beloved dead, have earned the right to an unending vigil.'[31] While Carter imagines these statues as deserving of respect, the monuments are more ambiguous signifiers elsewhere in writing of the period. For instance, white novelist Ben Haas juxtaposes respect for the Confederate dead with the disenfranchisement of poor southerners when he opens his novel *Look Away, Look Away* (1964) with a description of the Great Depression in the 'typical' Southern town: 'You could see them in the courthouse square of every little Southern town, then, in the spring of 1932 – the dispossessed [. . .] on the courthouse steps or on the benches around the inevitable bronze Confederate soldier.'[32] Haas opens his novel with a familiar scene of the southern town, but his comment on the inevitability of the Confederate monument serves to critique the Lost Cause narrative of southern history. The misplaced pride that some southerners place in Confederate history is satirised by the poverty that surround the garish bronze statues. The recurring trope of the monument to the Confederacy that persists in fiction and non-fiction depictions of southern towns throughout this period signifies the white supremacist appropriation of American history, as well as challenges to such revisionism. In southern agrarian Allen Tate's poem 'Ode to the Confederate Dead' (1937), a speaker looking out onto a Confederate graveyard considers nostalgia a force for arresting development: 'The brute curiosity of an angel's stare / turns you like them to stone.'[33] In Tate's poem, the act of observing a monument to the past threatens to stifle contemporary action. The ubiquitous monument to the Confederate dead is an ambiguous signifier of the 'typical' southern town's past and constitutes a site of internal conflict over the right to identify the town's political and historical identity.

In *The Reivers*, Jefferson's town square is both the space through which Priest seeks to strengthen his narrative authority and a symbol of the town's collective identity for which Priest is unable to speak. In my reading, because Priest's narrative constitutes a prolonged act of evasion, he is selective about the elements of the geography he wishes to represent, as when he and Boon drive the car away from Jefferson avoiding the square: 'if we go the back way, we can dodge the Square' (66). Using the back roads means that Priest only describes those elements of the town that are conducive to his history. The novel's opening scene is set one year after *The Reivers'* primary adventure story, and relates Boon's failed attempt to shoot an African American coachman who, like Boon, works in the Priest family livery stables. After relating the first story of Boon's aborted murder of Ludus, Priest digresses to describe the introduction of the automobile to Jefferson in the previous year, 1904. The introduction of the car is the catalyst for the novel's main plot as it unfolds over the course of twelve of the novel's thirteen chapters, while the ancillary story depicted in the first chapter is self-contained and distinct from the narrative proper. This opening scene also provides a microcosmic exploration of the themes and narrative strategies Faulkner deploys in the novel as a whole (7–20). Tellingly, this rehearsal is sited at the geographical heart of Faulkner's fictional town, indicating that Priest's attempt to orient the space and social hierarchy of Jefferson is analogous to Faulkner's own construction of the town. In the ancillary narrative, Priest insinuates himself into the centre of Jefferson in order to cast himself as its representative by relating a childhood job collecting 'freight bills [. . .] around the Square' (7). This ostensibly trivial job functions to make Lucius appear indispensable to Jefferson's commercial centre. Even as a child, Lucius is employed as an overseer and mediator of the town's economic affairs, literally responsible for moving things around the town and exacting a price for the service.

Fittingly, this first narrative takes place entirely in the fictional town of Jefferson, while the rest of the novel is largely set outside its limits, and positions the text so that the town square becomes its geographical and ideological centre of gravity. The ancillary story rehearses motifs, metaphors and narrative strategies that persist, more elaborately, in the main narrative. By siting this first story in the square, Priest stakes his claim to representing the identity of the town and he makes the town's centre an emblem of its holistic identity as he seeks to co-opt both. This constitutes a revision of Jefferson's physical geographical centre as a space that is figuratively sanitised for Priest's use of it to his advantage. However, Faulkner peoples the square with characters from his fiction that pre-exist Priest. Boon, Isaac McCaslin and Ned McCaslin, a new character in the cycle, hinder Priest's attempt to speak for Jefferson because pre-existing, or, in the case of Ned, allegorical, co-texts supersede Priest's revision of Jefferson.

Comparative Boons: Unincorporated Characters and Faulkner's Parable of the Talents

The novel's opening scene depicts Lucius as a necessary part of the town's social centre and also articulates a version of Boon Hogganbeck that is contradicted by earlier, third-person portraits of the town. Priest attempts to reimagine Boon in order to make him, and his white masculinity, more palatable. Alongside this revisioning, Priest seeks to neuter earlier depictions of Isaac McCaslin as an ascetic who rejects capitalism because of his shame over his family's racial history. Priest recrafts each of these characters into more appropriate models for white supremacist masculinity, but his attempts are undermined by Faulkner's already-established constructions of the characters and of Jefferson. Priest is unable to successfully incorporate Boon and Isaac into his story because they pre-exist it. Priest is unable to fully incorporate Ned into his white-washed narrative because Faulkner constructs Ned intertextually by making him an allegorical figure outside of Priest's authority. Knowledge of Faulkner's town denies Priest the authority to tell Jefferson's history because a scene he describes in which Boon attempts to murder an African American man contrasts with a very different representation of the same scene earlier in Faulkner's fiction that resists Priest's revision.

In both versions, Boon is wronged by a black man, attempts to shoot him but misses five times, and, instead, wounds a black woman who is walking past. While these details remain consistent, the particulars change drastically. The scene in *Go Down, Moses* dramatises Boon's poor marksmanship:

> He had never hit anything bigger than a squirrel that anybody ever knew, except the negro woman that day when he was shooting at the negro man. [. . .] Boon shot five times with the pistol he had borrowed from Major de Spain's negro coachman and the negro he was shooting at outed with a dollar-and-a-half mail-order pistol and would have burned Boon down with it only it never went off, it just went snicksnicksnicksnicksnick five times and Boon still blasting away and he broke a plate-glass window that cost McCaslin forty-five dollars and hit a negro woman who happened to be passing in the leg only Major de Spain paid for that [. . .].[34]

In this scene, the McCaslin who pays for Boon's broken window is not Isaac but his cousin, McCaslin Edmonds, because Isaac is a child during the incident. The onomatopoeic effect of this passage signifies the black man's gun failing to fire, but in missing the man Boon hits a black woman in her leg.

This episode is depicted very differently in *The Reivers*. In the later rendition, Boon steals the gun from John Powell, a co-worker at Lucius's father's stable, rather than borrowing it from de Spain's coachman, and his dispute is with an African American co-worker named Ludus, left unnamed in the earlier telling. In the version recounted in *The Reivers*, Lucius pursues an enraged Boon and witnesses the episode in person:

> We hadn't even reached the end of the alley when we heard the shots, all five of them: whow whow whow whow whow like that, then we were in the Square and (it wasn't far: right at the corner in front of Cousin Isaac McCaslin's hardware store) we could see it. (17)

The onomatopoeia represents five shots successfully fired by Boon's gun rather than five failed shots from his target's, and Priest goes on to describe how

> one of Boon's bullets (they never did find where the other four went) had shattered after creasing the buttock of a Negro girl who was now lying on the pavement screaming until Cousin Ike himself came jumping out of the store and drowned her voice with his. (17)

An especially significant divergence in the two representations is the role that Isaac plays, both in the incident and in Jefferson's economic life. Rather than the property-eschewing Isaac of *Go Down, Moses*, Priest describes him as owning property in the square, at the centre of Jefferson's social economy.

In contrast, Ike's earliest published appearance, in the opening pages of *Go Down, Moses*, immediately identifies him as a character who has removed himself from Jefferson's capitalist economy:

> McCaslin, 'Uncle Ike,' . . . uncle to half a county and father to no one . . . who in all his life had owned but one object more than he could wear

and carry in his pockets and his hands at one time [. . .] who owned no property and never desired to since the earth was no man's but all men's, as light and air and weather were.[35]

Go Down, Moses begins with a clear and unambiguous portrayal of McCaslin's ascetic lifestyle and his symbolic – and racially loaded – honorific status as 'uncle' to Jefferson's white population. This depiction of Isaac predates his depiction in Priest's narrative and, because it is related by an omniscient narrator, has greater narrative authority to define Isaac in relation to the other citizens of the town. Priest, on the other hand, ensures that his representation of Isaac is less morally ambiguous.

Perhaps because of the closer familial relationship, Priest refers to Ike as 'Cousin Isaac', 'Cousin Ike' and even, in a direct address to the narratee, 'your cousin Ike' (17, 22, 23). Isaac is relegated from uncle to cousin, and the principles he represents in *Go Down, Moses* are similarly undermined. The Ike of the earlier novel refutes all his worldly possessions in an effort to escape the shame of his grand-father's adulterous and incestuous affair with his enslaved daughter. While Priest does refer to Isaac's 'abdication' of inheritance, he does not explain his cousin's act as a conscious refutation of ownership in the specific context of a shameful racial history (21). Instead, Isaac's act of repudiation is elided in Priest's conservative retelling, and is not permitted to undermine his white supremacist agenda. Ike's job in the town square is not itself a shocking revision of the town's history, but his ownership of the store is.

In *The Mansion* (1959), Isaac is also described as working in the hardware store Mink visits shortly before he murders Huston: 'he crossed the Square and entered the hardware store where McCaslin was junior partner.'[36] As in *The Reivers*, the hardware store is located on the courthouse square, signalling the significance of McCaslin's role in the town's economic infrastructure. However, in *The Mansion*, McCaslin is described only as 'junior partner', in keeping with his reluctance to assume the full responsibility of material ownership. In this earlier rendition, McCaslin works in the store, rather than owning it. It is an inconsistency in Priest's narrative that a character who, from his earliest appearance in the cycle, is described as unwilling to own property should own a business that sells material to others. The hardware store represents not only ownership but also the facility to maintain and create new items of property, and represents an investment not only in the real estate of the town but also in the town's collective ability to exploit black labour. Between the two iterations of the shooting, the personnel is changed almost entirely, as is the date on which the incident is supposed to have occurred. *Go Down, Moses* makes it clear that Isaac gives up his inheritance in 1888 at the age of twenty-one, and the shooting is described as having happened some years earlier. In this narrative, Priest would not have been born, let alone capable of witnessing the events. Priest is precise in locating the scene chronologically – 'this was 1905, remember' – but the scene could not possibly have occurred at that point in Faulkner's extended fictive chronology, despite the narrator's insistence that it did (16).

Not only does Priest misrepresent Isaac as deeply invested in property, but he also depicts him as more concerned with the maintenance of his property than with the welfare of Jefferson's black population. Isaac drowns out the voice of the young black woman with his own, an action that symbolically undermines his decision to, effectively, speak for his African American relatives by renouncing the racialised burden of his inheritance. Priest alters Isaac to more easily fit his paradigm of southern masculinity in the early part of the twentieth century. Isaac's compromising involvement in the town's economic life coincides in this opening narrative with a legally suspect arrangement between Lucius's wealthy white family and their employees. Black and white labourers are subjected to the bargaining of wealthier white representatives of the Jefferson legal system in *The Reivers* in a scene that Priest presents as humorous but which I read as pointedly troubling. Through metaphor and creative interpretation of the law, Judge Stevens and Maury Priest establish arrangements that effectively constitute bonded labour. Stevens agrees to financially punish Boon or Ludus for doing anything that 'don't suit' Maury (19). Stevens, notionally the representative of federal and local law in the town, is depicted by Priest as having a laissez-faire attitude and exploiting black and white labour: 'if such a bond is not legal, it ought to be' (19). Priest stages a metaphor for enslavement involving one black and one biracial character (although Boon's Native American heritage is consistently marginalised in Priest's narrative) as a joke, but Faulkner presents the scene as ironic.

Boon's identity within the town is conceived by Priest as itself a commodity jointly owned by a number of the town's prominent families as his ability to work is legally owned by Maury Priest. Boon is a 'corporation, a holding company in which the three of us – McCaslins, De Spain and General Compson – had mutually equal but completely undefined shares of responsibility' (21). Rather than a member of the community, Boon is 'a mutual benevolent protective benefit association' (21). The description of Boon as a 'holding company' recalls Emily Grierson's status as a ward of the town where she is described as

> A tradition, a duty, and a care; a sort of hereditary obligation upon the town, dating from that day in 1894 when Colonel Sartoris, the mayor – he who fathered the edict that no Negro woman should appear on the streets without an apron – remitted her taxes.[37]

In the story, racial etiquette is inextricably bound to the office of the mayor and the town-wide regard of Grierson as an embodiment of the Lost Cause.

While the codification of racial etiquette is explicitly outlined in 'A Rose for Emily', it is masked and obscured in *The Reivers*. In both cases, these characters are figured as economic commodities or unavoidable overheads in the financial life of the town rather than being conceived of as persons by the town's population at large. As a result, Boon is effectively the property of the town in Priest's revision of the cycle, and Priest does this in an attempt to assert his authority over the town. Faulkner's earlier work, however, has previously established a claim of authority over the depiction of Boon that conflicts directly with Priest's.

In my reading, Priest's story is one among a number of competing narratives that Faulkner deploys and which collectively constitute the fictional town of Jefferson by representing different corners of its history from text to text. In staging these discrepancies across his fiction, Faulkner positions Priest's narrative as one voice among many, each of which is of Faulkner's own invention. I interpret these discrepancies as indicative of a satire of white supremacist ideology in the South at mid-century drawn out of the dramatic irony present in Priest's retelling of Jefferson's story. Faulkner simultaneously invents an ideologically biased narrative and undermines it through the recurrence of tropes and characters that he defined earlier. Faulkner further undermines Priest's narrative by populating it with at least one Jeffersonian who does not pre-exist Priest and yet cannot be incorporated into Priest's self-sanctioned revision.

Priest's revision is evaded by the black Jeffersonians he describes, especially in the case of the character whose naming is most reflective of a personal relationship with the town, Ned, who insists on introducing himself on numerous occasions in full as 'Ned William McCaslin Jefferson Mississippi'. Ned cannot be successfully incorporated into Priest's self-sanctioned history because his relation to the Priest family is burdensome and his persistence in their daily lives is their inadvertent 'inheritance' from their philandering ancestor, LQC McCaslin: '. . . he – Ned – was a McCaslin, born in the McCaslin back yard in 1860. He was our family skeleton; we inherited him in turn . . .' (32). Furthermore, Ned is drawn through intertextual allusion to biblical sources and Faulkner positions him in opposition to Priest's conservative agenda. Subtexts such as those through which Ned's character is developed undermine Priest's claim to authority. When the trio of reivers returns from Memphis to Jefferson, Ned makes his manipulation of the town's racist economy apparent, and, I argue, Faulkner stages this manipulation as a biblical allegory, underscoring Ned's resistance to Priest's dominant narrative. This intertextual construction establishes Ned's resistance as more than simply the mischief that Priest routinely incorporates into his paternalistic narrative. Ned's shrewdness also sets him apart from the Priest family's privileged position as employers. Ned's self-interest is made legible when the novel is read through New Testament biblical analogues. Firstly, Ned, Boon and Lucius's encounter with the 'mud farmer' at Hell Creek Bottom is a parody of the Exodus myth and Moses' crossing of the Red Sea. Rather than a doorway to freedom, the 'sea' the trio must traverse in order to reach Memphis is an exploitative, economic trap (82). Bobo Beauchamp's financial difficulties are consistently cast as analogous to the parable of the Prodigal Son, reimagined in the context of race relations in the South. In Ned's words, Bobo has 'give[n] up Missippi cotton farming and take[n] up Memphis frolicking and gambling for a living in place of it', but when he returns to his employer he is not welcomed back as in the biblical narrative (272). Instead, Mr van Tosch assumes a paternalistic tone when discussing Bobo with Ned: '"But why didn't he come to me?" Mr van Tosch said. "He did," Ned said. "You told him No"' (269). The capital N of Ned's final 'No' is a typographical effect that represents the nuances of Ned's speech on the page and underscores the divergence from the source parable. Comparing this typographical effect with the starkly separated phrase that opens the novel, 'Grandfather said', suggests that van Tosch's position as a benevolent patriarch is as unstable as Priest's claim to narrative authority.

More specifically, Faulkner constructs Ned in a way that I interpret as highlighting Ned's challenge to Jefferson's social economy. Faulkner's use of biblical analogues conveys Ned's shrewd behaviour in the light of the New Testament Parable of the Talents, from Matthew 25, and the related Parable of the Minas in Luke 19. In Matthew's parable, an absentee 'lord' divides his belongings into talents, a unit of currency that represents the worth of 6,000 denarii. One denarius constitutes payment for one day's labour, and a talent represents the worth of 6,000 days labouring, roughly sixteen and a half years. In an economy such as this, the equivalency between labour and capital is more direct and acute than in a modern capitalist economy: money is a more direct metaphor for time spent labouring.[38] In Matthew, a landowner leaves five talents to one servant, two to the next, and one to the third 'to every man according to his several ability'.[39] The master's trust in his servants is predicated on their value as workers, with each entrusted with capital equivalent to the master's esteem. The first two servants invest the money and double its value before the master's return, while the third hides his talent for safekeeping. When the lord returns from travelling he rewards the first two servants for increasing his financial worth and punishes the third for failing to accrue interest. The third servant is described as 'wicked and slothful' for failing to invest the money.[40] The details of the parable are much the same in Luke, in which a 'nobleman' gives each of ten servants a mina, and, upon his return, receives ten from a first servant and five from a second.[41] The first is awarded with dominion over ten cities in the man's kingdom, and the second with five. As in Matthew, a third servant is punished for returning his master's money without interest.[42]

Conventionally, these parables are interpreted as allegories about rewarding hard work and good service. Each parable ends with the master declaring that 'every one which hath shall be given; and from him that hath not, even that he hath shall be taken away from him'.[43] These sentiments are usually interpreted as encouraging people to make the most of their personal 'talents' and achieve success in their lives. However, the mercenary punishment exacted by each biblical lord contradicts other New Testament parables, especially Christ's teaching that 'blessed are the meek', that 'it is easier for a camel to go through the eye of a needle, than for a rich man to enter the kingdom of heaven', and that 'the last shall be first, and the first last'.[44] These better-known ethical directives suggest that earthly structures of wealth are anathema to Christian morality, and that worldly poverty is rewarded while avarice is punished. In contrast, both the Parable of the Talents and the Parable of the Minas seem to advocate brutal and violent punishment for servants who fail to return a master's money 'with usury'.[45]

In the parables, the rewarded servants do not profit from their shrewdness but from their master's supposed benevolence. In contrast in *The Reivers*, Ned profits directly from his shrewdness and duplicity in the horse race, while Boss Priest makes a financial loss for having trusted his employee to serve Priest's interests over Ned's own. Ned anticipates this outcome early in the novel when he excuses trading the automobile for the horse, observing 'it would have tooken a braver man than me to just took his automobile back to him. But maybe this horse will save you' (113). In my reading, Ned manipulates the parable's mandate to usury to his own advantage as an excuse for his illicit behaviour. After Ned profits by betting on the opposing horse in the race against Acheron, he excuses his decision not to repay Boss Priest's investment in the race, alleging that it would be an 'insult' to do so:

'When I offers to pay his gambling debt, ain't I telling him to his face he ain't got enough sense to bet on horses? And when I tells him where the money come from, I'm gonter pay it with, ain't I proving it?' (284)

Not only does Ned masquerade as a faithful 'servant' by pretending to return his employer's investment with interest, but he also takes advantage of the deference expected of him for his own financial interests. Ned has no reason to be anything other than self-serving, just as the biblical servant who refused to deposit money in a bank is not 'wicked and slothful' but self-interested. In *The Reivers*, the Parable of the Talents is a metaphor for the exploitation of black labour in the South and for resistance against such exploitation.[46] Faulkner's rewriting of the parable inversely echoes Priest's rewriting of Faulkner's town. Priest's attempt to rewrite the town's history is an attempt to neutralise the racial complexes of the cycle, but Faulkner ensures that the Yoknapatawpha cycle survives Priest's assault. Priest's revision of the cycle is mirrored in the novel's cyclical narrative structure, too.

Just as prominent events and characters recur across various novels and stories, so too this novel is structured cyclically, and in this way Faulkner reasserts his claim to authority. The novel's opening phrase, 'Grandfather said', is echoed in its closing line. On the first occasion it is printed in stark capitals, which, with the inclusion of a colon, act as a visual marker of narrative distance (7). The phrase is separate from everything that follows and the immediate past indicated by the use of 'said' suggests a temporal moment subsequent to that of the narration which is 'past' at the moment of transcription. The temporal confusion inherent in this ostensibly simple phrase serves to distance the grandson from the grandfather's narrative, and the grandfather from the moment of narration. While Priest is careful to avoid locating himself in the present moment of narration rather than the historical moment being narrated, his removal from the idealised Jefferson he both depicts and seeks to represent is covertly signalled in the novel. Privileging Jefferson's traditional treatment of elderly whites, Priest is bitter in his reference to nursing homes as 'cubicled euphemisms with names pertaining to sunset' (45). Tellingly, this description is itself a euphemism, with Priest strenuously avoiding outright discussion of nursing homes, or suggesting that he is resident at one at the time of his narration, preferring to site his narrative in Jefferson's central town square in the first instance.

In an echo of the novel's opening phrase, *The Reivers* concludes when Lucius is introduced to Boon and Everbe's baby and is made aware that the child has been named in his honour: '"What are you going to call it?" "Not it," she said. "Him. Can't you guess?" "What?" I said. "His name is Lucius Priest Hogganbeck," she said' (284). This brief exchange also draws attention to the faux-orality of Priest's narrative through repetition of the word 'said'. The novel ends, as it begins, with reported speech and allusion to earlier instalments in the cycle, as well as characters created by Faulkner that predate Priest.

While it closes the circular narrative of *The Reivers*, the exchange above also invokes earlier moments in the Yoknapatawpha cycle, signalling the novel as the culmination of a wider narrative. Everbe invites Priest to 'guess' the name of her son, while readers of Faulkner's earlier works will be familiar with the name before it is even spoken, because Lucius Hogganbeck appears in Faulkner's published fiction earlier than Lucius Priest. Apparently inheriting his father's fascination with cars, Lucius Hogganbeck is described in *The Mansion* as the proprietor of an 'automobile jitney' in Jefferson's town square before Mink Snopes murders Jack Huston, thereby locating him more securely in the economy of the town square than in Priest's recollection of collecting freight bills.[47] Within the chronology of *The Mansion*, this would locate Hogganbeck's taxi business in 1908, during Eula Snopes's pregnancy.[48] This timeframe would either make Lucius Hogganbeck a singularly enterprising three-year-old or Lucius Priest an unreliable narrator.

Priest reworks the history of the town in order to communicate a narrative in which his white supremacist agenda is successfully imparted to his grandson, and, in doing so, he restructures the physical layout of Jefferson at its very centre. Pre-existing histories of the town challenge his revisions and the courthouse square presented by Priest as the seat of his narrative authority is instead a textual rejoinder to Priest's attempt to co-opt the history of the town. For instance, when Priest locates Isaac McCaslin in the square's economic nexus, earlier representations of both the square and Isaac undermine his narrative. The superficial reading of *The Reivers* encouraged by its first critics overlooks how the meaning of the square within a typology of the archetypal fictional town can derail Priest's agenda, denying, as they do, that Priest has a political agenda at all.

Writing about another novel published in 1962, David Bradley condemned *The Reivers* as 'less a reminiscence than an avoidance'.[49] While I agree with Bradley's assessment, I argue that it is Priest and not Faulkner who avoids discussion of 'a time when southern conflicts were so much a part of the national consciousness'.[50] Bradley reads *The Reivers* in contrast to William Melvin Kelley's *A Different Drummer* (1962), and while Faulkner's last novel is 'remarkably mute' on direct action against segregation, Kelley's first novel is anything but. In *A Different Drummer* a fictional southern town is the setting through which an African American writer is able to imagine immediate and wide-ranging action against segregation in the South. In the novel, every black inhabitant of a fictional southern state deliberately abandons their home. This mass exodus leaves white men like Lucius Priest to understand and record the history of race in the South.

CHAPTER 6

Knowing How to Curse:
William Melvin Kelley's Sutton

In an essay for a 1968 issue of *The Partisan Review*, poet Calvin Israel recalls a chance meeting with William Faulkner in Washington Square Park in New York in 1956. The title of the article, 'The Last Gentleman', is suggestive of Walker Percy's 1966 novel of the same name and positions Faulkner as the last vestige of a southern literary aristocracy. Israel describes the ageing Nobel Laureate as 'a quiet center of great activity' amid the bustle of the city park.[1] When Israel notices Faulkner's 'detachment' from people around them, he confronts the author about his controversial stated views on racial gradualism. Faulkner responds with the single word 'Violence' before abruptly ending the encounter.[2] Israel underscores Faulkner's legacy as it was understood in the late 1960s: he is made redolent of a lost tradition and epitomises a failure to act against racial segregation.

Coincidentally, Israel's memoir of Faulkner is preceded in the same edition of *The Partisan Review* by 'An Appeal' issued by John Young, Chairman of the Boston chapter of the Congress of Racial Equality (CORE).[3] Young's letter makes a plea for aid to 'Negroes in rural Mississippi areas subsisting partially on grass, and begging for food and / or money at Civil Rights headquarters in their various localities'.[4] Poverty and hunger are presented as facts of life in the 'various localities' of typical southern towns. Young's emphasis on how a clear and present threat to black life exists 'not in some economically backward country . . . [but] in the United States of America, the richest country on Earth' throws Faulkner's anachronistic gradualism into relief.[5] Young's and Israel's very different pieces of writing represent two voices in the discourse of race in the South at the end of the 1960s. The same issue's main feature, a symposium of black and white intellectuals on the topic of Black Power, represents still more voices. Included in the (all-men) group of black and white activists are Ivanhoe Donaldson and Abbie Hoffman, Norman Mailer and Nathan Wright Jr. and New York–born African American novelist William Melvin Kelley. In his essay, Kelley aims his acerbic commentary on American race relations directly at an imagined white reader. He describes the emergence of the ideology of Black Power as a necessary outcome of racial difference, both cultural ('I thought that everybody knew the difference between James Brown and Elvis Presley, or Willie Mays and Mickey Mantle . . .') and historical ('Our ancestors did not want to come to the United States, yours did').[6] In this chapter, I argue that Kelley's first novel, *A Different Drummer* (1962), represents a departure from the models of the fictional southern town explored earlier in this study. His fictional southern town, Sutton, is a thought experiment concerning a hypothetical, racially separatist, reconstitution of the South's social landscape.

The model of developing the setting of the southern town as a subtle critique of segregation was not enough for Kelley. Unlike the novels discussed in earlier chapters, *A Different Drummer* is not content with positioning an archetypal town as a fly in the ointment of segregationist ideology. Instead, Kelley demands that the critique inherent to the portrayal of the small town be felt throughout the nation. This chapter argues that Kelley's engagement with the trope of the town first engages with the existing typology in his treatment of a grocery store porch before expanding his critique beyond the town of Sutton, first through the South and then to the entire nation. In the novel, Kelley imagines the literal manifestation of the intellectual difference along racial lines that he would later describe in 'Black Power'. It is a depiction of a typical small town that must come to terms with a new, mono-racial identity following the sudden departure of all of its African American citizens. In Kelley's short essay, he asserts an essential difference between white and black Americans that derives largely from his assessment of Old World traditions: 'You remained, essentially, a European people. We remained an African people.'[7] In Kelley's essay, one of the most fundamental issues of divergence between what he sees as white and black American cultures is the rift between the written and the spoken word: 'You had books, libraries . . . And we, those of us whose ancestors came from Africa, we had, still have, an oral tradition.'[8] It is this perceived rift in heritage, between the closed, written tradition, and the relatively accessible oral tradition that brings Kelley to his stark conclusion on the origins of the Black Power movement: 'We are different.'[9]

The juxtaposition of Israel's memories of Faulkner's detachment and Kelley's intellectual engagement with black power in the same issue of *The Partisan Review* is striking, especially given the further coincidence that Kelley's first novel, *A Different Drummer*, was published in the same year as Faulkner's last, *The Reivers* (1962). Kelley's remarks on orality and written discourse are anticipated and problematised in *A Different Drummer*. Kelley dramatises how white-authored narratives – both oral and written – about African American and southern histories consistently fail to account for the sudden departure of a fictional southern state's entire African American community. The community space of the porch of the town's grocery store is the hub for white narratives of the town, and I read the men on the porch as a microcosm of the white men of Sutton and the South. The grocery store itself serves the function within a typology of the fictional southern town of providing food and other goods for consumption. White men who represent different offices, and different social strata, congregate in the public and commercial space of the porch. While Kelley, like the white authors discussed in previous chapters, imagines the town of Sutton as 'typical' of southern towns, the larger context in which he places the town is atypical. Kelley imagines an entire American state that is decidedly different from any recognisable, existing state in the Union. He deliberately eschews representation of an identifiable southern state in order to better imagine the hypothetical ramifications of his invented exodus on the South and the rest of the nation.

As was the case with Lillian Smith and Carson McCullers, reviewers dismissed Kelley's narrative technique as secondary to his political engagement, and tend not to consider how the novel's form and plot are shaped by his racial politics. One critic condemns the novel as neither 'fresh [nor] imaginative' and as suffering from similarities to other novels of the period, making it merely 'another poignant study of the injustice and moral corrosion of race prejudice and racial discrimination' that fails because its author is 'intensely interested in social protest'.[10] Another reviewer writes that Kelley 'has put an effective prose style at the service of an aroused social conscience instead of his imagination'.[11] This critical ambivalence to the novel is reflected in a tension between literary esteem and financial success: he was awarded $2,000 by the National Institute of Arts and Letters in 1963, with judges commending the novel as a 'considerable literary achievement, although not a commercial success'.[12] However, as Eric Sundquist describes, the novel 'faded from view after very brief acclaim'.[13] Over the last two decades, critics have sought to recuperate Kelley's novel within the southern literary canon, with Trudier Harris describing *A Different Drummer* as 'a fertile point of departure' for studying 'the development of southern black fiction',[14] and Eric Gary Anderson responding by decrying the 'general critical ignorance' of Kelley and his work.[15] Rather than placing the novel in a temporal trajectory of the 'development' of African American southern fiction, I trace the development within the novel of competing narratives of southern identity.[16] The current chapter argues that Kelley's radical departure from the racially liberal deployment of the southern town reflects that radicalisation of the black freedom struggle that would continue through the rest of the 1960s.

When the novel opens, the mass exodus is an event that has irrevocably altered the social make-up of the South and is already a matter of historical record in the fictive present. An extract from the fictional *Thumb-Nail Almanac* stages the fictive present as 1961 before the narrative proper reorients itself to June 1957, the month in which *'for reasons yet to be determined, all the state's Negro inhabitants departed'*.[17] The *Almanac* sites the narrative that follows in the same historical moment as William Faulkner's *The Reivers'* framing narrative. Lucius Priest seeks to co-opt the history of the South in service of segregation, but Kelley explores an anti-nostalgic recent past. Complementing the cold factual account of the almanac, Kelley depicts another narrative delivered to a group of white men on the porch of Thomason's grocery store in the small town of Sutton. Mister Harper, the keeper of the town's collective memory, is driven by partial local knowledge and myth surrounding Tucker Caliban, whose actions instigate a wholesale exodus from an unnamed southern state, and his enslaved ancestor named only as 'the African'. When the African is finally killed in the midst of a slave revolt, his son is taken as property by the town's prominent Willson family. Willson's son Dewey – who would go on to become a celebrated general in the Confederacy – names the child Caliban after the character in Shakespeare's *The Tempest*. Generations later, 'Caliban' has become the surname of a family of African Americans who continue to work for the Willson family until, in the fictive present, Tucker Caliban manifests his namesake's threat to Prospero: 'You taught me language; and my profit on't / Is, I know how to curse.'[18] Tucker Caliban and his wife Bethrah destroy and abandon their property in Sutton before leaving the state for ever. Kelley's Caliban salts the earth on the small farm he owns and burns his home to the ground before abandoning his town and state. Although Caliban never intervenes in the lives of the rest of the state's black citizens, every one of them follows suit and abandons the state in a mass exodus.

This fable-like plot has encouraged readings of the novel as an allegory for the black freedom movement, with Erica Edwards highlighting the novel's treatment of a diffused, grassroots model of black leadership: 'the black residents who depopulate their segregated town are political agents arching toward something else in the interval between the known and the unknown, the seen and the unseen, the here and the there, the shouted and the hushed.'[19] In Edwards's reading, the exodus of the black people of Sutton forces them into an interstitial, undefined space, while Sundquist argues that 'exile is presented not as a problem of epic global migrations but rather as a philosophical conundrum to be teased out on a local scale' in what he describes as 'Kelley's Afro-Zionism'.[20] In my reading, the black residents' action neither remains local nor is it merely a retreat into the liminal. Rather, the impact of the exodus from Kelley's invented small town, and his imaginary state, is felt in the rest of the nation. It restructures the racial landscape of the entire United States by displacing millions of black southerners. Kelley presents a white southern community that is entirely unable to understand the newly all-white space of the town of Sutton. Where Byron Herbert Reece's *The Hawk and the Sun* depicts a white lynch mob enforcing racial integrity, in *A Different Drummer* Sutton is rendered wholly white as the result of black self-determination. Where James Loewen conceives of 'the sundown town' as one that is 'all-white on purpose', for Kelley's Sutton it is the African American residents, not the whites, who desegregate the town 'on purpose'.[21]

The cumulative voice of the white southern community is crucial to an understanding of the imaginative construction of Kelley's Sutton. Kelley's white porch-sitters are presented as a microcosm of the typical white South. Kelley explores how a white southern mentality confronted with, what is to them, an inexplicable and sudden desegregation of the South. Kelley dramatises the process through which white children are socialised into the masculine community of the porch and examines the failure of a white-community narrative to account for black civil disobedience. Because the group is typical, it responds to change and confusion with recourse to racial violence. While Sutton breaks the mould I outline in earlier chapters, it remains structured by the principles of racial etiquette and violence. The construction of this condensed and representative unit of the imagined southern white community is most fully realised when the group vents its frustration through the lynching of the last remaining African American in the town.

The Porch: Kelley's Microcosm of White Community

The spatial organisation of the town of Sutton is geographically and ideologically grounded in white-led narratives of southern history, similar to the one Lucius Priest invents in *The Reivers*. Kelley positions the men on the porch as observers of the passage of time and of the drastic change in southern demographics that he depicts, drawing as he does on the literary tradition of the southern porch in black and white southern fiction. Simultaneously, the voyeuristic group of men is itself the subject of observation as Kelley demonstrates the processes of socialisation that make up such a group. The white boy Mister Leland's childhood is a process of development into the raced and gendered community of the porch. Kelley represents the porch as a venue for a second-person narrative voice when Harper directly addresses his neighbours with his story of the town, and Kelley's literary technique exposes how contemporary white thinking on race fails to account for the sudden exodus sparked by Tucker Caliban. Kelley, unlike Lillian Smith, Reece and Carson McCullers, refuses to site optimism for racial progress in a gradualist conviction in progressive generational change

Kelley's narrative of the southern town differs from the white-authored novels I discuss elsewhere because he refuses the paradigm whereby individual representatives stand for an entire community's capacity for change. Instead, he presents a white community that has already failed to accommodate sudden racial change. Kelley not only figures white southerners as incapable of overturning segregation, but also consistently negates their ability to narrate and define desegregation. *A Different Drummer* effectively addresses and discards the motifs for understanding segregation through the metonymic fictional towns that I have traced in white-authored fiction from *Strange Fruit* to *The Reivers*. While I have argued that these white southern novelists were not, as novelist David Bradley suggests, 'remarkably mute' in representing segregation in fiction, none of the novels I have explored provides so stark a conclusion to segregation as Kelley's.[22]

In opposition to the paradigmatic treatments of the southern town, segregation in *A Different Drummer* is observed only in retrospect. Following a dispassionate historical record of local racial history, the narrative proper begins with the line: 'It was over now' (5). The confused temporality of this brief and stark opening sentence features both the past and present, announcing the narrative's retrospective focalisation and the text's concern with the 'now'. Kelley imagines a South in which exploited African Americans are themselves the architects of desegregation, and he does so by exploring the failure of the abandoned white community to understand the ramifications of the racial sea change. The imaginative experiment of Kelley's exodus is tested in the laboratory of the fictional southern town established over the previous three decades. Kelley organises the entire town around principles of white supremacy predicated on a white-governed sense of southern tradition and the statue of General Willson in its square geographically centres the town. As in Faulkner's *The Reivers* and McCullers's *Clock Without Hands*, the town square, complete with Confederate monument, symbolises the ideological centre of the white population's collective identity. Radiating out from this centre is assembled a socially representative group of white men through whom Kelley explores the town's failure to understand or adapt to the exodus.

In the novel's fictive present, Civil War 'hero' General Willson continues to anchor the town both spatially and ideologically, because the statue erected in his honour stands 'in the center of town' (28). The nominally objective account of the town's history recorded in the almanac suggests that the process of becoming a symbolic ideological leader can be fatal:

> *On April 5, 1889, having just returned from the dedication of a ten-foot bronze statue of himself which the townspeople of Sutton had erected in their Square, [Willson] was stricken and died. He is considered by most historians to have been, after Lee, the Confederacy's greatest general.* (4)

This short passage describes, in very quick succession, Willson's transformation into the symbolic centre of his hometown, his death, and the subsequent academic consensus of his contribution to the Confederate cause. If the national memory of the Civil War remembers Willson as second only to Lee, the town of Sutton remembers Lee as second only to Willson: 'Lee Street' runs east to west through the square that commemorates Willson (29).[23] Kelley positions the white supremacist 'Lost Cause' narrative of the Civil War as a physical structuring principal for the town, suggesting a corollary ideological foundation.

Sutton is insular and static within the broader geography of the novel and is only described in relation to other places in the state. General Wilson and Mister Harper are educated at West Point, but the New York academy is not positioned in relation to the town or anywhere else in the state (3, 7). On the other hand, the grocery store porch on which Harper and the other white men congregate is defined as a point between the state's capital and its major port:

> being on the Highway between New Marsails and Willson City, [the men]
> had watched the line of cars crammed with Negroes and enough belong-
> ings to convince the men that the Negroes had not gone to all this trouble
> to move a mere hundred miles. (6)

In this passage, 'the Negroes' are consistently figured as the object of the sentence, for which the white observers are the collective subject. This same position on the highway recalls Dewitt Willson's search for his escaped enslaved African during which he and the militia he gathers are 'camped a little north of New Marsails' (21). The narrative colonialism of Harper and the other men is thereby implicitly connected to Dewitt Willson's project of ownership. In Harper's telling, the African is larger than life and capable of impossible feats and needs to be shot multiple times before succumbing to his injuries (23–4). Harper tells his tale on the communal porch, between the commercial space of the grocery store and the highway. The porch is a space from which the white men observe and recall the state's shifting racial landscape while they remain physically and ideologically static. Within the geography of Sutton, the men on the porch are uniquely positioned to witness and report the exodus. They occupy a space on the town's main road; they are stationary but they witness and comment on the movement of others and they are led by the most stationary of them all, the wheelchair-bound Mister Harper.

Kelley's Harper, like Reece's Harker, is the subject of nominative determinism. Harper's role in the community is to 'harp' on the subject of local racial history. Harper is drawn in overt opposition to the mobile and migratory black population of the state:

> So, thirty years before, he decided life was not worth meeting on foot,
> since it always knocked you down, and seated himself in a wheel chair to
> view the world from the porch, explaining its chaotic pattern to the men
> who clustered around him each day. (7)

Harper's elected stasis signals his ideological opposition to the mobilisation of the state's African Americans who escape its 'chaotic pattern'.[24] Harper's belief that 'life was not worth meeting on foot' suggests that he will be utterly incapable of composing a narrative to explain millions of people mobilising to extricate themselves from segregation As Stephanie Li argues, 'Mister Harper's story reveals more insight into the nature of whiteness than into the reality of black subjects.'[25] I would add that his narrative simultaneously buttresses a white supremacist ideology and seeks to maintain the town's existing racial epistemology, despite its obvious irrelevance after the exodus.

Harper conceives of Caliban's sudden civil disobedience through pseudo-scientific recourse to his African heritage. Harper insists on a biological imperative, saying, 'But the way I see it, it's pure genetics: something special in the blood [. . .] It's got to be the African's blood! That's simple!' (8) Harper's insistence on a genealogy of dissent against the South's racial order is predicated on white racial anxieties evident in the novel's white community. 'Black leadership', as Edwards summarises, is 'the white characters' worst nightmare and their preferred model for making sense of their social reality.'[26] This paradox explains Harper's compulsion to understand Caliban's revolutionary act from within an epistemology that can no longer adequately account for the South's shifting racial identity. Harper's insistence on old narratives and old modes of thought is analogous to his, and his observers', failure to metaphorically move with the times. If the Exodus narrative in African American culture represents, in Anna Hartnell's terms, 'an entrance to and an exit from the privileged [. . .] terrains of US national culture',[27] then Kelley's choice to locate his pseudo-Greek-chorus on the road to and through the town of Sutton allows the white men to observe the exodus from the state as a trajectory through US national and racial identity. By situating his abandoned white community on the porch, Kelley also reorients the typical significations of the porch in southern literature and culture.

Jocelyn Hazelwood Donlon addresses, albeit in a sentimental tone, the symbolic relationship between the southern porch and community-wide nostalgia when she writes:

One prevailing notion that spans cultural boundaries and characterizes the South as a whole is that the porch, though used less frequently today than in the past, remains integral to a southern identity. Though we routinely sound the death knell of the front porch, it continues to endure – if not always in reality, at least in our memories.[28]

Donlon replicates the nostalgic and utopian image of white southern community that Kelley undercuts in his deployment of the trope in *A Different Drummer*. Donlon proposes a totalising southern community, represented by the pronoun 'we', defined by a stable and shared sense of identity and a collective and idealised vision of the past. As I argue in the previous chapter, these same presumptions and the same politics of memory underscore the narrative discourse Faulkner deploys in *The Reivers*. In that novel, Lucius Priest looks back over his life in the small southern town of Jefferson and in looking backwards forges his own idealised history of the South in the twentieth century. In *A Different Drummer*, Kelley creates and critiques a community of Lucius Priests who collectively and individually seek to understand a suddenly desegregated present solely through recourse to a heroic and digestible narrative of a coherent southern past.

The porch on which the action of *A Different Drummer* takes place is not the entrance to a private home but to a small business serving the practical needs of the community. In Zora Neale Hurston's *Their Eyes Were Watching God* (1937), the porch is a linguistic synecdoche for the African American women who share it, as when the protagonist Janie walks away feeling 'the porch pelting her back with unasked questions'.[29] In this passage, the African American women on the porch metaphorically assault Janie with their gossip. On the other hand, the porch in *Their Eyes Were Watching God* operates as a space of intimacy in a way that the porch in *A Different Drummer* does not. When Janie tells her story to her friend Phoeby the porch comes to signify their homosocial community, underscored by Janie's description of their dialogue: 'mah tongue is in mah friend's mouf'.[30] In Kelley's novel, the porch occupies a position in a typology that makes it primarily the site of commercial transactions rather than intimate friendships.

As the entrance to a business, Kelley's porch complies with other conventions of the front porch in the literature of the South, such as those depicted in McCullers's 'The Ballad of the Sad Café'. In this earlier novella, the porch is a space of community in which the white people of the fictional small town congregate, but it remains a space of potential violence. The hamlet reacts with a collective expectation of violence when the protagonist, Amelia, is insulted by her estranged husband: 'So now if Miss Amelia had split open Marvin Macy's head with the axe on the back porch no one would have been surprised.'[31] Here, the proprietor of the business to which the porch is affixed has a symbolic ownership of her patrons and the image of the porch is more threatening.

The place of the porch in an iconography of the rural South is such that, in Edward Albee's stage adaptation of McCullers's novella, the porch constitutes an important part of the visual grammar of the southern town:

> Miss Amelia's *house must be practical, in the sense that its interior will be used, both upstairs and down, and, as well, we must be able to see its exterior without entering it. The main street of the town runs before the porch of the house, parallel to the apron of the stage.*[32]

Albee's stage directions make evident the role of the porch as a means of visualising the intimate space of a home from the public space outside by highlighting the significance of seeing inside Amelia's home without entering. Albee chooses to stage the town's main street and the building's porch as two layers of distance from the apron of the stage and the viewing audience beyond. The staging helps to elaborate on Kelley's aesthetics of voyeurism in *A Different Drummer* and helps to explain the ways in which front porches operate as both intimate and public spaces. The porch's capacity to allow people to see inside the business from without is played out in particular in a scene in the novel in which Mister Leland remembers his first meeting with Caliban.

On a summer morning in 1956 Mister Leland observes as Caliban 'entered the store and purchased a bag of feed, started out, then stopped and pointed to the window, speaking to Mister Thomason, who weighed out a full pound of peanuts and poured them into a brown paper sack' (49). The topography of the porch allows Mister Leland to see, but not hear, Caliban's interactions with the store-owner. Caliban's inaudible communication in this passage complies with Li's contention that Caliban '[a]lmost entirely renounces language, affirming that freedom will not be found in words but in action'.[33] The geography of the porch enables Mister Leland to observe Caliban's actions without hearing his words. When Caliban presents Mister Leland with the bag of peanuts and instructs him to 'tell your pa I knows what he trying to do with you', the boy is initially confused, and his father's explanation that 'your mama and me is trying to make you a passable human being' does nothing to allay his confusion (49). In effect, Caliban is rewarding Harry Leland and his son for Harry's efforts in raising Mister Leland to eschew the overt racism of the other white men in Sutton, as when Mister Leland feels guilty for using a racial slur: 'He had been told not to use NIGGER' (33, emphasis in original). This brief exchange on the porch elaborates on the process through which Harry Leland begins to socialise his son into the white community, represented by the men on the porch; Leland's parenting is an extension of a paradigm of racial improvement. Kelley presents the model of gradualist improvement only to roundly reject it by showing how Mister Leland is implicated in existing paradigms of white male sexuality in the town.

As in the other novels I have analysed, unmarried women are spatially and socially marginalised in Sutton. Like Smith's Miss Ada, Kelley's Miss Rickett is maligned in the white community as a sexual predator. When Harry Leland's wife asks him to pay his respects to Miss Rickett because she is ill, he demurs:

Let the boy do it; I'll send the boy over. That woman gives me the willies. I can't see how Marge can't know about her and what she does. But I know she wants a screwing and I ain't about to give it to her. I'll just send the boy. (28, italics in original)

While Leland doesn't expect his son to be a 'victim' of Miss Rickett's desires, he remains willing to sacrifice his son and, by extension, incorporate him into the town's adult sexual economy. By sending Mister Leland into what he thinks of as a *'she-lion's den'*, Harry Leland implicitly sanctions his son's transition from sexual ignorance – what Marge Leland *'can't know'* – to mature, masculine sexual knowledge – *'I know she wants a screwing'* (29). Even though nothing happens to the child, Harry Leland is willing to sacrifice his son to the sexually predatory woman in order to save himself from unwanted attention. He thereby introduces Mister Leland to the sexual norms of white masculinity in Sutton and undermines his own project of raising Mister Leland as 'a passable human being'.

A similar childhood sexual rite is explored and anticipated in 'The Turtles' (1956), an early short story by Ernest J. Gaines. In the story, a young African American boy is pressured by his father into having sex with an unmarried woman, who lives 'back in the fields' away from the rest of the rural black community, in order to make the boy 'a man'.[34] While Gaines's story depicts a reluctant son and a forceful father, in opposition to Kelley's characterisation of the Lelands, Mister Leland's proto-sexual encounter in *A Different Drummer* nevertheless suggests that the child is in the process of becoming another of the men on the porch, with all the ideological baggage that invokes.

The assortment of Sutton's citizens who congregate on the grocery store porch is carefully organised to cross the social barriers between the town's lower and middle classes. Crass Bobby-Joe McCollum, who spits and condescends to Mister Harper, is a crudely drawn archetype of a poor white while Loomis, who 'had been upstate to the university at Willson', is representative of the town's white middle class (7). In racial politics, too, the group represents a cross-section of white attitudes ranging from conservative 'righteous anger' to the racially moderate: 'Harry Leland had gone so far as to express the idea that the Negroes had the right to leave' (6). Leland's position is marked as unusual in the manner in which the omniscient narrator describes a simple opinion on freedom of movement as having 'gone so far'. While the group is relatively inclusive it remains restrictive; only working- and middle-class whites are included in the group and the abiding atmosphere is one of racial conservatism.

The character of the group is mediated by Mister Harper, and the social differences between the other men are rendered moot when he begins to speak. Harper's authority over the group is signalled when he begins his tall tale concerning the African. As the men 'coax' Harper into telling the story, with each instance of reported speech signalled in the text by quotation marks, this practice abruptly shifts, following a line break, as soon as Harper begins his narrative (8, 9). Kelley allows the form of the novel to acquiesce to Harper's authority by altering the punctuation rendered in the text. These visual markers of textual difference subtly indicate a shift in narrative technique from an omniscient third-person voice to a second-person monologue in which Harper directly addresses the assembled group of men.

While relatively rare in literature in English, the second-person narrative voice is unusually prevalent in southern literature at mid-century. I have already discussed how the second-person narrative voice operates in Smith's *Strange Fruit* to conflate the subject positions of fictional characters and an imagined reader and how Faulkner's narrator in *The Reivers* stages his narrative for his grandson in order to predispose an imagined reader to his revisions. In *A Different Drummer*, the second-person voice operates along similar principles, as Bradley recognises: 'Kelley uses precisely the same techniques that Faulkner uses [. . .] and to precisely the same end: to humanize and sympathize characters whose points of view readers might have ignored.'[35] By transposing Harper's narrative from reported speech into a direct address to a named group of narratees, Kelley incorporates an imagined reader into Harper's fantastical tale.

In the southern literary tradition, this form of direct address can be used humorously and to incorporate an imagined reader into the narrative. The opening line of Mark Twain's *The Adventures of Huckleberry Finn* (1884) is comically metafictional even while it constructs a sense of intimacy with the eponymous character: 'You don't know about me without you have read a book by the name of *The Adventures of Tom Sawyer*; but that ain't no matter.'[36] In this case, the fictional character directly addresses an imagined reader, inventing an atmosphere of hospitality in the first-person narrative. Hospitality is used as a form of misdirection, as in Eudora Welty's *The Ponder Heart* (1954). Edna Earle Ponder narrates her family history to a travelling salesman. The novel's fictional Beulah Hotel is a component of the typology of the fictional town that relies on movement through the geography of the town. Edna Earl's coercive hospitality allows the narrator to mediate the narrative as it is received by the narratee and, by extension, an imagined reader. In *A Different Drummer*, Harper excuses his tall tale by describing it as analogous to the biblical story of Samson: 'Might not all be true as you read it in the Bible; folks must-a figured if you got a man just a little bit stronger than most, it couldn't do no real harm to make him a whole lot stronger' (9). Harper directs his listeners, as well as the novel's imagined reader, to a particular mode of reading the narrative of the African. Harper represents the coercive narrative architecture on which Sutton is built.

The second-person narrative voice can also function to incorporate an imagined reader into a collective southern 'memory', as in the section of Shelby Foote's *Jordan County* (1954) titled 'The Freedom Ticket'. This chapter features a monologue that depends on an imagined question asked by an addressee but unreported in the text: 'You ask about that old time. It aint nothing I cant tell you. Kluxers, smut ballots, whipping-bees, all that: I'm in a position to know and I remember, mainly on account of my mamma.'[37] In this passage, 'memory' is a hereditary property: the narrator is able to remember because of similar stories his mother has told him. The narrative is instigated by an imagined question and relayed as though in response to that same fictional question. Similarly, Harper assumes the role of arbiter of Sutton's collective memory and the amassed white men consume his narrative as a founding text of the fictional southern town centred on the Willson family: 'Well, that's the story and you all know as well as me how that baby got named Caliban by the General, when the General was twelve years old' (25). The young Dewey Willson is twice described here as 'the General' despite the anachronism the title engenders in Harper's story. This strange temporality, in which a twelve-year-old is a Confederate officer, underscores the degree to which General Willson is located as the defining figure in the town's collective history, and Kelley explores the coercive ends to which direct narrative address may easily be put.

General Willson's place in white memory translates into a geographical and social prestige for the General's descendants. David Willson is even further removed from Caliban's departure than the white men on the porch. Willson, who stands as Kelley's critique of white southern liberalism, reacts to the event that sparks the exodus in a personal. Willson is a component of the same cultural economy as the working- and middle-class men on the porch but is socially removed from them through his wealth. Willson relates a trip to town immediately following Caliban's migration, dated 31 May 1957:

I walked downhill and into the Square and across to the store. (There were two or three men and a boy there this morning, unusual for that hour: about 7:30. I did not speak to them of course; I do not know any of them. None work my land.) (152)

His walk through the town's centre, past the statue of his ancestor in the square, indicates that Willson is a component of the town's collective social identity, but the symbolic geography of his walk 'downhill' underscores his position in the town's social elite. In the typology of the fictional town, Willson – the wealthy landowner – is dependent on and distanced from the other offices that make up the town. His habitual journey from his home to the centre of the town marks his inclusion in the town's social and commercial economies, even while his status as a landowner and employer governs his relationship to his neighbours. Whether or not he 'knows' the men on the porch is contingent on whether they work on his land. That the description of the group is rendered entirely in a parenthetical aside underscores the social remove at which Willson observes his fellow townspeople. This distance is compounded by the rhetorical addition in the journal entry of the phrase 'of course', which takes for granted Willson's social distance from the men on the porch.

Kelley's represents Willson as a person *of* the white community of Sutton who is nevertheless consistently positioned at a remove from the men on the porch. A former journalist, Willson receives the news of Caliban's dramatic act from still another apparently dispassionate and factual source, a brief newspaper article. The newspaper, in turn, has received its information through oral narratives passed along by the men on the porch: '*Witnesses stated the fire was started deliberately by Caliban, a Negro, himself. Those interviewed said they had watched Caliban most of the day . . . Caliban was not available for comment*' (153). Willson is distanced from Caliban by at least two removes: the men who witness the event narrate their account to the local journalist who renders it into written text before Willson peruses it in his home atop a literal and figurative hillside, overlooking the white and black residents of Sutton who have had more direct access to Caliban's departure. The narrative is contingent on the local flow of information, and it is compromised following multiple layers of mediation.

Through diary entries from the 1930s Kelley locates Willson on a contrasting but parallel ideological trajectory to Caliban. Unlike the perennially silent Caliban, Willson writes anonymously in local newspapers, decrying what he calls 'the corrosive effect of segregation' on the South (175). Upon being discovered and 'blackballed' in the state's newspaper industry, Willson contemplates a move from the segregated South to New York City, an act of migration that would have anticipated Caliban's departure from the state (175). However, the uncertainty of such a move with a pregnant wife dissuades Willson from action:

> But I cannot pack up Camille now and make a total move. Suppose I could not get anything in New York. We would be even worse off. I have to find something here. Perhaps this will all die down, and someone will take a chance on me. (176)

Willson chooses to content himself with patiently awaiting a shift in the state's racial temperament. Anticipating the possibility that the white supremacist backlash against his journalism will 'all die down', Willson implicates himself, in the privacy of his diary, as a racial gradualist. Kelley critiques Willson's beliefs by unambiguously contrasting him with Caliban. Bethrah Caliban is pregnant when she and her husband destroy their property and abandon the segregated southern town. Caliban's personal situation at the time of the exodus is so similar to Willson's in the 1930s as to highlight the contrast in the courage of their political convictions.

Kelley is more critical of his representative poor white, Bobby-Joe, than he is of the wealthy liberal Willson. Harper's presence on the porch is coercive, but it nevertheless lends the conversation 'form and scope' (29). In his absence, the white men act violently on their white supremacist convictions, marshalled by the uneducated and spiteful Bobby-Joe. Kelley's final chapter, 'The Men on the Porch', depicts a southern town in which bigotry and racialised violence persist after desegregation. As in George Schuyler's satirical novel *Black No More* (1931), the eradication of a colour line provokes a desperate white population to locate anyone who is racially 'othered' on whom to vent frustration. In Schuyler's novel, a white clergyman in the fictional southern town of Happy Hill prays for 'a nigger for his congregation to lynch' after a new medical treatment has eliminated racial difference.[38] Similarly, the white men of Sutton alleviate their frustration by humiliating and lynching the last African American in the town, northern activist B. T. Bradshaw, who has come to the state to witness the aftermath of the exodus.

Bradshaw, the leader of a fictional black church in New York, visits the Caliban farm in an attempt to make sense of the exodus. Bobby-Joe begins to fixate on what he imagines as Bradshaw's role as a leader of the exodus: 'That nigger preacher come driving by here and we just sat here watching him like he was the President' (191). In the white imagination, black leadership can only be imagined in relation to accepted norms of representative governance, and Bradshaw is facetiously compared to 'the President' as a means of incorporating the black freedom movement into those accepted norms. By scapegoating 'agitators' or 'fellows what come in and stir up trouble' (192), the white men seek retribution against Bradshaw as a representative leader of his race. Bradshaw's claim to leadership is tenuous; he merely 'wishes he could say he had been the instigator' and seeks to manipulate the exodus to his own benefit (197). In the absence of Harper as the group's moderator, Bobby-Joe takes over the role of the group's ideological leader.

As the last African American in the state, Bradshaw becomes a fetish for the white men's frustrations. As Bobby-Joe says: 'You fellows know this is our last nigger? Just think on that. Our last nigger, ever [. . .] The only niggers we'll ever see, unless we go over to Mississippi or Alabama, will be on the television' (199). Kelley ends *A Different Drummer* with the persistence of violent white supremacy in the de-segregated South. This dénouement locates the novel in opposition to the other texts I have discussed, each of which ends with the implication that the white South is making progress towards coherent integration.

The small town of Sutton represents Kelley's convictions that white and black Americans are irreconcilably different and that racial segregation could not be ended by the efforts of well-intentioned white southerners. Kelley makes the men on the porch symbolically analogous to the unnamed state in which they are located; they remain constant even as they observe and react to the sudden movement of the state's African American population.

Like their home state, the men in the town of Sutton can only look backwards, and Kelley seems to hold little hope for the future of the town of Sutton. However, if the town and the state are both lost causes, Kelley's imaginative construction of the state suggests that the Union of which it is a component can still make progress in racial politics.

An Impossible State: Kelley's Invented South

In imagining a thoroughly unique and idiosyncratic state in which to incorporate this typical fictional town, Kelley further problematises the paradigm of the fictional southern town as synecdoche. Kelley rejects a narrative of racial progress in favour of a complete overhaul of America's racial systems. By imagining the exodus of an entire black population, Kelley severs ties between his novel and the facts of the segregated South, proposing instead a hypothetical post-segregated South. His state is an entirely imaginary construction, underscored by detailed description of its dimensions, population and identity. Kelley's description of the state's geography, in the *Almanac*, is so clear as to preclude any confusion with an existing southern state: '*An East South Central state in the Deep South, it is bounded on the north by Tennessee; east by Alabama; south by the Gulf of Mexico; west by Mississippi*' (3). This catalogue of the state's coordinates within the nation locates it, from the very beginning of the novel, in a geographically impossible position, wedged between Alabama and Mississippi. From the start, then, Kelley codifies his state as discrete from the geography of the region.

While earlier chapters have argued that analogues with real-world coordinates cement the invention of towns in southern fiction as synecdoches that are representative of 'typical', real-world southern towns, Kelley's invention does not gesture towards any such coordinates, but is consistently marked as atypical by its author from the novel's opening pages: '*Today it is unique in being the only state in the Union that cannot count even one member of the Negro race among its citizens*' (4). Kelley's state is not offered as representative in the sense of being an archetype. Rather, it is a prototype, explicitly figured as unlike any real-world southern space. Trudier Harris argues that Kelley 'creates a mythical southern state to enact his narrative of black and white relationships'.[39] The imaginative construction of the unnamed state allows Kelley to contemplate a black-led revision of the South's segregated racial structure. Kelley's practice of inventing his hypothetical and impossible state operates along similar principles to the imaginative work of inventing southern towns of the other novelists. However, Kelley's politicised aesthetics are predicated on a separatist rather than an integrationist ideology.

In an essay published after *A Different Drummer* and following the legislative changes engendered by the Civil Rights Act of 1964 and the Voting Rights Act of 1965, Kelley expresses a decidedly separatist ideology: 'Separation is indeed the answer – not to flee the evil of whiteness but to create an economic unit which can bring an end to exploitation.'[40] In *A Different Drummer*, Kelley dramatises the 'economic unit' that would be left in the wake of such an immediate separation. Through his imaginative construction of an all-white state, Kelley begins to develop an aesthetic to imagine an America devoid of racial segregation and bifurcation. While earlier chapters examine how authors return to fictional towns, Kelley's novel signifies the beginning of a pattern that would continue across subsequent fiction. This pattern is overtly constituted by linguistic experimentation. An alliterative pattern can be discerned when considering the titles of Kelley's books following *A Different Drummer*: the short-story collection *Dancers on the Shore* (1964) and the novels *A Drop of Patience* (1965), *dəm* (1967) and *Dunfords Travels Everywheres* (1970). Through the repetition of the 'd' sound, Kelley suggests that his work constitutes a larger project with characters who appear in *A Different Drummer*, especially members of the Willson and Bedlow families who recur in later texts. The titles echo the onomatopoeic sound of drumming, his first novel inaugurating an aesthetic predicated on linguistically constructed, racially separatist spaces.

The same separatist sentiments are evident in Kelley's dedication to *dəm*, which asserts that America will not adequately incorporate an African American population: 'This book is dedicated to the black people in (not of) America.'[41] The title of Kelley's later novel is the idiomatic, African American pronunciation of the word 'them', rendered in the International Phonetic Alphabet. Kelley invents a linguistically constructed, imaginary America across his fiction, which is inaugurated and codified in his first novel. Across his novels Kelley articulates a connected and revisionary view of American racial structures, and the first building block he depicts, his imaginary state, departs significantly from existing literary tropes.

While other fictional southern states either provide a setting for satire and comedy or are closely modelled on real states, Kelley's is a canvas on which he can explore the principles of segregated southern society. When fictional southern states appear in satire, state names tend to be intrinsically comical, as in English novelist Thomas Love Peacock's Apodidraskiana, the setting of *Crotchet Castle* (1831). In other cases, the comedy derives from a name's obvious relation to recognisable states, such as in Missituckey, the setting of the E. Y. Harburg and Fred Saidy's Broadway musical *Finian's Rainbow* (1947). In this case, the comedy arises from the manner by which the naming of the state indicates a generally southern setting rather than specifying any particularities of location.[42] That Kelley's state remains unnamed, despite details of its constituent towns and cities being clearly depicted, indicates that the satire and fantasy that define the plot of *A Different Drummer* are never allowed to undermine the usefulness of his invented state by making of it a punch line.

The most famous fictional southern state to be clearly modelled after a real state is Thomas Wolfe's Old Catawba, a fictionalised representation of North Carolina, depicted in *Look Homeward, Angel* (1929) and also in the short story 'Old Catawba' (1935). In the story, Wolfe describes the state's location, dimensions and demographics in more oblique terms than Kelley does for his later imagined state:

On the middle-Atlantic seaboard of the North American continent and at about a day's journey from New York is situated the American state of Old Catawba. In area and population the state might almost strike a median among the states of the union: its territory which is slightly more than fifty thousand square miles, is somewhat larger than the territories of most of the Atlantic coastal states [. . .] Upon this area, which is a little smaller than the combined areas of England and Wales, there live about three million people, of whom about the third part are black. Catawba, therefore, is about as big as England, and has about as many people as Norway.[43]

While Wolfe's description is informative, it is full of prevarication. The details he provides add texture to the fictional state without ever firmly and unambiguously fixing any of its coordinates. Aside from the frequent choice of mediating phrases such as 'almost' 'about' and 'less than', Old Catawba is geographically located in relation to New York, based on the speed of travel on an unspecified conveyance. Wolfe does not even make his state average, as it 'almost strike[s] a median' in terms of area and population. To make the state exactly average would be to make it distinctive. On the other hand, Kelley's description of his state is concise, definitive and eschews Wolfe's equivocations.

The impossible state was admitted to the Union in 1818, and this year's numerical symmetry and the rhythmic repetition of 'eighteen' echo Kelley's title by suggesting the rhythm of a drumbeat. The state's motto, 'With Honor and Arms We Dare Defend Our Rights', is immediately suggestive of a fierce local identity. The term 'rights' suggests the phrase 'states' rights', especially when the 'arms' alluded to likely signify the Civil War (3). The state's motto, then, resonates with its southern heritage and indicates a collective identity among the white population predicated on racial superiority and regional exceptionalism. The state's physical dimensions are catalogued with great detail, down to the last square mile, '50,163', and its population, according to data from the '1960 Census, preliminary', is exactly '1,802,268' (3). While the state is self-contained, and unique among the real United States, Kelley borrows liberally from the state's neighbours.

Kelley's state is not only geographically positioned between Alabama and Mississippi but is, on every level, constructed as a precise amalgamation of the two most 'deeply southern' states in the Deep South. Its motto is a conflation of Alabama's – '*Audemus Jura Nostra Defendere*', or 'We Dare Defend Our Rights' – and Mississippi's – '*Virtute et Armis*', or 'By Valor and Arms'. Kelley's motto compounds Alabama's state identity as defensive of local freedoms, with Mississippi's assertion of traditions of chivalry and, again, armed 'defense' against the 'invading' forces of the North.

Kelley's state is admitted to the Union between Mississippi, the twentieth state accepted to the Union in 1817, and Alabama, the twenty-second, accepted in 1819.[44] In area, Kelley once again locates his state between Alabama, with an area of 50,744 square miles, and Mississippi, with an area of 46,907 square miles. According to the US Census Bureau, the populations of Alabama and Mississippi in 1960 were, respectively, 3,266,740 and 2,178,141. Each of these numbers is considerably larger than Kelley's fictional population until the populations of African Americans (980,271 and 915,743, respectively) are removed from each state.[45] This would leave the population of Alabama, following a mass exodus, at 2,286,489 and Mississippi at 1,262,398. Kelley's fictional population of '*1,802,268*' is once again occupying a middle space between Alabama and Mississippi (3). Overwhelmingly, the various social and geographical dimensions of Kelley's imagined state signify the conflation of Mississippi and Alabama. Kelley's construction of the demographic, physical and cultural shape of the state is painstaking and deliberate. The impossible state is a synecdoche for the Deep South that does not claim to represent any specific state, but is representative of the South broadly conceived. Like the anthropologists I discuss in Chapter 1, Kelley constructs a stable and representative subject of analysis. Unlike those social scientists, Kelley's makes no claim for objectivity. Rather than the conflation of Alabama and Mississippi making the state analogous to either, Kelley insists on his own, newly defined paradigm of southern space and identity.

Kelley positions his state between Mississippi and Alabama not just geographically, but demographically, ideologically and in area. In doing this, Kelley makes his state atypical: it is not a metonym for any southern state, nor is it a fictionalised version of a single, identifiable state. Rather, Kelley constructs an imaginary landscape in which segregation has been immediately and wholly dismantled by African American southerners. Within the novel, characters are described traversing the space of the state as when the poor white character Bobby-Joe McCollum travels 'upstate to the university at Willson' (7) and when Dewitt Willson hunts the escaped African 'all along the Gulf Coast almost to Mississippi and the other way into Alabama' (19). The narrative is bounded by the state, even as it ranges across Kelley's invented space. Having invented an integer, a complete and functional state-wide municipal and social complex, Kelley goes on to explore the hypothetical impact that a mass exodus from such a state would have on both the United States at large and the intellectual principles of the exodus narrative in African American culture.

In Kelley's text, the trope of the exodus narrative departs from Robert J. Patterson, in whose analysis 'African Americans have long appropriated and typologically identified with [the biblical Exodus narrative] to argue that their civil rights are God-given and divinely protected'.[46] In Kelley's novel, Caliban's instigation of the mass exodus from the state precedes failed white attempts to commit the event to written and oral narrative. Rather than a biblical Exodus narrative providing a textual basis for African American civil rights leadership, Kelley depicts a mass migration from the segregated South that produces a narrative of exodus rather than being constituted from such a narrative. While the biblical Exodus story is, as Hartnell summarises, 'a myth central to America's national, religious and racial self-identity', Kelley proposes a new mythological centre for African American identity.[47] Due to the nature of the mass exodus, the impact of this new identity cannot be felt anywhere in the fictional state in which it originated. Instead, in the novel's fictive present, the unnamed state is uniquely ignorant to the changes that have occurred in African American ideology as a result of the exodus.

The state's racial 'integrity' is a matter of record by 1961, and the mass exodus that defines it is represented as being felt throughout the rest of the United States. When Wallace Bedlow, an African American leaving Sutton, is confronted by the group of white men on the grocery store porch, they ask where he is going, but they are already certain of the answer: '"You moving into the Northside?" The Northside was where New Marsails' Negroes lived' (56). Initially the white men are unable to conceptualise a black migration in which one segregated town or city is not merely traded for another. Bedlow responds that he is moving to New York, leaving the men unable to respond except to say 'Oh' (57). In this way, Kelley's vast and sudden migration ripples through the rest of the union, changing not only the demographics of his invented state, but of the real United States in which it is wedged. Kelley's narrative suggests that, although the white population of the fictional state will not and cannot learn from its sudden desegregation, the rest of Union will be more capable of developing racial tolerance as a result.

In *A Different Drummer*, the fictional state is a crucible for a new racial epistemology and the southerners who migrate away from the state may propagate that new ideology to every state in the nation except the one that they have abandoned, as they 'journey toward the state's borders, to cross over into Mississippi or Alabama or Tennessee, even if some (most did not) stopped right there and began looking for shelter and work' (5). The fictional state is the epicentre for a new mode of racial thinking, and Kelley depicts the dispersal of that mode as a radiation outwards. While Kelley refuses to leave any hope for racial improvement in the fictional town of Sutton, he simultaneously depicts capacity for fundamental racial progress, presided over by African Americans, throughout the rest of the nation. Through this expansion of narrative focus, Kelley extends the practices of imagining fictional small towns that I have discussed across this study in order to explore the ramifications of desegregation, not simply on a single, representative community, but on the entire Union.

Kelley's novel represents a departure on a number of levels. In the literal sense, of course, it offers multiple, often competing, narratives of a mass departure from the South. More than that, and pointedly in the context of this book, the author departs from the literary conventions of the segregated town that I have discussed at length in this book and that are – by 1962 – recognisable touchstones in narratives of the contemporary South. Kelley's rejection of an ameliorative, integrationist mode of thought on desegregation coincides with his decision to construct a broader imaginative landscape through which to explore those ideas.

Kelley's fictional town exists in a radically reimagined southern landscape: the author expands on the common deployment of the fictional southern town by imagining an outright and immediate end to its segregationist structure that would require the development of a new typology of the southern town. Sutton is incompatible with a narrative of progressive improvement, and its fictional history bears out Kelley's radical racial politics. For Kelley, and in

Sutton, nothing less than a total overturning of the architecture of the southern town is sufficient improvement for black Americans. Where Nonnie Anderson, the farmer Abraham, Jester Clane and Ned McCaslin represent decisive shifts in their towns' racial landscapes, Tucker Caliban burns Sutton's racial architecture to the ground, ensuring that no one other than he may enjoy the product of his land.

Conclusion:
(De)Generative Ground –
The Field and the Segregated Town

Rachel Carson's pivotal book on ecology, *Silent Spring* (1962), was published in the same year as William Faulkner's final novel and William Melvin Kelley's first. Carson opens the text with a self-described 'fable' of American life:

> There once was a town in the heart of America where all life seemed to live in harmony with its surroundings. The town lay in the midst of a checkerboard of prosperous farms, with fields of grain and hillsides of orchards where, in spring, white clouds of bloom drifted above the green fields.[1]

Carson goes on to describe the 'strange blight' that 'crept over the area' and how 'Some evil spell had settled on the community'.[2] Carson ends her opening chapter, titled 'A Fable for Tomorrow', with an admission that she has constructed a synecdoche: 'This town does not actually exist, but it might easily have a thousand counterparts in America or elsewhere in the world. I know of no community that has experienced all the misfortunes I describe.'[3] Carson chooses not to describe a real town that has suffered from unsustainable industrial practices because her point is better served by an amalgamated, representative construct. Carson puts her scientific fiction of an archetypal town to use as a warning to take action on ecological stewardship: 'this imagined tragedy may easily become stark reality we all shall know.'[4] Carson was successful in instigating the change she wanted to effect with her writing, and *Silent Spring* led to the institution of bans on certain harmful pesticides for use in American farming. Crucial to Carson's extended metaphor of the town is the agricultural landscape that surrounds it. *Silent Spring* reflects on the inherent connectedness of the semi-urban community space of the small town and the agricultural industry that, literally and figuratively, feeds it.

Each of the towns I have mapped in *Living Jim Crow* is the centre of activity for a wider rural, agricultural economy. As sociologist Thorstein Veblen wrote in 1927, the American 'country town' exists in a symbiotic relationship to the neighbouring countryside:

> To an understanding of the country town and its place in the economy of American farming it should be noted that in the great farming regions any given town has a virtual monopoly of the trade within the territory tributary to it.[5]

In the specifically southern town, the surrounding farmland is even more closely tied to a town's identity. John Dollard observes that 'any study of the town inevitably involves the surrounding rural plantation region because the town itself is a depot for goods and services to the mass of the surrounding population'.[6] Similarly, Hortense Powdermaker asserts that 'the town is not, however, an entity distinct from its environs. Except for taxes and census returns, its borders mean little. In this agricultural region, town and countryside are interdependent.'[7] Carson differs from her scientific forebears because she takes advantage of the potential for fiction to elucidate real scientific issues. She follows their lead, on the other hand, by recognising the importance of the neighbouring landscape to the social and economic structures of the town. In the fictional towns that I have explored in depth, the economic symbiosis shared with surrounding rural areas is a crucial element of a town's social identity. In each text, the image of a field – a discrete unit of productive agricultural land – is depicted at some point in the narrative as a symbol of the town's entanglement with or ideological development away from the system of racial segregation and symbolises a given fictional town's capacity for racial progress. Across the novels discussed here, the metaphor of gradual progress becomes increasingly inadequate and this is mirrored in the authors' need for a total reappraisal of the typology of the segregated town.

In work by African American writers of the 1930s, the field is a threatening symbol of racist labour practices and exploitation. Like the town, the field symbolises oppression and violence for Zora Neale Hurston and Richard Wright. In novels by white racial liberals from the 1940s to the early 1960s, fields signify growth and development: they are sites of agricultural cultivation and also represent the germination of a town's collective identity.[8] In *Strange Fruit*, the image of the field suggests a cyclical narrative of white supremacist dominance in the town of Maxwell. In *The Hawk and the Sun* and *Clock Without Hands*, fields symbolise the gradual cultivation of new, racially progressive ideologies among white townspeople. In different ways, authors position the field as a signifier of a fictional town's political development. In *The Reivers*, the resonance of the field is overturned. In that novel, a 'mud farmer' exploits his property to inhibit progress in a literal sense by arresting the development of drivers on the road from Jefferson to Memphis. Finally, *A Different Drummer* explodes the recurring image of the field when Tucker Caliban carefully sows salt into the field on his property, ensuring that the land is never fertile again. The progression of this trope across these texts shows how imagery of complete overhaul supplants progressive racial change. The field that surrounds the typical southern town ceases to be productive in the 1960s and becomes instead an emblem of a reimagining of race in the region.

In southern literature, the field is an obvious signifier of labour and productivity. In Faulkner's *The Hamlet* (1940), for example, a young farmer studying at the University of Mississippi in Faulkner's hometown of Oxford is employed to prepare a playing field for American football. Labove, the farmer and student, is bemused that a prime stretch of arable land would serve no agricultural purpose:

> He didn't know then what a football field was and he did not care. To him it was merely an opportunity to earn so much extra money each day and he did not even stop his shovel when he would speculate now and then with cold sardonicism on the sort of game the preparation of ground for which demanded a good deal more care and expense both than the preparing of that same ground to raise a paying crop on; indeed, to have warranted that much time and money for a crop, a man would have had to raise gold at least.[9]

Faulkner's fictionalised version of his hometown of Oxford, Mississippi, is forty miles distant from the fictional Jefferson. In the invented Oxford, the space of the field is removed from a recognisable agricultural economy, a development that jars with Labove's understanding of the economy of the rural town.[10] Once the field is stripped of its economic meaning, the object of the American football is similarly reduced when Labove, now a reluctant athlete on the university team, thinks of it as a 'trivial contemptible obloid'.[11] At least as early as 1940, southern authors are exploring how the image of the arable field relates to the moral and social development of a small-town community.

In Hurston's *Their Eyes Were Watching God*, a move beyond the confines of Eatonville, into the labouring space of the field, also marks a resurgence of segregation. When Janie and Tea Cake turn to labour in the Everglades, they are – as Martyn Bone, Hazel Carby, Patricia Yaegar and others have noted – returned to an explicitly segregated economic order.[12] Tea Cake, who has spent a greater part of his life working with whites, jokes that 'God don't know nothin' 'bout de Jim Crow law' after being directed to segregate bodies for burial.[13] To Hurston, the coercive labour of the field undermines the already fragile utopian potential of the all-black Eatonville.

The story 'Long Black Song' in Wright's *Uncle Tom's Children* is set entirely on a farm near the unseen town of Coldwater, pronounced 'Colwatah' by African American characters.[14] Wright explores the interdependence of farm and town life when an African American woman, Sarah, is left alone while her husband visits town to sell their cotton. Wright signals his interest in the relationship between town and country in an epigraph that establishes an atmosphere of ill-ease from the outset: '*Go t sleep, baby / Papas gone t town / Go t sleep, baby / The suns goin down / Go t sleep, baby / Yo candys in the sack / Go t sleep baby / Papas coming back . . .*'[15] In this brief verse, the idea of the town shifts from a shorthand for opportunity – the potential reward and luxury of a sack of candy – to a metaphor for loss and isolation. More pertinently, the epigraph establishes the story's motif of 'going to town' as a mechanism of inclusion in the South's coercive capitalist economy. In this story, as in the others collected in *Uncle Tom's Children*, to inhabit the synecdochic southern town is to be subject to the economic and social hostility of racial segregation. The necessity of Silas 'going to town' to sell his crop leaves Sarah vulnerable to sexual violence at the hands of a white travelling salesman. The visit from the salesman, who insists Sarah buys a commodity she does not want, amounts to the town making a house call. After the salesman rapes her, Sarah feels 'the presence of the fields' surrounding her as an overwhelming burden.[16] Wright clearly implicates the physical space of the field in the exploitative and violent infrastructure of the archetypal southern town.

The racialised exploitation of labour in the rural South is an extension of violent racial terrorism. For example, following the lynching of Henry McIntosh, Smith's Maxwell begins to return to its former racially imbalanced state: Tracy's murder is 'avenged' and Maxwell's African American residents are terrorised into conformity in the town's collective identity. In the aftermath, two men who had been instrumental in forming the mob that murders Henry return to town from the outlying site of the lynching: 'Bill and Dee not talking, only hoofs and creak of wheels breaking the silence as the buggy moved under moss hanging low from great oaks, past ponds, past black clumps of palmetto . . . cotton fields . . . to the old house.'[17] During this scene of Maxwell, Georgia, in repose, Smith's inclusion of ellipses echoes the passage through space and highlights the cotton fields as the only natural marker that the men are not explicitly described as moving 'past'. Instead, the cotton fields are held constant and are the closest rural site to the 'old house' that marks a return to the town. After the murder and lynching, the cotton field remains an undisturbed feature of Maxwell's landscape. The field's coercive symbolism for African American labour is strengthened when Bill mockingly boasts that he will have 'no trouble' finding labourers to pick his cotton, after the spectacle of the lynching.[18] Here, the field symbolises how the town's white supremacist collective identity regenerates with force following the threat represented by Tracy's murder.

Elsewhere, the field can signify a productive organic cycle and suggest that the moral health of a fictional town is gradually improving. In Chapter 3 I explored how Abraham in *The Hawk and the Sun* represents the potential for cultivation, both in agriculture and as the father of 'strong sons' who are positioned to alter Tilden's racial politics. Reece combines these elements of Abraham's character in a scene in which the farmer's responsibility to his fields is portrayed as an analogy to his faith in his sons. Abraham reflects that one of his sons 'was a seed [. . .] in a pod of my flesh. For the farmer thinks in terms of planting and harvest and in that cycle of always-analogy, mostly the planting; the harvest is the Lord's.'[19] Here, the cycle of planting and harvest of an arable field is an overt allegory for Christian morality. The analogy of the farming cycle is implicitly tied to Abraham's role in encouraging a new generation of southerners to eschew racist violence. Immediately prior to the description of the field, the omniscient narrator describes how Abraham has trusted the maintenance of his fields to his sons:

> He had nothing to do before breakfast for he had entrusted the chores about the farm to his sons. Or rather they had inherited them on coming of age to do men's work, as Abraham had inherited the chores from his own father.[20]

When, much later in the narrative, Abraham makes good on his moral responsibility by refusing to take part in Dandelion's lynching, the implication is that the agricultural cycle of the farm will be mirrored and extended by his sons' ethical lives. The image of the field is an extension of Reece's construction of the farmer as a proponent of racial change. Reece implicitly advocates for racial gradualism by deploying a metaphor of intergenerational renewal and growth.

Abraham's confidence in his sons' moral commitment to the culture of their community anticipates McCullers's depiction of Jester Clane as a young would-be lawyer who is intent on improving his town's racial order. In Chapter 4 I examined a passage near the end of *Clock Without Hands* that describes Jester Clane's aerial view of Milan and its environs:

> Looking downward from an altitude of two thousand feet, the earth assumes order. A town, even Milan, is symmetrical, exact in a small grey honeycomb, complete. The surrounding terrain seems designed by a law

more just and mathematical than the laws of property and bigotry: a dark parallelogram of pine wood, square fields, rectangles of sward.[21]

In the chapter, I read this passage as an indicator of Jester's increasingly sophisticated understanding of his hometown's racial politics. In returning to the same passage now, the 'surrounding terrain' of the town, or what Veblen might call the 'territory tributary' to Milan, suggests a surface calm that Jester will be empowered to disrupt. That the collection of fields and forests is described as a 'parallelogram' suggests order, with four straight lines meeting at four corners, but it is also askew; the lengths of the line are uneven and unequal. That the town's neighbouring fields are described as sward, an upper layer of soil covered in grass, suggests a productive and fertile layer of earth, but one that does not extend much below the surface. Jester sees a productive surface layer of grass, on which livestock can graze, that belies the dirt underneath. McCullers lingers on this image of the field at the moment in the narrative when Jester's perception – and his commitment to a future as a liberal lawyer – is most clear and acute. The 'product' of the field in this passage is Jester's growing self-awareness; as such, the image is generative in McCullers's novel and it indicates a more cohesive racial future for Milan.

In contrast, the narrator in Faulkner's *The Reivers* seeks to halt any possibility of racial progress, and this desire is manifested in a representation of the field that diverges from those outlined above. Early in young Lucius Priest's adventure, on reaching the outskirts of Yoknapatawpha County, he encounters a rural entrepreneur who has made a business of cultivating an impassable road and charging motorists for his assistance in driving through it. When Lucius, Boon and Ned encounter a mud farmer, Ned is astonished that the white man 'works this place like a patch just to keep it boggy' to extort money from the region's new automobile traffic.[22] Ned makes an overt comparison between the mud farmer's unproductive labour and conventional southern agricultural work: 'This sho beats cotton. He can farm right here setting in the shade without even moving.'[23] Social scientists allude to this scene as an expositional metaphor for finance capitalism. Economist Randall Bartlett reads the scene as an example of 'ungranted event power'[24] that allows the mud farmer to profit from a crisis of his making, and legal scholar Fred S. Chesney deploys the scene as a metaphor for politicians' practice of 'rent extraction', writing that 'The essence of mud farming [. . .] is thus the mounting of a credible threat of loss, then selling back to those otherwise victimized reprieve from that loss.'[25] While each of these perspectives positions the mud farmer as financially exploitative, the specifically racial dynamic of the exploitation is neglected.

Unlike these spatially abstracted readings of the scene, historian Howard Lawrence Preston describes how 'unimproved roads were one of Faulkner's metaphors for a backward, underdeveloped South',[26] and others have read the scene as a narrowly avoided lynching in what they describe as an 'undercurrent of menace'.[27] In this reading, Ned capitulates to racial etiquette in his dealing with the mud farmer. As Barbara Fields and Karen Fields describe: 'This incident ends with a giggle; but it might easily have ended with fire and a rope.'[28] The mud farmer scene is a metaphor for Priest's white supremacist revisionist history in miniature. He masks violence with humour, but Faulkner is careful to maintain the implications of violence inherent in the exchange. Like the playing surface of the American football field in *The Hamlet*, the mud farm in *The Reivers* is profitable without producing any crops. Despite his exploitative and extortionate labour, the mud farmer maintains a position of privilege in the segregated social order and the fable of the mud farm resonates with Priest's attempts to halt southern history in his own metaphorical mud hole.

The irony in Faulkner's depiction of the field is that what is a metaphor for growth and progress in novels by Smith, Reece and McCullers instead becomes a symbol of arrested progress. This resonance is drawn out still more boldly in *A Different Drummer*. The catalytic moment in Kelley's narrative of escape from the southern town is Tucker Caliban's careful destruction of his own property. Caliban's action is directly compared to typical agricultural labour (an onlooker thinks that it's *'Just like he's planting seed. Just like it's spring planting time'*).[29] Caliban's attitude is methodical and precise; he is *'not running out like a mad dog and putting down salt like it WAS salt, but putting it down like it was cotton or corn, like come fall, it'd be a paying crop.'*[30] Kelley's depiction mirrors Reece's earlier portrayal of a typical and progressive agricultural cycle, with the growth of spring and the harvest in autumn, but only as a subject of parody. Because Caliban sows salt in the same way that he might a 'paying crop', Kelley suggests a radically different future for the fictional southern town. Caliban's final act as a resident of Sutton not only overturns existing trends in the depiction of the image of the field in southern literature but also ensures that it will never again be fertile in this case.

The novels explored in *Living Jim Crow* are narratives of cross-generational cooperation or rupture. In every case, the children of the southern town are positioned to make sense of its racial future. In Faulkner's and Kelley's novels both published in the early 1960s, the narrative of generational racial improvement has become less tenable. While Faulkner represents exactly how the young Lucius Priest would grow up to obstruct cross-racial understanding, Kelley's young Mister Leland is left without any African American neighbours on whom to exercise the tolerance he has learned from his father and Caliban. As the metaphor of the field suggests, southern fiction by the early 1960s had reimagined and refashioned the trope and imagery of the fictional Southern town; writers would begin to draw on new forms and techniques to critique the South's racialised geography.

The trope of the town develops and evolves in multiple directions following the early 1960s and continues to be a favourite recurring setting for southern writers. Wendell Berry's Port William, Kentucky, Donald Harington's Stay More, Arizona, Randall Kenan's Tims Creek, North Carolina, and Jesmyn Ward's Bois Sauvage, Mississippi, are four examples of fictional towns that anchor narrative cycles. In Kenan's and Ward's small towns, racial divisions persist, and the archetypal small southern town remains a potent foundation for racial protest. These diverse southern novelists inherit a tradition of imagining the small town as a model for the critique of white formulations of history and race. Bernice McFadden's *Gathering of Waters* (2012) takes the trope of setting as a tool for protest still further. Published in the wake of Trayvon Martin's murder by George Zimmerman, McFadden focalises her novel through the consciousness of a town made famous following the murder of Emmett Louis Till. She asserts her formal choice starkly in the novel's opening line: 'I am Money. Money Mississippi.'[31] By personifying the town in which Till's purported transgression of racial etiquette took place, McFadden deploys the archetypal mid-century southern town as a tool for contemporary protest in the era of #BlackLivesMatter.

The Black Lives Matter movement has encouraged African American writers to reassess their engagements with grief. For instance, personal grief is translated into national protest when novelist Ward remembers the sentencing of the white drunk driver who killed her brother in her memoir *The Men We Reaped*: '*Five Fucking Years*, I thought. *This is what my Brother's life is worth in Mississippi. Five Years.*'[32] Coincidentally, the contemporary movement has led to a resurgence of public interest in Kelley's life and work. In 2017 the *Oxford English Dictionary* added the word 'woke' as an adjective meaning political understanding and engagement and specifically cited Kelley's 1962 *New York Times* article 'If You're Woke You Dig It' as the earliest recorded use of the term in that context.[33] Being 'woke' has become a vital shorthand for a new kind of twenty-first-century protest that highlights individual engagement and a diffused leadership model. It is not surprising that the term has its roots in a body of cultural work that insists on the political weight of literary aesthetics. Throughout this book, I have applied a racially calibrated adaptation of the method of close textual analysis – divorced from the methodology's roots in a certain pocket of mid-century southern conservatism – to explicate how fiction contributes to a tradition of anti-segregationist protest. Close attention to literary form allows scholars to better understand and express the aesthetic and rhetorical techniques of racial protest since racial segregation, and especially in relation to the iteration of the black freedom struggle that came to the fore following Trayvon Martin's murder in 2012.

Notes to Introduction

1. Frank Capra, dir. *It's a Wonderful Life* (RKO Studios, 1946).
2. Kelley, 'On Racism, Exploitation, and the White Liberal', 10.
3. Ibid. 8.
4. Smith, *Killers of the Dream*, 154.
5. Ibid. 157.
6. Kelley, 'On Racism, Exploitation, and the White Liberal', 9.
7. Szalay, *Hip Figures*, 3.
8. Odum, *Race and Rumours of Race*, 4. Odum linguistically divides the population of the South along racial lines in this formulation, but he is by no means the first or last commentator to do so. As early as 1889, George Washington Cable, for example, anticipates a similar personification of the South when he described how resistance to the Civil Rights Act of 1875 imagined the South as an integral unit under threat: 'Says one opponent, imputing his words to a personified South, "Leave this problem to my working out."' Cable, *The Silent South*, 47.
9. Egerton, *Speak Now against the Day*; Hale, *Making Whiteness*, xii; McMillen, *Dark Journey*.
10. Bibler, *Cotton's Queer Relations*, 57.
11. The other defining features are 'an aesthetics of fear, and crucial scenes of cross-racial contact'. Norman, *Neo-Segregation Narratives*, 10.
12. Welty, 'Must the Novelist Crusade?', 150.
13. MacKethan, *The Dream of Arcady*, 181.
14. Such change can, of course, be progressive – as in the cases of Smith's Dessie and McCullers's Jester Clane – or regressive – as in the cases of Faulkner's Lucius and Kelley's Mister Leland. In either eventuality, the South is figured as in a moment of generational shift.
15. Brinkmeyer, 'Marginalization and Mobility', 225.
16. Williams, *The Country and the City*, 10.

17. Carter, 'Statues in the Squares', 239.

18. Haas, *Look Away, Look Away*, 1.

19. Cox, *Dixie's Daughters*, 67.

20. Romine, *The Narrative Forms of Southern Community*, 2, 4. James McBride Dabbs locates the idea of the town as coercive in a history of the North, and not the South, writing that 'one of the main reasons for the town was the Puritan desire for religious and moral control; this could be much better maintained in a town than in a sparsely settled countryside.' Dabbs, *Who Speaks for the South?*, 14.

21. Robolin, *Grounds of Engagement*, 13.

22. Yousaf, 'A Southern Sheriff's Revenge', 221.

23. Sheriff's departments are responsible for policing a county, where police forces tend to operate within a city or town.

24. Trefzer, *Disturbing Indians*, 5.

25. Davis, *Southscapes*, 2.

26. Bhabha, *The Location of Culture*, 61.

27. Gilmore, 'Fatal Couplings of Power and Difference', 16; McKittrick, *Demonic Grounds*, xiii.

28. Lefebvre, *The Production of Space*, 15.

29. Harvey, *Spaces of Hope*, 189.

30. Abel, *Signs of the Times*, 163.

31. M. Smith, *How Race is Made*, 115.

32. Williams, *The Country and the City*, 9.

33. Ibid.

34. Yi-Fu Tuan, *Topophilia*, 4.

35. Moretti, *Graphs, Maps, Trees*, 1.

36. Duck, *The Nation's Region*, 6.

37. Loveland, *Lillian Smith*, 129

38. McPherson, *Reconstructing Dixie*, 1.

39. Greeson, *Our South*, 7.

40. J. Smith, *Finding Purple America*, 22.

41. Romine, *The Real South*, 9.

42. L. Smith, 'The Role of the Poet in a World of Demagogues', 163.

43. Ransom, 'Introduction', *The Kenyon Critics*, vii–x, viii.

44. Brooks, *The Hidden God*, 4.

45. Handy, *Kant and the Southern New Critics*, vii; Cain, *The Crisis in Criticism*, 95.

46. Lentricchia, *After the New Criticism*, 25.

47. Godden, *Fictions of Labor*, 4.

48. Ibid.

49. Altman, 'The Bug that Dare Not Speak Its Name', 48.

50. Simmel, 'The Metropolis and Mental Life', 334–5.

51. Holland, *The Erotic Life of Racism*, 6.

52. Monteith, 'Southern Fiction', 89. Robert Penn Warren, in *Segregation: The Inner Conflict of the South* (1956), describes the 'bitter catalogue of paradoxes' that supports segregationist ideology, including the conviction that African Americans are unclean juxtaposed against white dependence on African American nurses and cooks. Warren, *Segregation*, 19.

Notes to Chapter 1

1.   Warren, *Who Speaks for the Negro?*, 12.
2.   Warren, 'The Briar Patch', 260.
3.   Bourne, 'The Social Order of an American Town', 227.
4.   Ibid. 227.
5.   Bourne elides the significance of race in his definition, writing 'It is a common enough saying that there are no classes in America, and this, of course, is true if by "class" is meant some rigid caste based on arbitrary distinctions of race or birth or wealth'. Bourne, 'The Social Order of an American Town', 228.
6.   Ibid. 236.
7.   Veblen, 'The Country Town', 407.
8.   Ibid.
9.   Ibid.
10.   Lynd and Merrell Lynd, *Middletown*, 5.
11.   Orvell, *The Death and Life of Main Street*, 139, 141.
12.   Lynd and Merrell Lynd, *Middletown*, 7.
13.   Ibid.
14.   Ibid. 8.
15.   For correctives to the Middletown studies that focus on Muncie's Jewish and African American communities, respectively, see Rottenberg, ed., *Middletown Jews* and Lassiter et al., eds, *The Other Side of Middletown*.
16.   Dollard, *Caste and Class*, 1n.1; Powdermaker, *After Freedom*, xliv.
17.   Dollard, *Caste and Class*, 1
18.   Ibid.
19.   Powdermaker, *After Freedom*, xliv.
20.   Ibid.
21.   Ibid. 7.
22.   Clifford, 'Introduction', 6.
23.   Ibid.
24.   Ibid. 7.
25.   Visweswaran, *Fictions of Feminist Ethnography*, 3.
26.   Geertz, *The Interpretation of Cultures*, 6.
27.   Bilbo, *Take Your Choice*, 165. Putnam, *Race and Reason*, 108.
28.   Ward, 'Truths, Lies, Mules and Men', 311.
29.   Boas, 'Preface', xiii.
30.   Hurston, 'How It Feels to be Colored Me', 827.
31.   Wall, *On Freedom and the Will to Adorn*, 20, 21.
32.   Hurston, 'My Most Humiliating Jim Crow Experience', 935.
33.   Hurston, 'Court Order Can't Make Races Mix', 956.
34.   Hurston, 'Crazy for This Democracy', 947.
35.   Ibid. 949. Emphasis and double exclamation in original.
36.   Hurston, 'How it Feels to be Colored Me', 827.
37.   Ibid. 826.
38.   Hurston, *Their Eyes Were Watching God*, 18. All further references appear parenthetically.

39. The territory on which the town is built is 'gifted' to the people of Eatonville by one Captain Eaton. Judith Newman reads Eaton's gift as incomplete and an act of bad faith. Judith Newman, '"Dis ain't Gimme, Florida"', 821.
40. Gates, *The Signifying Monkey*, 230.
41. Ibid. 186.
42. Veblen, 'The Country Town', 408.
43. Yaeger, *Dirt and Desire*, 22.
44. Hurston, 'The Eatonville Anthology', in *Folklore, Memoirs, and Other Writings*, 821. Emphasis in original. The same text has been included in collections of Hurston's essays and her short fiction. Hurston, 'The Eatonville Anthology', in *The Complete Stories*, 67–8.
45. Similarly, in the three-act play *De Turkey and De Law* (1930) the people of Eatonville congregate and gossip on the property of the town's 'Mayor, Postmaster, Storekeeper', Joe Clarke, an apparent rehearsal for the character of Joe Starks. As in the later novel, the post office in the play represents a hub of communication and commerce, and townspeople who come 'tuh git our mail out de post office' linger to share gossip. Hurston, with Langston Hughes. *De Turkey and De Law*, 155, 134.
46. Harris, 'Etiquette, Lynching, and Racial Boundaries in Southern History', 391.
47. Houston, *The Nashville Way*, 6.
48. Ibid.
49. Doyle, *The Etiquette of Race Relations*, xviii.
50. Ibid. xii, xviii.
51. Wright, 'The Ethics of Living Jim Crow', *Uncle Tom's Children*, 15. All further references to this collection will appear parenthetically.
52. Orvell, *The Death and Life of Main Street*, 134.
53. Racist naming practices are by no means unique to the South. Historian James Loewen visits the town of Anna, Illinois, whose name is commonly understood as an acronym for the phrase 'Ain't No Niggers Allowed'. Loewen, *Sundown Towns*, 3.
54. Parks, 'Towns and Cities', 515.
55. Ibid.
56. Couch, 'The Negro in the South', 451.
57. Gray, *The Literature of Memory*, 45.
58. Robolin, *Grounds of Engagement*, 8.
59. McKittrick, *Demonic Grounds*, xiv.
60. Henry Louis Gates identifies chiasmus as 'The overarching rhetorical strategy of the slave narratives written after 1845', arguing that African American narrative since the 1840s has made frequent and productive use of the technique. Gates, *The Signifying Monkey*, 186.
61. Himes, *If He Hollers Let Him Go*, 107.

Notes to Chapter 2

1. The Freedom Rides, a series of protests in 1961 during which white and black civil rights activists challenged segregation on interstate bus services, marked a

departure for the civil rights movement. Raymond Arsenault describes how 'the Freedom Rides sent shockwaves through American society' and that 'nothing in the recent past had prepared the American public for the Freedom Riders' interracial "invasion" of the segregated South'. Arsenault, *Freedom Riders*, 3. For other detailed accounts of the Freedom Rides, see: Niven, *The Politics of Injustice*; Barnes, *Journey from Jim Crow*, 157–75; and Thornton, *Dividing Lines*, 239–53.

2. Telegram, James Farmer to Lillian Smith, 27 May 1961, box 2, folder 15, Correspondence, C–K. Lillian Smith papers, MS1283.

3. Telegram, Lyndon B. Johnson to Lillian Smith, 1964, box 2, folder 82, Correspondence C–K, Lillian Smith papers, MS1283.

4. Ibid.

5. Ibid.

6. Jackson, *The Indignant Generation*, 181.

7. 'The Best Sellers of 1944', 356.

8. Loveland, *Lillian Smith*, 71–2.

9. King, *A Southern Renaissance*, 173–92; Brantley, 'Afterword', 121–45; Brinkmeyer, *The Fourth Ghost*.

10. L. Smith, *Strange Fruit*, 100. All further references to the novel will appear parenthetically.

11. Snelling, 'Preface', 11.

12. Ibid. 12.

13. The grandness and complexity of the novel did not translate well to the stage, despite Smith's insistence that the play cover as much of the novel's ground as possible.

14. Theatrical Programme, 'Maxwell Georgia', p. 4, box 40, folder 23. Lillian Smith papers, MS1283.

15. L. Smith, 'Extracts from Three Letters', 215.

16. Ibid. 214.

17. L. Smith, 'The Role of the Poet in a World of Demagogues', 163.

18. Theatrical Programme, 'Maxwell Georgia', p. 4. Lillian Smith papers.

19. 'Life with a Best-Seller', *The Atlanta Journal Magazine*, 14 January 1945, 5–6, box 46, folder 11. Lillian Smith papers, MS1283.

20. Wilson, *Shadow and Shelter*, xv–xvi.

21. Stowe, *Dred*. Historians have examined the role played by swamps within the Underground Railroad. See, for example: Preston, 'The Underground Railroad in Northwest Ohio'; G. Hendrick and W. Hendrick, eds, *Fleeing for Freedom*.

22. Wilson, *Shadow and Shelter*, 124.

23. See Loveland, *Lillian Smith*, 75. Smith's connections with the university persisted despite the controversy; she encouraged the casting of Dorothy Carter, whom she met while Carter was a student at Spelman, as Bess in the Broadway adaptation of her novel. Incidentally, Walter White's daughter – herself a Spelman graduate – played Nonnie in the same production.

24. Carter, specifically, drew Smith's ire as a proponent of racial gradualism, with Smith writing in letters to friends that Carter and other gradualists are weak-willed commentators 'whose fears have always kept them from speaking out

until it is safe to speak out' and that they are 'not real liberals'. L. Smith, *How am I to be Heard?*, 168, 191.
25. L. Smith, 'The Right Way is Not a Moderate Way', 68.
26. Hurston, 'How it Feels to be Colored Me', 828.
27. Faulkner, 'A Rose for Emily', 119; Faulkner, *Intruder in the Dust*, 75.
28. Lee, *To Kill a Mockingbird*, 119.
29. Ibid. 124.
30. McPherson, *Reconstructing Dixie*, 26.
31. Ibid. 26, 6.
32. Du Bois, *The Souls of Black Folk*, 3.
33. Monteith, *Advancing Sisterhood?*, 104.
34. Hunt, *Joanna Lord*, 34.
35. Roberts, *The Myth of Aunt Jemima*, 183.
36. Ibid. 185.
37. In Flannery O'Connor's *Wise Blood* (1952), Haze Motes establishes the 'Church without Christ', satirising Southern religious conventions. *Strange Fruit*'s engagement with Southern religious conventions is inclusive rather than satirical. O'Connor, *Wise Blood*, 71.
38. Smith's critique of Faulkner in the late 1950s is joyously scathing. To Smith, his characters are poorly conceived, but stylistically complex: 'They are moral sleepwalkers. [. . .] Once he has reduced them to moronic pygmies bereft of dreams he can do fabulous things with them. Whether it is worth the doing, I have never been quite sure.' L. Smith, 'A Trembling Earth', 123.
39. Sterling Fishman's definition of demagogue focuses on a politician's ability to influence his constituency, by proposing a 'popular crisis of psychology', inventing a scapegoat to blame, and finally, insinuating himself as the remedy for that crisis. Dunwoodie's manipulation of the townspeople certainly identifies him as a religious demagogue. Fishman, 'The Rise of Hitler as a Beer Hall Orator', 250–2.
40. Strict adherence to Christian teaching has already been marked out as antithetical to the ideology of the town, despite Dunwoodie's revival, earlier in the novel when atheist Prentiss Reed quips, 'If you practiced the teachings of that man Jesus here in Maxwell, we'd think you were crazy' (46). The revival's denomination is alluded to when Dunwoodie tells Tracy that he worked with his grandfather: 'Everybody knew Grandpa, everybody who was a Methodist – and that meant half of Georgia' (83).
41. Romine, 'Framing Southern Rhetoric', 95.
42. L. Smith, *Killers of the Dream*, 11. Emphasis in original.
43. Theatrical Programme, 'Maxwell Georgia', p. 4. Lillian Smith papers.
44. Jennifer Rae Greeson has written expansively on similar patterns of possessiveness during the nineteenth century in *Our South: Geographic Fantasy and the Rise of National Literature*.
45. Duck, *The Nation's Region*, 7.
46. Ibid. 196.
47. Ibid. 177.
48. James, 'Carson McCullers, Lillian Smith, and the Politics of Broadway', 46.

49. A passage from Laura's internal monologue suggests the intellectual satisfaction garnered from her friendship with Jane: 'And you knew you could talk to Jane, you could tell her about your sculpture and your verses, about your fears and your feelings' (246).

50. Slotkin, *Regeneration through Violence*, 5.

51. Wyatt-Brown, *Southern Honor*, 283.

52. Brundage, *Lynching in the New South*, 52.

53. L. Smith, *Now is the Time*, 73.

Notes to Chapter 3

1. Stanford, 'Byron Herbert Reece Highway Dedication'.

2. The Byron Herbert Reece Society, http://byronherbertreecesociety.wordpress.com/farm-2/ (accessed 5 June 2014).

3. Cunningham, 'Writing on the Cusp', 45. Emphasis in original.

4. Tishler, 'The Negro in Modern Southern Fiction', 4.

5. Watkins, *The Death of Art*, 3, 1.

6. Ibid. 28. Watkins also includes Carson McCullers's *Clock Without Hands* (1961) and William Faulkner's *The Reivers: A Reminiscence* (1962) within this category of 'racist' fiction.

7. Monteith, 'Southern Fiction', 91.

8. Dabbs, *Civil Rights in Recent Southern Literature*, 79.

9. Clark, 'A Kindred Spirit Moving', 157.

10. DeTitta, *The Reach of Song*, 29.

11. Ibid. 21.

12. Eller, *Uneven Ground*, 260.

13. Engelhardt, 'Trying to Get Appalachia Less Wrong', 4, 5.

14. DeTitta, *The Reach of Song*, 39.

15. Catte, *What You are Getting Wrong about Appalachia*, 35. Appalachia, of course, has a long history of anti-racist writing in addition to Dykeman and Reece. Most influentially, the school of Affrilachian poets, founded by Nikky Finney and Frank X. Walker in the early 1990s, has worked to centre the contribution of writers of colour in scholarly and popular understandings of the region's culture.

16. Letter, Byron Herbert Reece to Elliot Macrae, 26 July 1954, box 12, folder 5. Byron Herbert Reece Family Papers. MS 3055.

17. At the time of the novel's publication, the Tuskegee experiment had been under way for more than twenty years. Researchers at the Tuskegee Institute observed 399 black men with syphilis, and a control group of 201 uninfected men, all from Macon County, Alabama. Even after penicillin had been introduced as a successful treatment for syphilis, it was withheld from the infected African Americans. Harriet Washington, in *Medical Apartheid* (2007), interprets the Tuskegee experiment as 'one signal instance' of African Americans being exploited by immoral and criminal medical testing within 'a centuries-long history of such abuse'. Washington, *Medical Apartheid*, 10. See also Jones, *Bad Blood*.

18. De Certeau, *The Practice of Everyday Life*, 117.
19. Ironically, the absence of a 'sterile' winter foreshadows Dandelion's emasculation.
20. Yaeger, *Dirt and Desire*, 87.
21. This scene anticipates, on a smaller scale, the mass migration from a fictional Southern state imagined in William Melvin Kelley's *A Different Drummer* (1962), the focus of this book's final chapter.
22. Genesis 10:9. All biblical references are to the King James Bible.
23. Genesis 10:6, 8.
24. Tilson, *Segregation and the Bible*, 21.
25. For more on the usage of *hwæt* in Anglo-Saxon narrative, see Walkden, 'The Status of *hwæt* in Old English', 465–88.
26. Woodward, *Origins of the New South*, 23.
27. Franklin, *Reconstruction*, 211, 212. 'Copperhead' was the term used by Northern Republicans to refer to anti-Civil War Northern Democrats. For more, see Weber, *Copperheads*.
28. Foote, *Love in a Dry Season*, 95.
29. Cash, *The Mind of the South*, 30–60.
30. Ibid., 30.
31. Ibid.
32. O'Brien, 'W. J. Cash, Hegel, and the South', 382; Cobb, *Away Down South*, 183.
33. Lecture Notes, box 6, folder 7. Byron Herbert Reece papers.
34. Gray, *Southern Aberrations*, 232. Emphasis in original.
35. Appiah, *Cosmopolitanism*, xi.
36. Ibid. xiii.
37. Roberts, *Prizing Literature*, 13.
38. Letter, Byron Herbert Reece to Jimmy Winn, 11 November 1956, box 1, folder 2. Byron Herbert Reece papers.
39. Goyen, 'Headlong Toward Catastrophe', 4.
40. Letter to Jimmy Winn. Byron Herbert Reece papers.
41. Letter, Louise Townsend Nicholl to Byron Herbert Reece, 21 January 1955, box 12, folder 6. Byron Herbert Reece family papers.
42. Ibid.
43. Ibid.
44. Ibid.
45. Letter, Byron Herbert Reece to Louise Townsend Nicholl, 26 January 1955, box 12, folder 6. Byron Herbert Reece family papers.
46. Copy for the Press, 25 January 1955, box 10, folder 3. Byron Herbert Reece papers.
47. Letter to Jimmy Winn. Byron Herbert Reece papers.
48. Ibid.
49. Raymond Williams draws attention to the etymological relationship between 'culture' and 'cultivation'. See Williams, *Keywords*, 85.
50. Dante, *The Divine Comedy*, Canto XXXI, lines 358–9.
51. Letter to Jimmy Winn. Byron Herbert Reece papers.
52. Ibid.

53. 2 Sam. 5:6–7, and also 1 Chron. 11:4–5.
54. Jer. 52:12–13.
55. Jer. 52:6.
56. Harker can be read as representing what George Lipsitz has termed a 'possessive investment in whiteness' because of his unexamined capitulation to a perceived 'tradition' rooted in medieval Europe. In Lipsitz's formulation, whiteness is the 'unmarked category against which difference is constructed, whiteness never has to speak its name, never has to acknowledge its role as an organizing principle in social and cultural relations'. Lipsitz, *The Possessive Investment in Whiteness*, 1.
57. This textual allusion to James Joyce's Molly Bloom is further evidence of Reece's immersion in twentieth-century literature.
58. This phrase echoes the eccentric character Wing Biddlebaum in Sherwood Anderson's *Winesburg, Ohio* (1919) who 'talked much with his hands' and 'wanted to keep them hidden' to avoid betraying his secret homosexuality. Anderson, *Winesburg, Ohio*, 10. In both Anderson's and Reece's novels, hands represent a suppressed secret in a small, rural town.
59. Manuscript Draft, *Tents toward Sodom*, box 9, folder 6. Byron Herbert Reece papers.
60. Letter to Jimmy Winn. Byron Herbert Reece papers.

Notes to Chapter 4

1. The manuscript of the story is undated, though the editor of *The Mortgaged Heart*, McCullers's sister Margarita G. Smith, is certain only that the story predates *The Heart is a Lonely Hunter* and was likely written between 1935 and 1936. M. G. Smith, 'Editor's Note' in *The Mortgaged Heart* (London: Penguin, 2008), 21.
2. McCullers, 'Untitled Piece', *The Mortgaged Heart*, 111.
3. Ibid. 135.
4. Brinkmeyer. *The Fourth Ghost*, 310.
5. Adams, *Sideshow U.S.A.*, 18. Gleeson-White, *Strange Bodies*, 38.
6. Evans, *Carson McCullers*, 192.
7. Prescott, 'Books of the Times', 27.
8. Ibid.
9. Howe, 'In the Shadow of Death', 5.
10. Rubin, 'Six Novels and S. Levin', 509.
11. Emerson, 'The Ambiguities of *Clock Without Hands*', 16.
12. Carr, *The Lonely Hunter*, 490. Williams found the portrayal of Sherman, particularly in chapter 4 in which Sherman and Jester discuss Sherman's sexual abuse, 'especially objectionable'.
13. O'Connor, *The Habit of Being*, 446.
14. L. Smith, 'Letter to Margaret Long, Sept. 10th, 1961', in *How Am I to be Heard?*, 284.
15. McCullers, *The Heart is a Lonely Hunter*, 7.
16. While the definite article ordinarily creates specificity, I read it here as pertain-

ing to a thing rather than an example of a type of thing. A contemporaneous example of such usage is found in the title of Robert Penn Warren's *Who Speaks for the Negro?*

17. McCullers, *Reflections in a Golden Eye*, 7.
18. In this regard, McCullers anticipates other southern novelists who have used similar settings to view the southern town indirectly. William Styron explores a peacetime military camp during the escalation of the Korean War in *The Long March* (1952), and John Oliver Killens maps the training of African American soldiers during the Second World War in *And Then We Heard the Thunder* (1963). In each of these novels, soldiers stationed at the camp interact with neighboring Southern towns and, in each case, Fort Benning is a likely real-world touchstone.
19. McCullers, *The Member of the Wedding*, 32.
20. Ibid. 167.
21. McCullers, *The Ballad of the Sad Café*, 9.
22. Ibid. 22.
23. McCullers, *The Member of the Wedding*, 123.
24. Whitt, 'The Exiled Heir', xviii.
25. McCullers, *The Member of the Wedding*, 79.
26. McCullers, *Clock Without Hands*, 14. Further references to the novel will appear parenthetically.
27. As I described in the previous chapter, the phrase 'the church' is a *pars pro toto* synecdoche that places the responsibility of a religious denomination on its architectural representative.
28. McCullers, *The Heart is a Lonely Hunter*, 17.
29. Brinkmeyer, *The Fourth Ghost*, 239, 310.
30. Blount confides his politics to Singer, saying, 'Over there in my suitcase I have books by Karl Marx and Thorstein Veblen and such writers as them. I read them over and over, and the more I study the madder I get', and Copeland goes so far as to name his son Karl Marx Copeland. McCullers, *The Heart is a Lonely Hunter*, 64, 74.
31. McCullers, *The Heart is a Lonely Hunter*, 260.
32. Ibid.
33. Fred Hobson, *But Now I See*, 2.
34. Prescott, 'Books of the Times', 27.
35. A fictional building that similarly refracts and contains local narrative in another Southern novel is the Beulah Hotel in the fictional town of Clay, Mississippi, in Eudora Welty's novella *The Ponder Heart* (1954). The hotel in that text is the source of local gossip, mediated by its proprietor and the novella's narrator, Edna Earl Ponder. *The Ponder Heart*, like McCullers's 'The Ballad of the Sad Café', is an experiment in exploring Southern narrative through a single building. In each novella, events are grounded by these lone buildings, mediated by the experiences of their proprietors, through which entire fictional communities are concentrated.
36. McCullers, *The Heart is a Lonely Hunter*, 175.
37. McCullers, 'Author's Outline of "The Mute" (*The Heart is a Lonely Hunter*)', 138.

38. Hassan, *Radical Innocence*, 211.
39. McCullers, *The Heart is a Lonely Hunter*, 188.
40. Ibid. 189.
41. McCullers, 'Loneliness . . . an American Malady', 266.
42. Ibid. 265.
43. Sunita Rai reads the existentialist dimension of the novel as an extension of what she sees as the novel's theme of the 'loneliness that results from man's alienation from his own self', but does not excavate the significance of this reading to the construction of Malone's character. Rai, *Carson McCullers*.
44. As is also the case in Beckett's novel, Malone's name suggests that he is a bad (from the Latin *malus*) individual. In McCullers's use, the implicit malevolence in Malone's name refers simultaneously to his disease and his complicity in white supremacy.
45. Sartre, *Existentialism and Humanism*, 26.
46. Watson, *Reading for the Body*, 137.
47. Duval, *Race and White Identity in Southern Fiction*, 16.
48. Sollors, *Neither Black Nor White Yet Both*, 68.
49. Sollors, *Beyond Ethnicity*, 150.
50. McCullers is not alone among her contemporaries in portraying sickness and defective blood at the same time as the author is suffering from serious ill health. Susanna Gilbert has identified a relationship between Flannery O'Connor's lupus and the trope of blood in her work, writing that 'blood, like lupus, is systemic, everywhere and anywhere in O'Connor's work'. Gilbert argues that blood in O'Connor's fiction operates both literally and metaphorically: 'Obviously, blood was not simply an abstraction for O'Connor but a highly visible physical presence in her life.' Gilbert, '"Blood Don't Lie"', 126.
51. Lillian Smith calls this intrusion of Kierkegaard on Malone's convalescence a 'blunder', complaining that it was unrealistic to 'say [Malone] picked out of the reading cart in a small city hospital in a Ga. town one of Kierkegaard's books'. Letter to Margaret Long, 10 September 1961, in *How am I to be Heard?*, 284.
52. Alice Walker, quoted in Monteith, 'Civil Rights Fiction', 169.
53. Ibid.
54. *Clock Without Hands*, typescript and carbon copies with revision, no date, MS pp. 22, 23. Carson McCullers Collection, Box 4, Folder 1.
55. Weidenmier, 'Turning Points in the U.S. Civil War', 877.
56. The movement for reparations for African Americans began in earnest with the establishment of the Freedmen's Bureau in March 1865, immediately before the end of the Civil War. The Bureau oversaw the transfer of agricultural lands to formerly enslaved Southerners. By 1960 the forms that reparations would take had changed towards systemic reform, and Martin Luther King Jr's economic strategy 'largely revolved around more welfare services and more job opportunities' for African Americans. Henry, *Long Overdue*, 42, 58. From the perspective of Critical Whiteness Studies, Jennifer Harvey has argued that white Americans have been and continue to be 'unjustly enriched' by the exploitation of African American and Native American labour and land and that the redress of this exploitation is imperative. Harvey, *Whiteness and*

Morality, 144. Ta-Nehisi Coates renewed interest in the question of reparations in a 2014 article in *The Atlantic* in which he traces the history of the movement for reparations and asserts the need for 'a national reckoning' to redress America's history of racist exploitation. Coates, 'The Case for Reparations'.

57. James C. Cobb defines 'southern patriotism' as 'loyalty to the collective southern white cause' and as being historically contingent on Confederate nationalism. Cobb, *Away Down South*, 59–60.

58. Tushnet, '*Brown v. Board of Education*', 160.

59. Quigley, *Shifting Grounds*, 130.

60. Ibid. 217.

61. Warren, *The Legacy of the Civil War*, 4.

62. Ibid. 7.

63. Workman, *The Case for the South*, 219.

64. Woodward, *The Strange Career of Jim Crow*, 146.

65. The opinion reads: 'Therefore, we hold that the plaintiffs and others similarly situated for whom the actions have been brought are, by reason of the segregation complained of, deprived of the protection of the laws guaranteed by the Fourteenth Amendment.' 'The Unanimous Decision of the Supreme Court in *Brown V. The Board of Education of Topeka Kansas* (1954)', in Clayton and Salmond, eds, *Debating Southern History*, 172.

66. John Bell Williams, a congressman from Mississippi, first used the phrase 'Black Monday' in this context on the floor of the House of Representatives on 19 May 1954. McMillan, *The Citizens' Council*, 17n6; Brady, *Black Monday*.

67. Adams, *Sideshow U.S.A.*, 110.

Notes to Chapter 5

1. Letter, Benjamin Aslan to Bennett Cerf, 14 June 1962, MS1048, Box 52. Random House Records, 1925–1999, MS1408, Columbia University Rare Books and Manuscripts Library. Thanks to Nick Witham for generously sharing archival research.

2. Ibid.

3. The novel features three characters named Lucius Priest: the narrator, his grandfather and his grandson. In order to avoid (further) confusion, I refer to the elderly narrator as Priest, the younger self he describes as Lucius, and his grandfather as Boss Priest.

4. Costello, *Plantation Airs*, 95.

5. Arnold, 'Preface to the Second Edition', xi.

6. Fant and Robert, eds, *Faulkner at West Point*, 5.

7. Bassett, '*The Reivers*', 54.

8. Ibid.

9. Faulkner, 'Letter to Malcolm Cowley', 11 February 1949, in *Selected Letters of William Faulkner*, 285.

10. Faulkner with Stein, 'The Art of Fiction', 57. Faulkner and Stein began a romantic affair around this time, and the author's tone can be read as somewhere between flirtation and bravado.

11. 'Jefferson, Yoknapatawpha County, Mississippi', reprinted in Warren, ed. *Faulkner*, 303.

12. Granville Hicks, 'Building Blocks of a Gentleman', *The Saturday Review*, 2 June 1962, 27, reprinted in Fargnoli, ed., *William Faulkner*, 522.

13. James B. Meriwether, 'Faulkner's Gentle Comedy of Rustic Rustlers', *Houston Post*, 1 July 1962, 'Now' Section, 30, reprinted in Fargnoli, ed. *William Faulkner*, 540; George Plimpton, 'The Reivers', *New York Herald Tribune Books*, 27 May 1962, 3, reprinted in Fargnoli, ed. *William Faulkner*, 520; Irving Howe, 'Time Out for Fun in Old Mississippi: William Faulkner's New Novel Celebrates Three Innocents Play Hooky from Life', *New York Times Book Review*, 3 June 1962, 1, 24–5, reprinted in Fargnoli, ed. *William Faulkner*, 532.

14. John K. Hutchens, 'The Reivers', *New York Herald Tribune*, 4 June 1962, 21, reprinted in Fargnoli, ed. *William Faulkner*, 533; Clifton Fadiman, 'The Reivers' *Book-of-the-Month Club News*, July 1962, reprinted in Fargnoli, ed. *William Faulkner*, 538; James B. Meriwether, 'Faulkner's Gentle Comedy of Rustic Rustlers', *Houston Post*, 1 July 1962, 'Now' Section, 30, reprinted Fargnoli, ed. *William Faulkner*, 542.

15. Hönnighausen, 'Violence in Faulkner's Major Novels', 247.

16. Urgo, 'Introduction: Reiving and Writing', 3.

17. Railey, *Natural Aristocracy*, 169.

18. Faulkner with Stein, 'The Art of Fiction', 57.

19. Robinson, *Creating Yoknapatawpha*, 13.

20. Foote, *Love in a Dry Season*, 3.

21. Faulkner, 'A Rose for Emily', 122; Faulkner, 'Dry September', 174.

22. Faulkner, 'Death Drag', 197–8.

23. Faulkner, *Requiem for a Nun*, 28.

24. Ibid.

25. 'Jefferson, Yoknapatawpha County, Mississippi', reprinted in Warren, ed. *Faulkner*, 303.

26. Faulkner, *Intruder in the Dust*, 49.

27. Dollard, *Caste and Class in a Southern Town*, 4.

28. Powdermaker, *After Freedom*, 9.

29. Warren, *Segregation*, 9.

30. Ibid. 55.

31. Carter, 'Statues in the Squares', 239.

32. Haas, *Look Away, Look Away*, 1.

33. Tate, 'Ode to the Confederate Dead', 17.

34. Faulkner, *Go Down, Moses*, 167.

35. Ibid. 5.

36. Faulkner, *Snopes*, 706.

37. Faulkner, 'A Rose for Emily', 119–20.

38. This parable is the source of the modern English word 'talent', suggesting that aptitude and the ability to earn money are etymologically linked.

39. Matthew 25:15. All biblical references are to the King James Bible.

40. Matthew 25:26.

41. Luke 19:12–18.

42. Luke 19:21–27.
43. Luke 19:26, also similarly phrased in Matthew 25:29.
44. Matthew 5:5, Mark 10:25 and Matthew 20:16.
45. Matthew 25:27, Luke 19:23.
46. Richard Godden, in *Fictions of Labor: William Faulkner and the South's Long Revolution* (1997) and *William Faulkner: An Economy of Complex Words* (2007), relates a series of Faulknerian vignettes as metaphors for the South's exploitative economy and establishes the means by which I understand this biblical metaphor. Nevertheless, this specific financial analogy is not discussed in either of Godden's studies.
47. Faulkner, *Snopes*, 709. A 'jitney' is an illegal or unlicensed taxi service.
48. 'Snopes Geneology', in Warren, ed. *Faulkner*, 301.
49. Bradley, 'Foreword', xxvi.
50. Ibid.

Notes to Chapter 6

1. Israel, 'The Last Gentleman', 315.
2. Ibid. 318.
3. Young, 'An Appeal', 314.
4. Ibid.
5. Ibid.
6. Kelley, 'Black Power', 216–17.
7. Ibid. 217.
8. Ibid.
9. Ibid.
10. Prescott, 'Books of the Times', 29.
11. Lyell, 'The Day the Negroes Left', 25.
12. 'Painter and Novelist Win Prizes', 38.
13. Sundquist, *Strangers in the Land*, 240.
14. Harris, 'William Melvin Kelley's Real Live, Invisible South', 26.
15. E. G. Anderson, 'The Real Live, Invisible Languages of *A Different Drummer*', 49.
16. While Donald Weyl has read the progression of Kelley's 'philosophy' from *A Different Drummer* through his later work as a shift towards more overt symbolism, Thomas H. Nigel locates Tucker Caliban in a narrative of 'Bad Nigger' figures in African American literature, and Mark Bould has read the novel as a precursor to contemporary science fiction by African Americans, the current chapter locates the novel as a radical progression of the trope of the fictional Southern town. Weyl, 'The Vision of Man in the Novels of William Melvin Kelley', 15–33, 15. Thomas H. Nigel, 'The Bad Nigger Figure', 143–64. Bould, 'Come Alive by Saying No', 220–40, 228.
17. Kelley, *A Different Drummer*, 4. Italics in original. All further references to the novel will appear parenthetically.
18. Shakespeare, *The Tempest*, I, ii, 517.
19. Edwards, *Charisma and the Fictions of Black Leadership*, 113.
20. Sundquist, *Strangers in the Land*, 240.

21. Loewen, *Sundown Towns*, 5.

22. Bradley, 'Foreword', xxvi.

23. Kelley satirises white memory of the Civil War by making the date on which Willson is 'stricken' by an unnamed calamity precisely fifteen days prior to the birth of Adolf Hitler on 20 April 1889. Through this subtle analogy between the glorified leader of the Confederacy and another charismatic political leader in whose honour statues were erected, Kelley signals his satirical approach to 'great man' histories.

24. Carson McCullers's *The Heart is a Lonely Hunter* also features a character who elects to maintain a physical impairment. The deaf character Singer is able to speak but remains mute rather than entering the community of the small town.

25. Li, *Playing in the White*, 163.

26. Edwards, *Charisma and the Fictions of Black Leadership*, 149.

27. Hartnell, *Rewriting Exodus*, 16.

28. Donlon, *Swinging in Place*, 19–20.

29. Hurston, *Their Eyes Were Watching God*, 14.

30. Ibid. 17.

31. McCullers, *The Ballad of the Sad Café*, 69.

32. Albee and McCullers, *The Ballad of the Sad Café*, 11. Italics in original.

33. Li, *Playing in the White*, 165.

34. Gaines, 'The Turtles', 83, 86.

35. David Bradley, 'Foreword', xxvii.

36. Twain, *The Adventures of Huckleberry Finn*, 1.

37. Foote, *Jordan County*, 225.

38. Schuyler, *Black No More*, 201.

39. Harris, *South of Tradition*, 149.

40. Kelley, 'On Racism, Exploitation, and the White Liberal', 9.

41. Kelley, *dəm*, v.

42. A similar aesthetic practice of inventing a southern state between two recognisable, factual states is used as a trope in a novel published forty years after *A Different Drummer*, white novelist Michael Bishop's *Count Geiger's Blues* (1992). This superhero fantasy is set in the state of Oconee, located between Georgia and Tennessee.

43. Wolfe, 'Old Catawba', 214.

44. The state that historically emerged between Alabama and Mississippi was Illinois, the twenty-first state accepted to the Union in 1818.

45. Census of Population and Housing, 1960.

46. Patterson, *Exodus Politics*, 2.

47. Hartnell, *Rewriting Exodus*, 1.

Notes to Conclusion

1. Carson, *Silent Spring*, 21.

2. Ibid.

3. Ibid. 22.

4. Ibid.
5. Veblen, 'The Country Town', 412.
6. Dollard, *Caste and Class in a Southern Town*, 13.
7. Powdermaker, *After Freedom*, 7.
8. Mid-century literature in English beyond the US South positions the field as emblematic of colonial intrusion, as in Irish playwright Brian Friel's *The Field* (1965).
9. Faulkner, *Snopes*, 104–5.
10. Ibid. 106.
11. Ibid.
12. Bone, *Where the New World Is*, 39; Carby, *Cultures in Babylon*, 176; Yaeger, *Dirt and Desire*, 16–17.
13. Hurston, *Their Eyes were Watching God*, 254.
14. Wright, *Uncle Tom's Children*, 127.
15. Ibid. 125. Italics and ellipsis in original.
16. Ibid. 138.
17. L. Smith, *Strange Fruit*, 346. Ellipses in original.
18. Ibid. 347.
19. Reece, *The Hawk and the Sun*, 27.
20. Ibid. 26.
21. McCullers, *Clock Without Hands*, 202.
22. Faulkner, *The Reivers*, 82.
23. Ibid.
24. Bartlett, *Economics and Power*, 43.
25. McChesney, *Money for Nothing*, 3.
26. Preston, *Dirt Roads to Dixie*, 13.
27. B. J. Fields and K. Fields, *Racecraft*, 91.
28. Ibid.
29. Kelley, *A Different Drummer*, 40. Italics in original.
30. Ibid.
31. McFadden, *Gathering of Waters*, 15.
32. Ward, *The Men We Reaped*, 235.
33. Oxford English Dictionary, 'New Words Notes June 2017'. See also Kelley, 'If You're Woke You Dig It', 45, 50.

BIBLIOGRAPHY

Abel, Elizabeth. *Signs of the Times: The Visual Politics of Jim Crow* (Berkeley: University of California Press, 2010).

Adams, Rachel. *Sideshow U.S.A.: Freaks and the American Cultural Imagination* (Chicago: University of Chicago Press, 2001).

Albee, Edward and Carson McCullers. *The Ballad of the Sad Café: Carson McCullers's Novella Adapted to the Stage* (New York: Scribner Classis, [1963] 2001).

Altman, Meryl. 'The Bug That Dare Not Speak Its Name: Art, Faulkner's Worst Novel, and the Critics', *The Faulkner Journal* 9 (1993/1994), 43–68.

Anderson, Eric Gary. 'The Real Live, Invisible Languages of *A Different Drummer*: A Response to Trudier Harris', *South Central Review* 22(1) (2005), 49.

Anderson, Sherwood. *Winesburg, Ohio* (New York: Dover Thrift Editions, [1919] 1995).

Appiah, Kwame Anthony. *Cosmopolitanism: Ethics in a World of Strangers* (London: Penguin, 2006).

Arnold, David L. G. 'Preface to the Second Edition', in *Faulkner at West Point*, ed. Joseph L. Fant III and Robert Ashley (Jackson: University Press of Mississippi, [1964] 2002).

Arsenault, Raymond. *Freedom Riders: 1961 and the Struggle for Racial Justice* (Oxford: Oxford University Press, 2006).

Barnes, Catherine A. *Journey from Jim Crow: The Desegregation of Southern Transit* (New York: Columbia University Press, 1983).

Bartlett, Randell. *Economics and Power: An Inquiry into Human Relations and Markets* (Cambridge: Cambridge University Press, 1989).

'The Best Sellers of 1944', *College English* 6(6) (March 1945), 356.

Bhabha, Homi K. *The Location of Culture* (London: Routledge, 1994).

The Bible: Authorized King James Version (Oxford: Oxford University Press, 1998).

Bibler, Michael P. *Cotton's Queer Relations: Same-Sex Intimacy and the Literature of the Southern Plantation, 1936–1968* (Charlottesville: University of Virginia Press, 2009).

Bilbo, Theodore. *Take Your Choice: Separation or Mongrelization* (Poplarville: Dream House Publishing, 1947).

Boas, Franz. 'Preface', in *Mules and Men* (New York: Harper Perennial, [1935] 1990), xiii–xiv.

Bone, Martyn. *Where the New World Is: Literature about the U. S. South at Global Scales* (Athens: University of Georgia Press, 2018).

Bould, Mark. 'Come Alive by Saying No: An Introduction to Black Power SF', *Science Fiction Studies* 34(2) (July 2007), 220–40.

Bourne, Randolph S. 'The Social Order of an American Town', *Atlantic Monthly* 111 (1913), 246–65.

Bradley, David. 'Foreword', in William Melvin Kelley, *A Different Drummer* (New York: Anchor Books, 1989), xi–xxxii.

Brady, Tom P. *Black Monday* (Winona, MS: Association of Citizens' Councils, 1955).

Brantley, Will. 'Afterword', in Lillian Smith, *Now is the Time* (Jackson: University Press of Mississippi, [1955] 2004), 121–45.

Brinkmeyer Jr, Robert H. *The Fourth Ghost: White Southern Writers and European Fascism, 1930–1950* (Baton Rouge: Louisiana State University Press, 2009).

—. 'Marginalization and Mobility: Segregation and the Representation of Poor Whites', in *Reading Southern Poverty between the Wars, 1918–1939*, ed. Richard Godden and Martin Crawford (Athens: University of Georgia Press, 2006), 223–38.

Brooks, Cleanth. *The Hidden God: Studies in Hemingway, Faulkner, Yeats, Eliot, and Warren* (New Haven: Yale University Press, 1963).

Brundage, W. Fitzhugh. *Lynching in the New South: Georgia and Virginia, 1880–1930* (Urbana: University of Illinois Press, 1988).

Byron Herbert Reece Papers, MS 56, Hargrett Rare Book and Manuscript Library, the University of Georgia Libraries.

Byron Herbert Reece family papers, MS 3055, Hargrett Rare Book and Manuscript Library, the University of Georgia Libraries.

Cable, George Washington. *The Silent South* (Montclair, NJ: Patterson Smith, [1889] 1969).

Cain, William E. *The Crisis in Criticism: Theory, Literature, and Reform in English Studies* (Baltimore: Johns Hopkins University Press, 1984).

Capra, Frank, dir. *It's a Wonderful Life* (RKO Studios, 1946).

Carby, Hazel. *Cultures in Babylon: Black Britain and African America* (London: Verso, 1999).

Carr, Virginia Spencer. *The Lonely Hunter: A Biography of Carson McCullers* (New York: Doubleday, 1975).

Carson McCullers Collection 1924–1976, Harry Ransom Center, The University of Texas at Austin.

Carson, Rachel. *Silent Spring* (London: Penguin, [1962] 2000).

Carter, Hodding. 'Statues in the Squares', in *This is the South*, ed. Robert West Howard (Chicago: Rand McNally, 1959), 239–45.

Cash, W. J. *The Mind of the South* (New York: Vintage, [1941] 1969).

Catte, Elizabeth. *What You are Getting Wrong about Appalachia* (Cleveland: Belt Publishing, 2018).

Census of Population and Housing, 1960, https://www.census.gov/prod/www/decennial.html (accessed 15 August 2015).

Certeau, Michel de. *The Practice of Everyday Life*, trans. Stephen Rendall (Berkeley: University of California Press, 1984).

Clark, Jim. 'A Kindred Spirit Moving: The Rural Ethos of Byron Herbert Reece, Wendell Berry, and James Agee', in *Black Earth and Ivory Tower: New American Essays from Farm and Classroom*, ed. Zachary Michael Jack (Columbia: University of South Carolina Press, 2005), 156–67.

Clayton, Bruce and John Salmond, eds. *Debating Southern History: Ideas and Action in the Twentieth Century* (Lanham, MD: Rowman & Littlefield, 1999).

Clifford, James. 'Introduction', in *Writing Culture: The Poetics and Politics of Ethnography*, ed. James Clifford and George E. Marcus (Berkeley: University of California Press, 1986), 1–26.

Coates, Ta-Nehisi. 'The Case for Reparations', *The Atlantic*, June 2014. http://www.theatlantic.com/features/archive/2014/05/the-case-for-rreparations/361631/ (accessed 8 November 2014).

Cobb, James C. *Away Down South: A History of Southern Identity* (Oxford: Oxford University Press, 2005).

Costello, Brannon. *Plantation Airs: Racial Paternalism and the Transformations of Class in Southern Fiction, 1945–1971* (Baton Rouge: Louisiana State University Press, 2007).

Couch, W. T. 'The Negro in the South', in *Culture in the South*, ed. W. T. Couch (Chapel Hill: University of North Carolina Press, 1934), 432–76.

Cox, Karen L. *Dixie's Daughters: The United Daughters of the Confederacy and the Preservation of Confederate Culture* (Gainesville: University Press of Florida, 2003).

Cunningham, Rodger. 'Writing on the Cusp: Double Alterity and Minority Discourse in Appalachia', in *The Future of Southern Letters*, ed. Jefferson Humphries and John Lowe (New York: Oxford University Press, 1996), 41–53.

Dabbs, James McBride. *Who Speaks for the South?* (New York: Funk & Wagnalls, 1964).

—. *Civil Rights in Recent Southern Literature* (Atlanta: Southern Regional Council, 1969).

Dante Alighieri, *The Divine Comedy: Inferno, Purgatorio, Paradiso*, trans. Robin Kirkpatrick (London: Penguin, [1320] 2012).

Davis, Thadious M. *Southscapes: Geographies of Race, Region, and Literature* (Chapel Hill: University of North Carolina Press, 2011).

DeTitta, Tom. *The Reach of Song: An Appalachian Drama* (Atlanta: Cherokee Publishing Company, 1990).

Dollard, John. *Caste and Class in a Southern Town*, 3rd edn (New York: Doubleday, [1937] 1957).

Donlon, Jocelyn Hazelwood. *Swinging in Place: Porch Life in Southern Culture* (Chapel Hill: University of North Carolina Press, 2001).

Doyle, Bertram Wilbur. *The Etiquette of Race Relations in the South: A Study in Social Control* (Chicago: University Chicago Press, 1937).

Du Bois, W. E. B. *The Souls of Black Folk* (London: Dover Thrift Editions, [1903] 1994).

Duck, Leigh Anne. *The Nation's Region: Southern Modernism, Segregation, and U.S. Nationalism* (Athens: University of Georgia Press, 2006).

Duval, John N. *Race and White Identity in Southern Fiction: From Faulkner to Morrison* (New York: Palgrave Macmillan, 2008).

Edwards, Erica. *Charisma and the Fictions of Black Leadership* (Minneapolis: University of Minnesota Press, 2012).

Egerton, John. *Speak Now against the Day: The Generation before the Civil Rights Movement in the South* (New York: Knopf, 1994).

Eller, Ronald D. *Uneven Ground: Appalachia Since 1945* (Lexington: University Press of Kentucky, 2008).

Emerson, Donald. 'The Ambiguities of *Clock Without Hands*', *Wisconsin Studies in Contemporary Literature* 3(3) (Fall 1962).

Engelhardt, Elizabeth. 'Trying to Get Appalachia Less Wrong: A Modest Approach', *Southern Cultures* 23(1) (Spring 2017), 4–9.

Evans, Oliver. *Carson McCullers: Her Life and Work* (London: Peter Owen, 1965).

Fant III, Joseph and Robert Ashley, eds. *Faulkner at West Point* (Jackson: University Press of Mississippi, [1964] 2002).

Fargnoli, Nicholas, ed. *William Faulkner: A Literary Companion* (New York: Pegasus Books, 2008).

Faulkner, William. 'Dry September', in *The Collected Stories of William Faulkner* (New York: Vintage, [1931] 1995), 169–85.

—. 'Death Drag', in *The Collected Stories of William Faulkner* (New York: Vintage, [1932] 1995), 185–206.

—. *Go Down, Moses*, in *Faulkner: Novels 1942–1954*, ed. Noel Polk (New York: Library of America, [1942] 1990).

—. *Intruder in the Dust* (London: Penguin, [1948] 1966).

—. 'A Rose for Emily', in *The Collected Stories of William Faulkner* (New York: Vintage, [1950] 1995), 119–130.

—. *Requiem for a Nun* (London: Penguin, [1951] 1960).

—, with Jean Stein, 'The Art of Fiction', in *The Paris Review Interviews, Volume 2* (Edinburgh: Canongate, [1956] 2007), 34–57.

—. *Snopes: The Hamlet, The Town, The Mansion* (New York: Modern Library, [1959] 1994).

—. *Selected Letters of William Faulkner*, ed. Joseph Blotner (London: The Scolar Press, 1977).

—. *Collected Stories of William Faulkner* (New York: Vintage, 1995).

Fields, Barbara J. and Karen Fields. *Racecraft: The Soul of Inequality in American Life* (London: Verso, 2012).

Fishman, Sterling. 'The Rise of Hitler as a Beer Hall Orator', *Review of Politics* 26 (April 1964), 250–2.

Foote, Shelby. *Love in a Dry Season* (New York: Vintage, [1951] 1992).

—. *Jordan County: A Landscape in Narrative* (New York: Vintage, [1954] 1992).

Franklin, John Hope. *Reconstruction: After the Civil War* (Chicago: University of Chicago Press, 1961).

Gaines, Ernest J. 'The Turtles', in *Mozart and Leadbelly: Stories and Essays* (New York: Vintage, [1956] 2005).

Gates Jr, Henry Louis. *The Signifying Monkey: A Theory of African American Literary Criticism* (Oxford: Oxford University Press, [1988] 2014).

Geertz, Clifford. *The Interpretation of Cultures: Selected Essays* (New York: Basic Books, 1973).

Gilbert, Susanna. '"Blood Don't Lie": The Diseased Family in Flannery O'Connor's *Everything that Rises Must Converge*', *Literature and Medicine* 18(1) (1999), 114–31.

Gilmore, Ruth Wilson. 'Fatal Couplings of Power and Difference: Notes on Racism and Geography', *The Professional Geographer* 54(1) (2002), 15–24.

Gleeson-White, Sarah. *Strange Bodies: Gender and Identity in the Novels of Carson McCullers* (Tuscaloosa: University of Alabama Press, 2003).

Godden, Richard. *Fictions of Labor: William Faulkner and the South's Long Revolution* (Cambridge: Cambridge University Press, 1997).

—. *William Faulkner: An Economy of Complex Words* (Princeton: Princeton University Press, 2007).

Goyen, William. 'Headlong toward Catastrophe', *New York Times Book Review*, 11 September 1955.

Gray, Richard. *The Literature of Memory: Modern Writers of the American South* (Baltimore: Johns Hopkins University Press, 1977).

—. *Southern Aberrations: Writers of the American South and the Problems of Regionalism* (Baton Rouge: Louisiana State University Press, 2000).

Greeson, Jennifer Rae. *Our South: Geographic Fantasy and the Rise of National Literature* (Cambridge, MA: Harvard University Press, 2010).

Haas, Ben. *Look Away, Look Away* (London: Peter Davies, [1964] 1965).

Hale, Grace Elizabeth. *Making Whiteness: The Culture of Segregation in the South, 1890–1940* (New York: Vintage, [1998] 1999).

Handy, William J. *Kant and the Southern New Critics* (Austin: University of Texas Press, 1963).

Harris, J. William. 'Etiquette, Lynching, and Racial Boundaries in Southern History: A Mississippi Example', *The American Historical Review* 100(2) (1995), 387–410.

Harris, Trudier. *South of Tradition: Essays on African American Literature* (Athens: University of Georgia Press, [1997] 2002).

—. 'William Melvin Kelley's Real Live, Invisible South', *South Central Review* 22(1) (2005), 26.

Hartnell, Anna. *Rewriting Exodus: American Futures from Du Bois to Obama* (London: Pluto Press, 2011).

Harvey, David. *Spaces of Hope* (Edinburgh: Edinburgh University Press, 2000).

Harvey, Jennifer. *Whiteness and Morality: Pursuing Racial Justice through Reparations and Sovereignty* (New York: Palgrave Macmillan, 2007).

Hassan, Ihab. *Radical Innocence: Studies in the Contemporary American Novel* (Princeton: Princeton University Press, 1961).

Hendrick, George and Willene Hendrick, eds, *Fleeing for Freedom: Stories of the Underground Railroad as Told by Levi Coffin and William Still* (Chicago: Ivan R. Dee, 2003).

Henry, Charles P. *Long Overdue: The Politics of Racial Reparations* (New York: New York University Press, 2007).

Hicks, Granville, 'Building Blocks of a Gentleman', *The Saturday Review*, 2 June 1962,

27, reprinted in *William Faulkner: A Literary Companion*, ed. Nicholas Fargnoli (New York: Pegasus, 2008), 522.

Himes, Chester. *If He Hollers Let Him Go* (London: Serpent's Tail, [1945] 2010).

Hobson, Fred. *But Now I See: The White Southern Racial Conversion Narrative* (Baton Rouge: Louisiana State University Press, 1999).

Holland, Sharon Patricia. *The Erotic Life of Racism* (Durham, NC: Duke University Press, 2012).

Hönnighausen, Lothar. 'Violence in Faulkner's Major Novels', in *A Companion to William Faulkner*, ed. Richard C. Moreland (Malden, MA: Blackwell, 2007), 236–51.

Houston, Benjamin. *The Nashville Way: Racial Etiquette and the Struggle for Social Justice in a Southern City* (Athens: University of Georgia Press, 2012).

Howe, Irving. 'In the Shadow of Death', *New York Times Book Review*, 17 September 1961.

Hunt, Mary Fassett. *Joanna Lord* (London: Hutchinson's Universal Book Club, [1954] 1957).

Hurston, Zora Neale. 'The Eatonville Anthology', in *The Complete Stories*, ed. Henry Louis Gates Jr and Sieglinde Lemke (New York: HarperCollins, [1926] 1996), 59–72.

—. 'The Eatonville Anthology', in *Folklore, Memoirs, and Other Writings*, ed. Cheryl Wall (New York: Library of America, [1926] 1995), 813–25.

—, with Langston Hughes. *De Turkey and De Law* in *Collected Plays*, ed. Jean Lee Cole and Charles Mitchell (New Brunswick, NJ: Rutgers University Press, [1930] 2008), 131–90.

—. *Their Eyes Were Watching God* (London: Virago, [1937] 1986).

—. 'My Most Humiliating Jim Crow Experience', in *Folklore, Memoirs, and Other Writings* ed. Cheryl Wall (New York: Library of America, [1944] 1995), 935–6.

—. 'Crazy for This Democracy', *Folklore, Memoirs, and Other Writings*, ed. Cheryl Wall. (New York: Library of America, [1945] 1995), 945–9.

—. 'How It Feels to be Colored Me', in *Folklore, Memoirs, and Other Writings*, ed. Cheryl Wall (New York: Library of America, [1945] 1995), 826–9.

—. 'Court Order Can't Make Races Mix', in *Folklore, Memoirs, and Other Writings*, ed. Cheryl Wall (New York: Library of America, [1955] 1995), 956–8.

Israel, Calvin. 'The Last Gentleman', *The Partisan Review* 35:2 (Spring 1968), 315–19.

Jackson, Lawrence P. *The Indignant Generation: A Narrative History of African American Writers and Critics, 1934–1960* (Princeton: Princeton University Press, 2011).

James, Judith Giblin. 'Carson McCullers, Lillian Smith, and the Politics of Broadway', in *Southern Women Playwrights: New Essays in Literary History and Criticism*, ed. Robert L. McDonald and Linda Rohrer Paige (Tuscaloosa: University of Alabama Press, 2002), 42–60.

John E. Bassett, '*The Reivers*: Revision and Closure in Faulkner's Career', *The Southern Literary Journal* 18(2) (1986), 53–61.

Jones, James H. *Bad Blood: The Tuskegee Syphilis Experiment* (New York: Free Press, 1981).

Kelley, William Melvin. 'If You're Woke You Dig It', *New York Times* (20 May 1962).

—. *A Different Drummer* (New York: Anchor Books, [1962] 1989).

—. *dəm* (Saint Paul: Coffee House Press, [1967] 2000).

—. 'On Racism, Exploitation, and the White Liberal', *Negro Digest*, January 1967.

—. 'Black Power', *The Partisan Review* 35(2) (Spring 1968), 216–17.

King, Richard H. *A Southern Renaissance: The Cultural Awakening of the American South, 1930–1955* (New York: Oxford University Press, 1980).

Lassiter, Luke E., Hurley Goodall, Elizabeth Campbell and Michelle Natasya Johnson, eds. *The Other Side of Middletown: Exploring Muncie's African American Community* (Walnut Creek, CA: AltaMira, 2004).

Lee, Harper. *To Kill a Mockingbird* (London: Arrow Books, [1961] 1997).

Lefebvre, Henri. *The Production of Space*, trans. Donald Nicholson-Smith (Oxford: Blackwell, [1974] 1991).

Lentricchia, Frank. *After the New Criticism* (London: Athlone Press, 1980).

Li, Stephanie. *Playing in the White: Black Writers, White Subjects* (Oxford: Oxford University Press, 2015).

Lillian Smith papers, MS1283, Hargrett Rare Book and Manuscript Library, the University of Georgia Libraries.

Lipsitz, George. *The Possessive Investment in Whiteness: How White People Profit from Identity Politics* (Philadelphia: Temple University Press, 2006).

Loewen, James W. *Sundown Towns: A Hidden Dimension of American Racism* (New York: Touchstone, [2005] 2006).

Loveland, Anne C. *Lillian Smith: A Southerner Confronting the South* (Baton Rouge: Louisiana State University Press, 1986).

Lyell, Frank H. 'The Day the Negroes Left', *The New York Times*, 17 June 1962, 25.

Lynd, Robert S. and Helen Merrell Lynd, *Middletown: A Study in American Culture* (New York: Harvest Books, [1929] 1956).

MacKethan, Lucinda. *The Dream of Arcady: Place and Time in Southern Literature* (Baton Rouge: Louisiana State University Press, 1980).

Massey, Doreen. *For Space* (Los Angeles: Sage Publications, 2005).

Maxwell, Angie. *The Indicted South: Public Criticism, Southern Inferiority, and the Politics of Whiteness* (Chapel Hill: University of North Carolina Press, 2014).

McChesney, Fred S. *Money for Nothing: Politicians, Rent Extraction, and Political Extortion* (Cambridge, MA: Harvard University Press, 1997).

McCullers, Carson. *The Heart is a Lonely Hunter* (London: Penguin, [1940] 1961).

—. *Reflections in a Golden Eye* (London: Penguin, [1941] 1968).

—. *The Member of the Wedding* (London: Penguin, [1946] 2008).

—. *The Ballad of the Sad Café* (London: Cresset Press, [1951] 1958).

—. *Clock Without Hands* (London: Penguin, 1961).

—. 'Author's Outline of "The Mute" (*The Heart is a Lonely Hunter*)', in *The Mortgaged Heart* (London: Penguin, 2008), 136–59.

—. 'Loneliness . . . an American Malady', in *The Mortgaged Heart* (London: Penguin, 2008), 265–8.

—. *The Mortgaged Heart* (London: Penguin, 2008).

McFadden, Bernice L. *Gathering of Waters* (New York: Akashic Books, 2012).

McKittrick, Katherine. *Demonic Grounds: Black Women and the Cartographies of Struggle* (Minneapolis: University of Minnesota Press, 2006).

McMillan, Neil R. *The Citizens' Council: Organized Resistance to the Second Reconstruction, 1954–1964* (Urbana: University of Illinois Press, [1971] 1994).

—. *Dark Journey: Black Mississippians in the Age of Jim Crow* (Urbana: University of Illinois Press, 1990).

McPherson, Tara. *Reconstructing Dixie: Race, Gender, and Nostalgia in the Imagined South* (Durham, NC: Duke University Press, 2003).

Monteith, Sharon. *Advancing Sisterhood?: Interracial Friendships in Contemporary Southern Fiction* (Athens: University of Georgia Press, 2001).

—. 'Southern Fiction', in *A Companion to Twentieth-Century United States Fiction*, ed. David Seed (Malden, MA: Blackwell-Wiley, 2009), 84–95.

—. 'Civil Rights Fiction', in *The Cambridge Companion to the Literature of the American South*, ed. Sharon Monteith (Cambridge: Cambridge University Press, 2013), 159–73.

Moretti, Franco. *Graphs, Maps, Trees: Abstract Models for Literary History* (London: Verso, 2005).

Newman, Judith. '"Dis ain't Gimme, Florida": Zora Neale Hurston's *Their Eyes Were Watching God*', *The Modern Language Review* 98(4) (October 2003), 817–26.

Nigel, Thomas H. 'The Bad Nigger Figure in Selected Works of Richard Wright, William Melvin Kelley, and Ernest Gaines', *College Language Association Journal* 39(2) (December 1995), 143–64.

Niven, David. *The Politics of Injustice: The Kennedys, the Freedom Rides, and the Electoral Consequences of a Moral Compromise* (Knoxville: University of Tennessee Press, 2003).

Norman, Brian. *Neo-Segregation Narratives: Jim Crow in Post-Civil Rights American Literature* (Athens: University of Georgia Press, 2010).

O'Brien, Michael. 'W. J. Cash, Hegel, and the South', *The Journal of Southern History* 44(3) (August 1978).

O'Connor, Flannery. *Wise Blood* (London: Faber & Faber, [1952] 2008).

—. *The Habit of Being: Letters of Flannery O'Connor*, ed. Sally Fitzgerald (New York: Farrar, Strauss, and Giroux, 1988).

Odum, Howard. *Race and Rumours of Race: Challenge to American Crisis* (Chapel Hill: University of North Carolina Press, 1943).

Orvell, Miles. *The Death and Life of Main Street: Small Towns in American Memory, Space, and Community* (Chapel Hill: University of North Carolina Press, 2012).

Oxford English Dictionary. 'New Words Notes June 2017', https://public.oed.com/blog/june-2017-update-new-words-notes/ (accessed 16 June 2017).

'Painter and Novelist Win Prizes', *New York Times*, 16 April 1963, 38.

Parks, Edd Winfield. 'Towns and Cities', in *Culture in the South*, ed. W. T. Couch (Chapel Hill: University of North Carolina Press, 1934).

Patterson, Robert J. *Exodus Politics: Civil Rights and Leadership in African American Literature and Culture* (Charlottesville: University of Virginia Press, 2013).

Powdermaker, Hortense. *After Freedom: A Cultural Study in the Deep South* (Madison: University of Wisconsin Press, [1937] 1993).

Prescott, Orville. 'Books of the Times', *New York Times*, 18 September 1961.

—. 'Books of the Times', *New York Times*, 8 June 1962.

Preston Jr., E. Dolores. 'The Underground Railroad in Northwest Ohio', *The Journal of Negro History* 17(4) (1932), 409–36.

Preston, Howard Lawrence. *Dirt Roads to Dixie: Accessibility and Modernization in the South, 1885–1935* (Knoxville: University of Tennessee Press, 1991).

Putnam, Carleton. *Race and Reason: A Yankee View* (Washington, DC: Public Affairs Press, 1961).

Quigley, Paul. *Shifting Grounds: Nationalism and the American South, 1848–1865* (Oxford: Oxford University Press, 2012).

Rai, Sunita. *Carson McCullers: An Existential Approach* (New Delhi: Classical Publishing Company, 2001).

Railey, Kevin. *Natural Aristocracy: History, Ideology, and the Production of William Faulkner* (Tuscaloosa: University of Alabama Press, 1999).

Random House Records, 1925–1999, MS1408, Columbia University Rare Books and Manuscripts Library.

Ransom, John Crowe. 'Introduction', in *The Kenyon Critics: Studies in Modern Literature from the Kenyon Review*, ed. John Crowe Ransom (Port Washington: Kennikat Press, 1951), vii–x.

Roberts, Diane. *The Myth of Aunt Jemima: Representations of Race and Region* (London: Routledge, 1994).

Roberts, Gillian. *Prizing Literature: The Celebration and Circulation of National* Culture (Toronto: University of Toronto Press, 2011).

Robinson, Owen. *Creating Yoknapatawpha: Readers and Writers in Faulkner's Fiction* (New York: Routledge, 2006).

Robolin, Stéphane. *Grounds of Engagement: Apartheid-Era African-American and South African Writing* (Urbana: University of Illinois Press, 2015).

Romine, Scott. 'Framing Southern Rhetoric: Lillian Smith's Narrative Persona in *Killers of the Dream*', *South Atlantic Review* 59(2) (1994), 95–111.

—. *The Narrative Forms of Southern Community* (Baton Rouge: Louisiana State University Press, 1999).

—. *The Real South: Southern Narrative in the Age of Cultural Reproduction* (Baton Rouge: Louisiana State University Press, 2008).

Rottenberg, Dan, ed. *Middletown Jews: The Tenuous Survival of an American Jewish Community* (Bloomington: Indiana University Press, 1997).

Rubin, Louis D. 'Six Novels and S. Levin', *The Sewanee Review* 70(3) (1962), 504–14.

Sartre, Jean-Paul. *Existentialism and Humanism*, trans. Philip Mairet (London: Methuen, [1948] 1980).

Schuyler, George. *Black No More* (Boston: Northeastern University Press, [1931] 1989).

Shakespeare, William. *The Tempest* (London: Arden, [1611] 2011).

Simmel, Georg. 'The Metropolis and Mental Life', trans. Edward Shils, in *On Individuality and Social Forms*, ed. Donald Levine (Chicago: University of Chicago Press, [1903] 1971), 324–39.

Slotkin, Richard. *Regeneration through Violence: The Mythology of the American Frontier, 1600–1860* (Norman: University of Oklahoma Press, 1973).

Smith, Jon. *Finding Purple America: The South and the Future of American Cultural Studies* (Athens: University of Georgia Press, 2013).

Smith, Lillian. *Strange Fruit* (Orlando: Harcourt, [1944] 1992).

—. *Killers of the Dream: Revised and Enlarged* (New York: Anchor Books, [1949] 1963).

—. *Now is the Time* (Jackson: University Press of Mississippi, [1955] 2004).

—. 'Extracts from Three Letters', in *The Winner Names the Age: A Collection of Writings by Lillian Smith*, ed. Michelle Cliff (New York: W. W. Norton, 1978), 12–18.

—. 'The Right Way is Not a Moderate Way', *The Winner Names the Age: A Collection of Writings by Lillian Smith*, ed. Michelle Cliff (New York: W. W. Norton, 1978), 67–75.

—. 'The Role of the Poet in a World of Demagogues', in *The Winner Names the Age: A Collection of Writings by Lillian Smith*, ed. Michelle Cliff (New York: W. W. Norton, 1978).

—. 'A Trembling Earth', in *The Winner Names the Age: A Collection of Writings by Lillian Smith*, ed. Michelle Cliff (New York: W. W. Norton, 1978), 121–5.

—. *How am I to be Heard? Letters of Lillian Smith*, ed. Margaret Rose Gladney (Chapel Hill: University of North Carolina Press, 1993).

Smith, Margarita G. 'Editor's Note', in *The Mortgaged Heart* (London: Penguin, 2008), 11–20.

Smith, Mark. *How Race is Made: Slavery, Segregation, and the Senses* (Chapel Hill: University of North Carolina Press, 2006).

Snelling, Paula. 'Preface' in *The Winner Names the Age: A Collection of Writings by Lillian Smith*, ed. Michelle Cliff (New York: Norton, 1978), 11–22.

Sollors, Werner. *Beyond Ethnicity: Consent and Descent in American Culture* (Oxford: Oxford University Press, 1987).

—. *Neither Black Nor White Yet Both: Thematic Explorations of Interracial Literature* (Oxford: Oxford University Press, 1997).

Stanford, Ken. 'Byron Herbert Reece Highway Dedication', *Access North Georgia*, 22 August 2005 (accessed 5 June 2014), http://www.accessnorthga.com/detail.php?n=128071

Stowe, Harriet Beecher. *Dred: A Tale of the Great Dismal Swamp* (Chapel Hill: University of North Carolina Press, [1856] 2006).

Sundquist, Eric. *Strangers in the Land: Blacks, Jews, Post-Holocaust America* (Cambridge, MA: Belknap Press, 2005).

Szalay, Michael. *Hip Figures: A Literary History of the Democratic Party* (Stanford: Stanford University Press, 2012).

Tate, Allen. 'Ode to the Confederate Dead', in *The Swimmers and Other Selected Poems* (London: Oxford University Press, 1970), 17–20.

The Byron Herbert Reece Society, http://byronherbertreecesociety.wordpress.com/farm-2/ (accessed 5 June 2014).

Thornton III, J. Mills. *Dividing Lines: Municipal Politics and the Struggle for Civil Rights in Montgomery, Birmingham, and Selma* (Tuscaloosa: University of Alabama Press, 2002).

Tilson, Everett. *Segregation and the Bible* (New York: Abingdon Press, 1958).

Tishler, Nancy. 'The Negro in Modern Southern Fiction: From Stereotype to Archetype', *The Negro American Literature Forum* 2(1) (1968), 3–6.

Trefzer, Annette. *Disturbing Indians: The Archaeology of Southern Fiction* (Tuscaloosa: University of Alabama Press, 2007).

Tuan, Yi-Fu. *Topophilia: A Study of Environmental Perception, Attitudes, and Values* (New York: Columbia University Press, 1974).

Tushnet, Mark. 'Brown v. Board of Education', in *Race on Trial: Law and Justice in American History*, ed. Annette Gordon-Reed (Oxford: Oxford University Press, 2002), 160–76.

Twain, Mark. *The Adventures of Huckleberry Finn* (London: Collins Classics, [1884] 2009).

Urgo, Joseph. 'Introduction: Reiving and Writing', *The Faulkner Journal* 13 (1–2) (Fall 1997/Spring 1998), 3–14.

Veblen, Thorstein. 'The Country Town', in *The Portable Veblen*, ed. Max Lerner (New York: The Viking Press, [1923] 1948), 407–13.

Visweswaran, Kamala. *Fictions of Feminist Ethnography* (Minneapolis: University of Minnesota Press, 1994).

Walkden, George. 'The Status of *hwæt* in Old English', *English Language and Linguistics* 17(3) (2013), 465–88.

Wall, Cheryl. *On Freedom and the Will to Adorn: The Art of the African American Essay* (Chapel Hill: University of North Carolina Press, 2018).

Ward, Cynthia. 'Truths, Lies, Mules and Men: Through the "Spy-Glass of Anthropology" and What Zora Saw There', *The Western Journal of Black Studies* 36(4) (2012), 301–13.

Ward, Jesmyn. *The Men We Reaped* (New York: Bloomsbury, 2013).

Warren, Robert Penn. 'The Briar Patch', in Twelve Southerners, *I'll Take my Stand* (Baton Rouge: Louisiana State University Press, [1930] 1977), 246–65.

—. *Segregation: The Inner Conflict of the South* (Athens: Brown Thresher Books, [1956] 1994).

—. *The Legacy of the Civil War* (Lincoln, NE: Bison Books, [1961] 1998).

—. *Who Speaks for the Negro?* (New York: Random House, 1965).

—, ed. *Faulkner* (Englewood Cliffs: Prentice-Hall, 1966).

Washington, Harriet A. *Medical Apartheid: The Dark History of Medical Experimentation on Black Americans from Colonial Times to the Present* (New York: Doubleday, 2006).

Watkins, Floyd C. *The Death of Art: Black and White in the Recent Southern Novel* (Athens: University of Georgia Press, 1970).

Watson, Jay. *Reading for the Body: The Recalcitrant Materiality of Southern Fiction* (Athens: University of Georgia Press, 2012).

Weber, Jennifer L. *Copperheads: The Rise and Fall of Lincoln's Opponents in the North* (New York: Oxford University Press, 2006).

Weidenmier, Marc D. 'Turning Points in the U.S. Civil War: Views from the Grayback Market', *Southern Economic Journal* 68(4) (April 2002), 875–90.

Welty, Eudora. 'Must the Novelist Crusade?', in *The Eye of the Story: Selected Essays and Reviews* (New York: Vintage, [1965] 1979).

Weyl, Donald M. 'The Vision of Man in the Novels of William Melvin Kelley', *Critique* 15(3) (1974), 15–33.

Whitt, Jan. 'The Exiled Heir: An Introduction to Carson McCullers and Her Work', in

Reflections in a Critical Eye: Essays on Carson McCullers, ed. Jan Whitt (Lanham, MD: University Press of America, 2008).

Williams, Raymond. *The Country and the City* (London: Chatto & Windus, 1973).

—. *Keywords: A Vocabulary of Culture and Society* (London: Fourth Estate, [1976] 2014).

Wilson, Anthony. *Shadow and Shelter: The Swamp in Southern Culture* (Jackson: University Press of Mississippi, 2006).

Wolfe, Thomas. 'Old Catawba', in *The Complete Short Stories of Thomas Wolfe* (New York: Simon and Schuster, [1935] 1987), 214–21.

Woodward, C. Vann. *Origins of the New South, 1877–1913* (Baton Rouge: Louisiana State University Press, 1951).

—. *The Strange Career of Jim Crow*, 2nd rev. edn (London: Oxford University Press, [1955] 1966).

Workman Jr., William D. *The Case for the South* (New York: Devin-Adair, 1960).

Wright, Richard. *Uncle Tom's Children* (New York: Harper Perennial, [1938] 1991).

Wyatt-Brown, Bertram. *Southern Honor: Ethics and Behavior in the Old South* (Oxford: Oxford University Press, 1982).

Yaeger, Patricia. *Dirt and Desire: Reconstructing Southern Women's Writing, 1930–1990* (Chicago: University of Chicago Press, 2000).

Young, John. 'An Appeal', *The Partisan Review* 35(2) (Spring 1968), 314.

Yousaf, Nahem. 'A Southern Sheriff's Revenge: Bertrand Tavernier's *Coup de Torchon*', in *Transatlantic Exchanges: The American South in Europe – Europe in the American South*, ed. Richard Gray and Waldemar Zacharasiewicz (Vienna: Austrian Academy of Sciences Press, 2007), 221–38.

INDEX

EU representative:
Easy Access System Europe
Mustamäe tee 50, 10621 Tallinn, Estonia
Gpsr.requests@easproject.com

www.ingramcontent.com/pod-product-compliance
Lightning Source LLC
Chambersburg PA
CBHW070633100726
47907CB00007B/1974